0064667

D0119574

PROVO

By the same author

SPIDER
PEACE ON EARTH
AND ALL THE KING'S MEN
SHADOWLAND

GORDON STEVENS

PROVO

HarperCollins*Publishers*

HarperCollins*Publishers*
77–85 Fulham Palace Road,
Hammersmith, London W6 8JB

Published by HarperCollins*Publishers* 1993

1 3 5 7 9 8 6 4 2

Copyright © Gordon Stevens 1993

The Author asserts the moral right to
be identified as the author of this work

A catalogue record for this book
is available from the British Library

ISBN 0 00 224180 3

Photoset in Linotron Aldus by
Rowland Phototypesetting Ltd, Bury St Edmunds, Suffolk

Printed in Great Britain by
HarperCollinsManufacturing Glasgow

TO DAVE

PROLOGUE

THE ANGEL OF DEATH stood in the graveyard and the priest waited at the door.

The Sunday afternoon was quiet, the faintest breeze stirring the foliage of the trees and rustling the hem of his cassock, the faded red brick of the Church of St Mary and St Phillip lost amidst the colours of summer.

It was two o'clock exactly.

The woman was in her late twenties or early thirties, dark-haired and tall, smartly dressed despite the heat. He saw her through the trees — as if she had suddenly appeared from nowhere. She smiled at him as she always did and went inside. In all the times they had met in such a way, the priest suddenly thought, the woman had never once spoken to him.

The church was cool, the image of the Virgin looking down and the candles on the right of the altar. The woman knelt, took one from the black metal box and held the wick against one of those flickering in front of her.

The wax ran down the candle and burned her fingers. Her face was still, as if she had not noticed the pain or was accustomed to it.

'Remember, o most gracious Virgin Mary, that never was it known that anyone who asked your help was left unanswered . . .'

The Memorare to her father, mother and her brother, and the plea for the salvation of their souls. Even now she remembered the day she had been taken from them, the days they had been taken from her. Even now the details of their deaths burned into her mind as the wax burned into her flesh.

There was no one else in the church. The woman placed the candle on the stand and stood up, the priest watching from the doorway. She folded a £20 note into the poor box and passed him, smiling her thanks as she did so, then she walked quickly through the churchyard. The priest closed and locked the doors and walked down the steps, along the path and paused under the headstone. The statue was of marble, the expression on the face was serene and the wings were folded. The Angel of Death to some, he reflected, the Saviour and Redeemer to others.

In life as in death, he supposed.

The afternoon was warm and the sweat trickled down the back of his collar. By the time he reached the gate the visitor had disappeared.

The car was parked half a mile away. Instinctively she checked the street – for the woman with the pram whom everyone else would accept as commonplace, for the motor-cycle which no one else would notice, for the car or van with the two people in the front seat – then drove the eight miles to the house where she had been raised. The tea was laid – Sunday linen and china, cucumber sandwiches and fruit cake. The french windows to the garden were open and the children were playing croquet on the lawn.

She kissed her father and her mother on the cheek and sat by her brother.

1

IN THE END, MCKENDRICK KNEW, it would all depend on the
man called Reardon: whether he followed the pattern of the past
weeks, whether his wife was at home when they called, whether his
son and daughter had gone out to play.

He woke at five, the sound of the pipes and the drums rattling
through his mind and the details of the next eighteen hours weaving
their apparently separate journeys through his brain. For thirty
minutes he lay still, staring at the ceiling, the pipes and drums still
haunting him and the Walther on his right side, beneath the sheet
where he had placed it five hours before, even in what he considered
a safe house, his hand resting on it all night and his fingers wrapped
around it.

Belfast, 12 July.

The day the Orangemen marched with their rolled umbrellas
and their bowler hats and banners. The day the Protestants stirred
their blood to the beat of the drums and the echo of the bugles in
commemoration of William's victory at the Battle of the Boyne
300 years before. The day the Brits and the RUC kept the Catholics at bay so that the Ulstermen could claim the Six Counties as
their own.

The sun touched the window. He rolled off the bed, washed,
shaved and dressed, and went to the rear door, not waking the family
in the bedrooms at the front. Even though it was not yet twenty
minutes to six, McKendrick waited till he saw Rorke in the alleyway
at the rear, and even then he did not leave the house. Rorke was
23, thinner than McKendrick, with longer hair, and had been his
minder for the past two years. He checked quickly and efficiently,
then nodded. McKendrick left the house and walked behind him to
the Granada parked at the end. The car was silver-grey and incon-
spicuous, registered to a baker in Springfield who was not on the
security checklist. The driver was smoking and the engine idling.

9

McKendrick slipped into the back seat, Rorke beside him, and the car pulled away.

It was still quiet, the first warmth seeping into the morning and the first security forces on the streets, the first surveillance helicopter chattering across the sky. When the patrols were out everything was normal, McKendrick knew. It was only when there were no patrols, no eyes in the sky, that you began to worry. It was then that they were clearing an area for the shoot-to-kill bastards from E4A or 14th Int or the SAS.

They turned into Beechwood Street. The houses were terraced with small gardens in front, the majority consisting of a square of grass surrounded by flowers but some of them paved. Most of the cars were second-hand and the curtains of the bedrooms were still drawn. In front of them the street curved slightly to the left, then straightened just before the point where Reardon lived. It was eight minutes past six, twelve minutes to wait. McKendrick tucked lower into the rear seat and wound down the window. The driver moved slowly along Beechwood Street, turned left at the end and stopped twenty yards from the junction so that they could see the van which came to pick up Tommy Reardon but would not be noticed themselves.

The planning had been immaculate, of course, the policy objective approved by the Army Council in Dublin and the military details agreed by the Northern Command. Knowledge of it had been restricted to those who would take part, and even then each section had been briefed only on the part it would play, unaware not only of the overall plan, but even unaware that an overall plan existed. Each of the North Belfast companies would be involved in the riots and bombings that day, each action soaking up more of the security forces, the timings and locations precise and vital, until the moment came when McKendrick and his people would take over. And seventy men coiled like springs in the Crum – the bleak and God-forsaken prison on the Crumlin Road. Seventy battle-hardened Provisional IRA men – bombers, gunmen and activists – with the explosives they would use to break their way to the main gate already smuggled in and only the gate between them and freedom. And all on Orange Day, all depending on the little bastard called Tommy Reardon. In the still of the morning – perhaps in the years of hatred captured and swirling in his mind – McKendrick heard the faintest sound of the pipes and the drums.

10

It was twenty minutes past six.

The Transit came down the road in front of them. The workmen were packed inside it and the vehicle had been sprayed blue, covering the name of the building company which had once been printed on its sides. Rorke left the Granada and walked casually to the junction, cigarette in hand. Sixty yards away Reardon left the house, climbed into the Transit, and the vehicle pulled away, the exhaust rattling and a thin line of blue smoke drifting from it.

Even though McKendrick had been baptized into the faith, it was of no concern to him that Reardon and his wife were also Catholic, or that their son and daughter were of the age where they would make their first Holy Communion. Reardon was a digger driver and the company for whom he worked did the occasional job for what might loosely be called the security forces. Both had been warned. Reardon was therefore a legitimate means to an even more legitimate end.

Rorke turned the corner, ground the cigarette on the pavement, and climbed into the car. McKendrick sat up and looked across at him. The minder nodded and the driver pulled away.

The site was surrounded by six-foot-high chain fencing and illuminated at night by spotlights. The Transit bumped across the ruts at the entrance and stopped by the Portacabin at the side of the agent's office. Reardon left his bag in the hut and collected the keys to the digger. The cab door was padlocked. He knelt down and examined the axle and undercarriage, his fingers searching delicately in the places where a bomb might have been concealed. The routine was as automatic as changing the Transit route to and from work each day when the job was outside Belfast. Only when he was satisfied did he unlock the door, climb in, wedge the photograph of his wife and children in the corner of the windscreen, and start the engine.

Tommy Reardon was 32 years old. He and Marie had married when he was twenty and she was nineteen. Their children were eight and seven, and there was a possibility – not yet confirmed – of a third. Reardon had left school at fifteen and served his apprenticeship at Harland and Wolff, losing his job when the yard cut back on its labour force. A year later he had begun work at the De Lorean car plant, leaving when it closed. After his second term of unemployment he had found work with the building firm of Ellis and Knight. Ten months later he had received his first threat. Six months ago an uncle in England had secured him a job at the Ford plant in Eastleigh, near Southampton. Two weeks before he was due to leave, the company had announced major cutbacks and voluntary redundancies for 500 of its existing workforce.

The morning was hot and the site busy. At eleven he stopped for ten minutes, pouring himself a coffee from the flask Marie had made that morning. At one he sat in the Portacabin with the other men from the Transit.

'So how's the Pope today?' The man who asked was a Protestant.

'Still blessing the world.' Reardon opened his sandwiches. 'Where's the umbrella? Thought you'd be carrying one.'

The conversation was quiet but cutting, each directing his words not at the symbols of the other's religion but at the bigotry of his own.

The Protestant looked back at him. 'Typical Taig.' He sniffed and looked out the window. 'No point carrying an umbrella unless it's raining, is there?'

The marching began just before nine, the surveillance helicopters in the sky above the Catholic areas of the city, the VCPs – vehicle checkpoints – suddenly and swiftly in place for fifteen minutes, then switched to another area of the Catholic heartland, and the army and RUC patrols sweeping the Catholic areas on the so-called census patrols, knocking on doors and checking on the whereabouts of males listed on the census reports, checking if known or suspected IRA activists or sympathizers were on the move. At one in the afternoon the first incident occurred – an apparently random attack on a security vehicle by a group of Catholic youths. Half an hour later a second incident took place, seemingly unrelated but provoking a Protestant reaction and sucking in police and army manpower; forty minutes later a third. By three in the afternoon the security problem was escalating, the incidents building suddenly and brutally into running battles, with police and army units intended to be held in reserve suddenly committed, and men not due to be on duty until the evening called in and placed on stand-by. At four the first petrol bomb was thrown, the crowd retreating quickly and orderly and the troops following, apparently beating them back but moving into the killing zone where the Provo snipers were waiting. At 4.20 the first soldier was shot by a gunman positioned at the Divis flats, ten minutes later a second, this time fatally. At 4.40 the *Belfast Tele-*

12

graph received the first bomb warning of the day. Half an hour later, with just enough time to clear the area, a five-pound bomb exploded in the city centre.

Tommy Reardon parked the digger, switched off the engine, padlocked the cab, returned the keys to the site office and walked to the Transit. It was six o'clock. The other men climbed in and the van pulled out of the gates.

At least it wasn't dark, at least they weren't in the country. Particularly after the first threats, and especially in the drives back from some of the sites twenty or thirty miles outside Belfast, he had prayed as they approached vehicles parked by the roadside in case they contained a bomb, or scoured the road ahead for signs of land mines and the countryside on either side from which the bombers would activate them. Had felt the panic every time a vehicle pulled in front of them in case it stopped and the men in the balaclavas leapt out and held them up, asked their names and religions, picked out the Catholics or the Protestants and took them to the ditch at the roadside. UFF or IRA, it didn't matter. All bastards.

The Transit turned into Beechwood Road and stopped outside his house. Reardon climbed out, shut the door, banged on the side, and watched as it trundled down the road, the exhaust rattling and the smoke hanging in the air. The street was quiet, a cluster of children playing ball and two women disappearing into a house twenty yards away. He smiled at them, walked up the path, unlocked the Yale and went inside. The smell of cooking and the sound of laughter came from the kitchen, at the rear. He dropped his bag on the hall floor, closed and locked the door, hung up his coat, kissed Marie and the kids and went upstairs. By the time he had washed and changed the supper was on the table.

The front door bell rang.

'I'll get it.' The boy pushed back his chair and ran into the hall. One of his son's friends, Reardon assumed. 'You can play after supper.' The boy stretched up and unlocked the door, his mother just behind him.

Rorke was wearing a donkey jacket and what appeared to be a woollen cap. 'Is Tommy in?' Even in the shadows of the hallway he sensed the way she tightened and smelt the fear which gripped her. 'He left his wallet in the motor, must have dropped out. I thought he might need it tonight.' He reached in his pocket.

13

The donkey jacket was the same as all the men wore. Marie relaxed, stood back. 'Come in, we're just eating.'

The Sierra at the top of the street edged forward.

Rorke stepped inside, pulled the balaclava over his face, and spun the woman round, his left hand clamped tight over her mouth to prevent her screaming and his right hand taking the Smith and Wesson from inside the jacket. The Sierra stopped outside the house, the two men stepped nonchalantly out and walked casually up the path and into the house, pulling the hoods over their heads and taking the AK47, with its folding stock, and the Czech CZ automatic pistol from their coats the moment they were inside.

'Who is it?' Reardon leaned across and saw the figures, realized. Tried to work out whether he could get through the back door before they shot him. Whether he could at least get his daughter out.

This happens to other people, not us, the thought screamed through Marie's head. She grabbed the boy and held him tight as Rorke pushed them into the sitting-room. Behind him one gunman bundled Reardon and his daughter into the room and the second closed and locked the front door, then the kitchen door at the back.

'Switch on the telly and close the curtains.'

Marie tried to stop trembling, to do as Rorke instructed. Then she stood in the middle of the floor, between the gunmen and her husband, the children clutching her skirt and the prayer running through her mind. They hadn't shot him yet. *Please, sweet Mary, Mother of God, may they have made a mistake. Please may they not have come for her husband after all.*

'Time to pay, Tommy.'

The children came out of the first shock and began to sob.

'Not here. Not in front of them.' Reardon moved slightly so that he was separated from his family, so that if they shot him they wouldn't hit his wife and children.

'You think we're going to stiff you?' There was amusement in Rorke's voice. 'You think I'm going to put the muzzle of this against your head or down your throat and blow your brains out?' His background had drained any mercy from him and his years with McKendrick had given his violence an edge, the beginning of a mirror image of the older man. 'No, Tommy boy. We just want to borrow you for a few hours, do a wee job for us.'

Both Reardon and his wife understood.

14

'Get on your working coat and boots. Don't want you driving through Belfast with your best clothes on, do we?'

Rorke followed Reardon upstairs. When they came down again Marie and the children were on the sofa, one of the gunmen in the armchair opposite them and the other by the door.

'Behave yourself and he comes back.' Rorke looked at the woman, then at Reardon. 'You do as we want and we don't touch her or the kids.'

The children were too frightened to cry.

'Nice and quiet, Tommy boy. Walk to the car and get in the back.'

He looked again at the woman. 'Don't worry, missus. You'll have him back by eleven.' If the bastard police and army could find enough of him to even fill a paper bag. No point in not giving them hope, though. Tell them the truth and one of them might try something; pretend to give them a chance and they'd do exactly as you said, even though they both knew what was going to happen. He pulled off the balaclava and the two of them walked down the path. Behind them one of the gunmen closed and locked the door. The driver of the Sierra glanced up at them and a second man opened the rear door. Reardon and Rorke climbed in and the car pulled away.

Seven o'clock, Rorke checked his watch. In five minutes the RUC would receive its third genuine bomb warning of the day, at eight its fourth. Everything on time and going to plan. The police and army already over-extended, the evening's bombs creating fresh diversions, the timing and location of each incident apparently random but carefully plotted to draw the security forces away from the route to the prison. And the lads waiting on the inside of the Crum for Tommy Reardon to drive his digger filled with high explosive into the front gate and blow it to kingdom come. Everything on schedule. Everything as McKendrick had foreseen.

'Now, Tommy boy. Where's that digger of yours?'

The gap in the curtains was less than two inches wide, and the curtains themselves had not moved. Perhaps it was because she was still in mourning that she kept them that way, she sometimes told herself. Perhaps because it prevented the sunlight from damaging the furniture. Perhaps because it enabled her to see what was happening without being seen herself. There were others in the street who kept a similar watch, she knew, but they reported to the

15

Provisionals. Beechwood Street, after all, was in Ballymurphy, part of the Catholic heartland.

Moira Sheehan was 66 years old and widowed for the last two. She was thin, with white hair, and walked with a slight stoop. Her fingers were bent and slightly arthritic. Moira Sheehan was also a Republican. In 1980 she had voted for the hunger striker Eamon McCann, officer commanding the Provisionals in Long Kesh, when – midway through his fast and in an attempt to gain publicity for it – he had stood for the British parliament. And six weeks later she had been one of the hundred thousand who had marched behind his coffin when his pitiful remains had been laid to rest in the Republican plot at Milltown cemetery. Even now she supported the Cause, gave money to it: even now she voted for Sinn Fein. But sometimes she wondered. About the men of violence and how they sometimes went about their business.

That morning Marie Reardon had told her the news about the baby, made her promise to keep it a secret until Marie had told her husband.

The Reardons had lived next door for the past nine years. During that time Moira Sheehan had grown close to them, had effectively become the grandmother to their children. Had shared both their dreams and their fears. Had sat with Marie one winter night when Tommy was working outside Belfast and the Transit had broken down, the night he had not returned home till midnight and they had feared the worst.

Now she watched as the Sierra drove out of Beechwood Street and turned left at the end. It was too soon for Tommy to be going out, she thought, there had barely been time for him to have his tea. And there had been something wrong. With the way the first man had gone in to the house, the way the others followed as soon as he stepped inside, the way Tommy had left with one of them.

Perhaps, in her heart of hearts, she already knew. Perhaps, in the deepest recesses of her soul, she knew what was going to happen to Tommy Reardon. She went to the kitchen, made herself a cup of tea, then resumed her position at the curtains and waited for Marie to come out with the children, waited to talk with them as she did every evening.

The bomb warning was exactly on time, giving a recognized code-word and location, and allowing thirty minutes for the area to be

16

cleared. The next genuine warning came fifty-five minutes later. Between the two there had been a constant stream of hoax calls via newspaper offices and radio and television stations, plus the normal emergency calls received every hour of every day.

It was sheer, bloody unadulterated luck, Halloran would reflect later, that he had offered to work overtime that evening, that for the first time in his life he was in the right place at the right time. That, above all, it was he who happened to be standing next to the constable when the call came in and was almost discarded in the cold and calculated chaos between the reports of bomb warnings from the journalists and switchboards receiving them.

'What is it?'

Halloran had been in the RUC for eighteen years, twelve of them as a sergeant, and – according to those close to him – would have made inspector, probably higher, if he had not voiced his opposition to certain aspects of Northern Ireland policing in the eighties quite so forcefully.

'Woman reports something funny with her next-door neighbours. No reply but she knows they're at home.'

'How?'

'Telly's on, she can hear it, and the curtains are drawn.' A burglary or a domestic, his shrug and the tone of his voice suggested, something CID could deal with in the morning.

'What else?'

'The kids aren't playing in the street as normal.'

'Who's at home?' It was instinct.

'The wife and kids. The husband left with someone else twenty minutes ago.'

Something the other man had missed, Halloran began to think, something the other man's lack of years had not picked up.

'Give me the name and number. I'll speak to her.'

The Transit had dropped Tommy from work as usual, Moira Sheehan told him. Half an hour later he had left with the other man. Marie hadn't brought the children out to play as she normally did. When she had knocked on the front door there was no reply and the back door was locked.

'But you're certain they're in?'

'Like I said, I can hear the television.'

'And the curtains are drawn?' The evening was still light – no need to draw the curtains.

'Yes.'

'What about at the back?'

'No, but the kitchen's empty.'

Halloran knew when not to ask a question.

'Funny though. The dinner's still on the table.'

'You said Tommy left with another man. Did he come home with Tommy?'

'No, he and the others came just after.'

The alarm bells began to ring.

'How many others?'

'Three of them altogether. Then there were the men in the car.'

Three in, one out with Tommy. Two still inside with Tommy's wife and children. 'What's Tommy do for a living?'

There was a commotion around him, another series of bomb calls being reported.

'He drives a digger.'

'Who for?'

'Ellis and Knight.'

Oh, Christ. Halloran knew what was happening. Oh Jesus bloody Christ.

The building site was deserted, the gate secured by a padlock. Rorke snapped through the chain with a set of bolt-cutters, pulled back the gate, and the Sierra drove through and parked behind the huts and Portacabins. Two minutes later a Transit, sprayed the same colour as those used by Ellis and Knight, drove in, a Cavalier close behind it.

There were three men in the Sierra, Reardon counted automatically, plus two in the Transit and four in the Cavalier, all armed with pistols or submachine guns.

'Keys?'

Behind them a gunman closed the gates and hung the padlock and chain in place.

'In the agent's office.'

Access was easy: a crowbar against the door, the lock holding but the wood around it splintering, then giving way. The office was neat and organized, a filing cabinet in one corner and a desk against the far wall, the site plans and charts stacked neatly on it. Beside the cabinet was a line of hooks with keys hanging from them.

'Which one?' Rorke was always behind him.

If he did what they said, Reardon thought, then at least Marie and the kids might live. His stomach churned with fear and he fought to stop his hands shaking. He took the keys and stepped outside. The digger was parked forty yards away, in the open. Rorke followed him across the site. Instinctively Reardon bent down to examine the underside of the vehicle for bombs.

'I don't think we need bother about that tonight, Tommy.'

He unlocked the cab, started the motor, and drove the digger to the side of the Transit.

'How's the fuel tank?' Rorke's attention to detail was as meticulous as McKendrick's planning.

'Half-full.'

'Check it,' Rorke ordered.

The back doors of the Transit were open. Two of the gunmen placed a plank against the rim of the floor, rolled out a forty-gallon drum, two hundred pounds of Semtex packed inside, then manhandled it into the bucket at the front of the digger. It was almost dusk.

'Time to go, Tommy boy.' Rorke pulled a canvas sheet over the barrel. 'The Crum and no stopping. Remember Marie and the kids.' He saw the look on Reardon's face. 'Don't worry, you'll have plenty of time to jump clear.' No point telling him the truth, no point telling Reardon that the IRA man in the first of the two escort vehicles would detonate the explosives the moment the digger rammed the gate.

The surveillance helicopter hovered in the sky and the army patrols swung into Beechwood Street and the terraces on either side, the Green Jackets piling out and knocking on the doors, beginning the census checks – the patrols leapfrogging house to house, the RUC policemen accompanying them.

'Dermot Wilson is registered here.' It was the second lieutenant's first Northern Ireland tour. 'Is he in? Where is he? What's he doing tonight?'

The woman slammed the door in his face.

'Michael Sullivan.' It was the officer with the second patrol. 'Does he still live here? Is he in Belfast? When did you last see him?'

It was no more nor less than the families in the street expected: the Brits putting on the pressure on Orange Day, the bastards letting them know who was boss. Piss off, Sullivan's wife began to say.

The patrol pushed past her and into the hallway, searching the rooms, downstairs, upstairs. Sullivan was different, Sullivan was on the security computer as a known Provo. His wife was shouting and his children screaming. The patrol hurried past them and out of the house.

The men in the patrol knew each other, had trained with each other, become accustomed to patrolling the streets together. Except for the two men who had joined them half an hour before and who had sat silently with them as the armoured personnel carrier swung into Beechwood Street.

The first patrol was already pushing its way in to the next doorway, the second lieutenant still questioning the family in the hallway and the rest of the patrol searching the rooms upstairs and downstairs, running down the stairs and pushing past, out into the street and to the next address on the list. The soldiers moving quickly and confusingly.

Six soldiers into number 47, only four out. Two — the two who had joined them thirty minutes before — through the trapdoor on the upstairs landing and into the roof space.

The patrols were still ten houses away from Tommy Reardon's. Abruptly the soldiers climbed back into the vehicles and the convoy screamed away as quickly and apparently as predictably as it had arrived.

The woman who left the slightly battered Opel by the shops three corners from Beechwood Street was in her late twenties, five feet six inches tall, with brown hair — Irish hair her mother called it — and thin attractive features. She spent the next fifteen minutes observing both the alleyway which ran behind Reardon's house, and the street itself. By the time she returned to the car it was positioned at the top of Beechwood Street.

Cathy Nolan had been born in Northern Ireland. Her family religion was Protestant, though she herself had slipped into something bordering atheism. For four years she had served in the Woman's Royal Army Corps, the last two of them in Germany, where she had volunteered for what was described — officially, at least — as an adventure training course, but which was a front set up by the talent-spotters and run by an SAS officer from the NATO Long Range School near Lake Constance. At the end of the course she had been taken aside and the suggestion made that she might

20

like to consider Special Duties. Three months later she had been given a new name and sent on the ten-week SAS course at Pontrilas for women undercover agents. At the end of that period, and with yet another identity, she had begun work with the 14th Intelligence Corps in Northern Ireland, based in Lisburn. For the past month she had been seconded to E4A, the RUC undercover surveillance department. The coat she wore was from Next, green but slightly faded, all the pockets with zips which she herself had added so that nothing would fall from them, and the 9mm automatic pistol she wore in the waist holster beneath the jacket was a Browning Hi-Power.

'All quiet?' Brady sat in the driver's seat. He was slightly older, fair hair and lean face.

The microphone in the car was voice-activated, the aerial concealed, and the two of them wore earpieces. Brady also wore a Browning Hi-Power in a waist holster on his left side, a Heckler and Koch MP5K lay on the floor between the driver's seat and the door, covered by a folded newspaper, and the two-man back-up car was three streets away.

'So far.'

Someone was being greedy — she had first felt the unease midway through the briefing, felt it again now. The SAS were dealing with the gunmen inside the house, plus the Provo team escorting Tommy Reardon and his digger. Assuming they found him in time. E4A were assigned to tailing any IRA men who might show during the operation. The two operations fine and logical, except they were being run together. And that was the problem. Either the SAS should be inside the house, or E4A should be waiting outside. Not both. Bloody typical, she thought. Different bosses playing out the same game. Herself and Brady in the middle.

Noel Ellis had been notified thirty minutes before and had telephoned RUC headquarters to confirm. The Special Branch man showed his identification and came straight to the point.

'An employee of yours, Tommy Reardon. We need to know where he's working.'

Ellis and a schoolfriend, Billy Knight, had formed the building firm twenty years before. Ellis was a Catholic and Knight a Protestant. When the other man had died two years ago Ellis had deemed it fit not to change the name of the firm.

21

'Why?' He poured himself a Black Bush and offered the policeman one. 'He's a good worker, took him on myself. Not the sort to get mixed up with the wrong people. Not in trouble, is he?'

The SB man declined the drink. 'What site's he working on?'

'Short Street, by the docks. I wouldn't normally know, but I was there this afternoon.'

'And he'd leave his digger there?'

Ellis began to understand. 'Yes.'

'Can I use the phone?'

The roof space was dark and dusty. Haslam and Phillips moved carefully, picking out the rafters in the beams of the streamlight torches and transferring their weight slowly and exactly, making no noise and counting the number of houses over which they passed. Each carried a Browning Hi-Power, with spare magazines in pouches on their belts. Each wore a remote earpiece, the microphones of their Mitre radios concealed and an induction loop passing through their clothing to the hand pressure switch by their wrists. Any messages they sent would be via the car parked three streets away, the car on remote and the message relayed to control, the net they were using dedicated to the operation and verbal signals kept to a minimum in case the IRA intercepted them or the people in the houses heard them. After eighteen minutes they came to the trap-door above the upstairs landing of Tommy Reardon's house. Haslam clicked the switch three times – the signal to the man on listening watch that they were in position – and waited.

In ten minutes he would die, Reardon knew. His palms were wet with sweat, and the fear drummed through his head and churned in his stomach. He followed the Sierra out of the docks area, under the motorway flyover and up Brougham Street. The route was as carefully planned as the pick-up: the building site was less than a mile and a quarter from the Crum, and where possible the route wound its way through back streets – all Catholic – with the houses on either side protecting the convoy from the eye in the sky. Only at three points would the digger be exposed, and the last of those was on the hundred-yard run-up to the prison itself.

The convoy filtered left along North Queen Street, the sound of the digger engine drowning the whine of the surveillance helicopter hovering high in the sky half a mile away above the Falls, then turned third right into Spamount Street. The terraced houses on each side were red brick and spotlessly clean, yet in the streets to the right many of the houses were boarded up and painted with INLA slogans.

McKendrick's Granada was waiting on the corner of Lepper Street. As the convoy approached he slid into the passenger seat. Rorke left the Sierra, joined him, and the convoy slipped past, along Lepper Street, the Republican slogans daubed on the walls and the sides of the tower blocks to Reardon's left. Five minutes to go, he knew, perhaps six or seven if he managed to slow down. He turned right into Churchill Street and tried to control the trembling.

'Any problems?' McKendrick sat back as Rorke spun the Granada round and headed for Beechwood Street. One last check before they cleared the area, he decided.

'Should there be?'

The Gazelle was half a mile from the convoy, the surveillance at an oblique angle to avoid detection. 'Red Nine, Yellow.' Communication from the helicopter was kept to a minimum, call signs omitted and codenames for locations pre-set.

The message was relayed to the two Macrolan Land-Rovers: Red Nine the code for the location where the digger had been spotted – and from this the suggestion that the Crum was the probable target – and Yellow the code for the fact that vehicles were following the digger. And that was the problem, the SAS commander in charge of the ambush knew. Because the explosives which Tommy Reardon was carrying were probably on a remote firing system – possibly others, but certainly a remote device as insurance in case the others failed or Reardon decided to make a run for it. So to save Reardon they would have to take out the command vehicle. But there was no guarantee that the vehicles in front of or behind Tommy Reardon's digger were part of the IRA operation.

McKendrick and Rorke saw it even before they passed the car. Two people sitting doing nothing at this time of night. Either the front car for an undercover operation, in which case it wasn't connected with Tommy Reardon and there would be a back-up three hundred yards away, or itself the back-up car, in which case the operation might concern Reardon.

Rorke drove past, ignoring the next turning left which led to

23

Beechwood Street. Only when he was a hundred yards on did he turn left, then left again, and accelerate up the road which crossed Beechwood Street twenty yards from the top and which ran parallel to the one on which the back-up vehicle was parked. Fifteen yards from the junction with Beechwood Street he stopped, then he and McKendrick left the vehicle and strolled casually round the corner.

The car was parked twenty yards away, the man and woman in the front seat and facing away from them. So what the hell was going on? McKendrick tried to work it out. Was the stake-out on Reardon's house, or was it just coincidence that the undercover car happened to be parked seventy yards from where Reardon's wife and children were being held? If the subject was Reardon, then what did the bastards know about the operation? But the fact that there was a car meant that even if the security forces suspected that something was up with Reardon, they didn't know what. Because if they did know they wouldn't have revealed that knowledge by putting an undercover car so close to the house.

He nodded at Rorke and thumbed the safety off the Walther.

They'd been in position too long, both Brady and Nolan knew, shouldn't be sitting in the vehicle like this. Should have left it and be standing on the street, lost in a doorway. Shouldn't be here in the first place. Except orders were orders.

'Oh shit.' He slipped the car into gear, released the handbrake, and held the car on the foot brake. 'McKendrick's behind us.' He warned Nolan, the message passed to control via the vehicle's voice-activated microphone. 'Rorke's with him.'

Back-up in now, Nolan knew Control was ordering. Except that was what Control was not doing. Because if Control ordered the back-up car in then it would confirm that they were a forward stake-out, but if Control didn't send the back-up in then she and Brady were in trouble. Therefore she and Brady had to react to protect themselves, but the moment they reacted they would blow the operation to rescue Tommy Reardon's wife and family.

Haslam heard the clicks on his earpiece. He eased up one edge of the trapdoor, Phillips covering him. Haslam opened the trap a fraction more. The only light came from below and the only sound was that of a television. He dropped through the hole and on to the landing, Phillips still covering him, took the Browning from the holster and covered the stairs as Phillips dropped from the roof space.

Two of the doors off the landing were closed and the third ajar. Haslam slid through the open door, clearing it quickly, and swept the room with the torch, holding it in his left hand and away from his body, the Browning in his right. It was a child's bedroom, bunk beds against one wall, a handful of toys on the floor, and empty. They cleared the other rooms, left the landing, moved down the stairs, and checked that the kitchen at the rear was empty. The door of the lounge was closed, from inside they heard the canned laughter from the television.

Rorke reached the front of the car as McKendrick drew level with the driver's door. The window was open. In one movement he stopped, bent and levelled the Walther at the man in the driver's seat.

'Wrong time, wrong place.'

Brady looked round and appeared to freeze, face suddenly white.

Rorke stepped in front of the car, the CZ pointed at the windscreen.

She and Brady had talked it through, so that each knew what the other would do and say, so that their movements would co-ordinate, so that one would create a diversion while the other went for his gun, so that the driver could reach the back-up weapon. But Brady's hands were on the steering wheel so that he couldn't go for his gun, and if she went for the Browning in her own waist holster they would see. Which left the MP5K on the floor by the driver's seat. But to get to it she would have to move across Brady's body. And to do that she would need a cover.

'Fuck you. You're setting me up, you bastard.' She directed her fear and anger at the driver. 'Not me.' She turned to McKendrick. 'I'm not with him. I'm nothing to do with this.'

She turned and tried to leave the car. Out of the passenger door or over the driver. Appeared to panic.

'So what're you doing if you're not with him?' McKendrick enjoyed the moment.

'What the fuck do you think I'm doing with him?' He picked me up in Amelia Street ten minutes ago: the implication and language were clear. Not if you're in the front seat with him: she saw the expression in McKendrick's eyes. Not if you've still got your pants on and your legs together.

25

'Not here.' McKendrick enjoyed the agony of the target before the kill. I know you. He tried to remember the driver's face.

'Ten quid. You must be joking.'

Finish it now and get out, part of McKendrick's brain told him. Enjoy it ten more seconds. 'Better give a condemned man his last wish, then.'

She couldn't, Nolan suddenly knew. She needed the gun but couldn't do what she had to do to get to it.

'Fuck off.'

McKendrick swung the Walther at Nolan. 'Do it.'

She wouldn't be able to. She leaned forward and slightly down, and undid Brady's trousers. The back-up had better come in carefully: too slow and they'd be too late, too fast and the bastards would see. And even if she could reach the MP5K it would only be with her left hand and the gun was pointing forward, for the driver to use, so she wouldn't be able to use it.

McKendrick chuckled, saw the way she glanced up at him before she reached inside the driver's trousers. The penis was limp. Slow everything down, don't do it yet, give the boys in the house a chance. She touched it. She couldn't, she knew again. No point in even trying, she knew.

'Do it,' McKendrick repeated.

She couldn't reach the MP5K, but she could reach Brady's Browning. She lowered her head on Brady's lap. A coffee after, she told herself. Large and Irish. Plenty of Black Bush. She let go with her right hand and held it only with her left. Slow down, she told herself, give the back-up and the SAS a chance. 'Do it,' McKendrick ordered her again. Nolan's mouth circled the head and her fingers felt for the Browning in the holster on the left side of his body.

He had already delayed too long, McKendrick told himself. He should have come in, done the job, got out fast. Five more seconds, he told himself.

What the hell was wrong? Nolan thought. Where the hell was the back-up? Her fingers were round the Browning and her thumb slipped the safety off. He's playing with you, she knew, had already given you thirty seconds more of life than he should have done. So why was she still delaying? Why didn't she do it?

Door hinges on left, Haslam rehearsed the movement in his mind: he goes left, Phillips right. It was thirty seconds to nine. He held the Browning Hi-Power in his right hand, the door handle in his left.

The television was in the right corner under the window. Marie Reardon pulled the children closer to her on the sofa, an arm over their shoulders and a hand half-covering their faces. One of the gunmen was in the armchair to her left, the pistol always pointing at her, and the other was on her right, what she thought was a Kalashnikov on his lap and also pointing at her. The gunman with the pistol stood up and switched television channels for the BBC news. At nine o'clock it will be all over, she suddenly realized, at nine o'clock Tommy will be dead. The programme ended and the door opened.

Gunman to left by television, pistol in hand, Haslam saw. He stepped left and cleared the space for Phillips to enter, crouched instinctively, the Browning already levelled at the gunman's chest. Squeezed the trigger. Phillips stepped behind him, swept right. Gunman in armchair, Kalashnikov across lap. The Browning was already on target. He double-tapped the trigger.

Marie jerked the children tighter to her and tried to turn, tried to protect them, put herself between them and the gunmen. Was too shocked to even begin to understand.

Haslam was still shooting, the man with the pistol was on the floor, the pistol still in his hand. Haslam squeezed the trigger twice more, saw the hand fall open. He dropped on to one knee, pulled out the mag, even though it still contained four rounds, took the spare from the magazine pouch on his belt and slid it in, the Browning on the gunman again. He edged forward, kicked the gun away, made sure the man was dead. To his right Phillips cleared the Kalashnikov.

'Friendly forces no casualties. Send QRF.'

Marie was in shock, shuddering with fright. She felt the hand on her shoulder and knew they were going to kill her, tried not to look round, looked round anyway. 'How many men are there, Marie?' The voice was English, a blur of sounds just as the events of the past thirty seconds had been a blur of colours and images. Leave the children, she tried to plead, for God's sake spare the children. Her brain was confused and her head was spinning. Phillips slapped her face. 'How many gunmen were there, Marie?'

For one second, perhaps less, the blow cleared her mind. 'Two.' The mist closed in again.

'Friendly forces no casualties.' Haslam repeated the message. 'Send QRF.'

The penis was harder, her mouth still around it. For Christ's sake do it, Nolan told herself. The shots from the house echoed up the street. She sensed rather than saw the moment, McKendrick's eyes flicking off her and down the road, Rorke glancing momentarily behind him.

She straightened, gun in hand, aimed at McKendrick. Shot twice then spun left, shot Rorke through the windscreen, missed, perhaps one shot on target, she wasn't sure. Brady slid his right foot off the brake and on to the accelerator, left off the clutch. Rorke moved, too slow and the wrong way. Finger pressing the trigger but the movement slightly altering his aim. The Opel slammed forward, into him, knocking him back and down. McKendrick was tumbling backwards, Walther discharging. Brady's foot was hard on the floor, Rorke on the ground in front. McKendrick was framed against the window behind the driver. Nolan turned, aimed behind Brady, fired at McKendrick through the window, the glass shattered. The Opel hurtled forward, over Rorke, and down Beechwood Street, the car bumping, not running smoothly. Nolan still facing back and checking, seeing McKendrick fall and looking for Rorke, Brady still accelerating and the engine screaming. They were twenty yards away, thirty. Something wrong with the car, she thought, something slowing it down. Rorke still underneath, she realized, Brady still accelerating to clear the area. The car freed itself of Rorke's body, the rear right wheel spinning on bone and flesh, then the torso flew out like a red rag.

The Land-Rovers of the Quick Reaction Force screeched to a stop outside Reardon's house and the soldiers of the Sherwood Foresters ran inside. Haslam and Phillips put on the caps the first officer gave them, left the house, climbed into the first vehicle, and the driver accelerated away.

The two Macrolan Land-Rovers screeched to a halt and slid across the road, slightly apart, the first blocking the left lane and the second the right, so that vehicles passing between them would have to drive through a chicane. Routine VCP – vehicle checkpoint – the watchers knew; in fifteen minutes the soldiers jumping out of the vehicles would jump back in and the Land-Rovers would scream away as quickly and suddenly as they had come. The soldiers were fanning out, the man with the GPMG – general purpose machine gun – taking a position behind a low wall thirty yards from the road block.

He had two hundred yards left to live, Tommy Reardon knew. Slow down and delay it. Accelerate and get it over with. Dear Mary, Mother of God, may it be quick and painless and may Marie and the kids be all right. He was wet with fear and shaking with nerves, his throat dry and tight and his bowels churning. They were almost at the end of the Antrim Road. The convoy turned right into Annesley Street and snaked through the alleyway behind the houses. Thirty yards up the back street turned a right angle to the left. To his right Reardon saw the glass and metal side of the Mater Infirmorum Hospital, the junction with the Crumlin Road twenty yards in front of him, and the prison itself a hundred yards away on the other side of the hospital. The command Sierra accelerated away from him, up the Crumlin Road, and the Cavalier fell back slightly. He came to the junction and turned right.

VCP, the Sierra driver suddenly saw, just where they didn't want it. Everyone in the car was armed, the front passenger carrying a Kalashnikov across his lap under a coat, and the rear with the remote firing device beside him. He was beginning to slow, still trying to decide what to do. Everything normal, he told himself, everything routine. Land-Rovers in standard position for a vehicle check, soldiers in position. Something wrong, it was a flicker in his mind, something about the soldiers. Not moving like ordinary squaddies, not the same age as ordinary squaddies, all slightly older, late twenties or early thirties. He swung the car left and swore a warning, the front passenger whipping the coat off the AK.

The night exploded. Gunfire in front of him, concentrated on the Sierra which had just passed him. Tommy Reardon jerked, foot stabbing the accelerator momentarily and the digger speeding up, then slowing slightly. The gunfire was deafening, unending. Sheets of sound pouring from the machine gun on the right of the road. The Criminal Court was on his left and the prison was on his right. He turned and glanced back. The Cavalier was still moving, the unseen men on either side of the road firing into it. He was confused, still terrified. Did not know what to do. Realized he was still moving and jammed his foot on the brake. The Cavalier bumped into the

29

rear of the digger. A car he hadn't seen before pulled in front of him, the men getting out even as it slowed, as he himself stopped. His foot was still locked on the brake, his body frozen with fear and the gunfire still crashing into the Sierra in front of him. A second car slammed to a halt, more men racing out, all armed, faces blackened. One of them pulled the cab door open and jerked him out, others surrounding and protecting them. A third car screamed to a stop, and the bomb disposal expert ran for the barrel of explosive, more men covering him.

'It's all right, Tommy.' He heard the voice as he was bundled out of the digger and towards the first car. 'Marie and the kids are fine.' He was pushed into the back seat, men clambering in around him and top of him. 'What did you say?' He was still confused, still frightened. 'Marie and the kids are okay. It's over.' The car accelerated away, men outside slamming the doors shut and the heavy duty rounds of the GPMG still battering the car with the remote firing device.

*   *   *

The water was piping hot. Doherty lathered the foam round his chin and jowls, and wet the razor under the tap. It was beginning to show, he told himself: the sinking of the eyes and the hollowing of the cheeks. He remembered the afternoon after the doctor had warned him of the possibility, the way it had passed, the last sun setting on the water at Kilmore, and the mountains fading into purple. Eighteen months, then he would face his Maker. He wiped the steam from the mirror and drew a swathe across the foam on the left side of his face.

So what will you say to him? He dipped the razor under the hot water tap and drew it round his chin, then down his throat. What will he say to you? Will the Holy Mary still smile her smile at you? And what will those you've left behind say? What sort of footnote will you have in the history of the struggle? It would be a small one, he was aware; perhaps even anonymous. Even in death it would not be possible to afford him the recognition he had so diligently avoided in life. For the past eight years Eamon Doherty, professor and family man, pillar of the community and the church, had been Chief of Staff of the Army Council of the Provisional IRA. For almost ten years before that he had served as a planner and tactician, and for the years before that in whatever role the movement required.

Bloody fiasco in Belfast, the anger broke his thoughts. Two dead at the house in Beechwood Street. McKendrick and Rorke butchered in the street. Eight shot to pieces on the Crumlin Road and seventy still trussed up inside the prison there. And all on Orange Day. The Prods chuckling all the way to the bank and the Brits laughing all the way back to London.

He wiped his face and dressed.

So who would begin the moves this morning? he wondered. Who would press for a major investigation into the identity of the member who had leaked the operation to spring the men from the Crum? Who would pick up on the McKendrick farce and turn it to his advantage?

Conlan or Quin, he knew; in the end it would come down to one of these. Both were respected in the Movement, both were playing for their places closer to the top of the pecking order. Both politicos, sharp tongues and sharper brains. Conlan tall, slender build. Quin bigger, using his bulk to disguise the speed at which his mind moved.

In a way the Movement was at yet another crossroads. There had always been discussion – often dissent – between the Republicans and the Socialists, even after the Movement had appeared to wither in the fifties and sixties. And in the seventies the Official IRA, the Stickies, had lost ground to the new heads and fiery demands of the Provisionals. Yet within the Provos there had also been disagreement – about the role of violence and the desirability of combining the gun with the vote. Now the new crossroads, Conlan and Quin already laying out their qualifications for the leadership, for the job of Chief of Staff. He finished dressing and left the house.

The Army Council met at eleven, seven men made up from representatives of the Southern Command, the Northern Command – the so-called war zone – and GHQ. The room in which the meeting took place had been electronically swept beforehand. For two hours they discussed the implications of the changes in Eastern Europe, the Middle East and North Africa, and how they would affect the financing of the Movement and the flow of arms, ammunition and explosives to it.

Conlan and Quin know, Doherty thought once; both have looked in my eyes and seen the shadow of the Maker lurking there.

For the next hour they discussed the quartermaster's reports on

31

the arms and explosives situation, the fact that although Libya had now said it would stop supplying the IRA, the statement made little difference given the volume already shipped to Ireland and stored there.

So how *would* he like to be remembered? The Bringer of Peace – if there could ever be such a person in that small corner of the world they called Ireland – or the Harbinger of War? What single action would mark the end of his stewardship of the Movement? And who would give it to him, who would give him what he now craved for more than peace or war?

They moved to the next item: the aborted attempt to free the men from Crumlin Road jail, the deaths which had accompanied it, and the political capital made by both the Protestants and the English. Who's going to move first, Doherty wondered, Conlan or Quin? The senior officer from the Northern Command briefed them on the background to the operation, the planning which had prefaced it, then the events of the day and evening.

'So what went wrong?' It was Quin.

The officer commanding the North Belfast Brigade shrugged.

'There was a leak?'

The man shrugged again. 'Possibly.'

'And what action has been taken to trace it?'

'A board of enquiry has been set up. The security section has already begun its investigations.'

The council was about to be split, they all understood, to be torn apart by the implications of the Orange Day fiasco.

'Who knew about the operation? Who knew enough to direct the security forces to Beechwood Street and to the Crum? Who knew about Tommy Reardon?'

The only people who knew the overall military details were the planners on the Northern Command. Therefore the leak must have come from one of them or their staff. With the implications for the Movement which followed from this.

'Gentlemen.' Conlan's voice was quiet, calming. Laying the groundwork for his move. That was the difference between the two men, Doherty understood. Quin would make his move, upfront and immediate. Conlan would lay the ground then withdraw, come back for the kill later. A come-on, just as the bombers sometimes left a small device by the roadside or in a car, but the main device in a second car or where they knew the security forces would wait while

32

the Bomb Disposal dealt with the first. 'There may or may not be a leak. If there is we must find it. If there isn't, we mustn't let the British con us into thinking there was and wrecking the Movement with a witch-hunt.'

The trap now, the execution later, Doherty knew for certain.

'I would only like to say one other thing. We all approved the operation.' Therefore we must all share the guilt – it was unspoken, but clearly meant and equally clearly understood. 'And that decision was a correct one. The political and military value of the operation had it come off would have been incalculable.' He turned to the officer commanding the North Belfast Brigade. 'Now perhaps you could tell us of any progress on the part of the security section.'

'So where was the leak in the organization?' Quin returned to his original theme. 'How does it affect future operations? What about operations on the mainland?'

What are you playing at? Doherty glanced at Conlan. Where are you taking us? He saw the way the other man was looking at him. You know, he thought again. You know what the doctor has told me to expect, you know the question growing in my mind.

'So what do we do?' The discussion continued for another forty minutes before Doherty gave Conlan and Quin their chance. Quin would move first, he supposed; Conlan would allow that, then check-mate him.

'A spectacular.' Instead it was Conlan, speaking first and more forcefully, though his voice was still quiet. 'One the bastards will remember for ever.' Conlan rarely swore, they all knew.

'Why?'

'For the morale of the Movement after Orange Day.'

A come-on, Doherty remembered, waiting for the moment.

'How?' Quin walked into the trap. 'We've already agreed that until we know otherwise we must assume that the units in the North and the ASUs on the mainland and in Europe might be compromised.'

Conlan paused. 'There's a sleeper.'

They would all remember the moment and the silence which hung round it.

'Where?'

'On the other side of the water.'

'Who?'

Conlan shook his head.

'Details?'

He shook his head again. Some disciplines in life were easy to maintain, others more difficult. Yet none compared with the discipline which he imposed upon himself when he thought about the individual they were now discussing.

'Who recruited him?' It was Quin.

'I did.'

'How long's he been in place?'

'Five, six years.' The answer was necessarily vague. 'Perhaps more, perhaps less.'

'But he's done nothing in that time?' Quin looked for the way out.

'A few jobs for the French and Germans, a couple for the Libyans and Palestinians. Occasionally for us as well, though it was always camouflaged, made to look as if it was somebody else's job.'

Doherty sensed the excitement round the table.

'So why haven't you told us about Sleeper?'

It was ironic, Doherty thought later, that it was Quin who gave the man his codename. Who stopped referring to him as simply *a* sleeper. Who provided the name which would immortalize him.

Conlan shrugged, did not reply.

'So what do we do?' Doherty moved them round the impasse, asked the question again.

'A spectacular.' Conlan repeated his previous answer. 'Something no one will ever forget.'

He's giving me my epitaph, Doherty thought, and in doing so he's staking his claim for my place when I go. But he's doing more than that. He's planning ahead, setting up an agenda for five, ten years' time. He's giving us what we have always lacked in the past. He's giving us the power. Not just the gun or the bomb, something much more.

Perhaps it was then that he began to see. The last option, he began to think, the one they had occasionally considered but always rejected.

'Where?'

'The mainland.'

'Where exactly on the mainland?'

'London.'

Doherty tasted the excitement, smelt it, savoured it, eating into the fibres of his body and the marrow of his bones. There had always

been four options for campaigns on the mainland: the first three –
the soft option, the military option and the political option – they
had planned for, sent the teams to the mainland for. Had hit the
soft targets; then the military, a barracks or a recruiting office; had
gone against the politicians, even mortared Downing Street. But the
fourth option was different. The fourth option was untouchable.
And now Conlan was about to propose it.

'Who?'

Even now Conlan could remember the street where he had been
born and in which he had been brought up. Could remember the
excitement which rippled through it when the pedlar came selling,
the bright colours of the ribbons and the glint in the boxes on the
wooden tray. Could remember what they called the pedlar, even
though it was a woman.

'Codename PinMan.'

'And who is PinMan?'

Doherty sensed the moment the others realized.

'The British royal family.'

2

THE EVENING WAS WARM, the first dusk lost in the lights of London, the dome of St Paul's behind and the Thames in front.

Major R.E.F. Fairfax – Marlborough, Sandhurst, the First Battalion the Grenadier Guards – stood straight-backed at the window in the officer's quarters of the Waterloo Barracks of the Tower of London and looked across the wasteland which was the City of London at this time of night. He was dressed in full uniform, his bearskin – white plume on the left-hand side – and sword on the stand in the small hallway.

Roderick Edward Fenwick Fairfax was 32 years old, six feet two inches tall, with a broken nose that was still slightly bent. His mother hunted with the Beaufort and his father had preceded him at Marlborough.

His guests had arrived an hour before. At twenty minutes to ten he telephoned the Spur Guard Room and asked the corporal to collect the party.

The quarters, up four flights of iron stairs, were functional rather than comfortable: a lounge, kitchen and bathroom, plus a small hallway off the main corridor. The six visitors gathered round the table in the lounge were formally dressed, the men in evening suits and the ladies in long dresses, and the champagne and food had come from Fortnum and Mason. Two of his guests that evening – the Japanese banker and the American corporate lawyer – were unknown to Roddy Fairfax. Sometimes a friend would ask him to arrange such an evening, the other guests usually from overseas and always business contacts. Occasionally, if the contacts were sufficiently important and it was the First Battalion which was mounting the Guard, Fairfax himself would take charge, even though it was normally the responsibility of a more junior rank.

The doorbell on the ground floor at the west end of the barracks rang. The guests left the officers' quarters, made their way down the stairs, then followed the orderly – dressed in civilian clothes – across Broad Walk and joined the tiny knot of people standing in front of Traitor's Gate.

It was ten minutes to ten. The Tower was still, the silence broken by the crash of the escort taking its position beneath the Bloody Tower. In the shadows along Water Lane, the cobbled street running inside the outer wall, they saw the first pinprick of light as the Chief Warder left the Byward Tower, the light growing brighter as he walked at the 'sedate pace' required by history. In his left hand he carried a lantern, the candle burning brightly, and in his right a ring of keys. At the Bloody Tower he turned left, handed the lantern to the man at the right rear of the escort, and fell in between the two leading soldiers. Then the warder and the escort marched back through the gate, wheeled right and disappeared in the dusk.

On the level stonework midway down the two sets of steps forming Broad Stairs the Guard took their position, the blood red of their tunics bright even against the dark. It was five minutes to ten, almost four and a half minutes. Fairfax checked his watch and waited. It was the done thing to cut it fine – no earlier than five minutes to ten, no later than two and a half – but God help any officer of the Guard who miscalculated. He stepped from the shadows and fell in in front of them, standing at ease, then standing easy, hands on sword, the tip resting on the ground in front of him. In the stillness he heard the commands as the Chief Warder locked the Middle and Byward Tower Gates and sealed the Tower for the night, then the crash of boots on cobbles as the warder and escort returned, and the challenge from the sentry at number three post.

'Halt. Who comes there?'

'The keys.'

'Whose keys?'

'Queen Elizabeth's keys.'

'Pass, Queen Elizabeth's keys, and all's well.'

On Broad Stairs Fairfax brought the guard to attention.

The escort and the warder swung under the Bloody Tower and marched up the gradual incline; fifteen yards from the bottom of the steps the escort to the keys stamped to a halt. The timing was perfect, the sound of the boots on the cobbles lingering as the clock on Waterloo Barracks began to strike the four quarters.

The last quarter ended. It was ten seconds before the hour. The

Chief Warder stepped forward and raised his bonnet. 'God preserve Queen Elizabeth.' His voice echoed back through history.

'Amen.' The voices of Fairfax and the guard joined his.

It was ten o'clock precisely. At the moment the barracks clock began to sound the hour the first note of the Last Post lifted like a ghost. The last chime echoed through the stillness and the last bugle note lingered in the dark.

By the time Fairfax dismissed the guard and returned to his quarters the champagne had been poured.

'Incredible ceremony. The timing was so precise, as if it was to a stop watch.' It was the Japanese banker.

'We've had a few centuries to practise.' The line always went down well.

'When you were giving orders you used the word "hype", not "arms".' It was the American. '"Slope hype, present hype."'

'From the French,' Fairfax's nod indicated his appreciation that the lawyer had noticed. 'The Grenadiers took it after they'd destroyed the French Imperial Guard at Waterloo.'

The conversation drifted over the history of the ceremony and on to the world economic situation and the possibility that certain countries might be climbing out of recession.

'Trouble is, of course, that when the upturn comes we won't be in a position to take advantage of it.' The guest had been with Fairfax at Marlborough and was now a senior analyst in a leading merchant bank.

'For example?' They had drifted slightly from the main conversation and were standing together looking out the window.

'Company called New World Electronics. Best research department in the country, but their order books are low because everyone's scared to invest at the moment.' And therefore the shares are at rock bottom, if anyone was reckless enough to buy.

So . . . Fairfax did not need to ask.

'By tomorrow evening Britain will no longer have a company which is a world leader in its field.' The accountant raised his glass. 'Thanks for tonight. I think our Japanese friend really enjoyed himself.'

At ten minutes to midnight Fairfax escorted his guests to the West Gate, shook hands with each of them, and watched as the gate was unlocked and they made their way to the limousines waiting on Tower Hill. At eight the following morning he telephoned his stockbroker, checked the price of shares in New World Electronics, and instructed him to buy five thousand.

At 11.30, when the Guard was dismounted, he was driven to Wellington Barracks near St James's Park, then returned to his flat in Onslow Square, two hundred yards from both South Kensington underground station and Christie's auction rooms, where he had bought most of his furniture.

There were six items of mail. Four were personal letters, the fifth contained statements for his various accounts at Coutts Bank in Kensington High Street, and the sixth was from the Swiss Investment Bank on Stockerstrasse, in Zurich's commercial quarter.

He skimmed the correspondence, showered and changed into civilian clothes, collected the Porsche – 944 Series 2 Cabriolet, Guards red – from the residents' parking area and drove to the San Lorenzo. The luncheon party was at a table towards the rear of the restaurant: one other man and two women. The head waiter was hovering, the manager was looking pleased but anxious, and the personal bodyguard was positioned at a table nearby.

Fairfax bowed slightly.

He had known her for five years, yet even now he would address her by her first name only if she so indicated, and then only in private.

'Hello, Roddy.' The Princess of Wales looked up at him. 'Family jewels still there?' There was a laugh on the face and a tease in the eyes.

'Last time I looked, Ma'am.'

The City of London was still quiet. It was not quite seven in the morning, the summer heat already settling between the concrete and glass fascias of the office blocks and the sky a brilliant blue. An inbound Boeing 747 passed overhead, the sun glinting on it, a white police Granada cruised slowly north along Old Broad Street and a dustcart trundled south.

Gerard Gray turned into the head offices of Barclays International, showed his ID to the security guards in the foyer and took the fast lift to his office. By 7.15 he had read the *Financial Times* and the *Wall Street Journal*, circling in red items he would follow up on later, by 7.40 he had speed-read the news and financial sections of the other quality dailies, including the *New York Times*, the European edition of the *Herald Tribune* and the *Irish Times*, as well as the city pages of the tabloids. By eight, when the next members of the department arrived, he had spoken to Tokyo and the Middle East.

Gray was in his early thirties, tall and well-dressed, with a first-class honours degree in economics from the LSE. Eighteen months previously he had been appointed Departmental Director, a promotion marking him for the fast stream. He lived in an apartment in one of the new blocks overlooking the Thames in the Wapping area of the old London Docklands, walking to and from the office each morning and evening. Despite his apparent acceptance of the life-style of a City executive he drank little; each morning before work he ran the Docklands section of the London marathon, and he played squash regularly. There was little trace of his Irish origins about him, the slightest hint of an accent creeping into his voice only when he chose, and he explained the scar which ran down his left shoulder by saying that he had been involved in a motor accident.

The morning was busy: at nine he held his first meeting with the management consultancy team brought in from Price Waterhouse to advise on information access to clients associated with the oil-producing areas, at one he met them for lunch in the executive dining suite. The only new member of the team, to whom he been introduced that morning, was a systems analyst, Philipa Walker. He guessed she was in her late twenties or early thirties. She was tall, dark-haired, slim and attractive, and dressed to match her position: lightweight dark blue pinstriped jacket with padded shoulders and matching skirt. When she talked it was in the fluent and efficient jargon he associated with the Price Waterhouse team; when she had nothing to contribute she listened carefully.

At four, when Gray checked the pound and the FT index, the only movement – and then only a minor flutter – seemed to have been be in the electronics and research sector where a company named New World Electronics had been taken over at a rock-bottom price by one of the Japanese giants which dominated the field. In the three hours since the announcement the value of its shares had quadrupled. Not that it would affect the world, Gray thought, most people probably wouldn't notice. Somebody might have made a killing, though.

He left the City, walked quickly to his flat, changed, collected the BMW from the parking bay below the block and cleared London before the main rush hour reduced traffic on the A12 to a standstill. By 5.45 he had passed Brentwood, just before 6.15 he pulled into the yard of the farm lost in the flatlands of the Essex countryside midway between Chelmsford and Colchester.

The farmer was standing at the kitchen door; the sleeves of his shirt were rolled up, he still had his boots on and his cloth cap was pushed to the back of his head. He shook Gray's hand and led him inside.

'Too nice an evening for London. Thought I'd get some practice in.' Gray accepted the mug of tea which the man's wife poured. 'Sorry not to let you know.'

'No problem. Danny'll pull for you.'

Fifteen minutes later Gray and the farmer's son walked through the farmyard to the clay pigeon shoot in the field behind the house.

'How fast?'

'Fast as you can.'

He waited. 'Pull.'

The clays spun into the air.

Not bad, he thought as they walked back to the house. At least he wasn't rusty. The drive back to London was relaxed. It would have been a good evening for a river trip down the Thames, he suddenly thought, a good evening to have invited Philipa Walker to dinner.

The following morning he was at his desk at seven; at ten he met the Price Waterhouse team. The day before Walker had been dressed like a city woman, almost severe, with her hair drawn back. Today, he noted, she wore a dress – casual though expensive – and her hair was looser, hanging round her shoulders. The agenda was tightly scheduled – Price Waterhouse, after all, was costing him a great deal of money – each of the management team leaving when his area of expertise had been covered. Perhaps it was coincidence, perhaps the way he structured the meeting, that the last item concerned computers and the last member of the team consulted was the woman called Walker. The discussion ended, he thanked her and gathered his papers together.

'I was wondering if you'd like a drink after work.' The invitation was either formal or informal, whichever way she chose to take it.

'Perhaps. Could be we'll still be working.'

Win some, lose some, Gray thought.

'Where?' She smiled as he held the door open for her. 'Just in case.'

41

'Gordon's Wine Bar in Villiers Street. A hundred yards up on the right from Embankment tube station.'

'What time?'

He shrugged. 'Five-fifteen, five-thirty.'

When he left at five the traffic was too busy to bother with a cab. He walked to Tower Hill and caught the underground to the Embankment. Villiers Street, sloping up towards the Strand and Trafalgar Square, was hectic, newspaper stands and flower stalls along the pavement and commuters rushing into the station itself. The first building on the right was dilapidated, a sandwich bar next to it, a lamp hanging from the corner and the name above the door. He went in, then down the stairs into the cellar. It was an odd place for a drink after the sanitized cleanliness of the City bank, he had thought the first time he had come, almost as if he was descending into the bowels of a London which no longer existed. Fifteen stairs, he had counted them the second time he had come, either out of historic interest or because of his fascination with detail.

The room below was built round a central column of brick and wood, the varnish peeling off the wall panelling and the anaglypta paper above it faded and yellow, and covered with old newspaper front pages and photographs. The bar was to the left, a portrait of Winston Churchill on the right. Already it was getting busy. He bought a bottle of Pol Roger, asked for two glasses, and went to the room to the left of the bar. The area was more like a vault than a room, the walls and ceiling curved in a half-circle and the centre of the ceiling less than six feet high. The bricks were grimy, and the only illumination came from candles on the ramshackle tables. The chairs were rickety and the wax ran down the sides of the candles.

He chose one of the three tables still empty, sat facing the entrance to the first room and poured himself a glass. Ten minutes later he saw Philipa Walker looking through the crowd and the half-light.

'Glad you could make it.' He stood up and held the chair for her.

'Amazing place.' She took the glass he poured for her, then left her briefcase under the table and walked round, easing between the people and looking at the newspaper pages framed on the walls.

The *Daily Mirror* of Friday, 21 November 1947: 'A Day of Smiles – The wedding of Princess Elizabeth.'

The London *Evening News* of Wednesday, 6 February 1952. The photograph of George V1 was in the centre of the page, the headline above: 'The King dies in his sleep at Sandringham.'

The *Daily Mail* of Wednesday, 3 June 1953: 'The journey to the abbey begins.' The main photograph was of the coronation procession beginning its journey from Buckingham Palace to Westminster Abbey, three smaller photographs to the left. The first was of two small children looking through a window, a nanny behind them, the second was of the girl, the third of the boy. Prince Charles watching his mother.

She pushed her way back to the table and sat down. 'This place is incredible. I never even knew it existed.'

He smiled and refilled her glass.

At 6.30 they left the bar, walked to Charing Cross pier, and caught a ferry to Greenwich, eating at a French restaurant close to the river.

Philipa Walker had a Bachelor's degree in modern languages from the University of Sussex and a Master's in business systems, analysis and design from City University – the information came easily as they discussed jobs and backgrounds. She had worked with a number of companies, specializing in fourth-generation computer languages before setting up her own consultancy. Her father was a retired solicitor, both her parents were still alive and living in Orpington. She had a brother, also a solicitor, who was married with two children.

At ten they left Greenwich and caught the ferry back to Charing Cross.

'Last drink?'

She shook her head. 'I still have some work to do.'

They climbed the steps.

'I was wondering what you were doing this weekend.'

'What are you suggesting?'

'There's a house party at Hamble. Dinner on Saturday evening, sail over to the Isle of Wight on Sunday.' He supposed he knew what she was thinking. 'No pressure, plenty of single bedrooms.'

She waved down a cab. I'll think about it. It was in the way she turned, the way she looked back at him as she gave the cab driver her address.

Dublin was warm. Conlan crossed the Liffy and turned along Bachelors Walk. Each evening, when possible, he strolled in the city centre, took a drink in one of the pubs in the spider's web of back streets and alleyways round Custom House and the Quays. Establish a pattern, have an identifiable and predictable routine which the

Special Branch tails would come to believe was normal, so that only if he did something outside that pattern would they become suspicious. Then build into it the tiny things – the contacts and the back doors out – which they would not notice.

If, of course, the SB knew about him. Even now he was uncertain whether his role in the Movement and his membership of the Army Council were known to the authorities, but he knew he could not assume otherwise. The surveillance on him so that the authorities could pick him up when they wanted, but also to protect him if London changed the rules and sent the SAS over the border to lift him or, in the euphemism he knew they used, to 'negotiate' him.

The lounge of Bachelors Inn was quiet and the floor freshly washed, so that it smelt of cold. Conlan confirmed there were no tails either in front or behind, ordered a Guinness and took it to the table in the corner. The bar was almost empty, a couple sitting against the opposite wall and the priest by himself, though there was nothing about his clothing or general appearance to indicate his calling.

Conlan pulled the ashtray in front of him, took a packet of cigarettes from his pocket, shook the last cigarette from the packet and lit it, dropped the empty packet in to the ashtray, then settled back and enjoyed his drink.

The meeting with Sleeper would be the last until the job was done. If the Army Council finally agreed, he was aware. If he continued to enjoy Doherty's support. And if Quin did not succeed in screwing him.

He downed the Guinness and went to the bar. As he did so the couple stood and began to walk out, past his table. For one moment Conlan froze, thought he had been wrong, thought that neither he nor the priest had spotted the tail. Behind him, he was aware, McGinty had taken a packet of cigarettes from his pocket, and would stretch across and take the ashtray from Conlan's table if the couple showed any interest in it. The couple thanked the barman and left.

Conlan asked for another Guinness, returned to the table and reflected on the irony that it had been Quin who had given Sleeper his name, on the historical quirk which had given Sleeper his cover. Even the smallest mistake on either of their parts, even the most inadvertent slip of the tongue on his own, and the essential cover which Sleeper enjoyed would be destroyed.

It was all part of the game. The Brits and the Provisionals playing their game against each other, himself and Quin playing their game

44

within the Army Council, and the Brits presumably playing their own internal games even though they were supposed to be on the same side. Everyone making their own rules and everyone applying their own assumptions and prejudices to the rules they assumed the other side would be making.

Put a team into London and the Brits automatically looked for them in traditional Irish areas such as Kilburn and Camden Town. Put in an active service unit, an ASU, and the Brits automatically assumed they would be working-class, with manners and covers to match and a safe house in the East End. Put in a shooter and the Brits would automatically look for an Irish accent.

Put in a sleeper, however, English university degree, impeccable qualifications and matching accent, and the cover of an expensive apartment and a job in the City . . .

He savoured the last of the drink, then thanked the barman and left.

After ten minutes the priest lit a cigarette – the last in the packet – then leaned across and took the ashtray from the table at which Conlan had been sitting. There had been no ashtray on his table – apparently by chance – and the cigarette he now smoked was the same type as the packet in the ashtray. As he drank he played with the packet; when he stood to leave the packet in the ashtray was his, and Conlan's – with its instructions to the priest and the coded message to Sleeper, to be placed in the personal column of the *Irish Times* – was in his pocket.

Two mornings later Liam Conlan packed the fishing rods and gear into the estate car, taking his time in case he was under surveillance, waved goodbye to his family, and drove the four and a half hours to the cabin set fifty yards back from the shore of Lough Corrib, in the west of Ireland. He had been a fisherman since boyhood, and the trips to Kilmore were as established a part of his routine as the strolls along O'Connell Street and the drinks round Custom House or the Quays. By one o'clock he was sitting, seemingly contented, the rod in his hand, the peak of his cap pulled down and the collar of his windcheater turned up, so that his face could barely be seen. At seven he returned to the cabin; thirty minutes later the smell of cooking and the sound of singing drifted from its door and across the lough. At ten, the dusk gone and the half-moon shining, the priest who had taken his place walked to the lough, the peak of Conlan's cap pulled down over his face, the collar of Conlan's windcheater turned up, and his hands stuffed into the pockets of Conlan's trousers. By the time he returned to the cabin Conlan was half-way to the location eighty miles away, the priest's car running smoothly and his own still parked by the side of the cabin at Kilmore. In the old days, he supposed, it would have a fishing boat, snuggled against a quay, the lights dimmed and the men hurrying in the dark. Tomorrow morning it would be a private airstrip and a Cessna 208A, Pratt and Whitney single turboprop engine and 1100-mile range.

Gerard Gray woke at five, ran his circuit of Docklands, showered, had a light breakfast, and was at work by seven as usual. The first newspaper he read was the *FT* and the fourth was the *Irish Times*. At 9.30 he rang the internal extension used by the Price Waterhouse team and asked for Philipa Walker.

'I'm sorry. Something's come up and I can't make the weekend party we talked about.'

'It's all right, I couldn't have come anyway.'

'Another time, perhaps.'

'Perhaps.'

The following morning – Saturday – Gray slept late, rising at seven, and running two Docklands circuits. By nine he was back at the flat. The day was hot and the sky a brilliant blue. He showered, skimmed the newspapers, including the personal columns, and left the flat.

Roddy Fairfax left Onslow Square at nine, taking the M4 west towards Bristol, the route already busy with holiday traffic. At junction 17 he left the motorway at the Cirencester exit, bypassed Malmesbury, then swung on to the Tetbury road. At 11.30 precisely he stopped the 944 at the gates which marked the beginning of the driveway to Highgrove. A police Land-Rover and two men, neither apparently armed though he assumed both were, were at the gates.

'Yes, sir.' The policeman bent over the car, the second standing back.

'Fairfax, I'm expected.' He showed his army ID card and knew they had already checked the registration number of the Porsche.

'Thank you, sir.' The policeman stood back and waved him through.

The driveway was short, curving right to the house, a number of other cars already parked. He just had time to pull the bag from the boot when his host appeared, the two boys beside him.

Initially at least, the Prince had always considered Fairfax one of his wife's circle, and her friends were not necessarily those he would choose for himself, just as his friends were not those she would choose. Fairfax was different, however. He was good company, talked not just about the London scene, or whatever the word was nowadays, but about other matters, politics and pollution. In the long and difficult months before the couple had separated Fairfax had refused to take sides, arguing forcefully and honestly with both of them. Even now, perhaps especially now, he remained friendly and loyal to both. And Fairfax was a soldier. Three tours in Northern Ireland, two of them at times when things weren't too pretty.

'Good to see you, Roddy.' Charles came down the steps and shook his hand. 'Glad you could make it for the weekend.'

An hour earlier, Gerard Gray had stopped outside the flats in Maida Vale. It was correct that there were single beds at the river party at Hamble, but there were also double ones, plus king size, and a water bed if you organized yourself properly. And if Philipa Walker was not sure about it, then he was better with someone who was.

Philipa Walker had woken on the first ring of the alarm at five. By 7.30 she was at Dover's Western Docks. She bought a return ticket to Ostend, paying cash, and caught the 0810 jetfoil, arriving at 1050 local time, taking the 1101 train to Antwerp, changing at Ghent. For the next hour she surveyed the restaurant tucked inconspicuously in the corner of the Handschoenmarkt, below the western façade of the cathedral. Only when she was satisfied that no surveillance was in place did she go in.

The restaurant was still full and the waiters busy. As she entered Liam Conlan rose to greet her.

The first and last cover, he thought, the single item he had driven deep into his subconscious as the foundation for the rest of his subterfuge. The one discipline above all others which he had fought to impose upon himself: in his discussions with Doherty, in his briefings with the Army Council, even in his sleep.

That he should always refer to Sleeper as *him*.

3

THE TARGET CODENAMED PINMAN, Conlan had said, a member
of the British royal family. The operation within the next twelve
months. She should aim to wrap up her preliminary research as
soon as possible, and communicate her decisions through the system
of codes and dead letter drops already in use. The Army Council
knew of the operation, but had not yet given its final approval. He
had been forced to inform the Council of the existence of Sleeper,
Conlan had also told her, but had given no details.

Walker's flat, on the third floor of a Victorian terrace close to
Primrose Hill in north London, was that of a successful and indepen-
dent professional woman. It consisted of two bedrooms, a large
split-level lounge with a marble fireplace and bay windows opening
on to a balcony, a smaller room off it which she used as an office,
plus a kitchen and bathroom. She had bought it when the property
market was still rising and redesigned it herself. Except for the study
the flat bordered on the luxurious without being ostentatious: the
furniture, decorations and lighting were modern; yet the hard edges
were softened by the small personal touches she had added – a
wall-hanging from Turkey, an icon from Russia, an Impressionist-
style painting she had commissioned from an art student after seeing
his work on the boarded-up window of a shop unit standing empty
in a new shopping precinct. The study, by contrast, was cold and
clinical – a world of computers and computer logic, shelves of
manuals and software, the black ash desk facing the window but the
sunlight from outside cut off by a blind, and the lighting efficient
and functional.

In many ways Philipa Walker's two lives were similarly organized. Just as there was no indication of the austerity of the study
in the rest of the flat, so there was no indication in her everyday
life of the second into which she occasionally disappeared. Her day-
to-day existence was also divided and equally organized: she had

professional colleagues and personal friends, the two rarely coinciding. Her affairs were seldom casual ones, almost always lasting more than six months; the most recent had ended two months before. It was a life-style Conlan had encouraged. Build a cover, he had told her the day she had committed herself, establish yourself so that no one will ever suspect. Continue the life to which her own background automatically pointed and she would be so immune she would be untouchable. Establish a career that allowed her to take time off, so that no one would even notice when she slipped from what had become her cover into the sub-world to which he had introduced her.

In the strictest definition, Walker was not a sleeper. A sleeper is an agent recruited from or infiltrated into an organization and required to remain inoperative until activated. Walker's role was neither of these, yet in a less traditional sense her background provided everything a sleeper could require: layer upon layer of cover built up over the years – in her case a background provided by the very establishment she now opposed.

She locked the flat and walked to the top of Primrose Hill. In the distance, glistening white, were the modern tower blocks of the City; in the middle ground Oxford Street; just below the hill, less than three hundred yards away, was London Zoo. Sometimes she would lie awake and pick up the faintest smells, reminders of those places her official passport said she had not visited. Sometimes – even at two or three in the morning – she would leave the flat and sit on the top of the hill, draw in the night air for a taste of those places. Occasionally, just occasionally, they would waft across the hill and drift through the window of the flat when she was making love. Then the images would come back to her: then she would slip into an almost subconscious memory of the places where she had executed the profession to which Conlan had led her. Not those where she had been trained. Rather, those where she put her craft into practice.

She returned to the flat, percolated coffee, poured herself a cup, and took it back into the study. It was 3.30 in the afternoon, the first children passing below the flat on their way home from school. The windows of the lounge were open and she could hear them laughing. It had been this time in the afternoon – the thought was not quite subconscious. Autumn going into winter, though, the smells of a new season and the first hint of cold . . .

*

49

. . . *she was fourteen, tall and thin yet becoming attractive, even in school uniform. She had forgotten a hockey boot – had thought she had packed both – and run home to pick it up. The day before she had brought home her school report, the evening before she had sat in the warmth of the sitting-room, the fire blazing in the grate, while her father read carefully through it in the manner she called his solicitor's style, her mother opposite her dwelling on every nod of his head. Grade 1 in every subject, it was no more than she had expected, had worked hard for. An outstanding student, the head teacher had written; we confidently expect superb examination results and university entrance.*

The house was quiet, the grandfather clock ticking in the hall. Her mother and her aunt were having tea together as they did every Wednesday. Quintessentially English, Walker would think in the years to come, when the hate was fired and burning in her. Quintessentially bloody bourgeoisie. She wouldn't disturb them, she thought, if she did she would have to explain, then she might be late for the practice. She ran quietly up the stairs, found the boot, and began to come down again.

The sitting-room door was slightly open. Her mother was show-ing her aunt her school report – she could tell by the conversation.

'She's done very well.'

'Very well indeed.' There was something in her mother's voice which took her by surprise. 'Considering.'

She stopped unseen on the stairs and wondered what her mother meant.

Even though she thought the house was empty her mother crossed the room and closed the door.

Considering what, the girl thought that night. She had every-thing, her parents were well-off though perhaps slightly old-fashioned, neither she nor her brother had ever wanted for anything. They lived in a large house in the Home Counties, had been educated privately from the age of four, and always been encouraged to study. Considering what? she was still thinking when she woke the following morning . . .

. . . the coffee was cold and the study was quiet around her.

Each of the jobs she had done for Conlan, or for others through Conlan, had begun differently. Some – the long-term jobs – had started this way: the months of detailed and often fruitless research.

50

Others had been more immediate: a dead letter drop where the weapon was waiting for her, the target details, a back-up supplying the way in and out. Always, however, Conlan had insisted on two fundamentals: that no one ever knew her identity, and that everyone assumed she was a man. As if he always had the spectacular in mind, she could not help thinking again, as if he always had her in mind for it. That was why he had not used her for two years, had allowed her to disappear into the shadows.

The afternoon drifted into evening. She left the flat and took the underground to the West End. It was eleven in the evening, the night still warm. The lights of Leicester Square and Piccadilly Circus were flashing behind her, the taxis filled with theatre-leavers and the streets busy. She left Trafalgar Square and walked through Admiralty Arch and into the Mall. The night was suddenly darker and colder and the pavements empty, only an occasional cab passing her. Six hundred yards in front of her she saw the lights of Buckingham Palace.

She would need access to the royal schedule, and one way to that was through the Wednesday List – the diary of engagements for each member of the royal family circulated by Buckingham Palace to the Newspaper Publishers Association and through the NPA to interested publications. The list, containing the skeleton of engagements for up to a year ahead and updated on a monthly and weekly basis, was sent out every Wednesday, hence its name. The PinMan operation, however, would require not just the official timetable of formal appointments where the target would be high profile and carrying massive protection, but – and more importantly – the details of the more informal and therefore probably more personal events, even though PinMan would still be accompanied by a bodyguard.

Buckingham Palace or the NPA? She was walking quickly, thinking quickly, weighing the options. If she accessed the computer system in the press office at the Palace she might also get inside the personal offices, get information not on the Wednesday List; if she made do with the NPA she might get less material but the risks were fewer. The computer security at the Palace would be more difficult to penetrate, yet in a way that did not concern her. What did, however, was the probability that at the Palace the system would, or should, pick it up immediately. And that might warn the security services.

A police car slid past her – the dark maroon of the Diplomatic Protection Group. She reached the Victoria Monument and stood looking up at the Palace, the standard fluttering from the flag pole. Queen's in – she remembered the day she had stood here with her mother, the way her mother had pointed out the flag to her, she in her best school uniform and her brother in his school blazer.

The NPA, she decided, keep the Palace as a last resort.

She turned down Buckingham Gate and into Petty France, the Passport Office on the right and the Home Office on the left; then she cut through to the Houses of Parliament and took the underground back to Chalk Farm.

The following day she began the process of building up a computerized file on PinMan. In doing so she was governed by one simple fact of life: that despite the system of passwords and other security measures which an individual or a company might build into a system, there was no such thing as computer security.

If the police or security services ever suspected her, the first thing they would do would be to search the flat. And the first thing they would do when they saw the computer would be to call in a specialist. By using a tape streamer, DOS operating system boot disk and a programmer's toolkit, an expert would first of all bypass the security and password system normally assigned to the C drive, access the hard disk and X-copy all information stored on it, even remnants of items which she had ordered to be deleted but which might not have been completely overwritten by the computer.

If she replaced the standard BIOS chips with chips carrying security passwords, they could replace those she had installed or circumvent them totally by taking the top off the computer, removing the hard disk, copying it, then replacing it. And if she had encrypted the material on the hard disk they would know she was hiding something and send it to the codebreakers at GCHQ.

For these reasons she would place no PinMan information on the hard disk. She would destroy all irrelevant material immediately, encrypt the material she wanted, using a standard software package, and place it on a floppy disk which she would in turn place in a bank deposit box hired under a false name.

The office was cool. She switched on the PC and checked the list of dial-up numbers she had acquired during her years in the City. Most were of banking, financial or related institutions, though four were of newspapers and the twenty-seventh was that of the Newspaper Publishers Association. She plugged the modem connection to the telephone socket, called up the communication software and keyed in the NPA number. The computer system at the NPA answered and she logged in. Eight minutes later she accessed the computer file based on the Wednesday List. On the pale amber of the screen were the outline schedules of every member of the royal family for the next twelve months, with the first six months of that period already highly detailed. She transferred the material from the NPA machine to her own and copied it on to a disk. Then she exited the NPA system, made herself a coffee, printed out the material and studied it.

The material was as she had suspected – useful but only as a starting point. Nowhere in it were the seemingly minor details, the unofficial functions or personal timetables, which she would need for the PinMan operation.

She burned the print-out and placed the floppy in the wall safe. The next morning she deposited it in a security box at a bank in the City, then returned to the flat, wrote out a list of publishers, and made the first telephone call. Two days later she entered the details of all books written about the royal family over the previous five years on the PinMan file, again placing the floppy in the bank deposit box.

Three of the books were out of print, two could be purchased over the counter, and five could be ordered, though the waiting time was up to five weeks. The following morning she went to the British Library, on the ground floor of the British Museum in Great Russell Street, and obtained a reader's pass in the name of Sampson, her application authenticated by a letter on University College headed notepaper which she herself had printed and on which she had written details of a fictitious PhD thesis. For the next ten days, in the vast domed reading room of the British Library, she worked her way through the books she had listed from the publishers' catalogues.

The following week she spent five days at the Press Association in Fleet Street, tucked into a corner in the newspaper cuttings library, again using the name Sampson and paying cash. On the first morning she asked for files on environmental pollution, with special reference to interest in the subject shown by the Prince of Wales; at the end of the morning she moved on to royal cuttings in general, taking the relevant folders from the filing cabinets herself and returning them once she had finished, so that there was no record of herself or which files she had consulted. The following week she spent four days in the British Newspaper Library at Colindale in north London.

The photograph was in the diary column of the *Daily Mail*.

Perhaps it was because she was concentrating on the content of the various reports, perhaps because the report in question was about a lunch party and therefore of little consequence, perhaps because the cutting at the Press Association library was slightly torn or the microfiche machine at Colindale was slightly out of focus, that she did not register it. It was only three evenings later that the feeling began to seep into her that sometime, somewhere, over the past days and weeks, she had missed something. Not something important, not something she could have used. And that was what annoyed her. Because not only could she not remember what she had seen or where she had seen it, but she did not even know why she should have noticed it or why it was surfacing from somewhere in her subconscious.

For the two weeks after that she concentrated on European and American magazines and newspapers specializing in scandal stories about the royal family. In each case the stories were more sensational, and less likely to be corroborated, than in the British newspapers, and the photographs were more intimate, or at least more intrusive.

September had slipped into October, and soon October would give way to November. Somewhere in the mass of information she had gathered together was the key to PinMan, she was aware; somewhere among what seemed like an industry in itself was the one person who could give her that key. Except that already she was running out of time.

Something she had seen in one of the photographs at the Press Association or at Colindale – perhaps she had been aware of the unease before, perhaps she had pushed it aside. Now it crept up on her again, only caught her because something deep in her psychology allowed it to. Not something about PinMan. Something about herself.

It was nine o'clock. She went into the lounge and switched on the television.

The *Sun* received the tip-off shortly before seven. Something important had happened in the life of the Princess of Wales, the source said; the previous evening she had toasted the news with close friends at one of her favourite restaurants.

'What news?' the deputy editor asked.

'The source wasn't sure.'

'How reliable's the source?'

On the fringe but reliable in the past, the reporter who had taken the call informed him. Offering the story on an exclusive basis but needing an answer fast. Or she would take it to another newspaper, the implication was clear.

'You've talked to the Palace?'

'They're making no comment.'

They wouldn't, unless you asked something specific, the deputy editor understood, and even then they normally didn't comment anyway. The story was weak – in a way it wasn't a story. Except that it might be, and someone else might have it. The editor was in Australia and the paper's royal-watcher was on holiday somewhere in the Far East. Buy the woman up and close the source, he thought, except that if she knew, then someone else probably did as well. And if another paper knew, they'd be running it that night.

'How much is she asking?'

'Five hundred.'

Go with it and she was right, and all he'd get was a pat on the back. Not go with it and somebody else had it, and his feet wouldn't touch the ground.

'Offer her one, the rest on results.'

'She'll take two-fifty.'

'Done. Guaranteed exclusive. How're you writing it?'

'I'm not sure.'

'Write it as a question. Expectations of major changes, speculation amongst close friends, etc. Pull in an astrologer, get him to confirm it in her stars. Last night's celebration in the third paragraph.'

That way he and the paper were covered. If there was a story. A bomb up every other paper's backside if there wasn't. And the classic spoiler if there was and someone else had it. And royal stories still moved copies, he could imagine the panic when the second edition came out, the rumours that would start in the other newsrooms even before that.

He rolled up his sleeves and telephoned the lawyer and picture editor in that order.

*

The story – or the first hint of it – broke at twenty minutes to nine. An hour earlier Patrick Saunders had returned to the flat which he used during the week. Saunders was 44 years old, fit for his age and occupation, married with two teenage girls, a country house in Wiltshire and a town flat in Barnsbury. He had joined the *Daily Mirror* seventeen years before, and was now what the newspaper liked to call the king of the royal-watchers.

The Cellnet, he noted as the telephone rang; the office getting hold of him in a hurry, not knowing where he was or having the time to find out.

'Yes.'

'Pat.' Only the news editor was allowed to call him Pat, and then only when he was in a hurry and the pressure was on. 'Big one breaking. A cab will collect you in two minutes.'

'What is it ?'

'The *Sun*'s carrying an exclusive on Di. We've just had the tip.'

Saunders's first reaction was shock and his second was a combination of disbelief and anger. So what was it, why didn't he know? Why hadn't his source given him the story first? His third, which over-ruled the others, was of self-preservation.

'You're sure?'

'We haven't seen it yet, but they're putting on extra copies.'

'You don't know what it is?'

'No.'

'On my way.'

He left the flat and ran down the stairs. The minicab was waiting. For Christ's sake be there, he thought. He sat in the back seat, balanced his notebook on his lap and dialled the number on the Cellnet. The contact answered immediately.

'Patrick here. Bit of a panic on.' There was no time for pleasantries. 'The *Sun*'s carrying a big story on Di.'

The contact began to laugh. 'Red faces all round, eh?'

Bastard, thought Saunders.

'Wrong Di, old man. One of the Princess's buddies, sort of lady-in-waiting, if you like. Just announced she's pregnant for the first time.'

'What about the Princess of Wales?'

'She's agreed to be godmother.'

You're sure? Saunders almost blurted. Head on the block time,

56

he knew. Of course I'm sure, he knew the contact would reply. 'Phone number?'

'She's ex-D.'

All of them were ex-directory, Saunders thought.

'Doesn't matter, though. She's not there.'

Stop pissing me about, Saunders glanced up as the minicab passed the Angel.

'She's with her parents.' The contact gave him the number. 'Old man's in *Who's Who*, that's where you got it, yah?'

'Yah.' Saunders clipped the cassette recorder on to the Cellnet and dialled the number the source had given him. The woman who answered sounded in her fifties, her voice pure Roedean.

'Mrs Wickham. This is Patrick Saunders.' He did not say he was from the *Mirror*. Some people would pay to get their names in the gossip columns of the *Mail* or *Express*; the same people, however, might consider the *Mirror* slightly the wrong colour and class. 'I wrote a small piece about Diana's marriage and wanted to congratulate her on the good news.'

I hope to Christ she *is* married, he thought.

'How nice. Would you like to speak to her?'

'If it's not too much trouble.'

Saunders heard the scuffle as the daughter picked up the telephone.

'Diana. Patrick Saunders from the *Mirror*. Sorry to trouble you, but you know what Fleet Street's like when a pretty girl has a baby.'

She knew the score, he guessed. Especially if she was a member of Princess Di's set. The woman laughed and he knew he'd won. For two minutes they talked about what she wanted, boy or girl, as well as details of her and her husband.

'Just a word of warning.' He slipped it in quietly, almost casually. 'I know you're a close friend of a certain other Di. Some people think it's the Princess who's got some big news coming.'

'How silly.' It was almost a laugh.

'But she knows?'

'Of course, we had a celebration last night.'

'Champagne?'

'Of course.'

'Any chance of Di being godmother?'

The woman laughed again.

They talked until the minicab stopped outside the *Mirror* building. Saunders thanked her, made a note to send her a large bouquet of flowers in the morning, entered the telephone number into the computer notebook, ran inside and took the lift to the newsroom. Just in time for the second edition, he thought.

The editor, night editor, news editor and lawyer were looking at the television screen, the Nine O'Clock News just starting.

'Photo of Diana Simpson, daughter of Brigadier and Mrs Wickham,' he told the pictures editor. 'Make it a happy one. Second picture of her with the Princess of Wales.'

He switched on the computer. The editor and news editor were behind him, the editor sweating slightly and the deputy fiddling with his braces. He ignored them and swore at the system to power up.

BBC running the story, the news editor shouted to him. The Palace are making no comment. Just what he wanted, he thought: everyone carrying the story and the silence from the Palace only fuelling the bonfire. His fingers were already on the keyboard.

The Princess of Wales is to become a godmother.

If it's a boy he will be called Michael James. If it's a girl she will be called Elizabeth Althea. And last night Kensington Palace was celebrating the good news.

Behind him Saunders felt the editor punch the air with a mixture of triumph and relief.

The evening was dark and cold, threatening rain. Walker told the cab driver to drop her by Chancery Lane, then walked briskly along Holborn. She was wearing what some might call her City clothes and carried a briefcase. The building which housed the Mirror Group of Newspapers was on the corner of Holborn Circus, the concrete and glass dominating the area, the main reception in front and the garage and works entrance in New Fetter Lane behind. In the daytime the lorries bringing the rolls of paper crowded the street, in the evenings the delivery vans lined the pavement waiting for the first edition.

There were two other features of New Fetter Lane which concerned Philipa Walker that evening. The first was the faded brick building, five hundred yards from the *Mirror*, which housed the headquarters of Her Majesty's Customs and Excise. The second was the White Hart public house opposite the rear entrance to the *Mirror* and known to its journalists as the Stab (short for The Stab in the Back).

The White Hart was quiet, the slack period after the City stock-brokers and money men left and before the journalists arrived. She ordered a gin and tonic, settled in a corner with a copy of *The Times*, and waited. It was the third time she had been there; on the previous two occasions the intermediary she had chosen had not come in. A first group of reporters arrived, then a second, the woman among them. She was smartly dressed though older than her photograph. After fifteen minutes the woman rose, asked the men she was with what they wanted to drink, and went to the bar. Walker finished her gin and tonic and followed her.

'Anything in tomorrow?' She stood next to the woman. Anything in tomorrow's paper, she meant.

The journalist turned.

'Helen Kennedy, aren't you?' It was both an explanation and the beginning of an introduction. 'Recognized you from your photograph.'

The woman laughed. 'Who are you with?'

'Which paper, you mean? I'm not.' She asked the second barman for a gin and tonic. 'Systems analyst consultant. Doing a job at Customs and Excise. Funny bunch, the Investigations lot.'

The journalist picked up the possibility of a contact. 'You by yourself?'

Walker nodded.

'Why don't you join us?'

An hour later Walker accepted Kennedy's invitation to join her for dinner at Joe Allen's, off Covent Garden. A table had already been booked, Kennedy explained, some other colleagues were already there. When they arrived the restaurant was crowded and the target was standing by the bar.

There were twenty three names of journalists, magazine writers and authors on the list she had compiled, each of them a possible way in to PinMan. Four nights before, however, only one of them had got it right.

'Patrick Saunders, Philipa Walker.'

Access Saunders and she might access Saunders's sources. Access Saunders's sources and she might access the private worlds of the

Prince and Princess of Wales. Access those worlds and she accessed PinMan.

'Should I bow or curtsey?' Walker's question was tongue-in-cheek and slightly challenging.

Saunders smiled as she knew he would. 'Bucks Fizz?'

'Why not?'

* * *

Belfast was quiet.

Nolan turned the unmarked car along Springfield Avenue – RPG Avenue as the locals nicknamed it. The Browning was in her waist holster and the MP5K was on the floor to the right of the driver's seat.

Work since the operation at Beechwood Road had been routine and on a downward spiral. Partly because after Beechwood Street everything seemed an anticlimax; mainly because she was winding down to the end of her Belfast tour. Not just her Belfast tour. Her last tour. She had already bent the rules, or persuaded others to bend them for her, so that she could stay on. Now London had decreed otherwise, had said that today was her last undercover day in Northern Ireland. Two weeks' leave, then they would pull her out.

There was something about the operation on Beechwood Street – occasionally the unease seeped through the block she had put on it, occasionally she found herself back there with McKendrick by the driver's door and Rorke in front. Mostly at night, when she was alone and trying to sleep, but occasionally even when she was working, when she was in the undercover car, particularly when they were ordered into the Ballymurphy area. Now it crept up on her again, black and cold, like a fog on the moors on a summer's day. One moment the sky was blue and warm, then the faintest strand of mist and the almost imperceptible finger of cold. Then it was upon you, engulfing and entrapping you.

She turned the car south and fought off the feeling.

'There's a rumour you're leaving as well.' She glanced across at Brady. Only once had they talked about what she had had to do in the car in Beechwood Street, and that was to invent a story which would explain how she was able to reach his Browning. Then they had agreed never to mention it again. And Brady had told no one.

60

Because at the end of the day there were a lot of things more important than a laugh between the boys, and at the top of that list was the fact that she had saved their lives.

'Possibly.' Brady had been with the RUC for nine years, the last three in E4A.

'Someone said Special Branch.'

Brady laughed.

'When?'

'Couple of months.'

It was six in the evening, the end of the shift. If they were pulling her out perhaps they should have done so after Beechwood Street when she was on a high, she thought. Now she was leaving as if the Belfast tour hadn't been part of her, or she part of it. There was no elation at what she had done, no relief that she was getting off the tightrope, just the immense and overwhelming feeling of anticlimax. Tomorrow she would slip away on leave. When she returned she would have her last talk with the CO, be told where she would be posted. And nobody would even notice.

'Fancy a drink?' It was Brady.

They turned into the barracks at Lisburn.

'Thanks.'

They parked the car and went to the team room. The corridor was empty and the room deserted. Hell of a way to go, she thought as she signed off. They left the block and went to the mess, Brady slightly in front of her, knowing what she was feeling. There would be a couple of people at the bar, he knew she assumed, they'd spend half an hour sipping beer, then she'd slip away by herself, nowhere to go and no one to go with. He opened the door and allowed her to go first. The room was full, the teams waiting for her – the men and women who would remain on the edge, the men and women who'd provided the back-up for her and for whom she had provided back-up.

'*Bastard*,' she whispered to Brady, and began to laugh.

The following morning Nolan collected the hire car and drove to the town where she had been born and where she had grown up. It was her first visit since the start of her Northern Ireland tour. That night she told her parents that she was on leave from Europe; the next day she drove to the west coast, on the other side of the border, where she had spent the occasional holiday as a girl.

The beach curved in an arc round the bay, the water was cold and the sand a glistening white. The October sun was warm – an Indian summer, she remembered her parents had called it. She took off her shoes and walked along the edge of the water, thought about why they were pulling her out of Northern Ireland and what she would do now.

It was obvious why they were pulling her, she told herself. Women were normally only allowed one tour, perhaps two. Yet the guys were allowed back – she felt the resentment rising. The guys were allowed back for tour after tour . . .

She wouldn't be able to do it, she knew. McKendrick was framed in the driver's window and Rorke was standing in front. Brady's hands were on the steering so he couldn't reach his gun, and if she went for hers they would see. The only chance was the MP5K by the driver's door, but to get to it she would need a cover. She couldn't, she knew again . . .

. . . the strand was so deep in her subconscious that she was not fully aware of it, was only aware of the defence mechanism it threw at her. It was as if she was running a security check on the computer, keying in the request, the computer flashing back that the information she wanted was blocked . . .

. . . a coffee after, she told herself. Large and Irish. Plenty of Black Bush . . .

. . . the tide washed in front of her. Twenty yards away a boy and girl played on a log which had rolled across the Atlantic, the seaweed hanging from it and the shells crusted round it.

So what now? Promotion probably. Germany again. Nice little desk job. And sheer absolute unadulterated bloody boredom. Perhaps she should resign, the thought came suddenly and unexpectedly. Cash in everything, get on a plane, and see where she ended up.

The office was empty, the boys out on a job, Nolan supposed. It was five minutes before the meeting. She cleared the few items from her locker and walked along the corridor. The colonel was sitting behind his desk, the paperwork in front of him and the blow-ups of street maps covering the walls. He was in his early forties and big built, his civilian suit slightly crumpled, the jacket hanging behind the door.

'Good leave?' He waved his hand for her to sit down.

'Fine.'

'Your next posting.' He spoke quickly, his voice matter-of-fact. Germany, she knew. Time to call it a day.

'Two-week refresher at Hereford, then The Fort.'

SAS at Hereford, MI5 at The Fort.

Somebody up there loved her, she could not believe it, wondered who. The relief was spinning through her head. And after The Fort, who knew what or where? No desk job, though.

But somebody up there also hated her, had it in for her. Because at Hereford the bastards would see. At Hereford they would find their way into her soul and chisel it open till it was a gaping chasm. At Hereford they would take her to the brink and make her walk over.

'Thank you, sir.'

The Hereford refresher began ten days later, eight men and two women from a range of backgrounds and regiments. On the third day of the second week the observation exercise began – five days in dug-outs on the Brecons, the exercise for real, as if it were Northern Ireland. Not just Northern Ireland. As if it were South Armagh.

The rain was cold and biting, driven by the wind. The two of them – Nolan and a corporal from Signals – were crammed together in the OP, the observation post, living off sandwiches and self-heating cans of soup. The cold had set in half-way through the first night, and the rain had begun seeping through the roof on the second day. They had worked as a team, two hours on, two off; one of them keeping the arms cache under constant surveillance while the other tried to sleep, the floor of the OP running with water and churning into mud. No complaints, though – if this was Northern Ireland they wouldn't complain, couldn't complain. If this was Northern Ireland and they were staked out in a roof space in the Falls or a field in South Armagh they would keep going, look after each other and watch their backs. And if you were training to go back into Northern Ireland, to do the job they would do, there was only one way to train for it.

It was two in the morning, the rain sheeting from the north, so that even with the image intensifier Nolan could barely see the target.

'ENDEX.' She heard the radio signal. Not just the end of the exercise, the end of the refresher. 'RV zero two three zero.' Thirty minutes to get to the rendezvous point, plenty of time if it was light and good weather. They were both moving quickly, the bergans packed. They left the OP and headed across country. 0215: half a mile to go and fifteen minutes to do it. Not so easy at night and in these conditions. They waded the stream, the rain driving down on them, and pulled themselves up the mud on the other side. 0220: ten minutes to the RV. Almost there. Hope to Christ they'd got the map reference right. 0225: they came to the road, checked they were in the correct position and sank back into the ditch which ran alongside it. 0229: they heard the three clicks on the radio, the pick-up on the way. The signaller clicked back, told the pick-up that they were in position. They checked left and right: nothing on the road, the rain still pouring down. They heard the next series of clicks and clicked back, knew the truck was closing on them, and scrambled out of the ditch. Everything about the exercise was still for real, even the drop and pick-up. Especially the drop and pick-up. In Northern Ireland the bastards would be listening for the noise of the engine, would be waiting to hear the change in noise if it stopped. That was why they had almost killed themselves five days ago, rolling out of the side doors with the car still on the move.

The van came from the right, headlamps dimmed and moving slowly, not stopping, the sound of the engine constant, the back doors held open by bungees and the bulbs of the brake lights removed. The van passed them and they began to run, the van not slowing. Bags in back, scramble in after them, Nolan pulling the signaller in or the signaller pulling Nolan, neither of them was sure. They were in, jerking the doors shut and settling down. There were two sleeping bags on the floor; they crawled into them and tried to warm themselves. Hereford in forty minutes, she thought, a hot shower and a mug of tea. Four hours' kip then the finish of the course and the train to The Fort. She snuggled deeper into the sleeping bag. Bloody well made it, the realization drifted through her head as sleep came on her, her mind and body relaxing. The van was swaying slightly. She ignored the movement, put her arm under her head and fell asleep.

The van crashed to a halt. Nolan was thrown forward with the impact, body and mind trying to tear themselves from sleep. She was still tucked deep in the sleeping bag, enjoying the warmth.

She heard the shots and the clang as the back doors opened, heard the voices. Kalashnikov, she suddenly realized. Out, the men were yelling, dragging her and the signaller from the sleeping bags. Her mind was still spinning, still trying to wake. *Irish accents*: she jerked awake and saw them. Four, five. Black balaclavas with eyeholes cut in them. She was pulled outside and saw the cars, the lorry pulled across the road in front of the pick-up truck, the rain still streaming down and the night still dark. She glanced to the left and saw the driver, half-kneeling, half-crouching on the ground, trying to fight back. Heard the shots and saw the moment his body jerked then crumpled to a heap. She and the signaller were being separated, one to each car, the men holding them, others frisking them, roughly rather than efficiently. The engines of the cars were running; she was pushed in the boot of one of them and it pulled away.

SAS, part of the bloody exercise? Or IRA? The fear pounded through her. A Provo kidnap squad. The car was being driven fast, sliding round corners in the wet and the mud of the Brecons, Nolan being thrown from side to side. How would the Provos know? They were going downhill, the road surface suddenly changing. She tried to brace herself and look at her watch. The road surface changed again and she knew they were on a larger road, knew they were trying to clear the area before Hereford realized what had happened. Calm it, she told herself, work it out. There was no way the Provos could know, no way anyone could know other than the course instructors. Part of the course, she told herself, let you think you'd finished, let you relax, and then they hit you, put you through the wringer. The car lurched right, across some broken ground, and slammed to a halt. The boot was opened and a hood was pulled over her head. Out, she was told, heard the accents again. South Armagh. All part of the exercise, she struggled to tell herself. She was bundled across the ground, tripping once, and into the boot of another car. The boot slammed shut and the car pulled away. What the hell was happening? She made herself calm down, told herself to get her hands in front of her body, pull the hood off her head. But keep the hood handy so she could put it on when the car stops again, try to see their faces but don't let them know. Don't let them see that you're thinking. The car slowed and stopped. Not a sudden halt. Traffic lights. She pulled the hood back and checked the time: 0430, two hours after the pick-up; the rendezvous point was only forty minutes from Hereford, so she had been in one boot or the other for at least án hour and thirty minutes. The road was changing again, motorway or dual carriageway. Was rougher again. She checked her watch, her head thumping and her body aching. 0700: she'd been in the car another three and a half hours. The car slowed, turned right, and bumped across what she thought was a field. Then it stopped for thirty seconds, the engine ticking over, and pulled forward. She barely had time to drag the hood down before the boot opened and she was manhandled out. The hands were holding her and the hood was pulled off.

She was in a barn, bales around the walls. The men round her wore balaclavas, eyes looking at her through the holes. Still part of the exercise, she tried to tell herself, still part of the Hereford refresher. Kalashnikovs. Anybody could have AKs, but two of the men were wearing Spanish Star and Czech CZ. SAS would carry Browning Hi-Powers.

The interrogation began.

You were in the front car at Beechwood Street. Who were you with? RUC or Army? How did they know about Beechwood Street? How did they know about McKendrick and Rorke? She was against the wall. The gunman asking the questions was short, not much more than five feet, thick Irish accent that even she could barely understand. How did they know about Tommy Reardon and the attack on the Crum?

The SAS know this, she told herself. This could all be part of the course. These men don't have to be Provos, they could be SAS.

The gunman moved quickly, as if he understood what she was thinking, hitting her across the face, all the power of his body behind it. She reeled over. One of the others pushed her back up and the interrogator hit her again, her head jerking back with the force. He hit her again, in the stomach, doubled her up, the air pushed violently out of her lungs. She was pulled across the floor, someone grabbing her hair. She was pushed down, almost kneeling, her head thrust forward and her face into the water. Her lungs were already screaming for air and her head was spinning. She tried not to breathe, knew she was going to. Her head was wrenched up and she opened her mouth, was pulling in the air when her head was pushed forward again, mouth and nose below the water and the rim of the bucket or the trough – whatever it was – cutting across her windpipe. She was struggling, trying to fight back. Her head was pulled up again, pushed down again.

Who told you about Beechwood Street? How'd you know about Reardon? Who told you what site he was working on? Who's the source in the Provos? How high up is he? What's his name? If you don't know then who would?

She was against the wall, had no idea how long she had been questioned. Abruptly the interrogator nodded and she was thrown into a corner, bales on three sides and straw on the floor. The interrogator and three others left, leaving two guards. She half-turned, tried to look at her watch. Part of the exercise, she still tried to tell herself, these men aren't Provos, these men are really SAS. It was 1700 hours, five in the afternoon. She should have left Hereford at twelve, was due at The Fort at eight the following morning. Her face was bruised and bleeding and there was a pain down her right side as if her ribs were broken.

The interrogator came back in, balaclava still on, and the questions began again.

Who was she with? Army or RUC? Military Intelligence or Special Branch? If she was sitting in a stake-out car then she would be E4A. Which meant she was RUC. Or on secondment to E4A from Military Intelligence. So who was the leak in the Provos? Where was the leak in the Provos? Where did the order come from to stake out Reardon's house in Beechwood Street? What time did it come? Who told her what about it?

He hit her again; face, body. Especially her body. Especially where they'd already broken her ribs.

It was night, morning again. She'd had two hours' sleep, nothing to eat or drink. At least she was dry, she told herself. The men pulled her up and led her outside. Make a break for it, she told herself, try to run. It was dark, therefore still night, felt as if the dawn was about to break. No way she would make it, the men all round her. The gunmen pushed her against a concrete wall and turned the hose on her, the water cold and the jet strong. She'd been against the wall five minutes, probably ten, was wet through and shivering. The gunmen took her back inside and the interrogation continued.

Who was she working with at Lisburn? Who else was on the squad? Who was the driver in the surveillance car?

It was midday. Past the time she was due to start at The Fort. It was as if the interrogator knew. Not knew the details as much as sensed that she had suddenly weakened. These men can't be SAS, she tried to fight back the thought, these men really are Provos. They threw her into the corner, left two men to guard her, and went outside.

She curled up and tried to sleep, tried to escape from the fear in her mind and the suffering in her body. Her hands were still tied behind her back. She bent her knees and pulled her hands forward. Two of them, she knew, no way she would get away with it. She curled up again and felt the piece of wood under her body. Not quite under her body, in the straw to the side. She moved slightly, ignored it. Tried to sleep. Felt for it beneath the straw. Not a piece of wood, the realization crept upon her, more like a handle. She turned slightly, made sure the guards weren't looking at her, and felt along it. Eighteen inches, then she came to the end, felt the ragged wood as if the handle had been broken. One of the guards turned and looked at her, did not notice that she had moved her hands in front of her body, looked away again. She felt the other way, felt the metal. The two prongs of the pitchfork. Her hands closed round it and she knew what she had to do. She began to turn, to check the guards. The interrogator came back in and the beating began again.

Who was handling the informant? Was the handler Special Branch or MI5? Who was the informant who told them about Beechwood Street? Was he being run from Lisburn? What about the FRU, was he working for them? Where did the orders come from? Someone must have said something, someone from SB or MI5 or the FRU must have let a name slip.

It was late afternoon, going into evening. They tossed her in the corner again, left her with one guard. The pangs racked her body and she wanted to die. Do it, she told herself, now while there's just one of them. But they could still be SAS, the thought held her back, it could still be part of the Hereford refresher. The bastards seeing how far they could push her before she cracked.

The interrogator returned and the questioning continued. Why were you in Beechwood Street? Who told you? What time did the orders come in? Who was the leak? Next time they pushed her in the corner, she told herself. But suppose they weren't Provos, suppose they had fixed it for her to arrive late at The Fort. Suppose they were SAS. She couldn't kill one if he was SAS, if he really was a Brit. The interrogator hit her again, the questions spinning through her head and confusing her. Kill them or don't kill them, the other question was like a vortex in her mind. Who the hell are they, what are they? Up to her, she told herself, whether she could do it or not. If she got the chance again. Should have done it before. The interrogation ended and she was pushed into the corner, two guards remaining. No chance to do it now, she told herself.

So what is it? she asked herself. What was she afraid of, why had she delayed before?

She was back in the stake-out car, McKendrick at the driver's window and Rorke in front, Brady's trouser zip undone and the Browning in his waist holster. She couldn't do it, she was thinking, was slowing down, telling herself she was stalling to give the SAS boys in Tommy Reardon's house a chance. She was in the car after, on patrol in the days and weeks that followed, was lying awake at night or walking along the beach on the west coast. The knowledge was deep in her subconscious, unavailable to her; the security block she had imposed upon it protecting her.

Beechwood Street, she made herself admit; she shouldn't have hesitated. Even now, even with the Provo guards ten yards from her, it was impossible to come to terms with. She had told herself she was delaying to give the men in the house a chance, but all the time she didn't want to do it.

Didn't want to do what, she asked herself.

She had to go down on Brady to get to the back-up gun, she knew the answer she had been giving herself. And ever since she had told herself that that was the thing she had been afraid to do.

But . . . she took herself on, pushed herself to the brink. But that had not been what she was afraid of. The sex wasn't relevant, wasn't even sex. It wasn't even a penis. It was just a way of getting to the gun. All the time it wasn't the sex that she had been afraid of, that she had known she couldn't do. All the time what she had been afraid of was actually killing someone.

One of the guards had left, the other sitting eating the supper they had brought for him, sitting with his back to her. The rope round her wrists had worked loose and she slid her hands from it. Do it, she told herself, do it now. These men aren't SAS, these men are Provisional IRA. If you don't talk soon they'll kill you. So kill them first.

There was no point. Even if she dealt with one gunman there were four, perhaps five more. Even if she got outside they would hunt her down. What you're saying is an excuse, she told herself.

69

Nobody likes killing, but sometimes it's necessary. Sometimes it's you or them. The gunman's back was still towards her, the man seated on a bale and crouched over the plate. She picked up the pitchfork and rose, stepped towards him. No noise, not even a rustling of the straw. She was four feet from him. Three feet. Two. His back was still towards her. Him or her. Him not her. She began to bring the pitchfork down.

'ENDEX.'

She heard the voice and froze. English. End exercise, the words pounded through her brain. The Provo gunmen stepped forward from the shadows; no balaclavas over their faces. Phillips turned round and looked at her.

Put her through it, Haslam had told him. String her out and see what happens. Take her down to hell and see if she comes back. Go down with her if you have to. Not for himself, not because it was Haslam who'd run the course in Germany where the talent-spotters had first picked her up, who'd drunk and talked with her and the others in the evenings, who'd taken her aside at the end and suggested that she might like to volunteer for Special Duties. But for her. Because at the end of the day she was worth it. And he couldn't do it because she would recognize him; then she would realize and throw up her defences; then she wouldn't admit what she needed to admit to herself. Then she would be lost for ever.

Unofficial of course, nothing to go on the record.

You . . . Nolan almost said to the man she had been about to kill . . . You were one of the men in the house on Beechwood Street.

Philipa Walker left the flat and took the Northern Line to the Newspaper Library at Colindale. Something about a photograph, she had been aware. At least one photograph, possibly two. Not something about PinMan, something about herself.

There were those who might have preferred to shrug off such a feeling, to let it slip away as if it had never existed. She herself did not subscribe to such a philosophy. If an item or detail existed she should face up to it even though she might not wish to. Control it, control herself, rather than allow things or events to control her.

The first photograph was in the diary column of the *Mail* – she remembered the type around it and the position on the page. The second, following the same logic, was in the *Sunday Times*.

She ordered the *Mail* for the years 1988 to 1990 – it was only

70

possible to order three volumes at any one time – and settled down to wait in the microfiche section at the rear. The boxes of film were delivered to her ten minutes later. She inserted the '88 cassette in the viewer and began her search. An hour and a half later she handed the boxes back and ordered the *Mail* for the three years beginning 1991. The photograph was in the *Mail* of April 1992. She recognized the page immediately – the headline and the layout triggering the subconscious layers of her memory. The picture spanned the middle two columns – the group at the restaurant table, the woman in the centre and the vague faces behind. When Walker had first seen it, it had been at the Press Association library and all the faces had been clearly defined. On microfiche, however, she could barely make out the faces of the two men behind the women. She noted the date of the newspaper, handed the cassettes back, and booked the *Sunday Times* beginning 1991.

The woman seemed asleep, the reading-room porter thought. He gave her the boxes of microfiche and was startled by the way she suddenly appeared to wake. Almost like an animal.

The story had been written before the separation of the Prince and Princess of Wales. It was trailed on the front page of the main section of the newspaper and dealt with in full in the News Review. Its theme was the distinct sets of friends enjoyed by the couple and the way in which this represented a crossroads in their life together. Again, however, the faces in the photographs which accompanied the article were indistinct. She read through the piece once, then went to the pay phone on the landing outside the reading room, telephoned the *Daily Mail* and *Sunday Times*, and confirmed that back copies of the relevant dates of each were available. Then she collected her coat and bag, walked to the tube station, and caught the Northern Line to Chalk Farm.

That evening she dined with Patrick Saunders at the White Tower restaurant in Percy Street. The relationship was developing as she had anticipated, indeed planned. In the almost twisted manner of the hunt, she even enjoyed it, enjoyed his company but also enjoyed the razor edge which came with the knowledge of why she was seeing him. As long as he was the key, as long as his source into the royal family was the one she needed. As long as she herself could access that source without Saunders or the source knowing.

At eleven next morning she collected the back copy of the *Mail*,

71

then went to a café two hundred yards away, ordered a cappuccino, and turned to the photograph on the diary page, ignoring the faces of the women at the table and concentrating on the taller of the two men standing behind them.

An hour later she collected the copy of the *Sunday Times*, returned to St Katharine's Dock, and ordered a Bloody Mary in the Thames Bar of the Tower Hotel. In the main, the article said, the Di and Charles camps were not compatible; the Prince thought his wife's friends too frivolous, and the Princess considered her husband's circle too serious, even boring. Only one person was welcomed in both camps. Major R.E.F. Fairfax of the Grenadier Guards, known to the royal couple as Roddy. Originally it had been the Princess of Wales who had welcomed Fairfax into her inner circle, the newspaper said. Charles, however, also thought highly of him, partly because he was a military man and had seen service in Northern Ireland, and had personally invited him to the royal home at Highgrove.

Of course Fairfax was a military man. Walker looked again at the photographs in the two papers and the name in the *Sunday Times*, felt the ice spreading. Of course the bastard had seen service in Northern Ireland.

Haslam had left Belfast ten days before, spending two days at Hereford and a further two checking airport security at Heathrow. He spent the night in London, left at 5.30 and liaised with the other men who would take part in the exercise at seven. At eight the three took the ferry to the island, enjoyed an hour-long breakfast, then caught the 10.30 return ferry as instructed.

The watchers from Five were waiting. Men and women. Fat ones, thin ones. Some looking fit as hell and others as if they could barely make it to the bar to get another drink. Double-sided coats, different colours each side to confuse the targets, wigs, bags, all the works. Spot them a mile off if you were expecting them and knew what you were looking for. Never see them in a month of Sundays if you didn't.

The latest graduates from the Firm's school at The Fort, SAS men playing the suspects they would tail in the end-of-course close-surveillance exercise.

He stepped off the ferry and turned up Lime Street.

'Charlie One Five. Green One.' The first tail picked him up, the streets already coded. Dead letter drops and pick-ups, contact with another suspect – it was all in the day's exercise.

Haslam reached the top of the street and turned left.

'Charlie One Five. Green Four.' The first tail dropped back.

'Charlie One Six. Green Five.' The second picked Haslam up from the other side of the road. Surveillance teams in front and behind. Vehicles on stand-by.

'One Six. Green Three.' The bus stop was seventy yards ahead and the tail thirty yards behind. Haslam glanced back and saw the bus; as it passed him he slowed and allowed it to stop at the stop, then sprinted for it as it pulled away.

'Charlie One Two. Blue Two.' The woman who had been waiting at the stop took the third seat in, downstairs, and watched as he went up the stairs to the top deck. 'Blue Three.' . . . Silver Street. 'Blue Four.' . . . Rodney Street. 'Blue Five.' She called the stops as the bus passed them. One car staying behind, the others moving ahead, dropping tails where the target might leave the bus.

This was their patch, Nolan thought; they'd practised on it and knew the streets backwards. Christ help them if the target decided to go AWOL, took the train to Bournemouth and got off at South-ampton, left them spread like confetti over the south of England. She slid from the car and looked in the window of the tobacconist next to the bus stop.

'Charlie One Three. Green Ten to Green Eleven.' . . . The suspect on foot in Vesta Road going towards Queens Road.

'Charlie Two One.' The next tail in position. 'Affirmative.' The tail slid in behind Haslam.

Bramshaw Road then Pembury Street, the railway line across the top and the footbridge to Marshall Place – the area map was imprinted on her mind. Cul de sacs at Bolsover Street and Duncan Road.

Haslam turned into the newsagents and waited for the tail to follow him in. 'Box of matches.' He paid, then browsed along the magazine shelves as the tail asked for a packet of cigarettes. It was time to start playing games, time to give them a run for their money. He left the shop and turned first right. The street was seventy yards long, turnings to the right and left at the top.

'Charlie Two Three. Green Eight.'

The tail was thirty yards behind and afraid to go too close. Haslam slowed and made the tail drop even further back, so that when he

73

reached the corner the man was almost forty yards behind him. He turned the corner and ran. Thirty yards, left; another forty, right. Left again and over the railway footbridge. The tail rounded the corner. 'Green Eight.' He looked right, left. Didn't know what to do or say.

Nolan heard, knew what the bastard had done. The pavement was lined with stalls. She pushed through them and slid into the back-up car. 'Marshall Place, quick, he's gone over the footbridge.'

The car accelerated, went through the lights on amber, and skidded across the level crossing at Fore Street as the barrier came down.

'One Three. Blue Two towards Black Four.' Haslam was fifty yards in front, walking away from them. The car pulled into a side street; she left it and followed him. 'One Three. Black Ten.' She turned right after him and realized. Bolsover Street, a cul-de-sac. He's going to sideline me, the thought screamed through her head, the bastard's going to eyeball me. Standard anti-surveillance if a target thought he was being shadowed – one of several. Turn, walk back past the shadow, stare him in the face. Let him know that you know. Put him out of the game.

Haslam turned and she saw his face for the first time. Understood.

Long time since Germany – he didn't need to say it. Long time since the adventure training course and the talk about Special Duties.

You – she was still walking towards him. You were the second man in the house on Beechwood Street. You were the one who pulled the strings and got me off the desk assignment and into the Firm. You were the bastard who arranged the little session at Hereford. You waited till it was me behind you before you turned in here.

Haslam was twenty yards from her, on the outside of the pavement, eyes straight ahead. They were ten yards apart, five. Both staring straight ahead. Good girl, the instructor whispered to himself, don't let him phase you. Just keep walking. Haslam was three yards from her, face set, Nolan still staring straight ahead.

As she passed him she winked.

4

THE ARMY COUNCIL MET AT TEN. Outside there was sleet in the wind; inside the air was mixed with cigarette smoke and the aroma of fresh coffee. Doherty was looking older, Conlan thought, the first cobweb of dark and wrinkled skin beneath his eyes and the eyes themselves darting as he had never seen them before. The evening before the doctor had confirmed what the Chief of Staff already assumed.

For the major part of the morning they discussed general issues – the escalating rounds of shootings and bombings, the income from the various fund-raising activities operated by the Movement and the laundering of that money through front companies on the British mainland. It was only as they approached midday that Doherty moved them to the item they had all anticipated.

'Sleeper and PinMan.'

Doherty had organized it well, Conlan thought, had guided the previous discussions so that the Council was already predisposed to agree to the PinMan project. Had added his weight only when necessary, and then merely to divert the tide of opinion in the direction he wished. Doherty was dying: he had suspected before but now he knew for certain, now he understood. Doherty wanted PinMan and what PinMan would give them as much as he himself did.

Doherty indicated that Conlan should brief the meeting. So what would Quin do, he wondered, how would Quin seek to counter Conlan?

'Sleeper has been activated, and is engaged upon preliminary research. I anticipate the project will take another three to six months.' He spoke for another two minutes only, deliberately vague about timings and other details, withholding as much as he could and knowing the direction the discussion would take when he had finished.

'Do we know which member of the royal family will be the target?' Quin stared at him through the cigarette smoke.

'Not yet.' Conlan wondered why he considered it necessary to lie.

'Assassination or kidnapping?' It was Quin again.

For the next two hours they discussed the range of alternatives and the various options within each, including the short-, medium- and long-term implications of whatever decision they reached. If assassination, what would be the effect on world opinion, including the Movement's supporters in the United States? How would the Catholic population in Northern Ireland react? What would be the response in the Republic? If kidnapping, what demands? Would the British try to hush it up? Would the Council let them? The discussion circled back on itself. What was the long-term aim, how would the various reactions further that aim?

Doherty had discussed it with Conlan the night before, Quin suddenly realized. Doherty knew who the target was and how it was to be done. Doherty dying – he looked into the man's eyes and knew for certain. Doherty on his way out and Conlan about to give him his footnote in history.

'I suggest we vote.'

Quin knows, Conlan suddenly realized: that he and Doherty had done the deal, that he enjoyed Doherty's full support.

The vote was unanimous. Outside it was already dark.

The following morning Conlan activated those he had already placed on stand-by.

McGuire, from Belfast. In his mid-thirties, lean and thin-faced, short dark curly hair. Married with two children. A good operator, one of the best.

McGinty, whose priest's collar and gentle manner gave him the perfect cover. Who loved fishing and who so matched Conlan in age and build that from a distance he could pass for him. Especially when he was wrapped in oilskins, woollen cap or dark glasses against the glare of the sun or the bite of the wind on the shores of Lough Corrib.

Plus the foot soldiers, the expendables. Clarke and Milligan, Black and Lynch. Hoolihan and Lynan.

But not Logan. Not yet. Logan was to come.

*

The morning was bright but cold, the white of the first snow lying on Divis Hill to the south-west of the city. When McGuire returned to the house his wife was in the kitchen.

'I'll be away a few days.'

Eileen McGuire was small, with bright eyes that hid her fear. She bit her lip and nodded.

'Don't worry. No problems this time.'

At least he was honest, she thought, at least he didn't say that every time he went away. He went upstairs to the bedroom at the front of the house. One day they would get him, the fear was always coiled in her. One day a shoot-to-kill unit from the RUC or the SAS would lie in wait for him and gun him down like a dog. One day the UFF would find out about him and slaughter him in his own front room. And in the meantime she would tell the children he was going away to work, a building site in Derry or wherever, and that he would soon be home again. She followed him upstairs and watched him pack the handful of clothes. When he finished she put the small bag into the large plastic laundry bag she used for shopping, went to the Sportsman's, dropped his bag in the back room, then returned to the house and carried on cooking.

At seven McGuire left the house and walked the three hundred yards to the bar. If he was under observation – from undercover motor vehicles, informants, OPs concealed in the roof spaces of surrounding houses, or high-altitude surveillance helicopters – there was nothing to suggest that he was doing anything other than going for a drink.

The Sportsman's was busy. After thirty minutes he muttered his excuses and went to the toilets at the rear, collected his bag and stepped into the alleyway behind. The car was waiting.

The shooting took place shortly after five the following day, outside a betting shop at the top of the Crumlin Road, on the edge of the Catholic Ardoyne area and close to the Protestant Shankill. The victim was a 32-year-old Sinn Fein politician whom the UFF alleged was a member of the Provisional IRA. The planning for the shooting which followed it took place the following evening and was led by the officer commanding the North Belfast Brigade of the Provisional IRA. The first part of the discussion was strategic – whether or not a shooting of a UFF activist was not only necessary but politically and militarily sound at that point in time; whether the UFF reaction to the execution of a member of its ranks would be counter-productive. The second part, which followed once the decision had been made, was tactical. The target would be a man known to be a planning officer for the UFF. The location and timing would be confirmed by the intelligence officer, the details to be supplied to the team assigned to the killing, and the weapon would be an AK47 supplied from one of the Provisionals' arms dumps in Myrtle Field Park, a middle-class street in a non-sectarian area of the city. The execution, as the Provisionals would describe it in the communiqué they would release later, would take place from a car stolen from the city centre. The driver would pick up the man carrying the gun fifteen minutes before the hit and the gunman himself ten minutes before. The gunman would leave the car as soon as they were clear of the area and in a neighbourhood considered safe; the man carrying the weapon immediately after, and the driver would abandon and torch the vehicle as soon as he could after that.

They came to those who would carry out the shooting, the gunman first.

'Clarke or Milligan.' The intelligence officer's suggestion was straightforward and logical.

'Out of circulation.' The OC – officer commanding – had not been told why.

'Black.'

The Bossman shook his head. Something happening, he had assumed when he had been informed by the Northern Command; something big if it required his three most experienced gunmen.

'Lynch.'

'Out of town.'

'Hoolihan?'

'Out as well.'

Five of the most experienced IRA gunman in North Belfast suddenly out of circulation.

'Lynan?' The intelligence officer knew the answer before he suggested the name.

The OC shook his head.

Six out of six. 'Who then?' Douglas, he knew, except that Douglas was young and still slightly brash, and the officer commanding would only use him if the rest of the team were older and more experienced.

'Frank.' Frank Hanrahan had been one of the best, but was now

78

in his late thirties. He had begun his Provo career as a teenager, done his time in Long Kesh without complaint; he had been on the Blanket then the Dirty Protest and – though he had denied it at the time, though he had volunteered for active service immediately he had been released – the years of confinement and hardship had taken their toll. He had married young, his boy and girl were now in their mid-teens, the boy coming up seventeen, but still Frank did the occasional job. Only when no one else was available, however, and only when they wanted an older hand to rein in the recklessness of the youngsters.

'Freddie's picking up the gun, Mickey's driving.' Both were young and both would be good. If they survived that long. But send them out with the gunman called Douglas and they would either wipe out half the Shankill or crash the car on the way.

Frank Hanrahan, they agreed.

Lisburn was quiet. Nolan sat back in the chair and looked again at the reports from the various agents which it was part of her job to analyse. She had returned to Northern Ireland four weeks before. When former colleagues recognized her she said simply that she was on a secure task, and no further questions were asked.

Perhaps something was running, perhaps not.

Clarke on the move. On the gallop, as the Provos called it. The information from E4A, the RUC undercover surveillance division.

Milligan on the move. From an informant in the FRU, the Forward Reconnaissance Unit, the wing of Military Intelligence dealing with agents and informants in the Catholic and Protestant paramilitary organizations.

She punched the names into the computer, checked on the background of each, and read through the reports for the third time. Nothing concrete yet, but something to keep her eye on. She left Lisburn and took one of the five alternative routes she had established to the flat she had rented in Malone Park in the south of the city.

Relatively speaking – everything in Northern Ireland was relative – the area was secure, not plagued by the violence suffered by the communities in and around the city centre. Most of her neighbours were young and professional class. Despite this she maintained a strict personal security. Each time she drove into the street she checked for the obvious signs of surveillance; each morning, when she went to the garage at the rear of the house where she had a first-floor flat, she checked the car for bombs before she started it, even though she had fitted the garage with special locks and an electronic door. Even when she went out to dinner in what was considered a secure area, with friends or colleagues, she timed the interval between ordering a meal and its being served in case someone on the staff was a Provo or UFF informant and had recognized her, had delayed the meal while a hitman was summoned.

Her cover story matched what appeared to be her life-style. She had lived in England for eight years, married, but was now divorced and living off the settlement paid by her former husband while she looked for a job. In case either side – PIRA, the UDA or the various organizations springing from them – had sources in the estate agent's office from which she had rented the flat, every month a cheque was paid into a bank account she had established. And in case the same organizations had a source in the bank, the money was paid from another account set up in England by a man alleged to be her former husband. In the flat itself, in case she was burgled, she kept solicitors' letters referring to the case, as well as the divorce papers themselves.

She hung up her coat, placed the Browning in the bedroom, and went to the kitchen. It was a strange life, she would have admitted; most people would not understand it. But in the end you were who you were. Even at the beginning . . .

. . . *she was nine, almost ten; long legs and awkward body. It was spring, going on summer, the children playing at the foot of the hill above the town. The game was hide and seek, the children divided into teams. She was on the catcher team, hunting through the trees and undergrowth for those hiding from them. The wood was quiet. She paused, not moving, not even shifting balance, totally alert, listening for the slightest rustle which would tell her where her quarry was hiding.*

The teams changed, the hunters becoming the hunted. Some of the children hid in pairs, but she was different, preferred to be alone, to take her chance alone.

The tree was covered with foliage. There was barely enough time to pull herself up and conceal herself before she saw the searchers below. The blood thudded through her head and she did not dare breathe. She knew the boys were looking for her, knew they knew she was close by them, looking at them. For five minutes she looked down on them, willed them not to look up, willed them to look for her somewhere else.

They moved off and she knew she had won, tasted the triumph and waited for them to come back, waited for the excitement of the moment again. The thudding eased and she was aware of the other sensation, though she would not have been able to express it, perhaps not even to identify it. Not just the emptiness of suddenly being out of the game. Something else. The emptiness of no longer being on the edge, no longer being in danger . . .

The following day she checked the reports for fresh information on Clarke and Milligan. The two were still on the move, one in Belfast and one in Londonderry. Plus a third gunman – Black, Alex – the intelligence on Black's movements from an SAS observation post.

Hanrahan reached the pick-up point thirty seconds early. The evening was dark and it was drizzling slightly. He waited, hunched against the weather, then the car stopped, the back door opened, he stepped in and the car pulled away. The men in the front seat were in their late teens, he guessed, certainly not in their twenties. The way they had all begun, what he himself had been like so many lifetimes ago.

'Which side?'

'Left.'

Hanrahan's mac was wet; he took it off and placed it on the seat. The man in the front passenger seat turned and handed him the gloves. Hanrahan pulled them on then took the Kalashnikov. The others were jumpy, he sensed, almost too keen, would go ahead with the job even if the Prods were waiting for them. It was already two minutes to seven. The car turned into Tennent Street. He checked the gun and wound down the window. The takeaway was fifty yards away.

'There he is.'

The driver pulled in to the pavement. Slightly too fast, Hanrahan thought, might have given the target some warning. He pressed the trigger and the car screeched away.

Farringdon was informed at eight the following morning; at 8.30 he included the information in his first meeting of the day with

Cutler. Cutler had been DoI, Director of Intelligence, Northern Ireland – the most senior MI5 position in Belfast – for the past three years; for the past eighteen months Farringdon had been his deputy.

The previous evening a man with links to the UFF had been gunned down in the Shankill, responsibility being claimed by the Provisional IRA. Cutler's briefing was to the point. The normal sort of job – the shrug said it – except that the driver of the vehicle used for the killing hadn't dumped it quickly enough. An RUC undercover car had spotted the vehicle, recorded as having been stolen earlier, and had arrested the driver for taking and driving away. At first it was thought that he had stolen the vehicle for a joy-ride; only later had it been tied in with the shooting. The driver's name was Flynn. During his interrogation he had admitted involvement in the shooting, but had denied knowing the identities of the others. Under pressure, however, he had given a description of the hitman which matched that of a Frank Hanrahan, a known Provisional IRA gunman with a prison record. Because of the possibility of Flynn being turned and acting as an informant, RUC Special Branch had been informed and had taken over the case, and had in its turn informed MI5.

'When are they picking up Hanrahan?'

'Now.'

'Any possibility of turning him?'

'Probably not.'

'Who are you assigning to the case?'

'Nolan.'

Nolan was relatively new, but she had come to him with a background unsurpassed by many of her more senior colleagues.

'Fine. Keep me informed.'

The interview room at Castlereagh was bleak and featureless, the desk and chairs of grey metal. Nolan sat patiently and watched the interrogation. Hanrahan against Brady – who had been with her in the forward surveillance car in Beechwood Street – and a Special Branch inspector named McKiver.

We all know why we're here, Frank. So what were you doing on the evening in question? How can you account for your movements? What were you doing between five in the afternoon and ten that evening – the hours were deliberately vague and loose, an attempt to draw Hanrahan in, make him admit something, anything, that they could check out. What clothes were you wearing, Frank? Same clothes that forensic are looking at now? You know about forensics, of course, what they'll be looking for? Fibre matches between your clothes and the car, traces of lead on your coat where you fired the gun.

Hanrahan was looking at his interrogators, absorbing their questions but saying nothing, not even acknowledging their presence.

They would get nowhere, Nolan knew: Hanrahan had done his time before and would do his time again. Not the breathtaking cold of the nights during the Blanket Protest, when the IRA prisoners had refused to wear uniforms; not the cells smothered with human excrement as they had been during the Dirty Protest which followed. Fifteen years, even twenty, cut by half in line with official policy, but a long time anyway.

Be careful with the questions, the interrogators knew. When Hanrahan was sent to Crumlin Road he would be debriefed by the IRA security section within the prison. Then the Provos' intelligence people would try to establish what the Brits or the RUC already knew from the questions his interrogators had asked him.

You won't make it this time, Frank. The two SB men were facing him, the use of his first name sometimes friendly, more often threatening and hostile. You remember what it was like when you were young, Frank, just imagine what it'll be like this time. So why do it, Frank, you hadn't done a job for a long time, why now?

Clarke, Milligan and Black still on the move – Nolan had checked that morning. Plus two more overnight – Lynch and Hoolihan.

Hanrahan's face was as grey and expressionless as the walls of the cell, eyes staring straight ahead, the thin scar which Flynn had described and which had pointed them to Hanrahan down the corner of his left eye. Somebody grassed, she read it in his face, somebody turned stag and when they find out who the boys will take him for his cup of tea.

The first day of the interview ended and Hanrahan was returned to the cell.

The overnight reports on the Provisional gunmen came through an hour before the interrogation of Hanrahan resumed the following morning. The five gunmen still on the move, now joined by a sixth – Lynan. Foot soldiers, Nolan knew, expendables like Hanrahan.

The interview recommenced at eight. Overnight they had assessed the possibility of Hanrahan cracking, had also looked at the possibility of Hanrahan turning, of Hanrahan becoming a CT – converted terrorist. Had gone through the files for the single piece of intelligence which might provide the key – gambling debts or affairs with other women were favourites; once it had been found that a Provo shooter had been having an affair with the wife of an RUC man.

You know the results of the forensics, Frank. You know we can put you in the car and that we have witnesses to say that that was the car used for the murder on Tennent Street. You know that we can prove that you fired a gun that evening. So be fair on yourself, Frank, have a think about it.

Hanrahan still had not said a word. Would not say a word, the interrogators knew. At eight that evening they finished the second day. The following morning they would formally charge him and the following afternoon, unless he said something worth listening to – unless he said anything at all – they would give up on him as they had known they would from the beginning, and Hanrahan would be detained at Crumlin Road jail. And two months after he would appear before a single judge sitting in a so-called Diplock Court – no jury because of the threat of intimidation – and be sent down for the required period.

That evening they scanned the Hanrahan file for what Nolan assumed would be the last time, that evening she returned to the flat in Malone Park and thought about the man who had still said nothing, about the details on his file. At six the following morning – two hours before Hanrahan's last interview was due to begin – she returned to Lisburn; at seven she made the request, at 7.45 she ran through the updates on the Provo gunmen still on the move in the North.

Clarke and Milligan. Black and Lynch. Hoolihan and Lynan. Plus a seventh.

McGuire. Not seen for four days.

She knew who and what he was but checked on the computer anyway.

McGuire, Kevin. Born 11.4.59. Married, two children. The details flickered on to the screen. Not a bomber or gunman, one of the men who ran the bombers and the gunmen. What the intelligence services would call an LO, a liaison officer.

She ran the reports together, logged a synopsis, and requested immediate reports on McGuire once he was sighted. Logical, she thought. The troops on the move and the handler out of sight. Almost too logical.

She left the office and went to the interrogation centre at Castle-reagh. Brady and McKiver were eating breakfast in the canteen; she collected a coffee and joined them.

'No problems about me asking a couple of questions today?'

McKiver was the problem, she and Brady had agreed: McKiver didn't even think MI5 should have been informed. The last day, they understood, therefore nothing would happen. Therefore she could join in.

'Fine.'

They went to the interrogation room, McKiver and Brady taking their usual positions along one side of the desk, the prisoner opposite them.

The forensics, Frank. Confirmation that the car was the murder vehicle and that you were in it. Ballistics suggest that the weapon has also been used in three other killings. The chances of them being put down to you, Frank. Might not carry in court, of course, but could affect the sentence.

Hanrahan sat impassive and said nothing, not even a flicker in the eyes. No response when they offered him coffee or a cigarette. At 10.30 they broke for five minutes. And when they returned Hanrahan would sit in the same position and not move until they led him out after charging him. There was a feeling of inevitability about the way they left the room, the knowledge that they had been through it before.

The documents she had requested had arrived. They probably wouldn't work, but it was worth giving it a try. She wouldn't mention it to McKiver though; despite his appearance and manner he was a good operator, knew when he was winning and when he was losing. And as long as he stood even the faintest chance he'd hang in. But the moment he knew he'd lost he saw no point in carrying on.

They returned to the interrogation room.

The evening in question, Frank. What time did they pick you up? Where did you leave the car after the job? What did you do after? Who told you about the job, gave you the instructions? Who decided it should be you, Frank, who gave you that pair to babysit?

There was no response, no reply or change in the facial expression.

'You were inside with Slattery, of course.' It was the first time Nolan had spoken. Fergal Slattery, gunman and bomber. So what the hell did Slattery have to do with it, thought McKiver. Slattery

85

had decided to call it a day, of course, get out while he could, but what bearing did it have on Hanrahan?

'You know what Slattery said, of course, don't you, Frank?'

So what the fuck should I know about what Fergal said, they read it in his face, in his eyes. Read something for the first time.

'He said that his children were nearing the age when they would be caught up in it, and that he didn't want them to go through what he'd gone through.'

The curtain drew again across Hanrahan's face.

'Good kids, Frank. How old are they now?'

She's blown it, Brady saw the look in McKiver's eyes as he glanced at Nolan. We had him going, were about to turn him. Now she's threatened his kids. Okay, so they weren't about to turn him, weren't about to make him even say a dickie bird. But kids were out of it. No way they threatened anyone's kids, not even someone like Hanrahan's.

'Good school reports, Frank. Boy did well at GCSE, A levels in a couple of years. The girl also expected to do well.' She put the copies of the reports on the desk. 'Pity they're going to end up like you, though. Because you know what's going to happen when you go down, don't you, Frank? The boy will end up like that pillock who was supposed to get rid of the motor. Be with you in the Crum by the time he's twenty. If he's lucky.' She leaned forward and moved the reports slightly. 'Same with the girl. End up pushing a pram for the rest of her life with the kids strung along behind and somebody like you for her husband.'

Know what I mean, Frank? Know what I'm talking about? 'Pity really.' As if there was an alternative. It was in her voice, in the way she leaned forward again and began to take the reports away then left them on the table. She sat back and the interrogation continued.

So what about the day in question, Frank? Where were you that afternoon? Go for a drink at dinner time? Where'd you go, what did you have? There were no answers, no movement in the body or the face. What about after, Frank? Did you go straight home? Or to a bar? Tell the lads the job was done?

'What's on offer?' Hanrahan stared past the two men at Nolan. No other words, no change in the face or the eyes. Just the three words.

'Good A-level results for the boy. You'll have to kick his arse, of course, make sure he doesn't let up.' I can fix the grades, but not that much, not so much it would make everyone suspicious. 'Place at a good university.' She looked straight at him. 'On the mainland. Not Dublin, not Trinity. You wouldn't want him becoming a thinking man's Provo, would you, Frank?'

Hanrahan smiled, Brady suddenly thought, Hanrahan the hard man actually fucking laughed.

'Same for the girl.'

Hanrahan's head and eyes dropped as quickly as they had risen and the interview continued.

So what about the gun, Frank? What about the fact that three other jobs have been done with it? Who did you see after? Suppose you had a Black Bush, celebrate like? Them telling you what a good job you'd done?

'What do you want?' It was only the second phrase Hanrahan had spoken since his arrest.

'You in the sweenies.'

She had balls, McKiver made himself admit. Nobody got anyone in what the Provos nicknamed the sweenies. The security section was the unit of the Provisional IRA which dealt with those suspected of being agents or informants for the Brits or the RUC. Get somebody in there and you struck gold.

Somebody else might have picked up on Nolan's suggestion, Brady thought; somebody else might have reinforced her offer about the kids. Somebody else might have blown it. Instead McKiver sat still and impassive, as if he and Brady were no longer there, nobody speaking – neither them nor Nolan nor Hanrahan. Five minutes, ten, gone fifteen. McKiver didn't even dare look at his watch. Probably twenty-five, almost half an hour. Nobody come in, dear God, nobody knock on the door and blow it.

'How?' Hanrahan had looked up again. How will you get me off the charge? How will you swing the forensics? How will you do it in a way that guarantees I don't get my brains blown out by my own people?

'You're charged, put in the Crum, appear before the court. With the evidence against you, you don't stand a chance. Except we'll change something. Everyone will know you're guilty but you'll get off on a technicality.'

'Guaranteed?'

'Guaranteed. You don't do anything for us until you've walked.'

Hanrahan wrapped himself inside himself again, head sunk into his chest and shoulders rounded. Not the way he had sat earlier, however, not the stance of prolonged and stubborn resistance. Everyone came to the end of the road sometime, he thought. Everyone came to the point where they looked back and saw what little they'd had, and how much more they wanted for their kids. Where they realized that all this stinking fucking cesspit was about was giving your kids a better start than you had.

'A good job afterwards.' He looked again at Nolan. 'The girl as well.'

'Agreed.'

The village of Rathmeen was tucked inconspicuously into the rolling hills some ten miles south of Lough Neagh, the border with the Republic twenty miles to the south as the crow flies, and the main A3 road between Craigavon and Armagh four miles to the west. The country road which wound down from the hills and ran through it served as its main street, most of the shops clustered round the small square in the centre and the houses running in terraces away from it.

Father Donal McGinty left shortly before eleven, driving south then picking up the A28 to Newry. The morning was cold and crisp, fresh snow in the fields. Half an hour later he drove through the town and began the climb up the hill to the border at the top. The first checkpoint was half-way up, the soldiers and police armed and wearing flak jackets, the machine gunner positioned in the sangar to his left and the Land-Rovers parked in the middle, armed patrols moving up the pavements behind him and a surveillance helicopter hovering in the sky to his right. The line of cars edged forward; he handed his driving licence to the RUC policeman, waited as the man scanned the details and waved him through. Ten minutes later, in the toilet of the Carrickdale Hotel, nine miles north of Dundalk, he took off the dark suit, ecclesiastical collar and black shirt, and replaced them with a sweater and sports jacket.

When he reached Dublin it was a little after two. He parked near the post office, put on an overcoat, and walked down O'Connell Street. The Joyce Bar at Madigan's was almost empty, only three people left from lunchtime. He asked for roast beef and Guinness and sat with his back to the wall opposite the bar from where he could see both the stairs at the rear and the door at the front. Conlan entered ten minutes later, bought a drink and sat at a table to his right. McGinty waited ten minutes, then rose and went to the toilets on the left of the stairs. As he came out, exactly two minutes later, Conlan went in. The envelope was switched as they passed.

McGinty finished his drink and returned to the car. The envelope which Conlan had passed to him contained a sheet of instructions and a second envelope. McGinty read the instructions, walked to the office of the *Irish Times* on D'Olier Street and placed an advertisement in the paper for the day after next, paying cash.

The afternoon was growing dark. He left Dublin and began the drive north, changing back into the priest's collar and black shirt and suit in a lay-by near Dundalk and reaching Rathmeen in the early evening.

Three mornings later McGinty drove to Aldergrove and caught the 1030 shuttle to London Heathrow. He was wearing his cloth of office. The flight was on time and because there was no computer file on him he passed through the security and immigration checks at both ends without being stopped.

In Belfast the morning had been cold but dry, at Heathrow it was beginning to drizzle. He ignored the signs to the cab ranks and walked briskly to the underground, choosing a seat next to a door. It was late morning, the stations busier as the train approached central London. The train reached Piccadilly, the platform crowded, people getting on and off. He sat still and waited. The doors began to close. Without warning he rose from his seat and squeezed between them, glanced left and right to check if anyone had jumped off the train after him. On the wall next to the exit was an underground map. He appeared to study it, waiting until the platform was almost empty, then walked briskly up the stairs marked NO ENTRY, turning sideways against the people coming the other way. At the top the hallway opened out, escalators leading up. He hurried past the busker playing Dvořák, checked if anyone had followed him, and took another escalator down. At the bottom he turned right again, along a second passageway marked NO ENTRY, and on to the Bakerloo Line platform. A train was leaving, the platform emptying. He ignored the exit signs and took an iron spiral stairway at the end of the platform to the labyrinth of interconnecting passageways at the bottom. Only when he was sure he was not being followed did he rejoin the Piccadilly Line, leave it at Finsbury Park in north London, and take the 106 bus to Stoke Newington.

Abney Park cemetery was on the right, entered through a set of large wrought iron gates. Opposite was a line of shops, two of the windows boarded up, and a café on the corner, flats above them and street stalls along the wide pavement outside. The pavements were wet, the coloured lights glowing on the stalls. McGinty left the bus, crossed the road, and went through the gates.

A straight gravel drive led from them to a dark red brick church 150 yards away. The first section of graves was well tended, the grass cut and the gravel of the drive free from weeds. Fifty yards in, however, it changed abruptly, as if he were crossing a border. The graves – with the occasional exception – were badly kept, weeds and grass growing round and over them. The church itself was drab, almost dirty, grime on its brickwork and the heavy wooden doors padlocked. Beyond it the cemetery degenerated into a jungle. The traffic hummed in the background and the water dripped from a broken gutter. McGinty confirmed he was alone, counted eight bricks to the right from the corner, three up, removed the loose brick, placed the envelope in the space behind, replaced the brick and left.

Walker wiped the condensation from the café window and confirmed that no one had gone into the cemetery after him and no one had followed as he left. She was wearing denims, sweater and a donkey jacket, her hair tucked under a woollen hat. She bought another cup of tea and waited. After half an hour she left the café, turned left down Stoke Newington High Street and right along Stoke Newington Church Street. A hundred and fifty yards along she turned right into Fleetwood Street, a cul de sac with the southern side wall of Abney Park cemetery at the bottom. It was empty. She checked again that she was not being followed, climbed the wall, dropped on to a path which was overgrown, the brambles reaching across it, and made her way to the church at the centre.

Eight bricks from the corner, third up – the drop was one of five she used. She removed the envelope, zipped it into an inside pocket, replaced the brick, and walked quickly through the trees and shrubs growing between and in some cases through the graves, to the northern side of the cemetery. The undergrowth was thick and the headstones ran up to the wall. She climbed on one, checked that the small crescent of houses on the other side was deserted, and dropped over. Only when she had returned to the flat near Primrose Hill did she open the envelope and decode the instructions inside, burning them when she had read them.

Her meeting with Saunders was at eight. She telephoned Iberia, the Spanish national airline, and booked a flight to Seville for the following morning, leaving the return open.

Saunders's day had been straightforward, no big stories and no scares that another paper had something he had missed. By five he had finished what he considered a minor item on the separation of the Duke and Duchess of York but which would still make the front page, copied it on to a floppy disk, entered the names and home telephone numbers of two new contacts into the computer notebook, and left the building.

He returned to the flat, copied the article and the contacts on to the relevant files on the PC in the spare bedroom which also doubled as his study – the bed a fold-up and the bookshelves filled with reference books – booked a minicab, then showered and changed. Forty minutes later the telephone rang and the minicab controller informed him that the car was waiting. He put the computer notebook and Cellnet in his pocket, locked the flat and was driven to Joe Allen's.

Philipa Walker arrived ten minutes later.

Sometime, he assumed, she would agree to go to bed with him. Meanwhile she was good company – intelligent and attractive.

Sometime, she assumed, he would let slip the remark that would give her the way in. And if he didn't, or if he wasn't the key she wanted, then she would have to look elsewhere. Meanwhile he was good company. Except that she was already three months into the schedule Conlan had given her.

'So what are you doing this weekend?'

'Wiltshire.' Wife, the girls and the ponies. 'How about you?'

'I'm away.'

'Skiing?' He had seen the snow reports.

'Spain. Way down south for the sun.'

'All right for some people.'

'The advantage of working for oneself.'

'Send me a postcard.'

By the time she returned to Primrose Hill it was 11.30. Twelve hours later she left the flat and took a cab to Heathrow . . .

. . . *it was the middle of the spring term, her first year at university. That summer she and the students with whom she shared a flat had decided to drive across Europe to Greece. The previous afternoon, therefore, she had collected the passport application form from the post office.*

She's done all right. Considering.

It was five years since she had stood on the stairs of the house in Orpington and heard her mother's voice, yet still the words haunted her. Not every hour of every day, not even every day of every week, yet always hanging in the recesses of her mind, sometimes conscious though most times not.

Birth certificate and two photographs – she checked the requirements for a full passport then went downstairs. The telephone was in the hall. She sat on the bottom stair, dialled directory enquiries and asked for the Orpington office of the Registrar of Births, Deaths and Marriages. The line was engaged. She waited two minutes then tried again. The woman who answered the enquiries number was friendly and helpful.

There were two types of birth certificate, both sufficient for a passport application. The short certificate gave merely the details of her name, date of birth and the registration district in which she had been born, and would cost £2.50. The full certificate would be a copy of her original birth certificate and would cost £5.50. She could come in person, or send a postal application stating full name, place and date of birth, plus a stamped, addressed envelope and a cheque for the relevant amount.

'How long will it take by post?'

'A week, perhaps ten days. No more.'

Post, she decided; there was no hurry and it would be simpler. She thanked the woman, returned to her room and wrote the letter.

Name: Philipa Charlotte Louise Walker. The names came from the two sides of the family.

Date of birth: 12.3.61. Each year, for as far back as she could remember, her parents had always given her a party.

Place of birth: Orpington.

She would have the full certificate rather than the short one, she also decided, even though it cost more. The document wasn't just a piece of paper, it was part of her life. She wrote out the cheque and posted the application that evening.

The stamped, addressed envelope which she included came back nine days later. It was lying on the hall floor when she and the others returned to the flat in the early evening. She slit the envelope open, already smiling. Her name, her date of birth. Her, officially

*recognized as a person for the first time. The thought was innocent
and enjoyable.*

*There was no birth certificate. Instead was her cheque and a
standard letter.*

Dear Miss Walker
*I refer to your recent application for a birth certificate. I
have made a search of our records for the relevant district and
period but I regret that I am unable to trace an entry.*

*The letter was signed by the Deputy Superintendent Registrar.
Typed below the signature was a note suggesting she applied – in
writing or personally – to the General Register Office, St Catherine's
House, Kingsway, London WC2 . . .*

. . . the late afternoon sun was low and the land was patchworked
brown and yellow, only the occasional green. The 727 banked to
port and she saw Seville: the heart of the old city with the newer part
sprawling out from it; the Guadalquivir snaking its way south-west
towards the Atlantic. Twenty minutes later Philipa Walker cleared
immigration and customs, collected a hire car and picked up the N4
motorway south, then switched to the toll road.

The temperature was still a pleasant 65°. A little over an hour
later she cut right towards Cadiz Bay. The city was opposite her,
across the causeway, the off-white concrete of the modern city
at the neck of the peninsula and the honeycomb streets of the
old quarter at the tip. She skirted Puerto de Santa Maria and
took the road to Rota. Three kilometres on she turned left into the
housing development called Las Redes, its streets named after the
oceans of the world, only the line of sand dunes between it and
the Atlantic.

The house on Mar Timor was two hundred metres from the sea,
protected by a whitewashed wall. She entered the security code,
drove into the garage, locked the door behind her, then tapped
the security code of the front door and went inside. The house was
cool and well-furnished, and the safe was concealed beneath the
flagstones of the small courtyard round which the house was
built.

She had not been operational for two years. She was still sharp,

93

her basic talents and instincts still intact, but it was logical both that Conlan should recommend a refresher and that he would arrange it this way.

That evening she ate in a fish restaurant close to the river in Puerto de Santa Maria, the streets cobbled and the smell from the sherry bodegas hanging in the warm night air. The next morning she placed her passport and personal documents in a deposit box in the Banco de Andalucía in the town centre, then spent three hours exploring the maze of streets and alleyways of old Cadiz; that afternoon she drove south to Tarifa, passing an hour in a café on the long, windswept beach to the north and two hours in the fortified part of the old town. That evening she filled out the postcards which had been placed in the floor safe.

Cadiz. *Amazing streets and houses. Can imagine Drake coming in with all guns blazing.* To her parents.

Tarifa. *Windy City, and I can see why. Great sailboarding if I wasn't too old. Southernmost point in Europe, you can almost smell Africa.* To her brother and his family.

Tangiers. *Couldn't resist a day trip. Soukh amazing. Another world.* To Patrick Saunders.

The cards would be posted over the next few days, confirming her holiday in Spain, the mileage on the hired car would show she had travelled a total of 500 kilometres, and her passport would be stamped to confirm the trip to Morocco.

At six the next morning she rose and showered, then dyed her hair blonde – including her pubic hair. At seven she left the house, picked up a bus into Puerto de Santa Maria, took the slow train to Seville and the AVE to Madrid. The Prado was ten minutes from the city's Atocha railway station, and the Mercedes was parked on schedule by the Goya entrance, the driver waiting. Walker recce'd the area for thirty minutes then closed on the car. Forty-eight minutes after she had arrived in Madrid, and under the identity of Katerina Maher, cover for an unnamed member of the German Red Army Faction, she approached the driver, gave the code, received the reply, and began the next stage of her journey to the training ground in North Africa.

The only thing she would not know, and Conlan could not have allowed for, was that on the day the postcard to Patrick Saunders was posted in Tangiers, whilst the main ferry service from the Spanish port of Algeciras sailed on schedule, the ferry from Tarifa, on the windswept northern promontory of the Straits of Gibraltar, was cancelled because of an engineering problem.

*   *   *

The sky was lead grey, Dublin waiting for the snow it had so far escaped. Quin parked at the side of the Post Office and waited for one of the telephone booths to become free.

It was not that he opposed Conlan's plan, the royal family was as legitimate a target as anything else British. Nor was it the first time one of them had been a target: Mountbatten had been blown up in his boat off Mullaghmore in 1979. And if a successful action against one of them was undertaken in central London, then the British and Protestant reaction against the Catholic population of Northern Ireland would be fearsome. That, in the long term, would serve the Cause far more than all the violence which had dominated the country for the past decades.

It was Conlan he opposed, just as Conlan opposed him.

Doherty was dying, and once Doherty went there would be a new Chief of Staff. If Conlan's plan succeeded then the chances were that he would take Doherty's place. And if that happened, then Quin was finished.

It was as simple as that.

Almost.

If Conlan's plan failed to give Doherty his place in history, then Doherty might even switch his support. Then his position would be up for grabs. Then it might well be he, Quin, who was in and Conlan who was out.

He stepped out of the car and into the telephone kiosk. There were three numbers from the time before, he had committed them to memory then, not dared write them down, and even now he still remembered them. The chances were that one at least would have been changed, two and he would be unlucky. Three disconnected and the Devil himself would be against him.

Nothing in life was ever straightforward, he supposed, yet in a way life repeated itself, the same pattern appearing time and time again. The conflict between the Provisionals and the Brits; the conflict in the Provisionals' camp and, he assumed, among the British as well. Yet sometimes, not often and not for long, the sides changed, allies became enemies and enemies became allies.

95

He lifted the receiver, inserted the phone card and dialled the Belfast code and the first number, cursed as he heard the unavailable tone. He dialled the second and heard the same tone. Even the Devil on the side of Conlan. He dialled the third and heard the ringing tone.

'Yes.' The voice was neutral.

'Is Jacobson there?'

Jacobson would not be there. Jacobson had been on the way up last time, would have moved on years ago.

'Who wants him?' There was no detail of the establishment he was calling and no confirmation that Jacobson existed. The same as last time, Quin thought, the alliance as unholy as they came, but something in it for both of them.

All games were dangerous, but that on which he was about to embark was more dangerous than most.

'Tell him Joseph wants to speak to him.' The biblical reference had amused them both. 'I'll phone tomorrow for a number.'

The telephone message from the man calling himself Joseph was logged at 3.56 PM, at 4.04 the codenames Jacobson and Joseph were run against the MI5 computer at Lisburn. Both files were blocked. At 4.18 it was passed to Farringdon and from Farringdon to Cutler. On the DoI's instructions the names were run again through the computer and the files – if any files existed, other than as simple acknowledgements that the codewords had once been used – were confirmed as blocked. At 5.18 PM, one hour and twenty-two minutes after Quin had made the telephone call, his message was passed to London.

In all except one detail, what had happened in MI5's offices in Belfast was now repeated in Gower Street. The two words *Jacobson* and *Joseph* were computer-run, and both files – again if they existed as more than codenames – were found to be blocked, with the single additional point of information that any reference or enquiry concerning the two should be made to T Department. At 5.53 the duty officer in T was informed and ordered a check to be run against the department's own computer system. The files were again blocked, with the instruction to refer any enquiry to the DDG.

Michaelmass was informed at 6.17.

John Petherington Michaelmass (Winchester and Balliol College,

Oxford) was 53 years old, tall, dark hair with the first traces of silver. After Oxford he had spent two years in the States, then returned to Britain to work with ICI. Three years later he had been loaned to the security services to assist in an enquiry in an area in which he was considered a specialist, and had remained. Like all intelligence chiefs he had the ability not only to absorb a considerable quantity of information, but to identify the strands or themes which might run through it. He was married with two children, a daughter who had graduated the previous July, and a son now in his final year. He lived in Kensington, with a country house in Buckinghamshire, both afforded by family money on his and his wife's side rather than his Security Service salary.

Five years before, Michaelmass had been promoted to Deputy Director General with special responsibility for T Department, which dealt with terrorism. It had not escaped his notice – nor that of the other Deputy Directors – that in two years' time the Director General himself would retire.

His office reflected what he considered to be his attitude to work. Tastefully though sparsely decorated (by which he would mean lean, trimmed to the bone) and functional (by which he would mean efficient). One wall was panelled, concealing his security safe, and the two others were a relaxing shade of white – not quite primrose – the watercolours on them his own property and the curtains covering the windows. His desk was mahogany, the telephones and their various attachments on a separate stand to the left, and the oval conference table – also mahogany – was in the corner opposite the window, also to his left.

The dark outside the window was the yellow-black of the city. Increasingly he wondered what the new headquarters at Thames House, overlooking the river, would be like when the Firm finally moved in. He swung in his chair, opened the curtains slightly, and sat looking across the lights of London and imagining the black and open spaces beyond. The only illumination in the room was the desk lamp. It was the way he finished each day. That evening he would change at the office and meet his wife at Covent Garden – Placido Domingo in a special charity performance.

The telephone rang.

'Do you have thirty seconds?' Penrose had been his assistant for fourteen months.

'If that's all.'

He closed the curtains and swung back to the desk. There was a knock on the door and Penrose came in.

'Half a minute, then I leave,' Michaelmass reminded him.

Penrose handed him a sheet of paper and sat down. 'Someone contacted Lisburn this afternoon on a direct line. Left this message. The Belfast files are blocked, the main files here say to refer to T, and our files say to refer to you.'

'To me personally or to DDG(T)?'

'The latter.'

Michaelmass tilted the desk lamp slightly and read the message. 'Thank you.' That's all, the edge of a smile and the nod of the head said it all, you can go now. Penrose left the room.

Joseph needing a number to speak to Jacobson. Michaelmass read the note again. Twelve years after the first contact and Joseph wanting another meet.

Joseph presumed to be Quin – it was only by selecting individual pieces from the various jigsaws which made up Northern Ireland and putting them together again, out of order and context, that Michaelmass had been able to come up with a possible identity.

When Quin had approached MI5 he had been adamant that he would speak only to what he called the top man. It was luck, though a man made his own luck, that the Director of Intelligence in Lisburn at the time was Michaelmass, and that Michaelmass made a point of personally examining every such approach to the Firm in Northern Ireland.

The deal – shortly before the Dirty Protest and hunger strikes which had marked the beginning of the eighties – had been of advantage to them both. Michaelmass had wound up a ring of the INLA and Quin had rid himself of a thorn in his side, plus a little more which Michaelmass had thrown in for good measure. Then the contact had been terminated, as abruptly as it had begun. Now Joseph again, seeking contact with Jacobson. A member of the Army Council of the Provisional IRA wanting to speak to a Deputy Director General of MI5. Both men older now, probably not a lot wiser though greyer, perhaps slower. But the game the same. And both men higher up the pecking order of their respective organizations, both men almost at the top. So what was Quin playing at? Something on offer, another deal? Or the second leg of a scam laid twelve years before? He reached to his left and dialled an internal extension.

'I need a new direct line into my office. The number effective

98

from eight tomorrow morning and to cease at six tomorrow evening. You and I only to know.'

The head of technical services gave him the number. Michaelmass thanked him and dialled a second number.

'I need a message sent to the Director of Intelligence in Lisburn. No reference to this department.'

Quin given his way in and all the other links broken – it was the way Michaelmass liked to operate. He changed and went to the opera.

The telephones which Quin chose at Dublin airport were in the departures area. His call was answered on the second ring.

'This is Joseph. You have a number for me.'

Contact, the MI5 officer manning the telephone alerted Farringdon. Putting you through now, he told Quin.

'Is that Joseph?' What was going on, Farringdon wondered, who was Joseph and who was Jacobson?

'Yes.'

Farringdon read out the number.

Inner London: Quin noted the 071 prefix. He left the airport and drove to St Stephen's Green, in the city centre. There were those who would have said that it was still too early in the operation for the watchers; in Quin's experience, however, it was never too early. Whichever side the watchers were on. He dialled the number from one of the kiosks opposite the Shelburne Hotel and heard the ringing tone.

Michaelmass was in the middle of a briefing, two senior officers sitting with him at the conference table. 'If you would excuse me for five minutes.' They understood and left immediately.

'Jacobson.'

'This is Joseph. I wondered if you fancied a Bushmills?'

Bushmills was the code for the bar on the waterfront at Wexford: Michaelmass remembered the details from twelve years ago. The Irish Republic, the alarm bells rang. So what was it that Quin wanted? The permutations had not stopped running through his mind since the first message.

'When?'

'Tomorrow.'

'Three o'clock.'

'Fine.'

'Someone might have to carry my bag.' Quin had delivered last time, and if Quin was contacting him he should respond. There was no way he would go without protection, however.

'As long as that's all.'

No microphones or cameras, Michaelmass knew Quin meant, the shadows to remain discreet. MI5 or SAS, Michaelmass considered. SAS, he decided, two men in tonight. 'Agreed.'

The call had lasted less than thirty seconds. Quin put the telephone down and cleared the area. For the next ten minutes Michaelmass sat at his desk, chin cupped in his hands and elbows on the desk top, and stared at the panelled wall opposite, body and mind apparently immobile. Then he lifted the telephone and requested an urgent meeting with the DG.

The next morning he was collected from his house in Kensington and driven to Heathrow for the 1105 Aer Lingus flight to Dublin. The passport he was using, in case he was checked, was in the name of Richards and the flight was on time and uneventful. He cleared immigration and customs, collected a hire car, and began the drive to Wexford. The MI5 resident at the Dublin embassy was waiting in the car park of the Glencormac Inn, near Bray; Michaelmass strapped the shoulder holster beneath his jacket, hung the Walther PPK in the holster, and continued south.

The waterfront at Wexford was cold – the boats moored along the granite quay and the railway line running along it. The bridge across the estuary seemed grey and colourless and the land on either side was flat and bleak. Michaelmass parked opposite Dixie's Bar, as the SAS had instructed him, then walked back towards the bridge. Quin was waiting in the rear bar of the Wren's Nest, his back to the wall, a yellowing poster advertising the 1899 Kilkenny Races above his head and the glass of Irish coffee three-quarters finished.

He looked confident, Michaelmass thought, authority sitting upon his shoulders, the whispers that he was on the Army Council correct.

The man he knew as Jacobson was going places, Quin knew by the way he walked, the way he sat down.

'So what'll you have?'

The bar was empty. They did not shake hands.

'Same as you.'

Quin ordered two Black Bush.

'There's something you might like to know.' He put the glasses on the table and waited until the barman went to the kitchen. 'We've activated somebody on the mainland.'

There were at least three ASUs in mainland Britain; what was different enough about this one for Quin to want to meet? Michaelmass downed the drink and they left the bar, crossed to the quay and turned left, walking side by side along the railway track. The fishermen's cars were parked by the boats, boxes stacked between them. Some of the boats were bright-coloured and new, others red-rusted and old.

'Who?'

'Codename Sleeper.'

Two of the boats were casting off, another coming in.

'Target?'

'Codename PinMan.'

Somewhere an SAS man was observing them in case a kidnapper was waiting, Michaelmass was aware, another making sure no one was slipping a bomb beneath the chassis of his car.

'And who's PinMan?'

It was part of the game, Quin spinning out the moment, setting the rules by which Michaelmass would be given the information, Michaelmass having to play his role, having to appear relaxed and noncommittal, almost uninterested. So why the contact after twelve years, Quin? What are you setting up?

'PinMan is a member of the royal family.'

Michaelmass would remember the moment, the way his mind splintered into a series of avenues, each with its own stream of thoughts and analyses. 'Tell me again.' Neither his voice nor manner had changed. If it was true, then why was Quin telling him? If untrue, if it was a sting or a come-on, then what the hell was Quin playing at?

Fifty yards in front of them the train rattled down the track. They stepped off the lines, still talking. 'The Provisional IRA have activated a hitman, codename Sleeper. His target is a member of the British royal family.' Quin spoke quietly, his words almost lost in the noise of the train, yet Michaelmass heard every syllable, every nuance.

'Which one? When? What? An assassination or a kidnapping? How?'

'I'm not party to that information.'

'What can you tell me about Sleeper?'

'Only what his codename suggests. He's been in Britain several years – nobody is allowed to know how many. He's done a number of jobs, for us and others, all of them attributed to someone else.'

'Where's he based?'

'All the indications are London.'

'How much lead does he have?'

If Quin was lying and MI5 acted on it, then so much of the British security services would be tied up that the IRA could do whatever else they wanted. But if Quin was telling the truth and MI5 didn't act, it might be responsible for the death of a member of the British royal family.

'Three months.'

Quin wouldn't be talking to him unless there was mileage in it for himself. Just like the INLA information twelve years ago, get the Brits to get rid of a rival. If Quin was telling him the truth.

'So why are you telling me?'

Quin shrugged.

Quin was playing his own game within the Provisional IRA, just as Michaelmass was playing his own game within MI5. Perhaps the Provos were playing their own game within Irish politics, just as MI5 was playing its own game with the other arms of the security set-up on the mainland.

'The number you phoned is dead. There's another one.' He gave Quin the details. 'An answerphone on it if I'm not there.'

They parted, Quin walking west and Michaelmass east to where he had parked the hire car. He waited fifty yards from the vehicle as instructed, allowing the SAS man – whoever and wherever he was – time to warn him if the vehicle had been booby-trapped, then he unlocked the door and began the return drive to Dublin.

The MI5 embassy resident was waiting at Bray.

'Change of plan,' Michaelmass told him. 'I need a secure phone to London.'

Fifty-seven minutes later, on a scrambler from a room in the British embassy, Michaelmass spoke to the Director General. One hour after that he left for London. When he arrived at Heathrow he was met at the aircraft exit, led discreetly away from the other passengers to his car, and driven to Gower Street. The Director General was waiting.

'The Prime Minister, Home Secretary and Commissioner of the Metropolitan Police have been informed.'

The DG's voice was bleak, as if he was preparing for something he had long feared. The Old Man had weathered the storms of the Cold War, Michaelmass thought, had been looking forward to the green and pleasant land on whose behalf he had fought so hard. And then the Cold War had ended and the DG's last years were to be plagued by the battle between friends as the various agencies of the security and intelligence services fought like dogs in the thinning job market which the so-called Peace Dividend had brought.

'Security for the royal family is already under review; in the meantime the Royal Protection Group is doubling its cover. Cobra meets tomorrow morning.'

All the royal family were targets, Michaelmass knew he must assume, yet when it came to the bottom line only three were likely – four depending on how he counted them. Nobody cared too much for Andrew and Fergie was out, Edward was a mere cipher, and the more distant members enjoyed a range of public attitudes from affection to something close to hostility. Which left the Queen herself, Prince Charles and Princess Anne. Not Princess Anne, he decided. Which left two. Three if he included the Princess of Wales. Even after the separation.

The Cobra committee met at ten, in one of the underground Cabinet rooms below Whitehall, and was chaired by the Home Secretary. Present, in addition to Michaelmass representing MI5, was a Deputy Director from MI6, the police commanders in operational charge of SO 12, the Special Branch, and SO 13, the anti-terrorist branch based at New Scotland Yard, the head of the Royal Protection Group, and the brigadier commanding Special Forces. The soldier, like the others, wore a dark pinstriped suit.

The room was off-white, the lighting sunk into the ceiling. The conference table was rectangular and designed for more than the eight men present that morning, so that they occupied only one half of it.

The chair at the head of the table was slightly different from the others, Michaelmass noted. It was unimportant though symbolic, he told himself. He settled back, waited for the Home Secretary to open the meeting, and for the first signs of conflict. Not open conflict, of course, and certainly not between the individuals on the committee, rather a tension between the organizations which they represented.

'Gentlemen, thank you for coming this morning.'

Sinclair had been Home Secretary for three years. He was 49 years old, public school and Oxford, a successful career at the Bar before entering politics. He was slightly overweight, despite the fact that he made a great point of his prowess at squash. Sinclair had been a contender in the leadership struggle when the premiership had changed hands and was still considered by many in the party as a future leader.

'You all know why we're here. MI5 has received information that the Provisional IRA has initiated a plan against the royal family. On the basis of that information I have convened this committee.'

No speeches, Michaelmass saw it in Denton's eyes, save the speeches for the punters. Denton had headed the Royal Protection Group, the RPG, for eighteen months. It was his men who would be the last resort, the bullet-stoppers, who if all else failed would put themselves between Sleeper and his target.

'Perhaps the DDG would update us.'

Michaelmass disliked the way Sinclair used the abbreviation. 'Thank you, Home Secretary.' Everyone playing the game, he thought, everyone believing they were in control. Too many ifs in the game for it to be controllable. *If* Quin hadn't played his own game twelve years before, *if* he himself hadn't agreed to play at least part of it with him; *if* part of the game Quin was now playing really did involve a hitman coded Sleeper and a target coded PinMan. *If* it had been somebody else who had received the information rather than himself, another organization than the Firm.

'MI5 has received intelligence that the Provisional IRA has authorized an operative, codenamed Sleeper, to plan and execute an attack against a member of the British royal family, codenamed PinMan.' Michaelmass's briefing on the events of the past 48 hours was succinct. 'The source understands that Sleeper is resident in London, and that he has been responsible for a number of assassinations, for PIRA and others. Sleeper was authorized to begin planning three months ago. Nothing else is known on Sleeper, nor are any other details available on PinMan. The identity of the target and the type and timing of the operation against him or her are also unknown.'

'May I ask the status of the informant?' The Deputy Director from MI6.

It was the first manifestation of the tensions each of them had brought to the table. During the Cold War MI5 and MI6 had enjoyed different areas of responsibility; with the break-up of the Soviet Union, however, both were looking for work and both were looking in the same place. In the past twelve months MI6 had reorganized and begun to concentrate its efforts on anti-terrorism, including Britain, which MI5 considered its domain. And most especially in Northern Ireland.

The question was relevant nevertheless, Michaelmass conceded.

'A senior member of the Provisionals. He sourced a project twelve years ago which led to the arrest of an INLA network. He approached us again the day before yesterday.'

'How senior? Military or political? Anywhere near the Army Council?'

'Senior.' Even on the Cobra committee Michaelmass refused to be drawn.

'How would you rate his information?' It was the commander in operational charge of the Special Branch.

Special Branch and the Anti-Terrorist Squad had lobbied long and hard to expand their jurisdiction outside London, and the police in the provinces had fought equally hard to maintain their own units.

'A1.'

Intelligence was rated on a scale A1 to F7, the Special Forces brigadier explained to the Home Secretary.

'Of course.' There was the slightest irritation in the politician's response, as if he already knew.

'But?' It was the head of the Anti-Terrorist Squad.

The competition between MI5 and the police over intelligence gathering and operational matters had been building up, the police claiming that MI5 was not only publicly unaccountable but inefficient, and MI5 arguing that the police had so far failed to provide an effective counter to terrorism on the mainland.

'But it depends which way we read it. What we see as the source's motivation for telling us. Whether we consider the information to be genuine, or a cover to soak up manpower whilst the Provos move against another target.'

They discussed the point, then moved on to the schedules of the individual members of the royal family – official and unofficial engagements, travel plans, locations and residences, even vacations. The use of the SAS in increasing the royal cover, but the legal and political implications of using the regiment in such a role. The degree of protection for the Princess of Wales now that she was effectively estranged from the monarchy.

The task was massive, summed up by the head of SO 13. *The Provisionals only needed to be lucky once*, he quoted the statement from the Provisional IRA after the bomb attack on the Grand Hotel in Brighton during the 1984 Conservative party conference. *The British had to be lucky all the time*.

'What about the royal skiing trip?' Sinclair turned to Denton. 'Do you need extra cover for that?'

'Already being looked into.'

'Nothing else on Sleeper, no indication whatever on the identity of PinMan?' It was the head of Special Branch again.

'Nothing.'

'What about the informant?' The MI6 representative returned to his original question. 'Who's running him?' It was another way of asking how important he was, how high up the PIRA structure MI5 had penetrated. 'Who's his handler?'

'I am,' said Michaelmass.

'So why's he talking to us?'

'There are a number of possibilities: old scores being settled, a power game within the Army Council, a testing ground between those who favour the ballot box and those who prefer the bullet.'

They discussed the range of alternatives within these.

'Which do you favour?' The MI6 representative looked at Michaelmass.

'At present I don't think we're in a position to decide.'

'You're sure it's not a Provo sting?'

'Same answer.'

'But you think we should treat the information as genuine?'

They were at the heart of the matter, they were all aware, whether the information came from what the Provos would call a stag, an informer, in Camden Town, an agent or double agent in Belfast, or a member of the Army Council in Dublin. That at the end of the day no one knew where the truth lay.

'As I see it we don't have any option.'

The Home Secretary nodded his agreement, then he summarized the decisions they had taken, informed them that he would brief the Prime Minister in the afternoon, suggested that until further notice they met weekly, and closed the meeting.

Sinclair was enjoying himself. Michaelmass looked at the way the Home Secretary shuffled his papers. Sinclair was efficient and had run the meeting well. But the bastard loved it. Loved calling the Cobra committee, even though it was his responsibility to do so. Loved the fact that he would brief the Prime Minister after. The fact that he had summoned them again for the following week, even though it was perfectly logical that he should do so. Yet Sinclair was the man each of the agencies was lobbying to secure their position in the future, and in the coming months it would be Sinclair who would decide the next head of MI5.

The kitchen was warm, the television on the sideboard in the corner and the breakfast plates laid on the table. It was six days since Eileen McGuire had taken her husband's bag to the Sportsman's, since he himself had gone to the bar that evening and not returned. She fussed over the knives and spoons and put on the milk for cocoa. It was the way she ended each day when he was away – the children fast asleep and the world to herself. Sometimes she wondered what it would be like the day the men came and told her that he wouldn't be coming home; how life would be without him, without the strain and tension his Republican loyalties imposed upon her. It was almost 11.45. She poured the milk into the mug and heard the noise at the back door.

The radio was playing, the bedside light was still on and the book lay open where Nolan had dropped it when she had fallen asleep. Salinger, *The Catcher in the Rye* . . .

. . . the black was like an envelope around her, sealing her in. The snow on the fields two hundred feet above was frozen hard and the waterfall which they had descended on a rope ladder had been freezing cold. She looked round her, seeing nothing, and tried to relax. She was on her back, the walls and ceiling tight round her, and only just enough space between the water and the ceiling for her to breathe.

It was the second term of her first year at university.

The duck and the sump and the birthday squeeze, they had joked to her. The duck where they would bail just enough water out of the tunnel so you could wriggle through on your backs, just enough air below the ceiling to breathe; the sump where the cave went underwater, where she would have to hold her breath, submerge herself and go through the narrow hole to the other side; the birth-day squeeze where it was so tight some people had to strip off everything to get through.

The wet suit was tight around her, the plastic boilersuit she wore over it to stop it tearing seemed caught, the hobnail boots were heavy and dragging, and the pot-holing lamp had been dislodged from the helmet and was somewhere in the water which covered most of her head and face.

So why the hell was she doing it, she thought, why the hell had she agreed?

Her elbows were bent and her hands were spread against the roof. She relaxed slightly and pushed herself along, the helmet banging against the roof of the duck and the lamp still dangling off it. The roof was slightly higher and the duck slightly wider; she tilted her head back so there was enough space to pull the lamp round, then clipped it back in place on the helmet.

Two minutes later she cleared the duck and waited with the others as the next one came through; an hour later she passed through the birthday squeeze, two hours after that the sump. Eight hours after the group had gone into the cave they climbed the rope ladder through the waterfall, scrambled up the last faces, and re-emerged into the world above. The night was dark, the snow was falling again, and the adrenalin pumped through her like nothing she could ever have imagined . . .

. . . the telephone rang and she woke with a start, made herself think clearly before she picked it up.

'Yes.'

'Murphy's home.' The voice of the duty officer; Murphy the code for McGuire.

Nolan looked at the clock. It was nearly 12.30. 'On my way.'

She dressed – Levis and sweater – strapped on the shoulder holster, the Browning Hi-Power in it, pulled a jacket on top, and went down-stairs to the garage at the rear. McGuire home and the others still running, she was thinking, the surveillance teams she had been allocated strung to breaking point across the Six Counties. She checked around and under the car, started the engine, opened the electronic door and drove out, stopping briefly to check the street and close the door. Taking a friend home – her mind automatically

invented the cover she would tell the neighbours in the morning –
a girl can't live on bread alone, but for God's sake don't tell the
ex-husband if he comes calling.

The coffee was bubbling in the corner of the ops room. Nolan
poured herself a mug and read the log.

'Front door or back?'

Front and it was McGuire pretending he was coming home from
the Sportsman's, back and there was a chance he might be leaving
again.

'Back.'

Clarke and Milligan in Londonderry – Nolan confirmed that the
surveillance situation hadn't changed since she had left the department seven hours before. Black in Coleraine. Lynch and Hoolihan
in Belfast, and Lynan in Strabane. The Provo foot soldiers crossing
and criss-crossing, trying to throw any tails into a tangle, the
shadows around them strained and exhausted.

And McGuire, the link man with the bombers and shooters –
what the Brits would have called a handler if he'd been running
agents for them – out of sight, now suddenly showing. Not showing,
she reminded herself. Slipping in the back door, when if he was
showing he would be using the front. McGuire breaking the rules
and unable to resist a warm night with the wife. McGuire about to
drop out of sight again.

'Take the teams off Lynch and Hoolihan and reassign them to
McGuire. Notify the teams on Clarke, Milligan, Black and Lynan
that they may be reassigned in the morning. Photo and description
out now.'

You're sure? she read in the duty officer's eyes. The men the
surveillance teams were following were terrorists. If she pulled
the teams off and any of them killed or maimed because of it, the
responsibility would be hers.

Her instinct, she reminded herself they had instilled in her at
Hereford, her decision. Ninety-nine times out of a hundred a man
and woman will make the same decision; on the hundredth the man
would act apparently logically and the woman would get it right.

'And tell the boys covering McGuire that they've done a good
job.'

The duty officer nodded. 'Your codename for the operation?'

Nolan remembered the book on the bed in the flat. 'Catcher.'

She went to the inner office, pulled a blanket over the camp bed, and lay down. Sleep is a friend, they had also taught her at Hereford. Use it while you can. Plan, check, then close your eyes and switch off. Be ready when it mattered . . .

. . . the face was looking at her, flashing in the windows of the bus as it passed. Her face. It was two years since she had finished university, good degree and matching job to follow. A job with prospects, good pension and liberal maternity leave, they had told her when she had applied for it. Everything ordered and routine, everything predictable. Two years in and she had been promoted twice.

She was standing on the pavement, the traffic busy and the shops and offices behind her and on the far side of the road. The face was still flashing at her, the different faces and the different memories. The girl in the tree so many years ago, heart pumping and blood racing; the emptiness when those looking for her had gone. The student stuck in the duck two hundred feet below ground and the fear streaming through her; the incredible, breathtaking exhilaration as she stood in the snow after and realized what she had done.

Of course she'd kept in touch with the old days, but somehow it was more difficult to fit everything in. Not everything, just the things like the pot-holing, the climbing, the para-gliding. The things which had taken her to the edge.

Successful career in front of her and everything planned. Plus a good pension at the end. They had emphasized that at the interview. Two years down and only twenty-eight to go. The traffic was moving more slowly and the army recruiting office was on the other side of the road. She dodged between the cars and went inside . . .

. . . the faces were looking at her: the Provo gunmen and bombers she'd released from the net in order to concentrate on the LO. The hand shook her shoulder.

'McGuire?' She was wide awake.

It was eight minutes past five, still two and a half hours of darkness left.

'Back door, ninety seconds ago.'

McGuire reached the safe house fourteen minutes later and remained there until the city had come to life and the streets were busy. Shortly after nine he left the house and walked to the car, the driver's door unlocked and the keys above the sun visor.

'Red three. Blue One.' McGuire taking the M2 north out of Belfast, the details of his car logged the moment he had picked it up and the radio messages kept to a minimum.

So where was NcGuire going, Nolan wondered, what was he playing at? 'Reassign the Clarke and Milligan teams.' They had worked through the plans since five that morning. 'Other units ready to follow if and when we know where he's going.' There were two cars behind him and one in front. She left Lisburn – false driving licence in case she was stopped, matching false passport, battered and dog-eared, in case McGuire went south – and joined the net. The Ford behind McGuire slid temporarily out of the pursuit and the Vauxhall in front took over.

'Red Five. Blue Three.' McGuire on the A6 towards Londonderry.

Ninety minutes later he entered the city. In the Catholic Creggan he left the car in a lock-up and went to a bar off Bligh's Lane. By five he was in what his shadows assumed to be a safe house in the Bogside.

She could break into the lock-up and either bug the car McGuire was using or put a tracer on it, but there was always the risk that McGuire had dropped the car deliberately, had it under surveillance to check if he was being followed. Leave it, Nolan decided, no chances.

The evening was cold and long, the night colder and longer. For one moment, somewhere round two in the morning, she considered the possibility that she was wrong: that McGuire was a front to pull the cover off the others, that even now one of the men whom she had let slip from her net was planting a bomb or pulling a trigger. She unscrewed the flask, poured two cups of coffee, passed one to the driver, and stared into the black.

The dawn was slow in coming and her back was stiff and aching. McGuire would move soon, should have moved already, should have left the safe house and picked up his motor. So where the hell was he? The teams were taking it in turns to grab breakfast; she ate the bacon and eggs as fast as she could and swallowed the tea even though it was scalding hot. Perhaps McGuire had slipped out during the night. Either through the back door, even though they thought they had it covered, or along the roof space above the houses and out through another house. It was almost 8.30.

'Red Two. Contact.'

'Red Three. Blue Nine.'

She checked the street map for the coded locations, the others doing the same.

'Red Five. Blue Two.'

McGuire picking up the motor, McGuire moving. This is it, she sensed in the voices of the tails. This is what we've been waiting for.

'Red Four. Blue Seven.' McGuire leaving Londonderry towards Belfast. McGuire making his move.

'Red Six. Yellow Three.' McGuire turning off the Belfast road and heading cross-country, going east towards Ballymena. She ordered the white and black teams in the direction he was heading, knew she had lost the front cars and hoped the others would get there in time, and wished to Christ that there had been a surveillance chopper available. But that might have given the game away.

'Fuck.'

She heard the driver swear and looked up, saw the army road block ahead, McGuire's car through and pulling away.

The soldiers were from 2 Para – even though they wore no insignia, there was something distinctive about them – the Land-Rovers pulled across the road to form a chicane, the GPMG to the right, one soldier covering the driver with an SA80 while a corporal checked his licence, a signaller close behind. The driver wound down his window and waited, held up his driving licence apparently for the soldier to inspect, then deliberately turned the page.

Surveillance vehicle. The corporal read the words. React too quickly or incorrectly and the people in the vehicles behind would notice, he knew; and among those people might be an IRA or UVF activist or informant. Undercover and on the job, he understood. Nice bit of stuff in the passenger's seat, though, wouldn't mind being on the job with her. He made a point of peering inside the car, then stood back and waved them on.

Bloody Brits, the driver in the vehicle behind cursed, bloody paras. Good man, thought Nolan. They rounded the bend, out of sight of the road block, and the driver accelerated.

'White Four. Yellow Three.' McGuire leaving Ballymena and heading west for the coast. Heading for Larne, the ferry connection to Stranraer in Scotland. McGuire heading for the mainland. Calm it, she told herself, McGuire heading *towards* Larne, not necessarily *for* Larne.

'White One. Yellow Two.' McGuire clearing the ring of hills skirting the town and turning left on to the dual carriageway.

'White Two. Yellow Three.' McGuire still on the dual carriage-way, ignoring the exit for the town centre.

The SeaLink Stella ferry leaving at 11.30 – Nolan checked the timetable. Blue Two in to terminal and buy ticket, she ordered; McGuire would presumably check behind him and the tail would be sitting in front.

'White Three. Yellow Four.' McGuire turning off the roundabout and towards the ferry terminal; stopping in the short-term car park.

McGuire collected a bag from the boot, locked the car and walked into the terminal. Someone else would pick the car up once the ferry had left; he himself would lose the keys on the boat, probably drop them over the side. McGuire at Larne ferry terminal, Nolan radioed Lisburn on the scrambler and alerted Farringdon, requested that London be informed. Possibility only at this stage, she warned, no confirmation that he was buying a ticket or boarding. McGuire a known Provo liaison officer, a man who ran the gunmen and the bombers, heading for the mainland.

The terminal was small and almost empty at this time of day at this time of year. McGuire would spot any tails a mile off. Blue Two, the first tail, in place but already sacrificed to confirm McGuire's movements. The 11.30 ferry would dock at Stranraer at 1.40, just in time for McGuire to catch the 2.35 train to Glasgow. One vehicle on the ferry, she decided; only the driver needing to enter the terminal to buy the ticket, and therefore also sacrificed, but the others in the car still secure. Two other cars on the 12.15 SeaCat from Belfast, she also decided, arriving five minutes after the ferry but having time to change plates and give her the full range of options, depending on what McGuire did when he reached the mainland. If that was why he was in Larne.

Sinclair straightened his bow tie and allowed his wife to brush the jacket of his dinner suit. The bodyguard was waiting downstairs and the Rover was outside. The reception that evening was at the Grosvenor House Hotel – the annual awards for the news and current affairs section of the television industry. As Home Secretary, and as guest of honour, Sinclair would be expected to be both informed and witty, the penetrating remark about the future of television combined with the carefully chosen asides, bordering just the right side of indiscretion, which those present would remember next time he did a live studio interview.

113

The reception began at seven-thirty and the dinner at eight, Sinclair positioned at the top table between the chairman, a distinguished journalist of the old school, and the chief executive of one of the new ITV companies. At 8.37 the duty functions manager approached discreetly and informed him that he was wanted. Sinclair excused himself and followed him out, fully aware that every eye in the room was suddenly upon him. The bodyguard was by the door. Telephone, he informed the Home Secretary; on the scrambler, he did not need to say. The manager escorted them to a private room. MI5, the minder told Sinclair when the manager left, and followed him outside.

'Sinclair.'

'Michaelmass. I thought you would wish to know. One of the IRA's top liaison officers has just entered the mainland.'

'Any connection with Sleeper?'

'Who knows?'

'Cobra, ten tomorrow morning.'

'Thank you, Home Secretary.'

Sinclair ended the call and followed the manager and bodyguard back to the reception, the minder taking his position at a table in the corner and Sinclair smiling as he took his own position at the top table. Sorry about that, the shrug said it all.

At seven the following morning, over breakfast at Downing Street, he briefed the Prime Minister. At ten he brought the Cobra committee to order and asked Michaelmass to update them on the latest developments. The tension in the room was both qualitatively and quantitatively different from that at the previous meeting.

'McGuire reached Birmingham at eleven last night and made his way to what we assume he thinks is a safe house. As of half an hour ago, he was still there.'

'So what do we do? Pick him up or let him run?' Sinclair was confident, almost abrasive. 'I assume the latter.'

For the next fifteen minutes they discussed the point and the matters arising from it: the coincidence of the IRA sending one of their top handlers into England at the same time as they had activated Sleeper; the possibility of losing McGuire if they let him run but the chance of missing Sleeper if they did not.

'What guarantee that he's connected with Sleeper?'

'None.'

But one hell of a coincidence if he wasn't.

'So we let him run.' Sinclair sat back in his seat and took his decision. The bastard was enjoying himself: Michaelmass remembered his reaction at the previous meeting.

'The royal family.' Sinclair moved the meeting briskly along. 'The PM agrees with me that they should be notified. His weekly audience with Her Majesty is this afternoon. The Prince and Princess of Wales have been requested to attend a special meeting immediately after. I myself will inform them.'

He turned to the Brigadier, Special Forces. 'When did Charles last do the course?'

'Five years ago.'

'Then I think it's time for him to do it again.'

He switched his attention to the head of the Royal Protection Group. 'What extra measures are you taking for his skiing holiday?'

'The SAS are already involved. Plans are also under way for additional protection using certain members of the royal party.'

Sinclair waited and Denton went into detail.

'What about Catcher?' It was the last item on the personal agenda Sinclair had drawn up overnight.

'I'm sorry, Home Secretary. What about Catcher?' Michaelmass knew what Sinclair was going to do and how he would set it up.

'Where is he at the moment?'

'Handling the surveillance in Birmingham. She had her own people follow McGuire that far by themselves and liaised with the London teams once everything settled.'

'She?' It was as if Sinclair had only just become aware that the person in charge of the operation was a woman.

'Yes, Home Secretary.'

'Has she *really* got the experience for this sort of thing?'

Some battles were worth fighting, others not; it was a fact of life. Just as it was a fact of life that if Sleeper really did exist and Cobra countered him, then Sinclair would emerge from the episode with a power base that most politicians would not even contemplate. And in the coming months the Prime Minister – on Sinclair's recommendation – was scheduled to appoint a new Director General of the Security Service.

'If that is your opinion, Home Secretary.'

'It is.'

The meeting ended shortly before eleven. They left the conference room and walked to the ground floor, Michaelmass and the Brigadier, Special Forces, slightly behind the others.

'Coffee?'

'Ten minutes at the Club.'

The Club was not well known, yet in a way it signified the separate establishment to which the two men, and in particular the brigadier, belonged. It was tucked inconspicuously in a side turning two minutes' walk from Sloane Street, a discreet security camera above and to one side of the black-painted door, no nameplate or other identifying feature visible.

The brigadier arrived first, told his driver to collect him in thirty minutes, pressed the entry buzzer, identified himself, and was admitted.

Rhodes was 46, not especially tall but still fit, and on his fifth tour with the SAS. The first, as a junior and inexperienced captain, had been twenty years ago; now he was back as brigadier. Even now, however – perhaps especially now – he still remembered two things. The first was the NCO who had given him hell on selection but had been beside him when they were both wounded at Mirbat. And the second was the first time he had stood on the stairs at the Club and looked at the photographs, two photographs especially.

Both men were colonels and both were young, one thin angular face and duffel coat, and the other bigger, broader shoulders. The first was a Scot, David Stirling, who in 1941 had founded the SAS, and the second was an Irish rugby international, Paddy Blair Mayne, who had served as Stirling's second-in-command then taken over 1 SAS after Stirling was captured.

Not all the photographs were of men, however: Andrée Borrel, the first woman to be dropped into occupied France during the 1939–45 war, Sonja Olschanesky, Vera Leigh and Diana Rowden: all four women Special Operations Executive agents, all four put to death at the Natzweiler concentration camp in eastern France in 1944. Noor Iniyat Khan, executed in the gas chamber at Dachau in September 1944.

He looked at them as he passed, and went to the bar. Michaelmass arrived thirty seconds later. There were two men at the bar itself and a second group at a table beneath a Stonehouse portrait of the Queen Mother. They went to the lounge on the ground floor, closed the door, and poured coffee themselves. The room was comfortable rather than large, a fire burning in the grate and bookshelves lining the walls.

'Perhaps we should consider the possibility that at some stage the

Cabinet might decide on a pre-emptive action.' Michaelmass was seated to the left of the fireplace.

'And therefore we should both be prepared.'

The decision to target the royal family had come from the Army Council of the Provisional IRA. Remove the Army Council, or those believed to constitute it, and you remove the threat – the conversation which followed was a rehearsal of what would take place within the secrecy of both Cobra and the Cabinet. By removing the Council, of course, one also opened the way to the possibility of the present members being replaced by men who were even more hard-line. Yet the present members had been party to a number of decisions which had resulted in massive blood-letting and carnage in Northern Ireland as well as on the mainland and in Europe. And they were using the immunity of another country as cover.

'I'll need an update on whoever you think fit.'

The legal, moral and ethical argument attached to the short and apparently simple statement would have been long and heated – at another time and in another place.

'You'll get it this afternoon.'

'In that case we'll go South tonight.'

Two hours later Denton left New Scotland Yard and was driven to Wellington Barracks. The guards on the front gate were expecting him: he showed his identity card and was waved through.

Roddy Fairfax had been informed at one o'clock. At five minutes past three he left the training exercise in the charge of a sergeant and went to the commanding officer's office. The colonel was behind his desk and a civilian – or at least a man wearing civilian clothes – was seated opposite him.

'Major Fairfax, Commander Denton.' The colonel introduced them and left the room.

'You're in the Prince of Wales's skiing party, I understand.' Denton showed Fairfax his warrant card and indicated that he could sit.

'If you say so.' Even in barracks Fairfax was always careful.

'We think it might be an idea for you to be armed when you go to Klosters with them.'

*   *   *

117

After the heat of the training camp Madrid was cold. The Mercedes dropped her at the Goya entrance of the Prado; Walker watched as it disappeared into the city traffic, then walked the ten minutes to the Atocha railway station, caught the AVE to Seville, and the slow train to Puerta de Santa Maria. There she collected her passport and personal documents from the deposit box at the Banco de Andalucía and caught the bus to Las Redes. The hire car was in the garage at the side of the villa – five hundred kilometres on the clock – and the postcards she had written had been removed from the floor safe. She dropped her bag on the floor and went for a shower.

The course in the desert training camp had been hard. Herself, one other student – a Palestinian in his mid-thirties – and three instructors. Her mind still reeled from the instruction and her body from physical exhaustion.

She sat on the floor of the shower and allowed the water to cascade over her. Ten minutes, she decided, then she would dry herself, change, and eat her final supper in one of the cafés facing across the square to the river. And at five the next morning, while the dawn was still grey and before the sea mist had lifted off the sand dunes, she would drive to Seville, catch the 11.55 flight, and be back in England by 1.30 . . .

. . . the General Register Office on Kingsway was busy. She found the register for the year 1961, turned to the relevant date, and scanned the pages for her name. It was not there. She looked again, knowing she must have missed it, then asked a clerk for help. Perhaps it was because the man understood, perhaps because he had dealt with the problem before. For the next twenty minutes he sat with her checking the register, then explaining to her the single devastating reason why she might not be on it, and the procedure by which she could apply for access to her original birth entry. The following week she was given counselling, the week after that she received a letter from the division of the General Register Office based at Smedley Hydro in Southport, authorizing access to her original birth entry, which she forwarded with the relevant fee to the office covering the Euston area of north London.

The stamped, addressed envelope which she had included was returned five days later. It was lying on the hall floor beneath the letter box when she returned from the university. The house was empty, the others still in the library. The copy of her original birth

118

entry was inside. This is me, she thought, this is the person I am as opposed to the person I thought I was. She sat on the bottom stair, half-leaning against the wall. She's done all right, considering – she was standing on the stairs in the house in Orpington four years earlier, her mother's voice drifting from the lounge, then her mother crossing the room and closing the door even though she thought the house was empty. The details rose up at her from the certificate, blurred then distinct then blurred again, the all-consuming knowledge of the three things which would change her life.

The first was that she was adopted, which she had known after her first visit to St Catherine's House in London.

The second was that she appeared to have no father.

And the third was that she was Irish.

5

CONLAN LEFT DUBLIN AT SIX in the morning, the wind rising and the wipers flicking the sleet from the windscreen. By 10.30 he was in the cabin on Lough Corrib; by eleven he was wrapped in oilskins, the whitecaps running hard and the far bank lost in the grey of cloud and the first white of snow.

Black, Lynch and the others still criss-crossing the North. The Brits would have spotted their movements a mile off, been tailing them ever since they started moving.

McGuire in Birmingham and about to move on, the tails also sitting on him, logging every move and waiting for the next. The Brits would have spotted him just as easily as they had spotted the others – a known LO like McGuire didn't drop out of circulation for more than a couple of days, three at most, before his absence was spotted and the alarm bells at Lisburn began to ring. And McGuire's orders had been strict and detailed, even down to the late-night visit to his wife and his departure by the back door at some ungodly hour in the dark of the following morning.

The rules of the game – except which rules and which game? The Brits thinking they were on to something – undecided whether McGuire and the others were connected, or whether the movements of Black, Lynch and the rest were a cover for McGuire – and piling resources into it. And the others, the real players and the real game, lying stone-cold and undetected.

McGinty tending his flock in Rathmeen and the European ASU waiting in Brussels.

Sleeper back from his training in North Africa – even in the isolation of the cabin at Kilmore, Conlan still maintained his discipline, still referred to Sleeper as 'he'. Sleeper about to move on to the next stage of his preparation.

Everything going to plan and time to bring in Logan.

He narrowed his eyes against the snow and tried to see how it might go wrong.

The snow had eased slightly. When he left Belfast it had been cutting, driving, whipped almost horizontal by the wind, and it had taken him nearly three hours to reach the border. Then the wind had died and the snow had fallen in huge feathers, deadening the sound of the world.

Michael Logan was 31 years old, five feet ten inches tall, with dark hair neatly cut. He wore a business suit, a hint of brown in the fleck, and a camel cloth overcoat. He was married, though childless, and his wife worked as an assistant bank manager. He had a degree in engineering from Manchester University and for the past four years had worked as marketing executive for an American-owned company with factories both sides of the border and with clients in Europe. He was considered by his and his wife's friends to be charming and amusing, with an uncanny ability to mimic both the accents and attitudes of the various countries he routinely visited as part of his job. He had no criminal or driving convictions, his credit card rating was high, and his name was not on the security list at Lisburn.

By the time he reached Dublin the snow had stopped and the clouds had cleared. He wound his way through the city centre, to the Westbury Hotel off Grafton Street where he always stayed when his work brought him to Dublin, parked the Granada in the garage beneath the hotel, checked in, and went to his room.

The driving licence and credit card were concealed in the false bottom of his briefcase. He took them out, put his own in their place, placed the briefcase and leather travelling bag in the wardrobe, and left the hotel. Then he collected the canvas overnight bag from the boot of the Granada and took a cab to the airport. The car rental booths were in the arrivals area on the ground floor; he went to the Hertz desk, smiled at the prettier of the two woman staffing it and asked for a Sierra, giving her the driving licence and credit card but arranging to pay cash and retrieve the credit card slip when he returned the vehicle.

'Thank you, Mr Donaldson.' She typed the details into the computer. 'Over here on business?'

'You can never call Dublin business.' His accent was English, matching the details on the false licence and card.

She flashed her smile at him and gave him the car keys. He collected the Sierra, left the airport, snaked his way through the north Dublin suburbs then picked up the N4. The afternoon was colder; west of Athlone the roads had not been cleared properly. By the time he reached Kilmore it was snowing again.

The hotel was small and set back off the road. There were two other cars in the park at the rear, one with Northern Ireland plates and one from the Republic. Even in the thirty seconds it took him to lock the Sierra and walk to the front of the hotel the cold was biting into him. The hall was empty, a reception desk to the left and the door to the bar on the right. He went in and felt the heat from the peat fire. There were three other people there, sharing a table; from their conversation Logan assumed the cars outside belonged to them. Two were American – a middle-aged couple – and the third, judging by his accent, was from Belfast.

'Welcome to Kilmore. You'll be Mr Donaldson.' The barman was in his sixties, white hair and smiling eyes. He passed Logan the guest book and asked him his fancy.

Logan looked at the whiskies along the shelves behind the bar, asked for a Bushmills and looked at the names in the book.

Alvin and Cy Morton: Milwaukee. Tourists.

Devlin Kelly: Belfast. Rep.

The peat smouldered in the fireplace and the smell of damp oilskins hung in the air. Outside it was dark, the sound of the world deadened by the snow. Conlan pulled on his overcoat, hat and boots, locked the cabin, and walked the mile to the Kilmore Hotel. By the time he arrived it was gone nine, the guests had finished their evening meal and half a dozen locals were seated close to the bar. He shook the snow from his clothes and boots, hung the coat and hat in the hallway and went in, nodding his greetings at those inside. 'How's the fishing?' the barman asked, and poured a Black Bush without needing to ask. When Conlan returned to the cabin it was shortly after midnight and the night was settled.

The hole in the ground was fifty yards from the cabin and freezing cold, despite the thermal underclothing the two men wore. They had just begun to eat – sandwiches and self-heating tins of soup – when the door opened and Conlan came out. They left the OP and followed him in the night, stopping outside the hotel but not going in, one waiting outside and opposite and the other checking the car park at the rear and noting the make, model and registration numbers of the vehicles parked there. Shortly before midnight they followed as Conlan returned to the cabin, scanning it with night sights in case he left again. At two, when they were satisfied he was asleep, one left the observation post and returned to the Kilmore Hotel. There were three cars in the car park. He noted the numbers again, entered the hotel by forcing the kitchen window, checked and recorded the names and addresses of guests staying in the hotel that night, then left by the same window, making sure he left no indication of his entry, and returned to the OP.

*　　　*　　　*

The royal party left Buckingham Palace at seven and consisted of the Prince of Wales, his two sons, their Royal Protection Group bodyguards, and a number of personal friends, all advanced skiers. Fairfax had joined them for breakfast. In his ski bag he carried a pair of Rossignol 4Ss and in the shoulder holster he wore beneath his casual jacket a service-issue Browning. Only the RPG members, however, had been informed of the last item, and of his dual role.

The morning was grey and the traffic light, the departure of the BAe 146 of the Queen's Flight from RAF Northolt unnoticed. At Zurich, however, the sun was in the sky and the drive to Klosters was less private. By early afternoon the group was established in the private chalet where Charles traditionally stayed, and the trusted locals whom they used every year as instructors and guides had joined him for a brief reunion. At four a senior member of the Prince's staff met with representatives of the press to discuss how the two sides might satisfy their opposed objectives — the press to secure pictures of the royal party and Charles to enjoy an undisturbed holiday.

At ten the following morning the Prince of Wales and his two sons posed for the agreed photographs on one of the gentler slopes near the village. Given the predictability of the photo call, Saunders had already written his opening paragraph and instructed his photographer of the shot he needed.

Saunders had arrived three days before, for two reasons: the first was that he enjoyed skiing, and the second was that it gave him two and a half days' start over the rest of the royal rat pack. In that time he had researched the slopes the royal party would be using and come to his arrangement with the men who drove the piste bashers, as well as getting on record a series of quotes from locals about the Prince, plus background pieces on the staff and instructors, in case he needed them in a hurry. In 1988 Charles had only narrowly escaped death when one of his party was killed and a second seriously injured in an avalanche.

That evening the royal group held the fondue party which traditionally marked the beginning of the more relaxed part of their holiday. The following morning, it was decided, they would also follow tradition.

Saunders received the call at eleven. He had eaten and drunk moderately, knowing what he might have to do the next day. He alerted the *Mirror* photographer, set his alarm for five – a request for an alarm call might have warned the other members of the rat pack – and went to bed.

The night was dark, the snow on the mountains almost ghostly. For one moment the Princess of Wales thought she was in Klosters with Charles and her sons, instead of in her rooms at Kensington. She was skiing down the black run the following morning, Charles and the boys around her and the circle of the moon thin against the sky. The boys were laughing, taunting their father to go faster. The moon was changing, was no longer a moon, was a face looking down on them. She was still skiing, still aware of the face looking at her. She was no longer skiing, was sitting up in bed and staring at the door, its shape barely distinguishable. Was unsure whether she was awake and looking at it or whether she was asleep and caught up in the nightmare. If she was awake she tried to sleep; if asleep she tried to wake. She was sitting upright, sitting in the room instead of Charles, staring at the door and waiting for it to open; was still in the nightmare, glancing at the figures around her but afraid to turn her head, afraid to even move or blink, knowing what would happen when the door opened. It was as if she was numb, either because she was drugged or through sheer unadulterated fear. The figures round her were still, almost unreal, inhuman. As if they had no flesh or blood in them. She tried to glance at them, look at them from the corners of her eyes, could not take her eyes from the front. Charles was to her right, even though she was not in the room, even though it was he who was sitting there and not her, even though she had taken his place. The door was opening, slow motion yet so fast, the thunder and lightning filling the room. Her head

124

was spinning, shrieking. The monsters were coming in, coming at her. Big and black, no faces, only eyes. The red and white spitting from them as if they were mediaeval dragons. They were grabbing her as if she meant nothing, tossing her between themselves as if she was a rag doll. The Princess of Wales woke and looked at the clock, saw it was five in the morning and realized she was bathed in sweat.

Saunders and the photographer left the hotel at 5.30, two and a half hours before the lifts opened. They carried skis, boots and rucksacks, and were dressed in light, almost colourless ski suits. On the opposite side of the valley the piste bashers were swarming up and down the mountains like fireflies. By 6.15 they were aboard one of them as it crawled through the black, its spotlights sweeping across the snow and picking out the pistes. By eight they were in position opposite the section where the royal family always stopped for their moment of private enjoyment, the lifts to the run closed and the area discreetly but firmly sealed off.

The two had worked together before and prided themselves on their relationship, on the secrets which enabled them to snatch so many exclusives. They concealed themselves along the edge of trees, fifty yards from the point where the black run angled sharply, slightly looking down on it and facing west, so that even though the sun was coming up they were still in shadow. The photographer took the cameras, short-leg tripods and telephoto lenses from the rucksack, set them in position – one camera shooting black and white and the other colour – and checked the focus. Saunders poured two mugs of hot goulash soup and they settled for the wait.

In the still of the morning he heard the voices. The photographer put the soup down and crouched by the cameras.

The bend opposite was icy, and he knew they would come off as they always came off. It was part of the tradition, the part the boys always insisted on skiing on the first day proper of the holiday. The snowball fight after.

Two figures came round the bend, skiing too well to be either the Prince or any of his guests. Instructors, Saunders assumed. The other figures appeared quickly, losing their edges suddenly and toppling over each other, everyone laughing, the cameras clicking. One of the smaller figures was already chasing the other, the skis slowing their progress, the Prince of Wales suddenly turning on his elder son and pushing him into the snow.

125

The skiers picked themselves up and moved on. Saunders watched as the photographer unscrewed the cameras from the tripods and began to pack, sensed rather than saw the movement, the combination of a change of noise and the landscape close to him shifting.

The shapes rose from the snow holes, one to his left and a second to his right, neither further than twenty metres from him. White camouflage suits, goggles, white gloves. The submachine guns also camouflaged. Either they had been there all the time and he hadn't seen them, or they had arrived after him and he had not heard them.

The two sets of eyes were looking at him. If he had put a finger out of line, he realized, if the photographer had been carrying a gun rather than a camera, they would have been dead fifteen minutes before the royal party had come into view.

Without speaking the figures clipped on their skis, hung the MP5Ks behind their backs, and disappeared down the slope.

Twelve days later, on the day the royal party ended their skiing holiday, Saunders returned to London. Coming home after such a trip was something he enjoyed, but only if it had been worth while, only if he had delivered something everyone else had missed. The return of the emperor, his wife had once joked. The car was waiting for him at Heathrow, the driver waiting in the crowd by the customs exit and holding up a copy of the *Mirror* with the Saunders exclusive splashed across the front page.

He returned to the office, spent thirty minutes with the editor, then telephoned his flat and checked the answerphone for messages. There were five, two from his daughters and one in which the caller had not identified herself but whom he knew to be Philipa Walker. The newsroom was clearing, most of the reporters leaving for lunch. He waved to them that he would join them, dialled her number, and found himself listening as the answerphone invited him to leave a message.

'Hello, Philipa. This is Patrick. Phoning lunchtime Friday.' He was due to drive home that evening, but the thought of the quiet of the Wiltshire countryside, the horses and a pint at the local somehow palled after the adrenalin of Klosters. 'Wondered if you could make dinner this evening. Eight o'clock at Wheeler's unless I hear from you.'

Sometime they would go to bed together. Not tonight, probably not for a while. But sometime. In a way it pleased him. It was rather civilized, he thought.

Philipa Walker received the message at three. Time was catching up on her. Suppose Saunders wasn't her route into the royal schedule; suppose he was but she failed to find her way in? She showered and dressed, then looked again at the copy of the *Daily Mirror* of eight days before: the photograph of the Prince of Wales and his two sons tumbling in the snow, apparently free from the attentions of the world, certainly oblivious to it. Suppose it had been she, positioned where the photographer was; she felt the first frost down her spine. Suppose it had been she waiting in the quiet of the snow. She left the flat and took a cab to Wheeler's.

Saunders returned to his flat at five, showered, transferred the Klosters material from the laptop on to the PC, then booked a minicab so that he would arrive at the restaurant at 7.45, assuming correctly that it would take him ten minutes longer than he calculated to get there, and therefore arriving five minutes early. Philipa Walker was on time. Philipa Walker was always on time, Saunders knew, her social life as organized as the systems analysis which was her work. He stood while the manager took her coat, then kissed her on the cheek.

'You look gorgeous.'

She was wearing trousers and ankle-length leather boots, both emphasizing the shape and length of her legs, and a lambswool sweater, intricately sequined.

'You look pretty good yourself.'

The skiing had left him fit and tanned.

She waved to the waiter and ordered champagne. Saunders's turn to pay for dinner, she acknowledged, but the drink was on her. A celebration of what had obviously been a successful trip for him.

'Thanks for the card.' What card? – he saw the question on her face. 'The postcard from Tangiers. It arrived just before I left.'

'Better not let the family see it.'

He laughed. 'So how was Spain?'

'Spain later. Tell me about the trip. How was it?' Tell me if you're the key. Tell me how I get to PinMan. The champagne was poured. 'So tell me.' She raised her glass and said it again. Tell me how it could have been me waiting for PinMan. Tell me if it really is you who will enable me to take PinMan out.

He told her about the royal arrival, where the Prince stayed, the antics of the rat pack, their efforts to get the royals to do something worth reporting and the ploys by each of them to make sure that he or she got that story, should it happen. He told her about the royals themselves, slipping into their first names occasionally, as if they meant something to him – Charles, William, Harry – then his voice hardening slightly, as if they were simply something to be hunted. Not quite that, she thought. Perhaps she was being unfair to him. More as if the tiny aspects of their lives which in any other family would go unnoticed were of earth-shattering importance to him.

The oysters were served.

'Tell me about the exclusive.' Her eyes were shining.

'I was lucky.'

'Not luck. You make your own luck.'

'True.'

'So how did it happen?'

'How do you mean?'

'How did you get a shot that no one else had? You must follow each other like hawks.'

Planning, he wanted to say. Good information rather than luck – as she herself had said, luck was something you made for yourself. Plus an alarm set for when the rest of the pack were just going to bed, and a flask of hot goulash soup. She would love the story, he knew, her eyes would flash and her head would shake with disbelief.

'We do,' he conceded.

'So how did you get away with it?'

He was enjoying himself. 'That's what everybody wanted to know.'

'But it wasn't just the photos, it was the words as well.' She was looking at him, the champagne glass in front of her and her eyes just above the glass.

'Talent.' He shrugged and laughed.

She laughed back. As if she understood, he thought, as if she enjoyed the conspiracy. It was almost like foreplay, he thought, as if they were engaged in sex, not conversation.

'You said there was an agreement, that in return for a photo call the press would allow the Prince and his sons their privacy.' She changed her questioning slightly, told herself to control the panic rising in her that he wasn't the key, that even if he was he wasn't going to give her the way in. 'So how did Charles react when your paper carried the pictures?'

'In a way he didn't, or couldn't mind. The pictures showed him in a good light, informal but happy family. Charles and his two sons enjoying being together.'

'But what about the agreement?'

'I didn't say there was an agreement. All I said was that on the first day the royals pose up, as we say, for a facility photo. After that, some press leave but others stay.'

'Why?'

'The first is the hope of getting a better shot, something no one else has.'

'And the second?'

'The Death Watch. Klosters is a long way from London if the Prince isn't so lucky off piste next time.'

'Bastard.'

They were drifting away from the conspiracy, from what she needed to know. She sipped the champagne and steered them back. 'But you got the pictures. What I mean is: it was you who got the pictures, not someone else.'

He shrugged. Smiled.

'Good, weren't they?' She wrapped the conspiracy round them again, as if they were about to make love. As if she were stroking him, teasing him.

'Very good.' He waved for another bottle of Bollinger.

'So how did you know they were going to fall off there?' The glass was in front of the face again and the eyes were glancing over it, flashing, challenging.

'They always do.' He sat back and allowed himself to enjoy the moment. 'Every year. Even if they could get round the bend it's a family tradition that they come off and have a snowball fight. Started when William and Harry were small and continued ever since.'

The waiter poured them each another glass and put the bottle in the ice bucket.

'So what time did you get up?'

She felt the excitement, the mix of cold and adrenalin.

'Five o'clock. It was bloody freezing, I can tell you.'

'But the lifts normally don't open until eight and the runs the royals were using would have been closed to the press and public.'

It was not like the schedule issued by the Newspaper Publishers

Association, was no longer simply the formal engagements on the Wednesday List at which PinMan would be untouchable. It was inside, touching on the personal details which would expose PinMan to her.

'That's why I went to Klosters before everybody else. I paid the piste bashers, got a lift up.'

'But how did you know?' Who's your source, how far ahead does he or she give you such information? How can I access it?

'Everybody has their sources.'

His voice and manner changed, were tighter, the doors in danger of crashing shut. She had almost gone far enough, she knew.

'But you must have been waiting up there hours.' She changed the subject as effortlessly as he would have done had he been talking to a contact.

'I was.' He was relaxed again, laughing at the memory.

'Tell me. From the beginning. Tell me everything.'

He told her. The exit from the hotel and the fear that another member of the press would see them. The rendezvous with the piste bashers and the trip up the mountain. The wait in the snow and the moment he heard the voices and knew it was them. The cameras, lenses and film the photographer had used and the exhilaration of the moment. The ski down the mountain after.

Saunders was the key, she understood as she listened, nodded for more champagne. All that remained was to find the way in.

Something he wasn't telling her, she was also aware. Not just the identity of his informant. Something else. Something she should push him on but couldn't.

So why didn't he tell her, he asked himself. He and the photographer had agreed never to disclose what had happened on the slope after Charles had left. The men – whoever they were – would have reported their presence, but their presence was known anyway because of the photographs. But as long as they kept quiet about the figures rising from the snow they had proved they could be relied upon, proved they could be trusted. Blow that trust by writing about it, even by idle gossip and the tips would stop.

Philipa Walker was different, though. She would enjoy the story and it would stop with her. So why hadn't he told her? Some misbegotten sense of duty, he laughed at himself, some misguided loyalty, even patriotism.

Tonight they had come so close, he thought as he returned to the flat in Barnsbury that night. Tonight he and Philipa Walker had almost gone to bed.

Tonight she'd come so close, she thought as she returned to the flat off Primrose Hill. Tonight she'd almost unlocked the secret of PinMan. She closed the curtains and went to bed . . .

. . . it was six days since she had sat at the bottom of the stairs and read the details on the copy of her original birth entry. Philipa Walker left the house, walked the half-mile to the station, caught the train to Victoria, and the underground to Euston, the carriage packed in the rush hour. In her small brown suitcase, in addition to the normal items, she carried a road map of Ireland, the envelope containing the copy of her birth entry, and a dress, coat and spare shoes. If she was going to meet her mother – if she managed to find her mother, if she actually went ahead with it – she should dress smartly, not the denims and sweater she normally wore.

Why hadn't she told anyone, why hadn't she confronted her parents and asked them the truth?

At Euston she bought the Daily Telegraph – old habits die hard, she thought, especially those instilled from childhood – and the Guardian. The train to Liverpool – change at Crewe for Holyhead – was waiting. She found a front-facing seat in a nonsmoking compartment and settled down.

So why hadn't she talked to her parents, she asked herself again. What was she doing now? Perhaps it was natural that she would want to meet her real mother, ask about her real father. Perhaps it was also natural that she should wish to make the journey by herself. Given the shock of the realization and the fact that she had discovered the details of her birth, rather than being told them by those she believed she could trust. Both journeys, she thought, the journey to Ireland and the journey to her past.

The doors closed and the train pulled out.

What did she expect? What was Ireland going to be like? How would she find her mother? Would she find her? The thoughts had not left her since she had read the words on the certificate and understood what they meant. She opened the case, took out the envelope, and read again the details of her original birth entry, the name she had originally been given before it was changed at adoption.

Date and place of birth: 12.3.61. London.

Christian name: Siobhan.

Father's name and surname: no details.

Mother's name and surname: Siobhan Mary O'Connell.

Rank or profession of father: no details.

Signature, description and residence of informant: S.M. O'Connell, the signature was thin but firmly written. Mother. Rathmeen.

There were fifty-two O'Connells in the telephone directory – she had checked at the public library – three in Rathmeen itself, but none with the initials S.M. If O'Connell was her mother's married name, she had thought, then the entry would be under her father's initials. One evening she had decided to telephone the O'Connells listed in Rathmeen, had actually begun, had heard the first number ringing and tried to imagine what Rathmeen looked like. Then she had panicked and put the telephone down before the call was answered.

Siobhan O'Connell. A good name, she thought, rolled it round her tongue, tried it with a touch of brogue. Laughed at herself. Almost cried. She cut off the emotion and opened the road map.

Rathmeen was in the North, in a tangle of country roads south of Portadown. In some ways it would have been easier to travel via Belfast, but she had been afraid. Belfast was racked by car bombs and shootings. The IRA prisoners in the H-blocks were protesting over the authorities' refusal to grant them political status. She had seen the television pictures. The Blanket Protest, even in the depths of winter the prisoners refusing to wear prison uniform and draping themselves only in blankets. Then the Dirty Protest, the human excreta the men – and woman – had smeared on the walls of the cells in which they continued to live. And now the hunger strikes, five men so far at weekly intervals.

For these reasons she had decided to avoid Belfast. Instead she would sail to Dun Laoghaire, near Dublin, then hire a car, and drive to a small but pleasant-sounding hotel on the River Fane, south of the border, which she had already booked. The following morning she would cross into the North, make the two-hour drive to Rathmeen, spending only as much time in the North as was necessary and returning that evening to the hotel. It was a very English way of organizing things, she almost laughed, a very English way of setting out to discover the truth of her past.

She put the certificate and road map away and read the newspapers, starting with the Telegraph. Overnight there had been more trouble in Belfast: the so-called officer-commanding the IRA Brigade at the Maze, Eamon McCann, had begun his sixth week of hunger strike, the event marked by two car bombs and one incendiary in a store in the city centre. The hunger strike was the second in the past six months: the first had ended when the prisoners had thought that the British government had agreed to certain of their demands; the second had begun when it had become clear that London had made no concessions whatsoever. It was a good decision to avoid Belfast, she thought again. She folded the papers and fell asleep.

The ferry from Holyhead left at two-thirty and berthed in Dun Laoghaire at six. By the time she had hired a car and driven to the hotel it was mid-evening. The hotel was slightly larger than she had expected, on the edge of the village, the river flowing opposite and the hills rising beyond. Her room was at the rear, small and comfortable and tucked beneath the eaves so that the ceiling sloped. That night she did not sleep. Instead she lay awake, looking at the stars through the skylight and wondering about the next day. At six she rose, took a long bath in the room along the landing, then dressed, putting on the dress she had brought with her. Breakfast was served from seven. She collected the copy of the Irish Times she had ordered the night before from reception, went through to the restaurant, chose one of the tables overlooking the street and river, and asked for bacon and eggs. The morning was bright and sunny. She unfolded the paper and read the front page.

Overnight the Provisional IRA had announced that the hunger striker Eamon McCann would stand for election to the British parliament at Westminster in a by-election caused by the death of a Northern Ireland MP. The paper gave his personal details, as well as the offences for which he had been imprisoned. In the centre of the page were two photographs, one of McCann before he had been arrested, and the second of him taken clandestinely forty days into his hunger strike and smuggled out of prison. The face was thin and the eyes staring. She looked at the face, at the way the eyes bored into her. How much is he suffering, she wondered, what physical pain is he going through? His fault, she also thought; he had made the decision therefore he should suffer the consequences. The waiter brought her breakfast. She folded the paper and put it into her bag.

Half an hour later she left the hotel, forty minutes after that she stopped at the border, handed her passport over for inspection, and drove into the North. It was like entering another land, she suddenly felt, like entering a war zone – the soldiers and the guns, the helicopter in the sky and the watchtowers in the hills. Instinctively she looked for gunmen and bombers concealed in the hedgerows. She was being stupid, she told herself, the people here spoke with the same accent, and the fields and hills rolled away in the same endless green. By this afternoon she would have found her mother, spent a pleasant two hours with her, promised that one day she would return, then crossed back to the South and be taking tea in the restaurant at the front of the Fane Hotel. And the following day she would drive to Dublin, take the ferry to Holyhead and never come back. She turned off the A28, checked the road map, and followed the B2 to Clare, then turned west. She might come back, she thought, she would send a letter at least, a card at Christmas.

She came to the summit of the hill and stopped, saw Rathmeen below, the road winding through it, the houses and a handful of shops on either side and the square in the middle, the church in one corner, a few more houses straggling out behind, then the road rising again, climbing the hill on the far side and leaving Rathmeen behind. It was so peaceful, she thought, so much like she expected of the Republic, nothing like the violence fifty miles away in Belfast.

She let off the handbrake, eased the car into gear, dropped down the hill and into the village.

The armoured personnel carrier was short and camouflaged, the rear doors open and a soldier with a rifle – she had no way of knowing what type – looking out from the back, aiming it. It was parked in a street just before the square, a second on a corner opposite, both concealed from the hilltop above the village where she had stopped. The women watched from the shop doorways and some twenty youths – late teens and all males – were clustered by the side. As she drove past the soldier followed her with the gun. She felt the fear and confusion and stopped, began to park, saw one of the women shake her head – the slightest shake, so that she almost missed it – telling her to move on. What's happening, she thought. Why Rathmeen? Why today of all days? She nodded – the movement again almost imperceptible – drove past the square and parked in one of the side streets. As she walked back an army lorry pulled into the village and stopped. She walked past it, to the two women.

I'm looking for someone called O'Connell, she almost asked, Siobhan Mary O'Connell. Realized how her English accent would stand out. 'I'm looking for the priest,' she said instead. *If her mother still lived here the priest would know, and he would keep quiet about her visit.*

'The house on the hill, overlooking the junction.' *The woman's voice was not friendly, not unfriendly.*

'Thank you.' *For the information, for the warning.*

The woman nodded.

She left the square and walked up the hill. Half-way up a road cut right, forming a fork before disappearing into the houses and trees beyond. Overlooking the junction was a medium-size house, set back slightly in its own garden, a door at the front and bay windows either side. She opened the gate, walked up the path, and knocked on the door. The woman who answered it was in her sixties, grey hair turning white and tied back.

'I'm looking for the priest.'

'May I say who it is that wants him?'

'My name's Walker.'

The housekeeper asked her to step inside, showed her into the sitting-room to the right of the hall, and offered her a seat. The room, like the house, was warm and welcoming, the furniture old and comfortable. Two minutes later the priest came in. He was tall, in his early forties. Reassuring – she did not know why she thought of the word to describe him – like the chair and the room and the house.

'How can I help you?' *He sat opposite her.*

'I'm looking for a woman called O'Connell.'

He turned his head slightly.

'Siobhan Mary O'Connell.'

'McCann.' *His voice was warm and he was smiling more.* 'O'Connell was her maiden name.' *He paused, inviting her to explain.*

'And she still lives here?'

'Of course.' *Again the pause.*

'Where?'

He gave her the address. 'It's on the left, in the centre of the terrace just off the square. Green door, you can't miss it.'

'Thank you.'

The nerves were suddenly consuming her, biting into her stomach.

'You'll be having a cup of tea before you go?'

She needed to go down the hill, to find the terrace, to knock on the door. 'No. Thank you, anyway.' Even now she did not know how she would react or what she would say, whether she would say anything. Whether she would even go to the terrace and knock on the door.

The priest walked with her to the garden gate and watched as she went down the hill.

The soldiers were spread across two sides of the square, RUC men in another line and the youths facing them. She was afraid but fascinated. The soldiers were in flak jackets and helmets, most armed though some carrying riot shields or long, heavy wooden batons. The number of young men facing them had doubled, probably trebled — fifty, probably seventy, even a hundred. Not all of them were local, she guessed. Why Rathmeen, she wondered, why here? Three cars drew up and the television crews jumped out.

It was all arranged, she realized: the TV crews and the youths and the army. Why, she still wondered. Mrs McCann, green door in the terrace on the left.

The first stones flew through the air; she did not see who threw them, just heard the massive shout that went up, then heard or saw them clatter against the reinforced plastic of the riot shields. More stones, more shouts. She was still walking down the hill towards the square, cutting left.

The bottle arced across the square. She saw it clearly and distinctly. Molotov, she thought she heard someone shout, sensed the moment the soldiers flinched. There was something in the neck of the bottle, something burning. The bottle bounced on a riot shield and shattered, the petrol inside ignited and the flames shot suddenly and terribly over the shield and along the ground, the soldier holding the shield pulling back, brushing frantically at his clothes, the flames up his front, others quickly and efficiently putting them out. There were more stones, two more Molotov cocktails, all directed at the same point, as if the youths had seen a weakness, almost as if they knew what they were doing.

The troops were moving forward, the youths pulling back then advancing, the troops holding their position. She was almost at the square. The youths were surging forward again, more Molotov cocktails streaming across the open ground. She heard the first crack of a rifle, did not know it was firing plastic bullets, realized how exposed she was. The left side of the square was clear of trouble; she made for it, almost ran. Shops and houses there, but the shop doors would be locked, probably the houses as well. She shouldn't have left the priest, she knew, but when she left the trouble hadn't started. There were more stones, more youths at the back of the main group lighting bottles, scarves over their faces. She heard the sound behind her and stopped, turned, was only aware of a blur as the two army vehicles stopped and the soldiers jumped out. The youths in the square saw, realized they were in a pincer, and began to scatter.

She was almost at the terrace. Tried one door, a second. Tried to get away. Was running, turning, not sure what she was doing. Someone went past, a man with a scarf over his face, soldiers chasing him, almost catching him. She tripped on the edge of the pavement and fell in front of the first soldiers, one of them stumbling over her and the others swerving or slowing, the man disappearing round the corner.

Sorry, she began to apologize. Bitch, she heard a voice. Hard and angry. It wasn't deliberate, she began to explain, I tripped, really I tripped. Two of them picked her up and flung her face first against the wall. Search her, she heard the order. Her arms were held tight above her head, her feet kicked away from the wall so that she was leaning forward and her legs forced open. She was dazed, confused, face grazed and blood trickling. And afraid. Not afraid, terrified. I'm sorry, she tried to say again, tried to turn her head to speak to them. The hand hit her, made her face the wall. She was sobbing, trembling. I'm English, she was shouting. No sound coming out. You can't do this to me. The hands ran down her arms and back, across her shoulders. Make it thorough, she heard the voice above the clamour, knew what the bastard meant, the soldiers round her and the two pinning her tighter. I'm English, she was still trying to shout. The hands came under her arms and round the front of her body, to her breasts. Held them, squeezed them hard. Left them and ran quickly down the outside of her thighs, up the inside. Inside her dress and pulling aside her pants, the gloved fingers thrust deliberately and viciously into her vagina.

I'm English, the last vestige of air was still trying to shout.

The hands left her and she slumped against the wall, still standing, trembling. Faced the soldiers. They were turning away, about to leave her. The battle in the rest of the square was continuing.

She saw the officer, didn't know his rank. Thanks for stopping them, she began to say. Thanks for pulling them off me.

'Wash your hands before you eat, corporal.' He was staring at her, she at him. 'You don't know where they've been.'

She heard the men round her chuckle. Knew that the bastard knew what they had done to her. Her reaction was automatic, instinctive. She stared at him, straight in the eyes. Spat at him. The saliva dribbled down his face and across his lips. Slowly, calmly, he drew his glove across his face and wiped it away.

'Irish tart.' He turned to the man on his right. 'She been searched yet?'

'No, sir.'

'Do it. Make a good job of it.'

The soldiers began to turn her, a line behind them sealing her off from the square. This time they would really hurt her, she knew, this time they would tear her to pieces.

'I think that's fine, lieutenant.' She was only just aware of the voice, did not even know it was the priest. 'I think the girl's had enough.'

She was slumped against the wall, trembling. The lieutenant nodded and the men dropped her. McGinty bent down and helped her up.

'Come on now, girl. Time for that cup of tea.'

They walked up the hill, his hand holding her arm and helping her when she stumbled. She was aware only of the thudding in her head, totally unaware what else might be happening around her. The housekeeper took her upstairs, ran the bath, gave her a fresh warm towel, and closed the door.

When she came down twenty minutes later the priest was waiting in the sitting-room.

'Thank you, Father.'

The housekeeper brought them tea, poured them each a cup, and left.

'So did you find Mrs McCann?'

She shook her head. What's happening here? she wanted to ask. Why the soldiers?

'Today's a bad day. You've had enough.'

She nodded again.

'Where are you staying?'

She told him.

138

He was nodding, smiling, as he had done earlier. 'You return there now. You go to your room and change. Have another bath if you wish.' His voice was different, almost undetectably so. As if he was giving her instructions. As if, she did not know, he was her handler. 'Then you go downstairs and have tea in the restaurant.'

Two hours later she crossed the border back into the Republic, forty minutes after that she reached the Fane Hotel. After the North the Republic felt secure, at peace. She parked the car and went to her room. Her pants were torn and she had bled slightly. No tears, she told herself, surprised at the calmness which had come upon her, no weakness. What should she do about her mother – it was like a sledgehammer, beating at her brain. Another day, another time, she told herself. She took a shower rather than a bath, changed, put on some perfume, picked up her bag and went downstairs.

It was four in the afternoon, the restaurant quiet, two couples at separate tables, and a man whom she barely noticed sitting alone. She sat at a table slightly back from the windows, but from where she could look out across the river to the fields beyond, and ordered tea and scones.

'Would you be minding if I joined you?'

She heard the voice – soft and friendly – and looked up. It was the man who had been sitting by himself. He was in his forties, possibly a little older, brown hair, wearing a well-worn tweed jacket slightly shiny at the elbows. A teacher, she thought. No threat, she understood. It was written all over him. A country doctor or a vet.

'Not at all.'

He sat down. 'You've been in the wars.'

She put her hand to the grazing on her face. 'I fell over.'

The waitress came with her tea, the man waited while she put it on the table then asked whether she would mind bringing another. You're on holiday, Philipa Walker knew he was going to ask. Where are you from? How long have you been here?

'So you're Siobhan.'

'I'm sorry?'

'I said you're Siobhan.'

'I'm sorry. I don't understand.'

'You're Siobhan McCann's little girl, O'Connell as she was.'

She felt the numbness, did not know how to react or what to say.

How do you know, he saw it in her face. Nobody knows. I haven't told anyone, not even the priest.

'The eyes,' said Liam Conlan. 'You're the image of your mother when she was your age.'

'You're my father?' *The words came out before she had even thought about them.*

Conlan shook his head. How do you know . . . the look was still on her face. How do you know who I am and why I'm here? The rules of the game, Conlan thought: both sides making their plans, putting their people in them, but the one thing no one could ever cater for, the one thing nobody would ever plan for, even if they knew.

The waitress brought him his tea.

'Tell me about my mother.' *Spoken. Tell me about me, who and what I am. Unspoken.*

'Giving you up – having you adopted – was the hardest decision of her life.'

A life of hardships and decisions, she heard it in his voice, felt it in the undercurrents of what he was telling her. She felt herself shivering, stiffening, the sudden electricity leaping, surging through her body. Felt the other feeling, the emotion draining away and the ice taking its place.

'You have two older brothers. Your mother is still alive, though she isn't well.'

'And she lives in the house in Rathmeen.'

'Yes.'

Why the demonstration there today, she thought, why the organized crowds and the police and army and the television cameras?

'My father?'

'Your father was killed ten years ago.'

Ten years after she was born.

'Tell me about them.' *Tell me who you are and how you know.*

'Your mother and father were married in 1953.' *His voice was soft, almost as if was telling her a piece of folklore. She loved the Irishness in it, in the story and the way he told it.* 'There are photographs if you wanted to see them. Their first son was born the following year.' *The softness disappeared as quickly as mist when the sun comes up.* 'By then your father was in prison. He did five years, no remission. Their second son was born nine months *later. By then your father was in prison again. Both the boys were brought up by your mother's parents.'*

'But why didn't my mother bring them up?'

'Because by then your mother was also in prison.'

'Why?'

'You come from one hell of a family, Siobhan McCann. Way back to your grandfather and great-grandfather, both sides of the family.'

'Tell me from the beginning.' The innocence, she would think in later years, when it had been drained out of her, when they had trained her, moulded her, into what they wanted. Into what she wanted.

Conlan nodded, allowed her time. The one thing that no one could foresee, he thought again. That some called Fate or Chance.

'Your father was called Daithi, Gaelic for David; your mother Siobhan. They were activists, both in the IRA – the Officials, as it was then. In the fifties the IRA's strength was waning, the Movement was being squeezed both in the North and the South. In 1960 there was an amnesty for men held in prison; most went home to their wives and families and severed their connections with the Movement.' He shook his head. 'They were sad times; sometimes people didn't even know why the men had been in prison. Worse still, didn't even care. It broke them, almost broke the Movement.'

We're talking about the IRA, she was aware. Not a romantic innocent movement, an organization which bombs and kills and maims.

'Your father went to the mainland, to keep the Movement going there. Your mother joined him and the boys were left with their grandparents. What nobody knew was that your mother was carrying you.' He paused again, remembering, or deciding how he should tell her. 'Everything seemed fine, except that the Brits found out about your father and he went on the run again. We tried to get your mother back to Ireland, but it wasn't possible. Then we arranged for her to have you in the safe house where she lived. The delivery wasn't easy. Someone panicked and she was taken to hospital. After that she had no option.'

She sat staring out of the window.

'So why did she give me up, have me adopted?'

'Partly because she was frightened for you, partly to protect your father, give the Brits one less lever against him. If the Brits knew

141

they would use you against her, use both of you against him.' It was something your mother always regretted, he did not need to say, something for which she never forgave herself.

So it wasn't that her mother hadn't wanted her, she felt the relief, almost the lightness. It wasn't that her mother had abandoned her, forgotten about her.

'On my birth entry my mother used her maiden name and there were no details of my father.'

'Correct.'

'Why?'

'To protect your father, as I've said.'

'That's not what I meant. Why use her own name, why take the risk of using even her maiden name? Why not make up one up?'

Fate, he might have replied, surprised not only at the question but the severity of it. Perhaps because she didn't know what she was doing; perhaps because she didn't want to sever the link totally; perhaps because she hoped that one day you might discover the truth and come looking for her. 'Who knows?' he said instead.

'Do my parents know all this? My other parents' – she corrected herself – 'the family in England.'

'Nobody knows. Your mother gave you up and disappeared.'

They sat without speaking again, barely sipping the tea.

'Tell me how my father died.'

It was thirty seconds before Conlan replied, and then it was with the smallest shrug of the shoulders or shake of the head, the almost unseen movement of the hand.

'To understand that you have to understand the history of the Movement. In the sixties the IRA – the Official IRA – seemed finished. According to some it was just something in the history books. The men in the North had lost faith with the leadership in the Republic, by 1969 military action had totally ceased.

'In the late sixties there were various civil rights campaigns and marches, most based in Derry. Increasingly they were met with violence. In 1969 the Catholics in Derry protested against the Apprentice Boys marching and the Bogside became a battlefield. This was followed by trouble in Belfast.'

What he told her next may have been factual. May, on the other hand, have been part of the Catholic folklore of the events which followed. May even have been his own account based on the first feeling – as yet unrecognized – of her future importance to him and the Cause.

'In August 1969 the RUC reported that the IRA was planning an uprising in Belfast; on the night you're asking about there were running battles along Divis Street where the Catholic and Protestant areas met.' Because she was English he avoided using slang. 'There was shooting, people fearing for their homes and moving out. The RUC sending in the armour.' Against us, he did not need to say. 'Just after midnight the Protestants began throwing petrol bombs at Catholic homes, the entire Divis was at risk. The key was St Comgalls schoolhouse.' The red-brick building positioned on a gentle rise in Divis Street and occupying a crucial position with a line of fire across the riot area. 'Seven men held it, kept the Prods at bay. Bloody pathetic.' The anger spat out, a sorrow and a pride tinged with it, the voice different again. 'The Officials had sworn to protect the people, but in the end they did nothing. So the men at St Comgalls were practically unarmed. A Thompson machine gun, a .303 rifle and four pistols, hardly any ammunition. They held out, though, that night they saved the Divis. Only pulled out when the guns were empty.' He turned to her. 'That was when your father was killed. On the way out.'

'My father was one of the men in St Comgalls schoolhouse.'

'Of course.'

She waited.

'We got his body out. Didn't leave him for the RUC or the Prods.'

'You were there as well?'

'Yes, I was there.' It was all he said.

And in the months that followed, he would explain to her later, and because the Official IRA – the Stickies as he would call them – had failed to defend the people, the Provisional IRA was formed. The bombers and the killers, part of her would have protested had he told her now, which was why he delayed till he had answered the personal questions he knew she would ask.

'My mother. Will I be able to see her?'

'Not this time.'

'Why not?'

'Because at this moment in time it would be difficult.'

Because at this moment in time it would expose you – perhaps it was then that the first thread drifted down, settling upon them,

143

wrapping itself round her and bringing her home. Perhaps it was then that he began to see, not knowing what he was seeing, not even aware he was seeing it.

'Why?'

'You don't understand, do you?'

'Understand what?'

He shrugged slightly, matched it with a wave of the hand.

'What about my brothers?'

'What about your brothers?'

'Who are they? Where are they? What do they do?'

'Your first brother is a priest.' He saw what he thought was an understanding in her eyes and corrected it. 'Not the priest in Rathmeen.'

'So I could see him?'

Conlan shrugged again.

'What about the second? Who is he? Where could I find him?'

'You still don't see, do you?' Of all the days for the daughter to come home, he thought. Of all the days and all the months and all the years. No more playing, he saw it in her eyes, no more myths and cobwebs. 'You've seen today's newspaper?'

'Yes.'

It was still in her bag from breakfast. He sat looking at her, not saying anything. She reached down and pulled the newspaper out.

The previous evening the Provisional IRA had announced that the man leading the hunger strike at the Maze prison was standing for election to Westminster. The photograph had been smuggled out of prison, the face thin and the eyes boring into her.

'Let me tell you what it's like on hunger strike.' Conlan faced her, turned the screw on her. 'The first days are marked by a feeling of great hunger, then the hunger pangs wear off and are replaced by a feeling of extreme nausea. Bowel movements cease and lack of vitamins affects the eyes. The hunger striker develops nystagmus, a condition in which he finds it hard to focus, and his gaze wanders. This affects balance which in turn produces a form of sea-sickness. For the first six weeks he vomits frequently.'

She wondered why he was telling her.

'After some forty-five days, there appears to be an improvement and the hunger striker is able to hold down fluids. As a result he seems more lucid, even demonstrates signs of recovery. But the *reason that he no longer vomits is that the brain cells that trigger the reaction are too damaged by vitamin starvation to work. As the brain damage develops the prisoner slips in and out of a coma, and is rambling and incoherent when conscious. The last days are accompanied by blindness and, if a man is lucky, unconsciousness. If unlucky, he suffers agonizing convulsions and has to be held down on his bed.'*

Even now you don't see — she read it in his face, in the tone of his voice. *What don't I see?* she almost asked. 'Is he going to die?' she asked instead.

'Yes,' Conlan told her.

'Why?' she asked.

'Because the Brits won't give in. Because he's the officer-commanding and therefore has to be the first, and after the failure of the last hunger strike he has to win or see it through.'

So why are you telling me this, she almost asked again, what is this to do with me? She looked at the newspaper again, stared at the face of the man, at the mouth and the eyes and the nose, looked again at Conlan.

'The first hunger striker. The one who's going to die. He's my brother, isn't he?' . . .

*　　　*　　　*

The meeting was at one, in Farringdon's office at Lisburn. Present, in addition to Farringdon, were Nolan and Brady. When the meeting ended Farringdon would brief Cutler, and Cutler would in turn brief London.

The following morning Frank Hanrahan would stand trial for murder.

'Everything's ready?' Farringdon's eyes darted between the two. 'The timetable's right, the evidence is in order, and Hanrahan's lawyer knows the hole?' And we're covered, he did not need to say; everything has been arranged so that the flaw in the prosecution case cannot be traced back to MI5 or Special Branch.

'Everything's fine.' It was Brady who answered. 'Tomorrow will be taken up with opening statements, the prosecution will begin its case on Wednesday morning. The first four or five days will be taken up with evidence about the shooting, sources of information, the usual arguments between counsel about the admissibility of certain evidence. They should get to the forensic sometime in the second week. We're not sure when the defence will spring their little trick, of course, though it will probably be in cross-examination.'

'Their case will be watertight?'

'Yes. They'll be able to drive a coach and horses through the prosecution.'

'And the RUC and Prosecutor's office will have no idea?'

'Not the Prosecutor's office nor the rest of the RUC. And the only people in Special Branch to know will be those with a need to.'

'When he walks out of court?'

'He begins work in the Provos' security section.'

'And we're sure he's ours?' We're sure the Provos aren't using him to feed us black information or setting us up for a sting? And if he is ours, how long can we run him, how far can we push him before the Provos find out?

They shrugged. Who knows, who can be sure of anything?

'What about Flynn?' The driver who had identified Hanrahan as the gunman.

'Special Branch are running him.' Not MI5's business, there was the faintest hint – we gave you Hanrahan, but some things we keep to ourselves.

'And he won't be jeopardized by the prosecution.'

Flynn was low-level but still important. Flynn wouldn't have the access Hanrahan would enjoy, but there was no way of knowing where the intelligence he would pass on might lead.

'Hopefully not.'

Farringdon closed the meeting and telephoned Cutler. The briefing, thirty minutes later, lasted twenty-five minutes and dealt in essence with the issues Farringdon had already raised with Nolan and Brady.

'How's Nolan reacting to the McGuire affair?' Cutler asked at the end.

How's Nolan reacting to being pulled off, he meant, how's she letting it affect her conduct and her judgement?

How d'you think she's reacting? Farringdon might have said. He knew Cutler well enough to be honest. 'She's fine. Not happy about the fact that she was pulled off, or the way it was done. But she's handled the Hanrahan case well, broke him when Special Branch couldn't.'

So what's happening with McGuire? he almost asked but decided not to.

McGuire pulling the surveillance teams thinner and thinner across Britain, Cutler had heard. Not formally, of course, simply in passing. London putting more and more effort into the McGuire operation, but nobody knowing why.

'Tell Nolan she's doing a good job.'

The office was quiet. Even after the word had been allowed to seep down from the Director of Intelligence that London was pleased, morale remained low, the adrenalin which had gripped the corridors vanished and the disaffection almost contagious.

Think positive, Nolan told herself, remember what you learned at Hereford. It was all in the head, win or lose – if you appeared to be winning or losing – even if the odds were stacked against you. Because in the end it was you who decided whether you won or lost, and nobody else . . .

. . . the figure was moving quickly, across the scree and into the woods. Everything apparently normal, she thought as the man reappeared then cut across the open ground in front of the barracks and past the guards at the main gate. Except –

It was four years since she had joined the army, the last two in Germany. In many ways the life was as she had expected it, in some ways not. Perhaps that was why she had seized on the two week adventure training course; get out of the routine, out of the office work which came with promotion.

There were ten of them on the course – most from the WRACs but two from the Military Police. Each day they worked hard, each evening they played and drank harder. Sometimes by themselves, sometimes with the main instructor. Quite often with the main instructor. Not that he was trying to get his leg over – she and the others had talked through it – though most of them wouldn't have minded. Most evenings he sat with them – sometimes with all or most of them, sometimes in smaller groups and occasionally with one of them by herself – and listened to their stories of army life. Most evenings they asked him about himself and received the usual put-offs.

Now she watched as he crossed the barracks, the mud caked up the side and back of the track suit, and disappeared into the sergeants' mess.

147

That much they knew about him — that he was a sergeant. And his first name. Dave. Probably Paras, except that he wore no insignia of regiment or rank, but no one would on a combat jacket anyway. One night one of the girls had asked him whether he ever jumped – with the obvious double meaning – and he'd joked about running out the back of a Herc. On another they'd worked out that he was on secondment and up from Lake Constance.

That evening he joined them in the mess. At nine, he asked whether she wanted to go for a drink in town.

The bar was busy and they sat in the corner.

'How's the hand?'

'Fine.' He looked at her across the table. 'Why'd you ask?'

'I saw you out running, thought you'd injured it.'

No . . . the shake of the head and shrug of shoulders said it.

They dropped the subject and began talking about other things: where she'd gone to school, why she'd joined the army. The girl in the tree and the student stuck underground. Not just why she'd done it, why she'd done it again. Plus less obvious issues: politics and the third world, freedom and liberty. Even fox-hunting.

'You hunt?' she asked.

He shook his head.

'Why not?'

'No fun.'

'Why no fun?'

She was back in the tree, the boys beneath looking for her, feeling the blood thudding in her ears and the disappointment as they went away, back in the duck of the pot-hole, back on the pavement the day she had signed up.

'Animals can't shoot back, can they?'

So what's going on, Dave? Why did you want to know so much about why I do things, about why I'm bored off my arse in the army? Who are you that you're armed even now? – perhaps the realization had been there all along, perhaps it came as a shock. Who are you that you carry a gun even when you're out jogging, a towel wrapped round it so no one will know? What's this course really all about?

'Another drink?' He sensed the moment she understood, the moment she knew who and what he was.

'Not yet.' Even though the glasses were empty.

So what is it, Dave? What are you going to ask me?

. . . bloody London. She kicked the metal wastepaper bin across the office floor, retrieved it, saw the dent she had made, and kicked it again. McGuire was hers. Then she'd been pulled off. Patted on the head, told she had been a good girl, and sent back home. So why had London taken the job from them? Why had London thrown in so much manpower? What was so important about McGuire that London wasn't telling? She was on a hiding to nothing, she knew. If the McGuire job came good then someone else would take the credit; if it fell apart then it would be down to her for initiating the tail in the first place.

Forget it, she told herself, forget McGuire and concentrate on the job in hand. She poured herself a coffee and turned to the intelligence reports which had come in since that morning.

Most were routine: updates on the Provos who had begun their movements when McGuire had first disappeared from view, four were now home and two were still moving. She looked for a pattern, gave up, and began checking the others.

The movement of prominent members of Sinn Fein. Reports that a television crew had filmed a staged incident near the border. Devlin Kelly observed in the Republic. Synopses of phone taps.

Who was Devlin Kelly, she thought, and turned back.

Kelly, Devlin. Park Road, Belfast. Observed at the Kilmore Hotel, Lough Corrib, two weeks ago.

Never heard of him, Nolan thought. She switched on the computer and checked the name against the security file, found nothing, and cross-checked the address. Still nothing.

Odd, she thought.

She looked at the report again. Intelligence grade F7. Intelligence was scaled from A1 down to F7 and most was F6 – reported but unconfirmed, probably from a snatch of conversation overheard by a low-level informant and unsubstantiated by anything or anybody else. But nobody would file F7 from the Republic: if it was from the South it wouldn't be low-level. But the grade it carried was the lowest of the low. So if that was the case why had they included it at all?

The coffee was cold. She threw it away and poured herself another. Forget Kelly, she told herself, Kelly was someone else's concern. Because tomorrow Frank Hanrahan would stand trial for murder, and she and Brady were Hanrahan's handlers. Therefore her sole function at the present time was to confirm that Hanrahan was on her side and protected.

So who are you, Frank? – the doubts came to her as they had come to her every day since he had agreed to be turned. Whose are you? What if –

She pushed the thoughts aside, switched off the computer, filed the Kelly report with the rest of the afternoon's intelligence material, took the Hanrahan documents from the security safe, and looked for the one thing she and Brady might have overlooked.

Michael Logan left home shortly before seven, took a minicab to Aldergrove, and caught the 0815 British Airways flight to Manchester. In the main body of his briefcase he carried a list of commercial appointments for the next eleven days; hidden in the false bottom he carried a spare driving licence, passport and credit card.

It was ten days since his visit to the South and his overnight stay in the hotel at Kilmore. The day before he had placed a coded entry in the personal section of the *Herald Tribune* notifying Kincaid of the meeting and specifying its date, time and place.

For the next 36 hours he kept the appointments he had made in England, travelling by train to Birmingham, Derby and Newcastle. On the evening of the second day he took a Sabena flight to Brussels. For the six days after that he kept his sales appointments in Belgium and the Netherlands. His only appointment on the eighth day was at nine in the morning and was finished by ten. His remaining – and last – appointment was at three the afternoon after next. He left Amsterdam at one, caught the train to Eindhoven, and checked in at the Holiday Inn, using the false passport and credit card but offering the card itself merely as a deposit and stating he would pay cash when he left. At four, discarding his formal business clothes for a leather jacket, denims and roll-neck sweater, he returned to the railway station.

Kincaid was waiting for him in the café off the ticket hall, his back to the wall so that he could observe the entrance to the station and the bus stop outside.

William Kincaid – called Billy by the few allowed to know his task or his whereabouts – was 34 years old, with a wiry body and short curly black hair. He had commanded the active service unit since it had been set up in Europe sixteen months before. In the first four months the ASU had carried out two operations, the bombing of the perimeter fence of the British army base in Dortmund, and the machine-gunning of a car driven by an air force corporal in Hanover. After that Conlan had pulled them off. For the past year the ASU had occupied itself researching and reconnoitring potential targets and establishing a network of safe houses, dead letter drops and arms caches across Western Europe.

'So, Billy, how's it going?'

Everything about Logan was different. His accent was sharper and harder, and his manner was decisive in a way totally different from the authority and leadership he showed in the commercial field. Though he listened to argument and reason, he brooked no dissent or indiscipline.

'Fine.'

They left the bar and drove to the safe house. A job at last, Kincaid knew, no more R and R — research and recce, the ASU's mocking adaptation of rest and recuperation.

'I need three targets. Each a Brit and each a shooting. The first within the next two weeks.' In case the ASU was discovered and the safe house compromised, Logan wore gloves. 'Single target, single gunman. I'm here to go through the list with you and work out how your team can provide the back-up and logistics.'

'We're not doing the hit?' There was a flash of anger in Kincaid's question which he regretted immediately.

'I obey orders, Billy boy. You obey them as well.' Logan's look was withering. 'You don't want to, or you want out, that's fine with me.' And then you're finished. Then you're dead and buried, because even though you don't know half what you think you know, you know too much anyway.

'What weapon?' Kincaid took the point.

'Ruger .357 with silencer. Soft-nose rounds plus speed loader.'

Not an indiscriminate target, not a haphazard swing of the AK. The target carefully selected, identified, and the hitman up close, eyeball to eyeball. One of the big boys coming in — Kincaid felt the edge of excitement — one of the heavies.

'No problem.' It was as close as he could get to conceding that he had been out of order.

They began to discuss the target and the arrangements.

'Venlo.' Kincaid's suggestion was firm and clear. 'Just inside the Dutch border with Germany.'

'Why Venlo?' Logan was clinical, analytical.

'There's a good store there, Maxis. Lots of squaddies come across to use it.'

'Which squaddies?'

'You name it, they're all just over the border. JHQ, NORTHAG, HQ BAOR, Ordnance.'

Ordnance provided the essential back-up for the British army in Northern Ireland – the technical teams, people like the surveillance technicians and the bomb disposal squads.

'Good choice.'

The following morning Logan and Kincaid drove the 50 kilometres to Venlo and walked the course, as Kincaid liked to put it. That afternoon they checked the location where the Ruger would be concealed, as well as the positioning of the getaway vehicles, should they be needed, the safe house and the back-up which the ASU would provide if necessary.

The morning after that Logan ran through the arrangements and location alone. Shortly before lunchtime he returned to Amsterdam, showered and changed. At four he kept his commercial appointment, then caught the evening flight to Leeds. For the next two days he attended further business meetings in the Midlands, then returned to Belfast.

The Hanrahan trial began well. At the appointed hour he was led in handcuffs through the underground passage connecting the prison on one side of the Crumlin Road to the Criminal Court on the other. The prosecution outlined what appeared to be a cast-iron case and the defence countered forcefully and vociferously, though apparently on weak grounds. On the third day, however, the presiding judge temporarily suspended the hearing due to the sudden and unexpected illness of the prosecution counsel, and the trial did not recommence until the Thursday of the following week. At all stages the Provo-spotters lounged unseen in the streets around the court, looking for the unknown face which might suggest that someone was a member of the police, army or security services. At no stage, therefore, did Brady or Nolan go near the court.

On the next Monday the prosecution reached the forensic section of its evidence. The first part of this related to the firearm involved, and the second concerned tests linking Hanrahan's clothing with what had already been confirmed as the stolen vehicle used in the

Tennent Street killing. The prosecution was expected to end its examination-in-chief of the key forensic witness the following day, Nolan was informed that evening.

Then the witness would face cross-examination. And the defence would drop its bombshell. The prosecution would stall, ask for an adjournment, try to counter the defence's case. And 48 hours after that Hanrahan would walk from court a free man.

The offices were quiet; it was mid-evening, the clock ticking on the far wall and the intelligence updates on the right of her desk. So how will Hanrahan react, she wondered, how far would she and Brady be able to push him? How deep would he be able to penetrate the Provos, given the extra cover the trial would have provided? How deep did Hanrahan want to penetrate the Provos? Who was running who, using who?

Devlin Kelly observed in the Republic. The name and information were still in her mind. Kelly, Devlin. Park Road. Occupation rep. Observed at the Kilmore Hotel near Lough Corrib. She had checked the name against the security file, found nothing, and cross-checked the address. Still found nothing.

Intelligence grade F7. It was lodged in her mind like the name Kelly.

She retrieved the relevant forms from the security cabinets, found the report and checked the source.

If the report originated in the Republic then it should be MI6 or Dublin Special Branch. If it was MI6 the report would have said so; if Dublin Special Branch then it might have come through Belfast Special Branch on the old boy network, or through MI5 in Dublin. But it was neither. It was 14 Int.

Some things in the North – certain sorts of things – were run by 14th Intelligence. But 14 Int also ran covert operations. More specifically, 14 Int also controlled SAS operations in Northern Ireland. But it was not unknown for the SAS to take the occasional holiday in the South. If the material referred to the Republic and was sourced 14 Int, therefore, the chances were that it came from the SAS. But if it was SAS, then it would have received a high classification, certainly not lower than A, probably not lower than A3. Never F6/7.

Somebody playing games and not telling anyone. London being London. Not her responsibility; her responsibility was Hanrahan. Interesting, though. She requested a low-priority surveillance on

153

Devlin Kelly, including a more detailed background check plus phone tap, and signalled London for additional information as well as the originating report.

The Hanrahan trial ended as abruptly as Brady had predicted and Nolan had planned. After one and a half days of forensic evidence, the defence lawyer rose to cross-examine. For the first three hours his questions were predictable and easily answered. It was shortly before midday that he asked, quietly and apparently simply, for the notebooks of the police officers and scientists concerned, and the log book of the items presented as forensic evidence.

No witness had identified Hanrahan as the gunman – the prosecution had successfully camouflaged the source of the information which had led them to Hanrahan, and Hanrahan himself had said nothing during his many hours of interview with the RUC. The main plank of the evidence against him, therefore, was forensic – that fibres from the rear seat of the stolen car used for the shooting had been found on clothing removed from Hanrahan's house, and that fibres from a coat and trousers belonging to Hanrahan had been found on the rear seat of the car. The chain of evidence was essential and straightforward, it was understood, the notebooks and logs confirming that the clothing removed from Hanrahan's house was the clothing forensically tested.

'Your Honour,' Hanrahan's lawyer paused for effect and looked at the judge. 'It is my contention that the clothing produced in court does not belong to my client. I refer you to the entry in the forensic log on the afternoon my client was arrested.'

The following morning Frank Hanrahan left court a free man.

So whose side are you really on? Nolan wondered when she was informed of the court decision. Whose game are you really playing? Whose rules are you running under?

What happens if one day the Provos say they're short of a shooter and need you to do a little job for them? What do you do then, Frank? What do I do if you come to me and tell me?

What do I say if the target is an innocent person? Do I sacrifice a life to maintain your cover, Frank? How do I weigh the life of a mother or father, a daughter or a son, against the security of the state? What's the balance?

And what if the target is a known terrorist? A member of the

INLA or the UVF or UFF, even someone within their own ranks whom the Provos want to get rid of? What do I do then, Frank? What if the target is someone I know is guilty, but against whom I don't have sufficient evidence to put down?

London's response to her request for more information on Devlin Kelly came through the following morning.

The Kelly file was blocked.

It was a mistake, she knew. She closed the office door, telephoned Gower Street, asked for Records and quoted the report number. The Kelly file was no longer blocked, she was informed. An error had been made and because the material was so low-grade it had been deleted and no longer existed.

The coded message to McGinty was in the *Irish Times*; the following afternoon he left Rathmeen, collected his instructions and placed his own message in the newspaper. Two days later he travelled to London and placed the message in the dead letter drop in the cemetery in Stoke Newington.

It was the way Conlan liked to operate, as many cut-outs as possible. McGinty knowing nothing of what or to whom he was delivering in London. Logan knowing nothing of McGinty, and McGinty knowing nothing of Logan or Kincaid and his ASU. No one knowing of Sleeper.

Two hours after McGinty left the cemetery Walker entered it. Three days later she took the train to Dover, caught the midday ferry, and slipped quietly and unnoticed into Europe . . .

. . . BBC Television's six o'clock news was half over. Each day now she watched the news, each evening she waited for the announcement. There was only one other student in the sitting-room, the others were in the kitchen.

'We are just getting news from Belfast.' The newscaster's tone was tense, urgent. 'The IRA hunger striker Eamon McCann is dead. The Northern Ireland Office announced the news minutes ago.'

The programme went live to the BBC correspondent in Belfast.

'Eamon McCann was the senior Provisional IRA member in the Maze prison. Late last night he was given the last rites by a priest, his own brother. According to prison authorities he died at two minutes past five this afternoon. This evening Belfast waits for the

IRA's reaction. Already there are demonstrations in the Falls Road and other Catholic areas.'

The newscaster began to question the reporter. Everyone had assumed that either the British government would give in or McCann would call the hunger strike off. Nobody had believed it would come to this. Therefore what did the future hold? What about the other men now close to death?

One of the girls in the kitchen shouted that dinner was ready. She turned off the television and joined them.

It was strange, she would reflect upon it later, how she could cut off her emotions, as if she had no emotions. How she could sit and eat while the others discussed the death of her brother.

At nine she watched the BBC news, at ten ITN, the scenes on the Falls Road and the pictures shot earlier that evening, the women banging their saucepans on the pavements, alerting the Catholic population, the people pouring out of their houses and the youths already building piles of stones. The black flags hanging from the windows. The images later, as the dark grew in and the violence began, the sky lit by the fires from the blazing cars, the colours dancing against the gauntness of the houses.

McCann's body would be released the following morning, News at Ten was able to report. It would be driven to his home on the council estate in the Twinbrook area of Belfast. The funeral service would take place the afternoon after that, in the small Catholic church at the end of the road, then he would be buried in the Republican plot at Milltown cemetery.

When the bulletin ended she waited till the others had gone to their rooms, then, although there was a telephone in the hallway of the house, walked to the public telephone kiosks two streets away. The day after her return from Ireland she had found the number in the telephone directory at the public library.

McGinty answered on the first ring, as if he had been expecting her to call, even though he had not given her the number and neither he nor Conlan had suggested she might wish to contact them again.

'I was just phoning to confirm that I'm coming over tomorrow.' She did not need to identify herself.

'We're all looking forward to seeing you.' It was as if they were discussing a family reunion. In a way, she supposed, they were. 'You'll be coming after work, of course.'

The instruction was disguised as a question.

'Yes.'

'Fine. I'll meet you off the six-thirty shuttle.'

The following afternoon she caught the train to Victoria and the underground to Heathrow. Her stomach was churning and she felt sick with nerves. The armed police patrols had been doubled in the other terminals, trebled in Terminal One. The entrance to the Belfast departure gate would be receiving special attention, she assumed. Of course they would ask her questions – the ice descended upon her as if she were two persons, as if she had left one persona and moved into another – of course there would be baggage checks and security screens. She walked across the floor of the terminal and saw the first policeman, saw the gun he was carrying. Don't hesitate, she told herself, don't even look at him. She passed the shops on the left and the cafeteria on the right and stopped in front of the ticket desk at the entrance to the hallway leading to the Northern Ireland flights.

'Belfast on the six-thirty, please.'

They were looking at her, were looking at everyone. What would she do if they stopped her, she suddenly thought, what would she say if they asked her why she was going to Belfast? Get it right next time – the thought was subconscious – your father or your mother or your brother wouldn't have come through without working it out first. She paid by cheque, collected the ticket, and walked through to the baggage X-ray. There were armed police beside it, more the other side. She ignored them and collected her bag. There's no problem, she told herself: you're English, you're carrying a genuine passport. They may have every right to stop you, but no reason. She smiled at the Special Branch officer and walked through to departures.

McGinty was waiting for her at Aldergrove. They shook hands as if they were friends, probably family. The car outside was a Ford, not his Nissan. The night seemed darker than in London; as they left the airport she saw the troops concealed in the hedges. Half-way into Belfast the priest reached into the back seat and gave her an anorak.

'Put this on, hood up when we stop.'

They entered Belfast, the streets suddenly harsh and hostile. All in the mind, she thought, all in her head. They skirted the city centre and stopped outside a terraced house. McGinty switched off the engine, took her bag and left the car. She pulled up the hood of the anorak and followed him into the house. The hallway was empty, no sound of anyone there even though it felt friendly and lived in. McGinty turned into what he would have called the front room. There was a television in the corner, switched off, sideboard to the left, settee and two armchairs, the floor carpeted and the curtains pulled tight.

'Put those on.'

On the back of one of the armchairs was a man's suit, shirt and tie, overcoat, scarf, trilby and gloves. Each of them except the shirt was black. On the floor was a pair of men's shoes, also black. On the arm of the chair was a pair of dark glasses.

She undressed and put the clothes on. Trousers, shirt and tie. Coat and shoes. Overcoat – collar turned up – then the scarf and trilby. The gloves and glasses last.

'You're ready, girl.' Conlan stood in the doorway, similarly dressed. There had been no indication that he was in the house. 'From this moment, until we get back here, until we've done what we have to do tonight, you don't say a word.'

She nodded, then followed him through the hall and kitchen and out of the back door to the alleyway at the rear. The Granada was waiting, the engine running and the gunmen around it. Four of them, she counted quickly, young and dressed in leather jackets, two with hand guns, two with submachine guns. The rear doors were open. Conlan chose the nearest, she herself walked quickly round the car to the other. One of the gunmen slipped into the passenger seat, two others on either side of herself and Conlan in the back, and the last remained at the house. The driver eased his foot off the clutch and the Granada disappeared into the night.

Only once in the next ten minutes did Conlan move, and even then the movement itself was barely perceptible – his right hand pulling down her left glove and his fingers on her pulse. Fifty-eight per minute when her heart should have been thumping and her pulse racing, he noted. He let go her wrist and stared straight ahead.

The night was darker, no stars. The Granada turned left, past the church on the corner, then swept right and stopped outside the eighth in a line of council houses. In front was a row of small gardens bordered by fences. The gunmen slid out, weapons ready and Conlan and Walker between them. There were men all round them, she knew, lost in the black but watching their every move, protecting those who came and guarding the shrine that was the house that night. From every window of the street hung black flags. In the house itself there appeared to be no light.

She followed Conlan through the small gate and up the path. As they reached the door another armed man opened it. There was one small light in the hallway, draped in black. She followed Conlan beneath it, through the door beyond, and into the kitchen.

The only illumination came from the candles on the mantelpiece. The coffin was on the bare wood table, the body laid out in it and the lid off. At each corner a man stood at attention, facing out. Each was dressed in trousers, roll-neck sweater, leather jacket and beret, all black. Each had his head bowed, and each carried an automatic rifle, reversed, the barrel pointing down. To the right of the coffin and facing it stood a line of four more people. Two women: one younger, one older, both dressed in black; and two boys, also dressed for mourning. The younger woman closest to them, the two boys, then the older woman. All standing to attention. Conlan stopped in front of the first woman, shook her hand and introduced her.

'Mrs McCann. Widow of Eamon.'

Her sister-in-law. Walker stepped forward and shook the woman's hand.

The daughter was taller than he remembered, Conlan thought, bigger shoulders, the image of her mother and her father.

'Young Eamon.'

The boy's face was blotched and red. Her nephew. She moved in front of him and shook his hand.

The ice was in her, no emotion, no querying why they should accept the stranger whom Conlan – if they knew his name – had brought to the house.

'Michael.'

Her other nephew. She stopped in front of him and shook his hand.

'Siobhan McCann, Eamon's mother. Who, of course, you know of.'

A legend in the Movement, he did not need to say. Widow of Daithi, husband and son martyred for the Cause, herself imprisoned.

Her mother.

She stopped in front of the woman.

159

Philipa Walker would have crumpled, Conlan knew, would have taken off her glasses and clasped her mother to her. Told her what it meant that she had come home.

Walker nodded and reached out her hand, took the older woman's. The grasps of both of them were firm, the handshake solid. The only concession, Conlan noted, the only difference from the other handshakes, was that as the daughter shook her mother's hand, her left hand came over to cement the mother's into hers. Then the moment was gone and the daughter straightened.

Conlan waited.

Walker turned, crossed the two paces to the coffin, and stood looking at the figure inside. What remained was thin beyond description; even Conlan, when he had first paid his respects, had needed to suppress his surprise at what little of Eamon McCann remained. It had been like looking at a skeleton. He stared again at the body then at Walker's face, at the way she stood. Shoulders straight, hands behind back, right hand in left.

This is my blood, the thought threaded her mind, this is my kith and my kin. This is my body and my soul.

She turned right and faced Conlan, held out her right hand, palm up. He understood, took the automatic rifle from the gunman at the door and gave it to her. She walked two more paces to stand between the two guards at the head of the coffin, facing out, feet apart, head bowed, weapon inverted.

The older woman moved forward, took the weapon and position of the guard of honour at the top right, the widow ushering her sons forward to take the weapons and positions of the guards at the other end of the coffin, then herself assuming the weapon and position of the sole remaining man.

Conlan left the room, the five men with him. When he returned ten minutes later the family was still in position. The guards took back their weapons and Conlan waited again, wondered for the last time what the daughter would do.

Her brother's face was so thin she could never have imagined it. She nodded slightly and Conlan cleared the room. For thirty seconds she held her brother's hand, holding it in one hand and stroking it with the other. Then she bent down and kissed his lips.

That night Philipa Walker did not sleep. For two hours after she and Conlan had left the house she and McGinty toured Belfast, the car he was driving passing with seeming impunity between the

160

official road blocks of the RUC and army, and the unofficial barriers of the Provisional IRA, the headlamps picking out the shapes of the gunmen in the shadows, and the wheels crunching over the carpets of broken glass.

Sometime that night she and McGinty rested in a safe house; sometime that night, with Conlan her only witness, Walker took the oath of membership of Cumman na mBan, the female wing of the Provisional IRA. At ten the next morning she stood silent and alone opposite the red-brick building that was St Comgalls school. At two in the afternoon she took her place with the crowd of thousands in the street outside the small council house and waited. Photographers and television crews had been stopped at the top of the street 200 yards away and round the corner. Even the army and RUC were absent, no helicopters in the sky. It was as if – no matter what happened on the route from the church to the cemetery – the 200 yards from the house to the church were sacrosanct.

The hearse was parked at the garden gate, the flowers and wreaths filling the inside and covering the roof, more on the roadway. The crowd was silent, waiting. The front door of the house opened and the men carried out the coffin. Young men, carrying it only for a few yards, clearing it from the doorway. The coffin was draped in a tricolour, on top of the flag were placed a black beret and two black gloves, one crossed over the other, in front of them a neatly folded belt. The crowd waited again, packed twenty deep either side of the roadway to the church.

The older men moved out of the house and took the coffin. They wore dark suits and overcoats, scarves and trilbies, dark glasses. The Big Men – she heard the gasp in the crowd – the full Army Council of the Provisional IRA breaking their cover and anonymity to pay their last respects. Among them, at the rear on the left, she saw Conlan.

The Army Council moved forward, carrying the coffin down the path, and stopped behind the hearse. The front door opened again and the four figures came out. The widow and mother of Eamon McCann dressed in mourning, his two sons in black jackets, berets and dark glasses. Slowly they walked down the path and took their place behind the coffin. The silence descended again and she knew what was going to happen, felt the electricity: in her body, in the air.

The gunmen filtered like ghosts from the crowd, each carrying

161

an automatic rifle, and stood in line to the left of the coffin, guns
pointing to the sky above it.

'Fire.'

She was not sure where the order came from.

The first volley echoed into the afternoon.

'Fire.'

The next and the next.

This is how I will end my days, she suddenly thought. This is
how I will cross the Styx, or whatever one crosses, to whoever or
whatever is on the other side. With a tricolour over my coffin, the
beret, gloves and belt on top, and a guard of honour firing my
farewell into the sky . . .

. . . she arrived at Venlo at eleven in the morning, 28 hours early.
The car she drove had been hired using a false identity and she had
worn gloves whenever she drove it, even when she signed the hire
form.

Maxis department store was in a shopping complex on the
Nijmegen road less than two miles from the border crossing into Germany, car parks on either side and other stores behind. The British
soldiers and their families were easy to identify, even though none of
the men were wearing uniform. She spent the next hour examining
the route in from the border crossing, and the next considering the car
parks at the shopping mall. Then she spent two hours analysing the
positions where the ASU would park the getaway vehicles, in case she
needed one, as well as the recommended routes out. At four she collected the hire car and drove the various routes, amending two slightly
as well as making plans for the roads she might take ten kilometres
from Venlo. Then she drove south and spent a further two hours
checking the countryside round the dead letter drop where she would
collect the Ruger the following day.

The light was gone.

She left Venlo and drove back to the pension at Helmond.

The following morning she woke at six, the adrenalin already
eating through her, and left at seven, her clothes casual and nondescript. By 8.30 she was in the area of the dead letter drop. The drop
itself was on the edge of a wood, the countryside flat and quiet. She
spent thirty minutes checking again that the hiding place was not
being observed, then parked the car and crossed to the wood. The
Ruger was in a shoe box wrapped in oil cloth, and buried eighteen

inches below the ground. She uncovered it, filled the soil back in the hole, swept the leaf mould over the top, returned to the car, brushed the soil from her shoes, and cleared the area. Only when she was five kilometres away and confident she was not being tailed, by car or surveillance helicopter, did she stop and open the cloth and box.

The cushioned rubber grip of the Ruger felt comfortable, even through the thin leather gloves she was wearing. She spread a clean cloth over her lap, so that any oil from the gun would not contaminate her clothing, and checked and oiled the cylinders, then checked the action. Although she assumed that the ASU would leave no fingerprints on the weapon she cleaned it anyway, then loaded it. The countryside round her was empty; she left the car, confirmed again that she was not being observed, and selected a target.

Go.

Automatically she dropped into a crouch, holding the weapon with both hands, right hand holding the gun and left wrapped round it, and fired. The trigger pull of the Ruger was a double mechanism: the first part pulling the hammer back and the second releasing it. Because the first was deliberately stiff – as a safety precaution – and therefore might affect her aim, she circumvented it by thumbing the hammer between each round. She reloaded, checked and loaded the speed loader, and burned the box and oil cloth. Then she drove back to Helmond, parked the car, changed her clothes – three-quarter-length wool overcoat, large and colourful neck scarf, dark blue trousers with lighter blue pinstripe, and black shoes that could have passed for men's – and returned to Venlo.

The early afternoon was cold, but the shopping mall was busy. She walked to the café on the corner of Maxis overlooking the car park, chose a seat near the window, and waited. The adrenalin was still there, but the ice was seeping through her body, as it always did at this moment.

She saw him the moment he drove in.

He was in his early twenties, civilian clothes but short haircut and military way of walking. VW Golf with German number plates – the order had been issued as a security measure after an ASU had singled out British soldiers by the registration details of their cars – but right-hand drive. So bloody obvious, she thought, probably had an official pass in one corner of the windscreen and the regimental magazine on the back seat.

Conlan bringing her up to a cutting edge, she understood. So this one would be easy, any others before the big one would be more difficult.

She watched as he left the VW and entered Maxis, confirmed there was no tail on the man, therefore no trap. Followed him into a shop and heard his English voice; confirmed he was a squaddie.

It was mid-afternoon.

She slipped through the other exit and turned right into one of the alleyways behind the other shops and warehouses at the rear. The overcoat was reversible, lady's blue on one side, gent's dark blue on the other. She took it off, pulled it inside out, and put it back on again. Then she pinned up her hair, took the man's cap and scarf from her pocket, put them on, and pulled the collar of the overcoat up. She had left the parking area outside Maxis as a woman, when she returned to it she passed quite easily for a man. The Ruger was in the right-hand coat pocket. She put on the soft thin leather gloves, and felt the butt of the weapon fitting comfortably into her palm, safety catch on, silencer fitted and speed loader in her left pocket. Then she crossed the parking lot and waited on the edge till the soldier appeared.

His arms were full of bags, mostly clothes and drink. He reached the car, balanced the bags against the side, and felt in his pockets for the keys. There was no one within fifty metres. She left the edge, right hand in right pocket, safety catch off. The soldier unlocked the doors, opened the back and put the packages in, then went to the driver's door and began to get in. It was cold, he thought, the road would be icy on the way back. He shut the door and looked up, saw the figure. Male, there was barely time for the image to register.

The Ruger was out of her pocket, held in her right hand. She swung the weapon in front of her, below the level of the car window, held it in the shooting position with both hands, and dropped into a slight crouch, the Ruger coming up. Pointing at him, at his head. She thumbed the hammer back, the movement smooth and practised, and pulled the trigger. Thumbed the hammer back again, eased the trigger again. The two soft-nosed rounds entered the soldier's head, the head still turning slightly. She thumbed the hammer and fired again.

6

THE ARMOUR-PLATED ROVER accelerated out of Queen Anne's Gate, the escort vehicle close behind, and cut ruthlessly through the traffic round Parliament Square.

Sinclair loved this moment: the bustle of London round him, the magnificence of Westminster in front, and the crowds wondering who was in the vehicle with the smoked-glass windows which slowed slightly then accelerated through Carriage Gates, the policemen on duty snapping to attention and saluting. Perhaps it was the speed – not necessarily of the official car, though that was a symbol. The pace of high office. The sense of slicing effortlessly through life while the poor bastards below struggled even to mark time.

There was only one moment which matched this, and that was arriving in Downing Street. One day . . . the thought was never far away.

The Rover circled the central island and stopped at the members' entrance. Sinclair walked briskly through the corridors, into the House, and took his position. Thursday afternoon, Prime Minister's question time. It was another moment he enjoyed, partly because of the knife-edge of debate – Sinclair himself was known to possess the niceties of a street-fighter when it came to such matters – but especially now that the proceedings of the House were televised and he could be seen on the front bench.

The questions were predictable, most passion being roused over the killing of the British soldier in Venlo for which responsibility had been claimed by the Provisional IRA. He pulled on his bulldog look and considered the implications. The PM's personal ratings were dipping, the Defence Secretary was known to be popular within the party should the PM fall under the proverbial bus, but now the Defence Secretary was in trouble over the Venlo incident. That evening Sinclair would address a meeting of the 1922 Committee to discuss the future of law and order in the country. Both the

165

committee and the issue would play pivotal roles in the future of the party, yet both involved considerable tightrope walking. Over the past months it had been Sinclair on whom the burden had fallen to return to the Court of Appeal a number of cases of what he referred to as *apparently* innocent members of the public sentenced on what *appeared* to be fabricated or misleading evidence. In so doing he may have won the support of the small liberal faction within the party; this evening he would make his peace with the main body.

He left the House and returned to the Home Office.

Cobra met at five. Sinclair thanked its members for attending and brought them abruptly to the first item.

Sleeper. There was no hard information on an IRA operation or hitman on the mainland. One of the problems, suggested Hamilton from Special Branch, was that the searchers could not name him in their enquiries, because by so doing they would provide the other side with precisely the sort of intelligence they themselves were trying to find. Yet by not doing so they would not uncover the information they needed.

McGuire. The Provo handler was still spreading the surveillance teams round the country like confetti, people were being pulled off other projects, overtime was up, and facilities were being stretched. With the dilemma that they wouldn't know if he really was leading them anywhere until they got there.

The killing in Venlo and the possibility of links with the McGuire investigation. No leads or connections, even pointers. Each topic discussed seemed burdened with a similar response.

The Army Council of the Provisional IRA. It was Sinclair who raised the subject, shoulders slightly bent and eyes darting. He assumed, he said, that should the Cabinet so decide, Cobra was in a position to take pre-emptive action.

Another tightrope, the Brigadier, Special Forces, knew, this time political. If his response was positive, then he would be confirming that his men had gone South, and to date there had been no political authorization for such an operation. But if it was negative then he might be accused of dereliction of duty. 'Yes,' he said noncommittally.

The contact Sinclair referred to as Michaelmass's man. No news from him. The Home Secretary came quickly to the point: was there any mileage, therefore, in contacting him? 'No.' Michaelmass's response was swift and comprised the single word, no discussion around it.

'And the royal family?' The royals are still okay? Sinclair meant; no problems with them?

'They've made it clear they dislike the extra protection, but they understand why it's there.' Denton, head of the Royal Protection Group, had not contributed a great deal to the discussion so far. 'They are prepared to put up with it for the time being.' But not *ad infinitum*: the addition was unsaid.

'Charles and Di are both at Hereford tomorrow. I'll discuss it with them then.'

Tomorrow the Prince and Princess of Wales would not be in a fit state to discuss anything, the Brigadier knew. It was fine for the Home Secretary to be glib about it, but he hadn't waited outside the door, hadn't sat in the room.

It was twenty minutes to his meeting with the 1922 Committee. Sinclair thanked them, stated again his original instruction that no one outside those present should know that the target was the royal family, confirmed the date of the next Cobra committee meeting and closed the discussion.

They were on a slippery slope with no way of getting off it – the mood as the others left the committee room was quiet. Professionals aware of the problems and fighting to overcome them, but caught in a cross-fire of contradictions and losing ground no matter what they did. The whole problem created by the intelligence delivered by Michaelmass's source; no way of checking whether it was correct; but no way, therefore, that they could ignore it. The same with McGuire: the LO leading them nowhere except up the proverbial garden path, but no way they could drop the operation on him.

'What time are they doing the course tomorrow?' Michaelmass asked Rhodes as they left.

'Midday.'

'Poor bastards. Your people still in place, I assume.'

The SAS still south of the border.

'Of course.'

Eldridge woke at three. In the two years since he had become head of the Anti-Terrorist Squad he often woke in the middle of the night. The bedroom was dark, his wife apparently sound asleep to his left. Go back and check – it was the way he always thought, the grounding he had received so many years before at the training school at Hendon – look for the obvious. But perhaps what they were looking for wasn't there yet, perhaps they were looking for something that didn't exist. The royal family, though, the Prince or Princess of Wales – in the quiet of the night the thought filled him with more horror than it did at any other time. The death hour, he sometimes called it, when the chill crept into the bones and the fear into the soul.

On his left his wife lay still and felt the tension in him.

At six he went to the kitchen and made a pot of tea. By seven he had left the house. At eight he was in his office at New Scotland Yard. At nine he briefed five of the six team leaders available, the other absent because he was liaising with an enquiry in the north of England.

'Sleeper's getting important.' Christ, what an understatement, when had the bastard not been? 'He's now priority. Go through all sources again. Pressure on informants, political and criminal. Give the undercover boys a session, tell them how much we're relying on them.'

That was unlike Eldridge, the team leaders thought; Eldridge was fair, took the pressure on himself, didn't put that sort of strain on the guys already on the edge in the field.

'Check the routine stuff, the stuff we wouldn't normally bother with because we know we won't find anything there. Membership of Irish clubs, raffle ticket holders if you can get the stubs, subscriptions to anything connected with St Patrick. Run them through the computer. See if we can get a match anywhere.'

'Gun clubs?' Sleeper wouldn't belong to a gun club, but Sleeper wouldn't be buying raffle tickets or drinking in Kilburn or Camden Town. 'Football teams with Irish connections?'

'Anything.'

Haslam woke at six. At seven he drove through the security gate at Stirling Lines, the barracks of the Special Air Service set incongruously close to a housing estate on the southern edge of Hereford, deep in the Welsh border country. By eight he and the teams were in the shooting ranges in the killing house in the centre of the complex. At ten they moved to the killing room itself.

*

Sinclair began work at eight. At nine he spoke to his constituency agent, at 9.25 he was joined by his Parliamentary Private Secretary, at ten he was informed that his car was waiting.

The Princess of Wales breakfasted at seven. At eight, because the schedule for that day had been disrupted by the Home Secretary's request, she held her daily meeting with her personal staff. At nine she was informed that Charles had arrived. It was strange seeing him at Kensington – he looked as uncomfortable as she felt. She wished him good morning and they left for Hereford, escort vehicles in front and behind, and one bodyguard in the front of the Jaguar, the Prince of Wales sitting quietly and thoughtfully in the left corner of the rear seat and the Princess in the right. Only once did he look across at her, and even then his face was expressionless. She remembered the last time he had gone into the room, remembered the nightmare when he and the boys were in Klosters.

Stand by, stand by. The voice of the operations commander echoed through Haslam's head. Stand by, stand by. He sat in the chair, the mug of tea on his knee, and tried to relax. Stand by, stand by.

Four-man team, full anti-terrorist kit: body armour and gas masks, stun grenades and Heckler and Koch MP5Ks (abbreviated to Hocklers), live ammunition. Himself and Phillips in front, two others tight behind. Door opening right to left. Stun grenades in. Himself in first, going right and clearing the door space, Phillips left. The next two in immediately, clearing the door frame. The room itself divided into sections, each man allocated a section and dealing only with that section. They had practised it so many times, worked out the positions and angles. Watched from the observation room above, or sat in the room itself, when the other teams went through their routines.

A system – that was the secret. Knowing what you and the men with you would do. Just as he and Phillips had known when they went into the sitting-room of the house in Beechwood Street. Yet in a way the training exercises at Hereford were no different. The stun grenades were the same, the procedure was identical and the ammunition was live. And amongst the dummies representing gunmen and hostages in the killing room were real people, live people, normally colleagues but sometimes VIPs being trained.

169

Today, however, was different. Even in the team room he could feel it.

They had stopped twenty minutes before, yet still wore the assault suits and body armour. The telephone rang. Phillips picked it up and passed it to him. 'He's ready.' Haslam heard the colonel's voice. 'He'll be coming through in ten minutes.'

At least the welcoming committee was restricted, the Princess thought, at least they weren't expected to make polite small talk. The brigadier, the colonel – wearing civilian clothes – the squadron major and a sergeant. And the bloody Home Secretary. The colonel put the telephone down and nodded to Charles. 'We're ready.' Now that the introductions were over his manner was polite but functional, no frills and no formalities. Get it right because we've got to get it right, next time it may not be a rehearsal.

The brigadier invited Diana, Sinclair and the two others to go with him, leaving just the colonel and the Prince. 'You did well last time, you'll do well this.' She heard the colonel's voice as she left, low and matter-of-fact. 'Just remember the instructions.' She turned back into the room.

'If my husband is doing it, then I should as well.'

The room, she meant. Not just the house clearance, like last time.

'You can't.' Sinclair's reaction was immediate.

'Why?' Rhodes looked at her.

'Because he may or may not be the target. If he knows what happens, then I should as well.'

They all looked at Charles.

Before the separation the answer might have been different. 'Her Royal Highness's decision,' he said simply.

Not the two of them together, the brigadier insisted. Make a mistake and wound one of them . . . Something goes wrong, even a ricochet, and kill them both, however . . . He and the Home Secretary left the room.

'If you would wait here with Her Royal Highness,' the colonel ordered the sergeant, then he and the Prince also left.

The room was quiet, not even a clock ticking. She shouldn't have suggested it, Diana suddenly thought, she should have contented herself with the formal instruction like last time. What's it like? she wanted to ask the man sitting opposite her. Have you done it? The colonel came back in. Everything's fine, his nod said. She followed

170

him out of the room, down a corridor, through a set of doors and into another corridor. Neither of them spoke, the building suddenly quiet. The colonel smiled at Diana and opened the door in the middle of the wall to their left.

'Don't worry. Everything will be all right.'

They stepped into the room. The walls were padded to prevent ricochets, the furniture was spread as if it was a normal sitting-room, and the lighting was low. She didn't see the darkened glass of the observation room, only the dummies. Three seated, three standing, lifelike in dress and appearance and guns in their hands. There were two empty chairs. The colonel told her to sit in the one on the right as they had entered, he himself sat in the other, to the left. A sergeant entered and adjusted the dummies, so that one was sitting next to the colonel and two were standing by him. The nerves churned through her stomach and she could barely control the urge to leave. If it's ever for real, she suddenly thought, please may it be Charles or me. Please God may it not be the boys. She was making a mistake, she suddenly thought, was tempting Fate. By sitting here now she was provoking the real thing, challenging Fate to make it happen. The sergeant repositioned the remaining dummies: one in the centre of the room, immediately opposite and facing the door, and two close to her, one standing and the last sitting. Then he left the room and closed the door behind him.

'You know the history of the regiment, of course. Founded by David Stirling in 1941.' The colonel was talking to her, telling her about Hereford. 'The barracks here are named after him.'

In two minutes it will all be over, she told herself. In two minutes she would be able to stand up and walk out. She was afraid to move, afraid to even breathe. Ninety seconds, she looked at the colonel and tried to smile. Hardly heard his words. Did not know that among them would be the trigger word to the men outside.

She couldn't stand the waiting, couldn't bear the fear. She was back in the room the last time she had been here, back in the hotel room in Klosters, being told that Charles had almost been killed in an avalanche. She was shaking with fright, almost crying, too tense to move yet every muscle and fibre in her body trembling. Let me out, she almost broke, almost did not stand the pressure. Almost moved.

'Stirling's dead now, of course, but some of the originals are still around. Tough old rogues. We call them the Dirty Dozen.'

The men outside heard the codeword.

'Go.'

The door slammed opened and the air exploded, her head and body bursting with the sudden noise and flashes. She was too frightened to move, too frightened to stay still. Tried to look for the colonel, tried to reach out for his hand, and saw the monsters. Froze in her seat.

Stuns in, two seconds, in and clear door. Haslam was moving fast right, clearing the door space, Phillips behind him going left, the two others behind them. Di seated. One gunmen standing to her right, second seated to her left. Haslam was not aware of what was happening in the rest of the room, concentrated on his sector.

She saw the flashes and remembered they were shooting live ammunition. Her head was still reeling from the stun grenades and her nostrils sniffed the first gas.

Hockler up, three-round burst first gunman. Switch target. Three-round burst second. Back to first.

The dummy fifteen inches from her head disintegrated, the shock of the bullets vibrating through her own body. More bullets, thudding round her. She wanted to run again, wanted to curl into a ball, was too tight and frightened to move. The second gunmen was twelve inches from her shoulder, also disintegrating. The first again, suddenly exploding. More shooting, round her, round the colonel, all round the room. Someone was grabbing her, roughly, no ceremony. Picking her up as if she were a rag doll. A line of monsters, black clothes and hoods and gas masks, guns over their backs. Throwing her out of the room faster than she could have run or they could have helped her. She was bouncing through the door and into the corridor, her head still spinning and her body churning.

Silence. Absolute peaceful wonderful silence.

She looked round and tried to focus, realized she was slumped against the wall at the end of the corridor, the colonel beside her. The men were round and above her, still dressed in armour and masks, the guns still in their hands or round their shoulders. More men retreating from the room, covering each other.

The door to her right opened and Sinclair came in.

'Well done –' he began to say.

'Out.' Haslam's bellow brought her to life.

Sinclair was still coming through the door, not understanding. The Princess looked up and saw one of the monsters reach out, tower over the Home Secretary, gun in one hand and the other on

Sinclair's chest, lifting him and pushing him backwards through the door. Someone else closing it.

The corridor was silent, just herself, the colonel and the men who had come into the room. Haslam put the Hockler on safety, pulled off his gas mask, and looked down.

'You all right?'

She realized how much she was shaking and tried to control it. Felt the thrill, the sheer absolute intoxicating charge of adrenalin through her body.

'Not bad for a practice.' She took his hand and pulled herself up. 'What's your name?'

'Dave.'

'Thanks, Dave. It'll be all right on the night.'

At seven-thirty that evening the Princess of Wales attended a charity gala in the West End of London. The next day she lunched at Kensington Palace. Her only guest – invited that morning – was Major Roderick Fairfax.

It was an interesting lunch, Fairfax thought as he returned to his flat afterwards, the Princess had been as he had never seen her before. Quiet, almost introspective. Even contemplative. Almost more than that.

You know what it's like, don't you – she had asked once. You understand Northern Ireland. You've served there. It was the sort of conversation he was more accustomed to having with her husband. Something's happened, he thought, felt for one moment she was going to tell him. Then the moment was gone and the royal silence prevailed.

The following day – Monday – was busy with preparations for the battalion's German tour and its transfer to the barracks at Münster. The next day Fairfax came off duty at twelve, returned to the flat, changed, and took a cab to the White Tower in Percy Street.

The restaurant was outside the normal haunts of both himself and the person he was meeting. If he saw anyone in the street whom he knew he would not go in. If he saw anyone inside whom he knew he would pretend he was looking for someone rather than go to the table reserved in the other person's name four days before.

The street was clear. He paid the driver and went inside, checked quickly, then smiled at the manager and allowed himself to be shown to the table in the corner.

173

Patrick Saunders rose and shook his hand. By the time the wine waiter reached them they had filled their own glasses from the Bollinger in the ice bucket.

In some ways the two were similar: both were self-motivated and ambitious, yet both were basically honest, even loyal. There were some things about the royal couple which Fairfax would never pass to him, Saunders knew, some things he might even lie about in order to protect them. And when Fairfax gave him the computer disks containing the engagements of the Prince and Princess of Wales over the next six months, he would have wiped from it anything which he considered personally embarrassing or a security risk. For some time now Saunders had assumed that the leaks were designed to help the couple – both of them: even that the leaks were authorized. It did not concern him, in some ways it even pleased him. Though Saunders believed deeply in his role as journalist, he believed equally passionately in the importance of the monarchy. He would report on the possibility of a royal separation or divorce, and argue with Fairfax that it was in the public interest, quoting the abdication of Edward VIII as precedent. Would debate with Fairfax on the need for the monarchy to pull itself into the twentieth century. But he also took pleasure in the mantle of royal-watcher, as distinct from member of the rat pack. Took pride in the fact that the Princess of Wales had once publicly commented that although she did not necessarily enjoy all he wrote about her, at least Saunders got his facts right. In the fact that at the reception she had thrown for journalists at the end of her Egyptian tour, it was Saunders whom she had singled out to talk to first.

'There's one thing I was going to ask.' He still remembered Klosters, the wait in the freezing cold of early morning, the shapes rising out of the snow and the stare of the men who confronted him. 'There were a couple of soldiers on the opposite slope.' Anything special, he meant, anything he could use?

'Just an exercise.' Fairfax looked him square in the face. 'Nothing worth bothering about.'

The following evening Saunders had arranged theatre tickets for himself and Philipa Walker to attend the opening night of the new Ayckbourn. They arrived early and spent thirty minutes chatting in the bar. Before they went through Saunders ordered champagne for the interval. When they returned the area was crammed, the queue at the bar itself some three deep, but the champagne was on a table in the corner. Saunders poured them each a glass then grimaced as the manager informed him that he was wanted on the telephone.

'No Cellnet?' Walker taunted him.

'Left it at home. I could tell the news desk not to phone during the performance but none of them can tell the time.'

She laughed and watched as he took the call. 'Sure, sure.' She could only hear part of the conversation above the noise of the bar. 'I have a number that might be useful.'

He took the computer notebook from his pocket, flicked open the lid, retrieved the information and read the number to the news editor, then crossed back to her.

Of course, the realization pounded through her. It was so bloody obvious. 'Very impressive.' She was smiling at him, eyes slightly teasing. 'I thought you still used a quill.'

'Not quite.' The interval was almost over; he poured the rest of the champagne. 'Computers in the newsroom, of course, but I also have a back-up system at home.'

'At home or at the flat?' Why hadn't she seen it? Why had she assumed she was the only person in the world who used a computer?

'The flat.'

They began to return to the auditorium.

'What do you use it for?'

'Everything.'

*　　　*　　　*

Belfast was quiet – no bombings or shootings. Nolan left the flat at 7.30 and was in her office in Lisburn fifteen minutes later. Overnight two surveillance teams had been pulled out of Belfast and sent to the mainland. The McGuire case, she knew, *her* case. She made herself forget the anger – set it aside rather than overcome it – and read through the fresh reports on Kelly.

What was she going to do about Kelly? How was she going to explain that she had ordered surveillance on him, background checks and phone taps, and now the reason for that operation – the original report – no longer existed? Why even bother about him? The intelligence had been low-level, a mistake. Except that it was not a mistake. Of that she was sure.

She made herself coffee, ignored the others in the office, and began at the beginning.

Clarke, Lynch and Black and the rest of the foot soldiers on the gallop – she used the Provo term. McGuire going quiet, disappearing for a few days then re-surfacing. Logical. Almost too logical.

Then McGuire – the LO, the link man with the bombers and shooters – in England.

Something not right. It was like a fishbone in her throat.

And Kelly.

But Kelly was so squeaky clean he was unbelievable. Nothing from the phone taps or the tails, nothing from background. Either he was a consummate pro, or he really was as white as he seemed.

Not Kelly. In the end even the pros resorted to certain tricks of the trade. But Kelly was so *transparently* clean that it hurt. Yet he had been named on a 14 Int report from the South. Then the file on him had been blocked; not only blocked, had disappeared completely, as if it had never existed.

It was not her business, she told herself. London was in charge, and if London pulled a file then London had a reason. But if Kelly really was so clean, then Kelly might not be the reason for the file being pulled. And if he wasn't, who or what was?

She sat back and switched herself off from the noise around her.

The report referred to the Republic and was sourced through 14 Int; the section of 14 Int most likely to be operating in the South was the SAS; therefore the report itself probably originated with the SAS. The report was blocked either because the SAS were not supposed to go South, or because of some other aspect of the operation from which the report had come. Then some desk johnny had slipped up, let part of it through, even though it was downgraded to F7. And now London was getting its knickers in a twist and pretending the file – and therefore the operation which had provided the intelligence for it – had never existed.

Probably, she thought. At least possibly. The games people play. Except this one wasn't hers. Her game at the present time was the informant Hanrahan, now in the Provos' security section. The next evening Brady would have his first meet with him.

It was interesting, though. As if she had thrown a pebble into a pond and was watching the circles spreading from it, then the surface of the water settling and no one knowing that she had thrown the pebble. Except that *she* knew.

There was one way to find out, and even that might not come off. She dialled the number, beginning with the 0432 prefix. Official, through Lisburn or MI5 in London, even through 14 Int, and she would get nowhere. Unofficial and she might stand a chance.

'Yes.' The voice was male, no identification of the number.

The sergeants' mess at Hereford was in a modern block at the side of the main barracks area, with access through its own security gate.

'I'd like to get a message to Dave.' She was not even sure it was his correct name.

The caller was Irish, the man who had answered thought immediately, possibly IRA. So how did she have the number? Why was she phoning the sergeants' mess? Two sergeants with the first name Dave.

'I met him on a selection course in Germany eighteen months ago; I assume he was up from the Long Range School.'

Haslam had been in Germany about that time, Haslam had instructed at the NATO school at Lake Constance. And Haslam's first name was Dave. 'Who wants him?' he asked.

'The name I was using on the course was Maggie. I'll give you a number.'

The caller was genuine, he decided, too much confidence, too much authority to be otherwise. Haslam pulling rank with a WRAC and getting his leg over, he also thought. Except that Haslam was too careful for that; Haslam would have covered his tracks or made other arrangements.

The number of the flat in Malone Park or her office in Lisburn, Nolan wondered. Home and the line would not be secure. She gave him one of the direct lines. 'If you can't pass it on could you come back to me?' If he's away, she knew she had been understood, if for some reason he's out of bounds.

At seven that evening Nolan, Brady and Farringdon met to discuss Brady's meeting with Hanrahan – where Brady was seeing him, whether any back-up was necessary and how much pressure they should be putting on him. It was interesting, Nolan noted, that while she and Farringdon both referred to Brady – a colleague and, as far as she was concerned, as close to a friend as one could be in this business – merely as Brady, they referred to Hanrahan – an IRA killer turned informant – as Frank.

At 7.30 Brady left Lisburn. Nolan received the telephone call from Haslam at eight.

'Where are you?' He did not identify himself.

'Work.'

Both lines were therefore secure.

'Fine.'

'Thanks for phoning.' Why hadn't she raised the Kelly issue with Farringdon, she wondered, why hadn't she brought it up after Brady had left for the meet?

'We're running something on a Provo suspect named Kelly.' She almost expected Haslam to interrupt, to say that he knew the man. 'He was included in a report from 14 Int. We've been looking at him but he seems whiter than white.'

'They do.'

'This one is.'

So what's the problem – the silence again.

'The question is: if he's clean, then why is he on an intelligence report?'

'You've tried your own people?'

'I've asked for more details but there are problems.'

'Why should that be the case?'

'Probably because the report stated he was seen in the Republic.'

'In that case it wouldn't be us. Probably Dublin Special Branch.'

'It was sourced 14 Int.' Therefore not RUC or SB, north or south of the border. Therefore you or us. But we don't go South. Therefore you.

'What's so important about him?'

'I'm not sure.'

'Give me the details.'

Brady was late. He should have finished his meet with Frank Hanrahan and been back by nine. The office was like a morgue. It was the wrong thing to think, Nolan knew. She sat at her desk, the fear gnawing through her stomach, and waited. Of course there were reasons why he was so late, she told herself: Frank had something for him and they were going through it, making sure Frank was delivering, making sure Frank was covered. At 10.30 she heard a noise in the corridor.

'He didn't show.' Brady slumped in the chair and took the glass of Bushmills which Nolan poured him. 'I waited an hour, thought I was being set up and almost pulled out, but nothing.'

'You should have requested back-up.'

Except that back-up sometimes gave the game away, exposed you as much as it protected you. Depending on where you were and who was providing it. She splashed some whiskey into a glass for herself and refilled Brady's.

'I'll run a check on his house.' She reached for a telephone.

'No point. I looked on the way back. Nobody's there – wife or kids, even his car.'

It was gone eleven. There was nothing they could do tonight. Not much they could do anyway. She washed the glasses and drove to the flat. The telephone rang at five. She reached for it and made herself stop, gave herself time to wake up and checked that the Browning was by the bed. Nobody phoned at such an early hour. Except the Provos. If the bastards had found out where you lived and were checking you were at home before they threw a bomb through your window or machine-gunned you to death.

'They've found a body.' She recognized Brady's voice immediately. 'Near Keady.' Keady was in South Armagh, close to the border.

They wouldn't go near it yet in case it was a come-on. In case the Provos had put a sniper in the hills above the body, or a pressure pad bomb beside it, or where they would stand as they waited for the area to be cleared.

'On my way.'

Lisburn was bleak and grey, even inside. Nolan made them each a coffee while Brady confirmed the details with the RUC and arranged transport. By seven they were sitting in the rear seat of an army Land-Rover, the dawn still half an hour off and the rain sheeting down. The road in front of them was taped off and the body was in a ditch on the right, the soldiers unseen in the fields around and the sniffer dogs checking for explosives.

Sorry, Frank, she almost thought. If we hadn't turned the screw on you you wouldn't be lying there now, the holes in your head and your blood trickling into the mud. Your decision in the first place though, Frank, your decision to join the Provos, to take part in the Tennent Street job. We only used you for what we believed was right. Don't worry, though, we'll stick to our part of the bargain, make sure the boy and girl get their ticket out of Belfast.

The army captain came up the road and stopped by the window. 'It's clear.'

179

They left the Land-Rover and followed him, under the tape and past the Green Jackets and RUC patrols, both Nolan and Brady wearing combat jackets, bullet-proof vests and woollen hats pulled down. The spooks: the soldiers watched them and nodded to each other. The stiff in the ditch was somehow connected to the security services.

The body was face up and naked, the hands tied behind the back, and black tape had been wound round the head, covering the face, the two holes in it – round the eyes – where the executioner had placed the weapon.

Not the right build for Frank, the thought seeped into her, wrong colour hair above the death tape. The wrong height and body for Frank, for a man Frank's age and background. She watched as an RUC inspector knelt by the body and wound the tape off the head, the face beneath it white but blotched with red where the blood had run.

'You know him?' The inspector looked up.

Flynn, the getaway driver for the Tennent Street killing, the informant who had fingered Hanrahan in the first place.

'No.'

So now we know, Frank: whose game you're playing and whose rules you're playing to. And now you're in trouble, Frank. You and the wife and the kids.

They thanked the policeman and walked back to the Land-Rover.

The message appeared in the *Irish Times* that morning. The following day Logan left Belfast, drove to Dublin, checked in to the Westbury, used the false driving licence and credit card to hire a Hertz car, then drove west to Lough Corrib. Because he was a careful man, however, he stayed at a different hotel, in a different village.

Haslam's call came at five. All day Nolan had waited – for the reports of the post mortem and any news of Hanrahan.

'The case you were asking about. Nothing to do with us.'

Our job and our information, she heard it in his voice. The line secure against the other side but not necessarily against our own people.

'Thanks, anyway.'

'Give me a call next time you're over.'

'I'm in London tomorrow. Any chance of a drink?' Am I reading you correctly? What exactly *are* you saying?

'Have to be a quick one. What flight?'

'The eight-fifteen.'

'I'll meet you.'

She checked for updates on Hanrahan, signed off and returned to Malone Park. The next morning she drove to Aldergrove, arriving early so that she was guaranteed a seat. In the twenty minutes that she waited in the departure lounge she recognized two of the other passengers, one from the Firm and the other an SAS sergeant from 14 Int, though she acknowledged neither and neither acknowledged her.

At Heathrow she let the two men leave the plane first, cleared the Special Branch checks and followed the maze of corridors into Terminal One. Arrivals was on the first floor, departures on the ground, the escalator and stairs to her right. Nolan took the stairs – it was difficult to turn and run on an escalator – walked past the baggage carousel, and waited by the enquiry desk. The lounge was busy, humming with noise. Haslam passed her and walked to the short-term car park. Nolan checked that he was not being tailed and followed. As she entered the car park the Audi stopped, Haslam leaned across and opened the passenger door, and she got in. Fifteen minutes later they were ordering coffee in the lounge of the Holiday Inn on the fringe of the airport complex.

'The intelligence identifying Kelly was from an SAS report based on an operation in the Republic.' Haslam was seated so that he could observe those around him, Nolan similarly positioned. 'Kelly was seen in circumstances which roused suspicion. The identification of Kelly, and others, was not the reason for the operation, but because of the circumstances our people on the ground reported back on everything they saw.'

'It was sourced 14 Int.'

'Yes and no. Yes in that 14 Int was the formal channel. No in that the report went straight to London.'

'Why?'

'No idea. You know how the system works as well as I do.'

The coffee was served.

'So why was Kelly's name included if he wasn't on file before and we can't find anything on him in Belfast?'

'Again, no idea. I wasn't on the operation.'

'You said Kelly was seen under suspicious circumstances. What exactly?'

Haslam seemed to sweep the lounge before he spoke, no movement of the head, simply of the eyes, and then almost imperceptible.

'Six weeks ago the regiment was ordered to stake out certain individuals in the Irish Republic. One of the teams was assigned to a man who takes fishing weekends on Lough Corrib.'

Which individuals, she wanted to ask, why were they being targeted? How did you know about them, what was the object of the exercise? Haslam would only tell her if he wanted to, she understood, and he himself might not know the details. It was the way both the Firm and the regiment worked.

'The team in question were in an OP near the cabin which this particular individual owns. One evening he went to a local hotel. There was nothing unusual about that, there are several in the area and he visits them all regularly. But because of the nature of the operation a note was made of who was in the hotel at that time. Kelly was one of them.'

'Why was the operation so important?'

The question was both reasonable and unreasonable. Why did your people think it necessary to note those in a hotel visited by your target? Why did they think it important enough to include them in their report?

Haslam swept the lounge again, as if he was checking, as if he was deciding whether or not to tell her.

'The men we were targeting were all members of the Army Council.'

Christ, she thought, controlled it. What the hell was going on? What was the government playing at? There was always pressure on Whitehall because of the situation in the North, of course, and there was always talk that the security forces knew the identities and locations of the key decision-makers. Always the demand, when an incident exceeded being a shooting or bombing and became an atrocity, for the government to deal once and for all with the men at the top.

'It was purely an exercise, I understand.'

But there would be a reason. The SAS wouldn't be sent South, wouldn't be ordered to stake out the Army Council, merely as an exercise.

The items converged in Haslam's head: the SAS knowing where

the Provisionals' leaders were every hour of every day and the Prince and Princess of Wales at Hereford. Not just at Hereford, going through the ordeal of the killing room.

'How did your people get Kelly's name?'

'Vehicle registration plus hotel register. The lads weren't properly dressed to follow our man in, so they noted the numbers and details of the vehicles in the car park, then went in after the place was shut up and checked the register.'

'Kelly was on the hotel list?'

'Yes.'

Sloppy, they both knew.

'And one of the vehicles was registered to him?'

'Yes.'

Very sloppy.

'Northern Ireland plates?'

'Yes.'

Downright criminal. But only if Kelly had something to hide, only if Kelly was meeting someone he shouldn't have been meeting.

'Who else was at the hotel?'

'There were three other guests. Two American – a married couple – and one English. Both groups using cars rented in Dublin. The names and personal details on the register matched the details on the rental agreements.'

A member of the Army Council making possible contact in a bar. Four people in the bar – excluding the barman and any locals. Therefore four possible contacts. But only one Irish, therefore only one a real runner. The logic was solid, seemingly infallible. Typical London.

'Names?'

'The Englishman was Michael James Donaldson, Findlers Avenue, Hemel Hempstead.' He had committed nothing to paper. 'The Americans were Alvin and Cy Morton, of Milwaukee. Alvin Jnr,' he added with a smile. 'Cy short for Cynthia.'

'You said that the car rental details confirmed the hotel details.'

'Yes. According to the driving licence details Donaldson would be about thirty, the Mortons in their late fifties.'

'Which rental companies?'

'Both Hertz.'

He knew what she was going to ask next.

'Has anyone confirmed the car rental details?'

183

'I assume so. But not us. That's not our job.'

'Of course not.'

She sat still, running through the options and checking that she had missed nothing. 'What about the barman?'

'Clean.'

'Locals?'

'No names on file.'

'And your people are still there?'

'Yes.'

'Give me a number where I can reach you.'

The number Haslam gave her was a direct line into the operations room at Hereford.

'They'll be expecting you. What name shall I tell them?'

'Catcher.'

If she hurried, she thought, she might make the ten-thirty shuttle. 'Thanks for the help,' she said. 'Watch your back,' Haslam told her.

A message to telephone Brady urgently was on her desk. She tried the number, swore when it was engaged, poured a coffee and logged three requests, each through London. The first was for a check with the DVLC at Swansea on the driving licence issued to Michael James Donaldson, Findlers Avenue, Hemel Hempstead; the second was for an FBI check on Alvin and Cynthia Morton of Milwaukee; and the third was for copies of all Hertz car hire agreements made in Dublin over the past two months. The first would take minutes, an hour at most depending on who was on duty. The second might take several days and the third the same.

It was time to make it official, she told herself, time to cover herself. She tried Brady's number again, then Farringdon's. Brady was still engaged and Farringdon was in London. She spoke to Farringdon's secretary, requested an urgent meeting with him, confirmed that she would see him at 7.30 the following morning, and began to draft her report. She had finished the first two paragraphs when the telephone rang. Brady, she assumed, something about Hanrahan.

'Your DVLC query reference Michael James Donaldson.'

'Yes.'

'The name and address are not registered, and the licence number is incorrect. We're running cross-checks now in case any of the details are wrong, but I thought you'd like to know.'

None of the details were wrong, she knew. Neither Haslam nor the men who had broken in to the hotel at Kilmore would make that sort of mistake.

'Thanks. It's appreciated. I'll be waiting.'

Her fingers drummed the desk top and the nerves wound in her stomach. Something up and running, something Kelly had led them to but which didn't involve him. Her thoughts were cold and calm, trying to work out what it meant and what she could do. If the Americans were involved, perhaps it was connected with IRA money from the States, even weapons. She telephoned the number in Hereford, identified herself as Catcher and asked for Dave.

'He'll contact you in fifteen minutes.'

The telephone rang – London confirming the first driving licence report. The telephone rang again.

'Mick's back in town.' It was Brady, using their personal code-name for Hanrahan. 'I'm seeing him this evening.'

'I'll come with you.'

It would be against the rules, of course. Every informant or agent had two handlers, so that if one died or was killed, or simply disappeared, his or her knowledge would not be lost.

'I'll pick you up on the way.'

The telephone rang again. 'Dave.'

She recognized Haslam's voice anyway. 'Thanks for the coffee this morning.'

'Pleasure.' He knew the reason for the call.

'Kelly's clean. It's Donaldson. His documents were false. You said your people were still in place. It's unlikely he'll show again, but it's worth keeping an eye open for him.'

'I'll make sure the right people know.'

'One other thing. I'm passing it upstairs. The meeting's tomorrow morning at seven-thirty. I'm drafting the report now.'

'Good idea.'

You'll cover your source, of course, not say where you got the information. Unspoken.

Of course. Also unspoken.

She thanked him and settled back to the report, working out what she could say and how she could say it, how she could cover both herself and Haslam. The telephone rang again. Bound to be London asking what she was playing at. Thank God she had at least begun to make it official. She picked it up and snapped a 'hello'.

'Dave.' Haslam identified himself again, even though there was no need, and waited for her confirmation. 'We might be in business.' Why, she thought, how? 'Our man's going walkabout again. One of the cars in the area is a hire car. We have the details but haven't yet checked the hirer.'

'I'll arrange it.'

He read her the information.

'I'll get back to you.'

The other phone was ringing. She ignored it, checked the Dublin directory, and telephoned the main Hertz number.

'Airport here.' She read the vehicle details. 'One of our customers might have lost a ring down the seat. Could you tell me which office has it at the moment?'

'I'll check.'

She invented a story in case it was the airport branch which had rented out the vehicle.

'Upper Leeson Street.' The branch in the city.

'Thanks.' She checked the directory and dialled the number. 'Maintenance here.' She gave the vehicle details. 'We might want to have a look at it. When's it due back?'

She could have at least some surveillance in place in two hours, full teams within six. Once she'd contacted Farringdon in London and tried to explain it to him, once Farringdon had explained to Cutler why Nolan had gone out on a limb and not briefed him before. Low-level stuff, she decided she would tell him, simply finding out who Donaldson was and what he might be playing at.

'Mr Donaldson?'

Christ, she thought. Yes, she almost said. 'No idea, I just wanted to know about the car.'

'It was returned half an hour ago.'

Brady was grim-faced and both of them were armed, Browning Hi-Powers in waist holsters and the MP5K beneath the newspaper on the floor to the right of the driver's seat. Just like last time, she thought, except that it was she who was driving and except for the heavy knitted sweater laying apparently haphazardly on the back seat. Concealed in the sweater, the barrel down a sleeve and the pistol grip immediately accessible inside the neck of the sweater, was an eight-round Remington pump action shotgun, the barrel shortened and the butt removed.

186

In summer there would have been cars parked at the beauty spot, children playing and couples walking. Tonight the location was bare and bleak, the leaves gone from the trees and the ground hard and damp.

So what's up, Frank? It was Brady. Where've you been? Why didn't you make the meet? You heard about Flynn, Frank? Nolan took over. Course you heard about him. But when, Frank? Before or after he was stiffed? Coincidence? Chance that your wife's mother was taken ill and that you and the family went to visit her? Why didn't you tell us, Frank? It was Brady again. Why make us think you're not telling us the truth? We've kept our part of the deal, Frank, the first half of our part at least. Time for you to keep yours. Time for you to deliver.

So what *would* she have done if Frank had been involved in the Flynn shooting? What would she have done if he'd told her after the event, explained that he'd had no option, that the Provos' security section, the sweenies, had investigated Flynn and found him guilty. That either he had been the shooter brought in for the execution or, more likely, had been aware of what was about to take place but had been unable to stop it. And that was the way out, because if Frank had told her afterwards, then there was no way she could have prevented it. But what if he had told her before? But he hadn't. Hadn't known of the execution, hadn't even suggested he was involved.

'How's the boy, Frank?' They had begun to walk away from each other. Hanrahan turned back and looked at Nolan. 'A little something for you.' She felt in her coat pocket and gave him an envelope.

He slit it open and took out the contents, looked at her then back at them. The first was a prospectus from Imperial College, London; the second was a *curriculum vitae* – the name deleted – of an engineering postgraduate from Imperial; and the third was a copy of a letter offering him his first job.

Thirty grand a year and he was no more than 25 years old, Hanrahan read. Company car, company pension, favourable share option, whatever that meant. And when he himself had been banged up the Provos had paid his missus a pension of twenty quid a week.

''Night, Frank.'

*

187

Farringdon had read her report before the meeting. The offices were quiet, it was still too early for the others. Half an hour earlier Michael Logan had left Belfast for England and his next trip into Europe.

'Summarize everything for me.' Farringdon sat back and looked at her.

'Kelly was named on an intelligence report from London as being observed in the Republic. There was no other information and no security record on him. Surveillance and the normal checks also revealed nothing. Checks were also made of other guests who had stayed at hotels where he had stayed in the Republic. One of these, Michael Donaldson, was shown to be false – false name, false driving licence. The same man, again using the Donaldson identity, was in the Republic two days ago.'

Farringdon was still sitting back, still looking at her.

'What happened the first time you requested further information from the Kelly file?'

'It was blocked.'

They had already been through it.

'And the second?'

'London said it didn't exist.'

'You referred to checks on hotels at which Kelly stayed.'

'Yes.'

'How many?'

She shrugged.

'One or more than one?'

She shrugged again.

'It was good work finding Donaldson, whoever he is.'

But . . . she waited.

'But was it coincidence that you picked the right hotel, or did it come from information supplied by a source?'

'A source.'

'Who?'

She shook her head.

Farringdon pursed his lips and tried to work out what to do.

'Good work,' he repeated to himself. His hands were in front of his face and his fingers played against his lips. 'I'm seeing the DoI at ten. He and I will discuss this then he'll pass it up the line.' Farringdon was all right, she knew, Cutler as well. As long as they trusted you and as long as you delivered. 'London will make sure that its story on the Kelly file is watertight. I suggest you do the same with yours.'

Nolan was informed at four; at nine the following morning she waited in her office for the meeting with the unnamed man from London.

Two cars had been hired under the name of Donaldson in the past six weeks, the checks of hire car companies in Dublin had revealed, seven over the previous two years. All rented by presenting a credit card as deposit, then paying cash and retrieving the invoice when the vehicle was returned. Plus false driving licence. So who are you, she thought, what are you up to? Whatever it was it was nothing to do with the American couple called Morton; overnight the FBI had cleared both. She left the office and went upstairs.

Cutler was seated behind his desk, Farringdon to his right and the man from London to his left, one chair remaining empty. The emissary from Gower Street was seeking to exude the aura of power, she thought. He was younger than both Cutler and Farringdon, probably her own age, his suit was well cut and his tie expensive.

Officially, Nolan had been informed, he was here to consider her request for computer access to hire car rentals in Dublin and surveillance on the man calling himself Donaldson. Unofficially, she assumed, he was in Lisburn to find out how she gained information from a file which was blocked.

'The Donaldson material,' Penrose sat comfortably, arms spread and legs crossed. 'Perhaps you could explain.'

Too obvious, Nolan thought. 'Explain what?'

'The requests for access to the car rental computers and the surveillance stand-by.' What else could I ask you to explain, his smile said it all. Not just the smile, the way he smiled. What else do you have to answer for?

'Donaldson is a cover. So who's using it and why? Does it or does it not affect us? It seemed to me that there was one way to find out.'

'But why Donaldson?'

'How Donaldson, you mean.' It was interesting that boredom had already set in, that she already knew she could run rings round him. How she was aware that both Cutler and Farringdon understood and were merely waiting to see how she played it. 'How did we single Donaldson out in the first place? Why did we run the check on him which indicated that the name was false?'

It was not the way Penrose had intended to raise the matter, not the time in the interview at which he had planned to ask it. 'Yes.'

'Obvious.' She looked at the other two then back at him. 'A report from 14 Int names a Northern Ireland citizen, Kelly. We carried out standard checks and surveillance on him.' She was casual. Not quite casual. Matter-of-fact.

But how does that lead you to Donaldson, she knew he would ask. How does that take you south of the border?

'We checked on Kelly's movements.' She gave him no time to speak. 'He's a rep. We therefore checked on who he had visited and where he had stayed, then ran checks on the names that appeared.' She had pulled strings to get it done, had covered her tracks with the care that Farringdon had suggested, but even now there were holes. If the man from London was sharp enough to see them. 'That was how we came up with the Americans and Donaldson. The FBI have just cleared the couple, as you know.' It was a nice touch, Farringdon thought – suggesting that the man from London was in touch with the situation. 'Then the DVLC in Swansea came up with the fact that the name Donaldson, and the driving licence he was using, were false.'

The nameless man from Gower Street didn't know a thing, she began to think. Hadn't asked her directly about the report, hadn't asked what had led her to the car rental companies. The man wasn't big league from London, he was a postman, delivering questions and taking back answers. When she and Cutler and Farringdon were collecting their pensions the man from London would still be the same. Swanning in from Gower Street or Thames House and pretending he was God Almighty when all he was was a public school queen who'd made it as a delivery boy.

Someone in London was playing games, she understood, someone in London wanted to find out how much she knew. Even though they were on the same side.

'Excellent.' Penrose shifted in the seat and folded his legs the other way. 'The requests won't be a problem.' He spoke as if the decision was his. 'Let's talk detail.'

The meeting ended at 11.15. At 12.30 Penrose took the shuttle back to Heathrow. The debriefing with Michaelmass began at four.

Catcher was good, Michaelmass was aware he was thinking. Of

190

course she had enjoyed an advantage, of course she had known more than he had allowed Penrose to know. But she had still covered herself. Assuming, of course, that her account of how she had obtained the information on Donaldson was not entirely accurate. First the McGuire lead, even though it was getting them nowhere, now this. He was both listening to Penrose, interrupting when necessary, and thinking about Catcher. Interesting that he was still calling her that.

They moved to the logistic and political problems of the operations in the Republic and whether the authorities in Dublin should be informed. If so, what and how much they should be told, and if not, how the surveillance teams could be put in and kept in place. Whether MI5 should keep the operation to itself.

'Theoretically, of course, the Republic is the responsibility of Six.' Penrose used the word *theoretically* to identify his position on the subject. 'If Donaldson *is* IRA, then the chances are that he'll be coming back into our domain. Either the North or the mainland. And then, theoretically speaking again, Six should hand him back to us.'

But MI6 were also operating in the North – it was unstated. MI6 was in the same team, but MI6 was also the opposition. Especially in the present climate, especially when the death of communism and the new world order meant that each of the security services was not only seeking to protect its traditional but dwindling spheres of influence but also looking for new ones.

Is this Catcher or is it you, Michaelmass almost asked, knowing it was both. But with Catcher it was something else. McGuire was hers, he could imagine the way she would argue, then somebody took McGuire away. Now Donaldson was hers; she was the only one to even spot him, had broken the rules to get him. No way she was handing him on a plate to someone else, no way she was letting it go this time.

The two files were on his desk – he had flicked through them while Penrose was talking. The first was hers – the initial SAS course and the shooting at Beechwood Street; the refresher at Hereford and the Firm's course at The Fort. And the second was the complete file containing the reference to Kelly, blocked to everyone else. Yet somehow Catcher had found out, he thought, somehow Catcher had not only worked out something no one else had seen, but had also managed to cover her tracks.

'Thank you.' He nodded and Penrose left the office. Donaldson was theirs, Michaelmass was clear on the issue, they would keep him. He keyed Cutler's line on the scrambler and remembered when he himself had been Director of Intelligence in Lisburn. 'Reference the discussion this morning. Tell Catcher she's done a good job.' You and Farringdon as well for supporting her, it was unstated. 'The requests are authorized. Just make sure she watches her back for the opposition.'

'Which one?'

Michaelmass understood, and to show he understood he laughed.

Walker arrived in Mons the morning after leaving Dover and 24 hours before Conlan had specified. The town centre was smaller and more compact than she had imagined, the streets round the Grand Place narrow and winding. That afternoon she ran through the routine: the location of the hit, the streets leading to it and away from it, the positioning of the getaway cars and the dead letter drops where she would collect the weapon and dispose of it after the shooting.

Both the instructions and the target were more specific than on the last occasion, she had already noted. Mons was twenty kilometres from SHAPE headquarters, the target a specific soldier and a specific rank, even his timetable and the location of the killing provided for her. Conlan winding up the pressure, putting her through her paces, making sure she was still up to scratch.

There were difficulties, of course. The square where the captain would park was straightforward, she could identify him immediately. After that he would go to the fishing and sports gun shop, then to the delicatessen. Again not difficult, she could lose herself among the restaurant tables already positioned in the Grand Place, the people at them enjoying the early spring sun but nevertheless wearing overcoats. After that he would spend half an hour having his hair cut at a small salon close to the alleyway leading back to the square. That was when she would slip into the church on the western side of the square and change.

The problems were the number of people around – not that many, but more than in the car park at Venlo – and, again, the time of day. Late afternoon, when there were no shadows to hide in, no darkness to conceal her before and after. London would be the same, she knew. When she had decided how and where to go after PinMan. She was so close to PinMan now that she could sense it, feel it. One night with Saunders and she would have the key to his secrets. She thought about it, how he would react, how she herself would react, then walked to the Grand Place and took a coffee at one of the tables.

The next day – Saturday – was warmer. Even when she collected the Ruger from the wood outside the town she smelt a change in the seasons, as if spring was on the way. In Mons, even in late morning, there were more tables and chairs in the square and more people on the streets. She checked that the ASU had placed the getaway cars in position, then walked to the other side of the town, collected the car she had organized for herself, drove it to the side road under the bridge carrying the main road west, and walked the two kilometres back to the square.

It was midday, time ticking away.

She was wearing the same clothes as before. It was the last time the technique would work. Next time – she assumed there would be a next time – with the weather turning warmer and the evenings lighter, she would not be able to muffle her appearance with a hat and scarf.

It was almost one. The nerves were in her stomach, her entire body alert, and the Ruger was in the right-hand coat pocket. At two she checked the cars again, at three the square where the captain would park his Mercedes. It was almost 4.15, the nerves suddenly gone. She left the Grand Place and waited, saw the Mercedes turn into the square. Right on time, she thought, the ASU had done their job well.

The captain was in his late twenties: brogues, cavalry twills and tweed jacket, short sharp stride, almost clipped, as if he was on the square at Sandhurst. She watched as he visited the shooting and fishing shop, then the delicatessen, stood twenty metres from him as he entered the hairdressing salon. Half an hour to go, her mind ran through the timetable, broke it down into its constituent parts. Twenty minutes to wait, five to change, five to position herself at the top of the street near the alleyway leading to the square. She wouldn't be there too early, didn't want any witnesses remembering someone hanging round.

Twenty minutes before the target left the barber's. The Grand Place was busy, most of the tables filled. She walked through them, along the cobbles of the pavement opposite the town hall.

'Philipa.'

The voice was male. Behind her. She froze, did not show it. A set-up – the thoughts came fast – the handler tailed, a member of the ASU compromised. Someone low down tortured and turned; someone high up paid their pieces of silver.

Her hand was already easing off the safety catch of the Ruger. Bring it out of the pocket before she began shooting and the suppressor might hinder movement slightly – her brain worked clinically through the options. Fire through the cloth and reduce the chance of a first hit but increase the chances of the public not realizing it was her. Depends who it is, depends how many there are.

Volvo two streets away, the thoughts were thicker, faster. Audi and Opel also close. The Opel, she decided. If she got that far. West out of the town, leave the Opel and jump over bridge. The Merc below, where she had parked it that morning.

SAS, she knew. Four-man team, almost certainly back-up. She wouldn't even get the Ruger out of her pocket.

'Philipa Walker.'

She picked up the slightest trace of Irish in the voice.

Not SAS. The SAS chose their killing grounds more carefully – a back street or alley where they wouldn't be seen. Therefore she stood a chance. She began to turn. Not obviously slowly, but slow enough to take in everything and everyone. Her movement was a casual circle, right to left, seemingly innocent but deliberate, facilitating her gun hand and giving the gun itself more cover.

'Gerard.' He was rising, standing. It was happening so quickly, yet her instinct, her training, allowed her to see it in slow motion. One chance, she knew, finger increasing pressure on trigger. Not SAS, he was too slow. If he had been SAS she would have been dead by now.

'Gerard Gray. You remember. Barclays International last summer. You were doing a job for Price Waterhouse.'

Christ, she thought, felt one tension snap free and the other take its place. Eighteen minutes before the captain left the barber's shop, for her to change and be in position.

'Gerard.' She slipped the safety back on. ''Course I remember. How was the river party?'

He ignored the question and asked what she would like to drink.

It was almost as if Conlan had planned it, as if it was what she needed. The one thing you couldn't cater for, the one thing that tested how sharp you were.

'Mineral water, ice and lemon.'

194

Fifteen minutes before the alleyway. Five minutes with Gray, six at most. Then change and get in position. As long as nothing else happened.

'The last person I expected to meet here.' He called to a waiter and ordered her drink.

'So what are you doing?' She couldn't afford to delay, but had to spend at least a few minutes with him.

'Fed up with London and fancied a weekend break, decided to visit Waterloo.' The site of the battle was half-way between Mons and Brussels. 'What about you?' He was expansive, confident.

'More or less the same. Not the Waterloo bit, of course.'

Thirteen minutes. Time running out.

The waiter brought her mineral water.

She knows I opted out of taking her to the river party because I didn't think I'd get her into bed, he thought.

'Here by yourself?'

'Sort of, sort of meeting friends.'

Twelve minutes.

'How about dinner tonight?'

'Nice try, Gerard. Have to go.' She took a sip of the mineral water, kissed him on the cheek, and left before he could object.

Ten minutes.

The church was clear. She changed and walked quickly to the alleyway.

Four forty five. The Mercedes still parked and the captain on time. He was scratching his neck, as if the barber had not brushed away the hairs.

'Excuse me.'

She was three paces behind him.

He turned and saw the Ruger.

7

ELDRIDGE HAD BEEN AWAKE SINCE FOUR. One day the job would kill him, he thought, one day he'd hear a small sound behind him, see someone folding on to the ground and gasping for breath, and realize that he'd died of a heart attack. Except he'd be moving too fast to even notice.

The mug of tea was untouched, probably cold by now. He'd made it an hour before, and for the hour before that he had lain in bed, staring into the darkness and wondering about Sleeper. Please God may they get the bastard before he got the Queen or Prince Charles or Lady Di. If he actually existed, if the royal threat was real. He emptied and washed the mug, dried it and placed it neatly back on the shelf, and left the house.

It was not quite six. Early shift: he remembered the old days on the beat – how it was the shift he enjoyed the most, the pavements smelling of overnight rain and London coming to life. Most days now, especially after the last promotion and the danger the new job carried, he drove or was driven to work. Yet sometimes he felt this removed him from the man in the street, took him into the world of the Sinclairs and the Michaelmasses. And sometimes he needed to go back down to where he'd started, to walk through Shepherd's Bush market, Dalston Junction or North End Road, see the real world in which the bastards from the Middle East or North Africa or Ireland lurked. Not that he had anything against the peoples of those areas, just against the bombers and killers who came from their midst.

The station was almost empty, it was too early even for the commuters, no flower stall outside and the news stand not yet open, the clerk in the ticket office on the right staring at him bleary-eyed. He bought a single to Victoria and walked down the stairs to the platform. Miracle, he glanced at the board and thought, train in five minutes.

So where were they going wrong? Where the hell was Sleeper?

The train rolled into the station. He got on, closed the door behind him, and sat facing forward, the train pulling away. South London was still lost in the dark and he was the only passenger in the carriage. One day Sleeper would make a mistake, he told himself, one day something would crop up that Sleeper or his controller hadn't allowed for.

The train rattled in to Victoria.

Another day started, one day less to find Sleeper and tomorrow already lost. Tomorrow he would take part in a discussion on counter-terrorism and civil liberties at the Police College at Bramshill, attended by high-flyers in the service and the radical lawyers and solicitors who opposed them. Good for the image, the Commissioner had said, show the other side that the authorities were prepared to be open. He'd argued against it, would argue again today, plead the time it would cost him. But in the end he would lose, in the end he would waste half a precious day. He left Victoria and walked the 800 yards to New Scotland Yard.

Some of the team were already in, computer checking the information which had come through after the shooting at Mons and looking for a cross-match with the killing at Venlo. The department had its mix just as every department had its different types, he always thought: the gorillas who would put the fear of God into you, and the stiletto merchants who would slide their blades in before you knew they were there. He spent thirty minutes with the squad leaders then telephoned the Royal Protection Group, asked for Denton, and suggested breakfast. The Mess, the fifth-floor dining room for ACPO ranks, was not open until lunch. He went to the canteen, joined Denton in the queue, asked for bacon, eggs, sausage and beans, no fried bread, and a mug of tea.

'Any developments?' They were alone at the table.

'Not a lot. Apparently the same weapon was used for both the Venlo and Mons shootings, but nothing else.'

In eighty minutes they would attend the next meeting of Cobra.

'How's the overtime?'

'Going up and questions being asked.' It would be the same at MI5, probably more so. McGuire still moving, still being tailed wherever he went, but nothing to show for it.

Cobra would discuss the matter in detail: Sinclair playing the politician, giving support but covering his back. Michaelmass presenting the options and hiding the doubts he must be feeling. Hamilton from Special Branch admitting they were getting nowhere fast, and himself agreeing that the Anti-Terrorist Squad were also stuck in a rut. Denton reporting on the royals' growing irritation at the restrictions which the increased protection imposed upon them. Rhodes being quiet about what the SAS were up to in the Republic.

That had shaken Eldridge. Not shocked him, just brought the matter home where it hurt. That because the situation was so bad, because none of them had been able to come up with anything, they were considering sending the SAS into another country, to assassinate the political leaders of another movement, terrorist organization though it might be, in order to protect a part of their own constitution.

In the end, he knew, unless his people found Sleeper, and found him in time, there might be no other option.

He left the canteen and went back to the department. During the next fifty minutes he held two meetings in readiness for Cobra, one briefing him on the search for Sleeper and the other on the European shootings. At 8.40 he walked through the department, glancing at the computer screens and listening in on the conversations.

'What's that?' He had been glancing at the detective constable for the past five minutes, at the way he kept going back over whatever items he had on his screen.

'List of hotel guests, etc., in Mons over the weekend of the shooting. We're getting some more in this afternoon. Looking for cross-matches with names in Venlo.'

So what's wrong? Eldridge wanted to ask. Why keep going back? It was time to go.

'Anything?'

'Nothing at all.' The DC was still looking at the lists, scrolling down the page.

But . . . Eldridge almost said; sensed it, felt it about the way the DC was operating the computer. But there's something there and I don't know what it is, the DC might have admitted. I don't know what it is because I don't know what I'm looking for. All I know is that I've seen it and I've missed it.

'Go back.'

The DC scrolled back.

'Further.'

Further still.

'Stop.'

Eldridge leaned forward. 'Wrong spelling.' He pointed to the item the DC was looking for. 'Gray with an "a" not "e". Probably Scottish; if it's Irish it would be from County Mayo, most likely Achill Island.'

It wouldn't be Sleeper. Sleeper wasn't in Europe and Sleeper was nothing to do with the ASU responsible for the Venlo and Mons jobs. Whoever had done them was a pro, light years on from most of the boys in Belfast. Up close and eyeball to eyeball, not spraying a car with a Kalashnikov and hoping for a hit. Therefore not the type to use a name like Gray, or to leave any trace of an Irish connection.

He took the lift to the ground floor and walked with Denton to the Cabinet offices.

The Prince of Wales's meeting was at St Katharine's Dock at ten. Among the myriad organizations, charities and projects of which he was invited to be patron, the Global Trust was one which he had had no hesitation in supporting and which he enjoyed the most.

There had been two other similar projects which he had supported – Operations Drake and Raleigh. Two years before, however, Charles had been persuaded to lend his name to the Global Trust. Since then the organization had been busy raising funds for the clipper *Trelawney*, which would serve as a sea-borne base for the operation, and working out its structure. Nine months earlier it had begun advertising for volunteers, each of whom would have to raise the money for his or her participation in the scheme.

His arrival at the dock was discreet and unobserved, and the project leaders were waiting. At ten he settled into the worn leather seat to the right of the chairman, the coffee mugs spread casually amongst the paperwork on the oak table. It was the type of meeting he enjoyed – informal but efficient, the participants showing him politeness then getting on with the job, accepting his contributions when they agreed with them, arguing against them when they did not.

The third item on the agenda was the departure of the *Trelawney* from its home port of Falmouth in Cornwall, and the ceremony which would accompany the event.

'The *Trelawney* has now received her DTI certificate and will sail from Falmouth on schedule.' The chairman was a former marine commando. 'It would be marvellous, sir, if you could be present.' He looked at Charles from his wheelchair. A decade before Johnson had led an SBS raid on an Argentinian position in the Falklands and had lost his legs; since then he had fought another battle – for paraplegics. For that reason he had founded the Global Trust, with the simple but daunting philosophy that the project would not separate the able-bodied from the disabled but would put them side by side, make them face adversity together, whether it was on a mountainside in Nepal, a slum in Rio or a Force Ten off the Cape. For that reason the Prince of Wales had not simply agreed to be the project's patron, but had suggested it himself.

'Of course.' It had been part of the original plans, the details and timetable already provisionally agreed and entered into the Prince's schedule. 'Date?'

'July 12th.'

Charles entered it in his diary. 'Confirmed.'

Saunders was waiting in the bar on the fourth level of the Royal Festival Hall when Philipa Walker arrived. *Her* evening, she had told him: the BBC Symphony Orchestra under Andrew Davis playing Elgar, then dinner at Overtons. Wheeler's was good but there was something about Overtons: the stools at the bar downstairs, the tables packed together on the first floor. She had already booked, even ordered what they would eat and drink.

Life was a market, a place where things were bought and sold. Some things you paid for, others you bartered for. As long as you both had something the other person wanted. Today the Prince and Princess of Wales would carry out their respective official duties as detailed by the Wednesday List circulated by the Palace to the Newspaper Publishers Association and then by the NPA to the country's newspaper, radio and television services. But sometime, today or tomorrow, next week or next month, the Prince and Princess of Wales would slip out of the formal schedule, would do the one simple innocent thing that was not listed by the Palace or the NPA, the unimportant thing where their defences would be down and their minders slightly relaxed and off guard. And tonight she would find out whether Saunders was the person who would tell her that. Not tell her, but allow her access to it. Already she felt the nerves.

'You're looking good.' He was wearing a dinner suit, slightly patterned dress shirt with winged collar, purple matching tuxedo, bow tie and handkerchief.

'You're looking stunning.' He meant it, returned the greeting.

To what do I owe the pleasure of this evening? – he gave her the glass but did not ask.

'A celebration and a wake. I might be going away.' If she got what she wanted there was no point staying and every point in leaving, in wiping every trace of her from his life. And if she didn't get what she wanted, if he was not the person she needed, then there was equally no point in staying.

'Where? Why?' I'll miss you, he almost said.

'The States. I'll know in the next couple of days.'

'Congratulations.' He knew how he was staring at her, knew she was aware of it. 'Tonight's a nice thought.' He raised his glass. Tonight we're going to bed together, he suddenly thought, tonight we're going to make love.

The performance was due to start, she slid her hand round his arm and they walked through. He sat uncomfortably, staring ahead, his hand resting lightly on the armrest, her hand on his. When the concert ended they crossed the footbridge over the Thames and took a cab to Victoria. The restaurant was in a block opposite the station. Saunders allowed her to go in front of him up the stairs, watching as the manager greeted her as if he knew her.

'Nick, Patrick Saunders.' She introduced them, the two men shaking hands. The tables were all taken, mainly with theatregoers. The manager escorted them to the small room, up two steps, off the side of the main restaurant, and shifted the table slightly to allow Walker to sit against the wall on the left beneath the mirror. Even though the room was small it normally contained three tables; this evening, however, Walker had booked the room and two had been removed.

The Bollinger was already in the ice bucket. The manager opened the bottle, poured them each a glass, and left.

'What are you thinking?' Her eyes were bright, shining. She was near the edge, like closing for a kill, the adrenalin pumping through her and the ice descending upon her, consuming her.

'I'm thinking that I hope you do well.' He shrugged, aware that he was half erect. 'I'm also thinking that I'll miss you.'

She smiled. 'Good times. Thanks for them all.'

The waiter laid the salver of oysters on the table and they began to eat.

'What are you really thinking?' Their legs were touching under the table and she was still smiling.

Nothing lost, he thought, no harm in saying what he really felt. 'I'm thinking that I'd like to go to bed with you.'

'What are you thinking at this very moment?'

What the hell, he thought. Decided against it.

'Tell me.'

He could imagine how she would look, how she would feel. 'You'd slap my face.'

'Try me. See if I would.'

What the hell, he thought again. 'You're wearing suspenders and nylons?'

'Yes.'

So what are you thinking, her silence asked him again, challenged him.

'I'm thinking that it would be a real turn on if that was all you were wearing under that dress.'

She looked at him, helped herself to another oyster and looked at him again.

'Can I ask you something?' Her voice was straight, no surprise or anger in it.

'Of course.' It was not the reply he had expected. He raised the glass.

'How do you manage to sit like that at the moment?'

He knew what she meant and almost spilled his wine. How do you manage to sit with a tight evening suit and an organ that, judging by the look on your face and the glaze in your eyes, must be threatening to burst the zip? 'With difficulty.' He was still laughing, could not stop. He put down the glass, coughing, laughing again. Saw the way she was laughing. Was almost crying with tears. 'Great difficulty.'

She lifted the napkin and wiped her lips. The waiter checked they had finished the oysters and took away the salver.

'Excuse me a moment.'

She picked up her bag, Saunders standing and pulling the table back slightly to allow her to get out. She thanked him and went to the ladies' room. The toilet was at the rear, the washroom in front of it, the basins against the wall and the mirror behind them. She locked the door and placed her bag on the floor. Some things in life were business, some pleasure, only occasionally a mix of the two. She unzipped the dress, slid it down, stepped out of it, and hung it on the back of the door. Then she unhooked her bra and slipped it off. It was as if she was waiting in an alleyway in the Middle East, the heat of the night settling on her and the smells of the night closing round her. As if she was waiting in a street in Norway, the sky so clear and the air so cold it seared her lungs every time she breathed. Five minutes to the target, she was thinking, planning, every muscle and fibre in her body taut and expectant, the ice in her brain and the Ruger in her hand. She hooked her fingers in her pants and slid them off, the heat and smells of Africa and the Middle East seeped into her, excited her, the cold and grimness of Northern and Eastern Europe searing into her, intoxicating. Twice, just twice, the sounds and smells of America. The places where her skill had taken her, the tautness of the moments coming back to her. Pity she couldn't have him here and now, him against the wall, her against the wall, it wouldn't matter. Except that it would. Except here there was no computer to check after, here there were no details of the way into PinMan. She put the dress back on, smoothed her hair, folded the items she had taken off into her handbag, took a sip of water, and returned to the table.

It was 10.30, the other tables emptying. The wine waiter removed the empty Bollinger and brought an '87 Mersault; the assistant manager, checking and smiling in the background as another waiter brought the grilled Dover sole.

'We're not keeping you?' It was Saunders who asked.

'Not till half-eleven, sir.'

Saunders ate slowly, poured them each another glass. Realized.

'You're not, are you?'

'Not what?'

'You're not wearing anything underneath.'

'Not wearing anything underneath what?' She teased him, played him along. Smelt the smells again and felt the heat and cold.

'You took them off, didn't you? That's why you went to the bathroom. That's why you were so long.'

'Took what off?'

The wine waiter hovered near them, poured them each another glass.

203

'So what are you wearing?'

'What do you think?'

He shook his head. 'I wish we were somewhere else.'

'Long night.'

She straightened her leg slightly and brought her right foot up, rested it on the edge of his chair between his legs. Continued eating, drinking, talking as if she was not rubbing it against him, knowing he was enjoying it. He stopped eating, wiped his mouth with his napkin, and reached down, began massaging the sole of her foot, her toes.

'That's good.'

Her body was tingling. She knew what he was going to do, what he was going to do after. He unzipped his trousers and held her foot against him, brought his hand back above the table and forced himself to drink as she massaged him.

'What are you doing?'

He had bent down, right hand beneath the table.

'What do you think?'

He undid his shoe and took it off, took off his sock. Then he stretched his leg out and ran his foot along the inside of her thigh. The dress was slightly tight on the chair. She raised herself and loosened it. Laughed. Thank God they have long tablecloths here, the look said it. She felt his foot against her stomach, felt herself moving.

'Tell me what you'll do to me.' She reached for the bottle and poured him the last of the wine.

'What would you like?'

She felt the sensation as he slid his foot down and ran his toes through her hair, moved them, slid them lower. Felt almost sick with anticipation.

'I asked you.'

He moved his foot between her legs, felt her open and wet. Tensed and relaxed the tendons of his foot. She raised herself slightly then settled down on him, felt the penetration. Was aware she had closed her eyes with the sensation.

'You want to go?'

'Yes. And no. And yes.'

She called the waiter and asked for the bill.

The cab rank was thirty yards from the restaurant, under the canopy outside Victoria Station, ten taxis waiting. It was beginning to drizzle; they hurried across the road and he opened the door for her, allowed her to get in first.

'Lonsdale Square.'

They sank back into the seat, floated in the shadow land, tense yet relaxed. Balanced on the edge because of what they would do, yet pulled back from the edge because they knew they would do it.

'So what about this wonderful computer you're always telling me about.' She began the next game.

'You want to see it?'

'If you insist.' She took the game one stage farther.

'I insist.'

The cab turned into Lonsdale Square.

Saunders leaned forward. 'Half-way down on the left.'

She was almost sick with excitement again, one game playing off the other, feeding the other. As they stepped out she brushed against him and handled his erection. As he turned away from her and paid the driver she massaged his buttocks and ran her hand between his legs. They went inside and ignored the stairs, took the lift even though the flat was only on the second floor. The doors closed and he unzipped her dress, slid it down, sucked her nipples long and hard. They reached the second floor and the doors opened. She pressed the button for the sixth floor and the doors closed again. He was reaching down, pulling her dress up. She undid his zip and felt inside. His penis was hard and erect. She grasped it, stroked it, held it tight. They reached the sixth floor. She pressed the button for the second floor and felt the slight movement as the lift descended. As the lift stopped she bent down and took him in her mouth.

The flat was on the right. He felt for his keys, stopped, felt for her, then unlocked the door and let her in. The flat was neat and tidy, not as much of a bachelor apartment as she had expected. Hallway, sitting-room at the end, kitchen and bathroom to the right, bedroom and office to the left. He took her coat and asked if she wanted coffee.

'No.'

The furniture was a mix of dark wood and leather in some rooms, light and modern in others.

'Champagne?'

'Yes.'

He took the bottle into the sitting-room and drew the curtains, found two glasses. The lights were dimmed. He slid the top half of her dress down and the bottom half up. Knelt in front of her and kissed her thighs, the inside of her legs, drew her up and slid his tongue into her. She undid his trousers again, held his penis, knelt down and took it in her mouth.

'You want to see the computer?' he asked.

'No.'

He laughed and pulled her up, slid the dress back on to her shoulders and took her into the study. The walls were lined with bookshelves, the PC on a mahogany desk, laser printer at the side and swivel chair in front. He sat down and switched it on.

'What do you use it for?'

'Everything.'

She was standing behind him, bending forward, arms resting on his shoulders. 'What's everything?'

'Everything I do at work I copy. Not just the final pieces. Notes and everything.'

She was kissing his ears. 'You're writing a book.'

'One day.'

'Show me.'

He went into the main menu and called up the files. Interesting, she thought: no security code, either basic or built into the BIOS chips. Felt the slight fear that he might not have anything to hide.

He accessed the files. *Mirror. Book. Accounts. Overseas.* Her brain took in the details as he ran down the list. *Contacts.* No *Charles*, she thought, felt the excitement rising again, no *Di*. She wondered what he had done with the names and how he had disguised them.

'Am I on the contact list?' She had stopped kissing him, was relaxed over him again.

'Of course.'

'Don't you think you'd better take me off in case your wife finds out?' It was casually said, the voice slightly blurred.

'Good idea.' Not before tonight, he thought; after tonight, yes. He accessed the contacts file, found her name, and deleted it.

'Back-up disks?' She had undone his shirt.

He opened the bottom drawer on the right and ran his fingers over the disk box. 'Wish you'd do that to me,' she told him. He laughed, turned and kissed her. Put the disk into the computer and wiped her name and details from it.

'What about the notebook?' The computer notebook she meant.

'You're not on it.'

'Show me.' She took off his shirt and unbuttoned his trousers.

'It's in my jacket.'

She swung the chair round and knelt in front of him, took off his shoes and socks. Reached up, kissed him on the lips. Sat back slightly, took off his trousers and pants. His hands were on her shoulders, playing with her hair. He had a good body, she thought, leaner than she had expected. Penis rising from the short, dark, curly hair at its base. She bent over and held it as she held the Ruger, both hands round it, opened her lips and guided it into her mouth. He lifted her up and took her into the bedroom, laid her on the bed.

Her dress had ridden up her thighs. He pulled it higher and lay down, began kissing her, tongue playing against her, biting her. Tongue jabbing in and out, teasing her, the tip against her clitoris. She was pulling the trigger, pulling his head tightly against her. He straightened and slid off her dress, let it fall to the floor, went to the bathroom and returned with a small bottle, dripped the massage oil on to her stomach and breasts.

'Expecting someone?' she joked.

'Hoping.'

He ran the oil up and down her, rubbing her nipples between his thumb and forefinger. Sat astride her and massaged her neck, slid his penis between her breasts. Edged up her body and guided the penis along her lips.

'Turn over.'

He trickled the oil down her back and massaged her again. Hands stronger than she had thought, and the pressure deeper. He reached for the bottle again, oiled and massaged her buttocks, penis sliding across her. She was spreadeagled on the bed, hands holding the rails at the top. He held the head of the penis against her, played it against the mouth of her vagina. Allowed her to settle over him then withdrew, teasing her again.

'Ready?'

'Christ, yes.'

The room was dark. It was gone three-thirty, almost four. Saunders was fast asleep beside her. They had reached the flat at twelve and fallen asleep only half an hour ago. She left the bed, felt for her handbag and went into the lounge. Saunders's jacket was on the chair. She took out the computer notebook, accessed the contact list, and confirmed that her name was not on it. Then she put it back, removed the keys from the other pocket, made an impression of both the flat key and the front door key in the wax block she carried in a container in the handbag, cleaned the keys and returned them to the coat, and went back to bed.

The Police College at Bramshill is situated in a discreet country estate an hour's drive south-west of London. The day-long seminar on the relationship between civil liberties and terrorism began at ten and was attended by senior officers – assistant chief constables and above – studying at Bramshill, plus representatives of concerned parties such as Liberty, the renamed National Council for Civil Liberties.

Eldridge arrived at 9.45 and was introduced over coffee.

It was an interesting mix of opinions, he thought, not necessarily between the police and those who might be considered outsiders, but sometimes within the police ranks themselves. The selection of the barrister who chaired the seminar was also interesting – the man not merely a prominent Queen's Counsel, as would be expected, but one who had represented the appellants in a number of recent cases where IRA members had successfully appealed against conviction. It was a choice to which several had objected. The QC, they argued, would push them to the edge, might take them over it. The argument found no favour with Eldridge. For too long he had been so accustomed to living on the edge that the only thing which disturbed him was that it no longer worried him. He therefore sat quietly, listening to the discussion, and contributing only when directly asked.

The seminar moved quickly over the predictable areas, the discussion cut short by the chairman, and on to more philosophical topics: the basis of law and the range of moralities which a particular system of justice might encompass. Some of those present, and not just police officers, objected, preferring to stay with what they called the factual discussion.

Perhaps they might illustrate the discussions with case studies, the QC suggested. Not actual cases, theoretical instances which they all might be called upon to deal with in the future. Perhaps Commander Eldridge might like to begin.

Eldridge smiled and moved his hand slightly, apologetically rather than dismissively. A lot on my mind at the moment, he wanted to say. 'I think that's a good idea but I'm probably too entrenched in the system to take the lead. Perhaps someone else might start.'

The poor bastard hasn't slept for days, the barrister thought, if he wasn't careful he was in the fast lane for a coronary. 'As long as you think there's a chance they might jog you out of your trench.' He gave Eldridge the way out.

Thanks, the policeman wanted to say. 'Nothing's impossible.'

Suspected terrorist attack, the authorities have prior notice but not enough to counter it, someone suggested.

The discussion began well but deteriorated quickly along predictable lines: the rules of the game whereby the IRA coded some bomb warnings to prove they were genuine, *ipso facto* a form of agreement between the police and the IRA; the role of the press and the so-called oxygen of publicity. It was interesting, thought Eldridge, that the discussion was entirely about the IRA.

Suspected terrorist attack, prior notice, no way of stopping it. It was an Assistant Chief Constable from Lancashire, one of the recognized high-flyers. They had already discussed it, someone began to suggest. The ACC indicated he had not finished. Big target, important target; not just a railway station or an office block. Say a politician, say the Prime Minister. What do you do then?

Close to home, thought Eldridge.

What about pre-emptive action? It was one of the civilians present.

Too close to home, Eldridge remembered the tacit agreement on the SAS and the Army Council at the last two Cobra meetings.

A good point for discussion, the chairman observed, the sort of issue they should be considering.

Agreed, one of the younger ACCs responded. Perhaps they should begin by looking at what the present legislation enabled the police to do and what legislation should encompass in the future.

Fuck the legislation. Eldridge felt the anger. I have an IRA hitman in London. His target is the Queen. If not the Queen then the Prince of Wales. I can't find him, but I do know – or at least I think I know – who's giving him his orders. So if I can't get to him, do I stop him by taking out those behind him? Simple as that. Black and white. No fucking round with legislation and existing police powers. The Queen or the IRA.

Surely there were already enough provisions in the Prevention of Terrorism Act to allow the police to do whatever was necessary, one of the civilians countered. *Too many*, the suggestion was implicit.

Perhaps it wasn't as simple as that – it was as if Eldridge was having a separate discussion. If you did it for the Queen, then why should you not do it for anyone else? Put another way – what right did the Queen have that an ordinary man or woman in the street did not? Would he take out the Army Council if he knew they had ordered the assassination of the man who lived three doors from him? And by so doing could prevent the man's death, he added to himself. He took it on a stage. He didn't normally know in advance when the Army Council had ordered an operation, but he knew in general terms that they would. So if he was justified in taking them out because he had advance notice of a specific killing, then would he not be justified because of future killings in general? He knew the counter-argument – the pragmatic rather than the moral or ethical one. Take out this Army Council and you sowed the seeds of a whirlwind. Take these men out, and in this way, and those who replaced them would make the present lot look like angels.

Which still left him the Queen and Sleeper.

The others were still discussing the PTA, getting bogged down in minutiae. The door of the seminar room opened and one of the Bramshill instructors informed Eldridge that he was wanted on the telephone. He excused himself and went to the office along the corridor.

'You're on a secure line?'

He recognized the voice of one of his superintendents. 'No.' The portable scrambler was small enough to carry in his pocket. He clipped it on, asked the code the team leader was using, and keyed it in.

'Okay.'

'We have a cross-match.'

'Who?'

'Gray.'

'What?' Not the other European shooting; there was no record of Gray at Venlo. Unless they had turned up something else.

'The Sleeper file.'

Christ, thought Eldridge. 'Specifically?'

210

'He's recorded as being a member of a gun club. Stopped his subscription but he was on the backlist.'

Gray wasn't Sleeper. There had been no suggestion that Sleeper was involved in Europe, and Sleeper wouldn't use an Irish name and belong to a gun club. But an Irishman with a proven involvement in guns being present in a town which most people hadn't heard of and on the day when a British army officer was gunned down by the Provos . . .

'So what have you done?' There would be time for the fine print later.

'Checking on home address, occupation, place of work, general background details. Armed teams standing by. Sniffer dogs and search teams already on the way to his flat – he lives near Wapping, by the way, posh address. Arrangements for phone tap and other surveillance already in hand.'

The necessary warrants would be issued by a magistrate's court sitting in camera. By the time Gray returned home from work they would have turned his apartment inside out. Left it just as they found it except for the taps in the phone system and the bugs in the walls and furniture.

Gray wasn't Sleeper, he thought again, but there was always the chance of a connection with the ASU in Europe.

Better make it official – sometimes there was a temptation to cut corners, especially when the pressure was on. And better follow the command structure – him reporting to the Deputy Assistant Commissioner responsible for Special Branch and the Anti-Terrorist Squad, the DAC reporting in turn to the Assistant Commissioner, and the AC reporting to the Commissioner.

'Get everyone in place, but no action until my say-so.'

'When will that be?'

'Five minutes.'

He ended the call and dialled one of the direct lines into New Scotland Yard. The DAC was out of the building, he was informed. There was no more time to waste on the formal structure, he decided, and dialled one of the direct lines into the Commissioner's office. The Commissioner, he was told, was in a meeting and not available for the rest of the morning.

'Eldridge,' he said simply. 'Urgent.'

The Commissioner took the call fourteen seconds later. Eldridge detailed the situation: possible suspect in Europe, possible – though

211

unlikely – connection with the home enquiry. Action recommended immediately but the DAC unavailable. Home Office being informed and warrants already being issued.

Go, the Commissioner told him.

Eldridge telephoned the Home Office, spoke to Sinclair's personal assistant, and was informed that the Secretary of State was attending a Cabinet committee. Eldridge thanked him and phoned Downing Street. He spoke to a secretary from the private office and was asked to wait. Sinclair would love it, he thought, especially in front of the PM.

'Yes.' The Home Secretary's voice was distinctive.

Eldridge explained again, keeping the details to a minimum.

'I'm here for the next hour. Keep me informed. I'll explain to the PM later.'

Of course you will, thought Eldridge. He thanked the Home Secretary, called the department, and authorized them to contact the magistrate's court for the necessary documentation. Gray wasn't Sleeper, he thought again, Gray *probably* wasn't Sleeper. But at least they had something. Even start on the wrong road, his experience had told him, and it might just lead you to where you wanted to go. He returned to the seminar room, apologized that he had to leave, and went outside. His car was waiting.

'NSY,' he told the driver. 'Yesterday.'

Arthur Whyte was 53 years old and had served his apprenticeship in the toolroom of the light engineering firm on the outskirts of Colchester where he still worked. His habits were regular and precise. Each Christmas he helped deliver presents to the children's ward of the local hospital, the money raised by the cricket match he organized each Whit holiday. Every summer he and his wife took their two weeks in a former tin miner's cottage, high on the Cornish cliffs between St Ives and Zennor. On Sunday mornings he did the accounts of the savings club, of which he was treasurer, and the books of the gun club, of which he was secretary.

The request for him to report to the manager's office echoed over the Tannoy shortly after eleven. He switched off his machine, crossed the floor and made his way to the admin section. He knew the manager, had persuaded him to take part in the Whitsun cricket match, but still felt slightly apprehensive.

The manager's secretary smiled at him, knocked on the door to the inner office, and showed him in. Present, in addition to the manager, were two men, one in his mid-thirties and the other slightly younger. Both were big and wearing suits. The manager introduced them as police then left, closing the door behind him.

'He thinks we want to talk to you because you might have witnessed someone leaving the scene of a robbery, even though you weren't aware of it at the time.' The detective sergeant settled in the chair behind the desk. 'Stick to that if he asks you, say you weren't able to help.'

Whyte sat in the straight-backed chair facing him.

'Other than that, this conversation did not take place.' They had checked Whyte on CRO, confirmed he had no record, would not have expected him to have a record if he was allowed to own a gun.

What's happening, Whyte glanced at the other man, to his right. They hadn't shown him any identification, he thought, and asked them for it. The DS held his warrant card across the table. Metropolitan Police, Whyte noted, not local.

'The Essex Gun Club.'

He was secretary, Whyte began to say. They know that, he realized.

'Gerard Gray.' The DS had not stopped looking at him. 'Tell us about him.'

Whyte had always prided himself on his memory. 'Joined about four years ago, let his membership lapse last year. Nice sort of chap.'

'He lives in London. So why belong to a gun club here?'

'I'm not sure, really. I think he had a high pressure job in the City and liked to get away.'

'Come down often?'

'A lot at one stage. Fell off a bit at the end.'

'How about friends?'

'Not that I know of.'

'Good shot?' It was the other man.

'Pretty good.' He screwed up his face, thought back. 'No, I'm wrong. He was better than pretty good; he was fit, good concentration.' He thought he saw a slight flicker of the eyes, one man to the other.

'Ever talk about Ireland?'

'Not that I can recollect. Why should he?' Christ. He suddenly realized, understood who they were.

213

The DS saw the change in his eyes. 'Routine enquiry.' His voice was reassuring. 'We appreciate the help.'

There was a tap on the door and the manager's secretary came in, another woman behind her carrying a tray.

'The manager thought you might like some tea.'

They'd been breaking their balls trying to find Sleeper, the DS thought. Now they had their first lead, tenuous but at least a lead. And the manager thought they might like some tea. Only two cups, he noted. Bloody typical.

'Any chance of one for Mr Whyte?'

'I'll see what I can do.'

'Thanks.'

He gave Whyte his own cup and sat forward. 'So now you know who we are and why we're here.' The net went over Whyte and drew him in. 'Friend Gray.' Every word counted now, every nuance. 'Let's start from the beginning.'

The secretary brought another tea. Mug, they all noted.

'Sorry, old mate.' The DS did not miss the opportunity. 'Should have waited, you don't get anything in a piddling little cup.'

Whyte was relaxed, his mind going back, searching. 'You asked if Gray had any friends.'

The DS sipped the tea. Sometimes a silence helped someone remember.

'Not friends, exactly, but he used to do a bit of clay pigeon shooting. Chap called Holden, runs a smallholding.'

Eldridge's conference with the squad leaders was at four. In one hour Gray would leave work, therefore in an hour they would need to have made a decision.

Gray was right and Gray was wrong.

Gray was not only confirmed as a member of a gun club, he was an excellent shot with pistol and twelve-bore – an unlikely combination and therefore giving grounds for suspicion. He had been in Mons at the time of the shooting. And he was extremely fit. Almost military in his bearing and approach, it had been suggested. But there had been no trace of weapons or explosives in the flat, the dogs had been as bored as if they'd been visiting the Chelsea Flower Show; there was nothing on his telephone record; and if he was a gunman he would not have belonged to the club or used his own name in Mons. Yet he had concealed his Irishness, further

214

investigation had confirmed, even to the point of wiping any trace of accent from his voice when he so wished.

Pick him up for questioning or let him run and see where he led them?

Under the Prevention of Terrorism Act they could hold him for seven days, an initial two plus five. If they picked him up and he was innocent then the proverbial might hit the fan, but they would be ready for it. Pick him up and he *was* a Provo, especially if he was a gunman, and he would have done the course. And if the Provos had put him through the mill then he would take anything the police were allowed to throw at him, would probably sit silently and not say a word until the day he died or walked free. But let him run and he skipped the country . . . Let him run and he was an IRA shooter . . . Let him run and he was Sleeper . . .

'The tails are in place for the moment he leaves work?'

'Yes.'

'They're sure they know what he looks like?'

'Identified him at lunchtime.'

'Let him leave, see where he goes and what he does.' Decision time, he knew. No point delaying. 'Pick him up as he enters the flat.'

The warning bells were ringing.

'One last thing. Nobody mentions we're after someone called Sleeper.' Name the hitman and it might leak out. Allow it to leak out and the Provos might pick it up. 'If he comes out with it, then we go in after him. Otherwise it's taboo.'

The days were warmer and the evenings lighter. Perhaps he should do something different this spring, Gerard Gray thought. Pack up his job, travel. See the world before he was too old. It was what he thought each spring. Perhaps he should do something less radical, get an overseas posting: Hong Kong might be interesting. He left the bank and walked briskly along Old Broad Street. Perhaps this year he would do it. The walk did him good as it always did. He entered the tower block and nodded at the doorman. Someone was already waiting at the lift, getting in.

'Fourteen.' He noted that the man had already pressed the button. The lift stopped and the doors opened. Gray allowed the other man to get out first and followed him right, came to his own door, the other passing it, turning the corner at the end of the short landing. Gray felt for his key, opened the door and began to go in.

215

'Gerard Gray?' The second man was big, muscled. Already in the door after him. 'Yes?' Gray reacted automatically. 'Detective Inspector Hughes, Metropolitan Police.' The warrant card was held up for sufficient time for Gray to see it, not long enough to register the details. 'Perhaps I could come in?' He was already in, a second man behind him. The man in the lift.

'What is it?' Gray felt the fear, the gnawing in the stomach and the confusion in the head. 'What do you want?'

'A few questions, won't take long.' What did he feel like, smell like? Hughes knew Eldridge would ask. How did he react? The two of them stayed close to him, hardly letting him move, even though they knew the flat had been searched for guns. 'Not here, sir; if you wouldn't mind coming with us.' They steered him from the flat to the lift, one either side of him and towering above him, the doors held open by a third man. The foyer was empty, no porter, the car outside. He was pushed into the rear seat, the men still on either side, and the car pulled away.

The interview room was white and featureless, desk in the middle and chairs either side, tape recorder on the desk and video camera on the wall.

'Your name is Gerard Gray. You are an Irish subject resident in Britain.' The voice was hard, harsh. The recorder was ready for Gray's first words and the camera zoomed into close-up on his face, Eldridge in the next room looking for the slightest expression, the single flicker of the eyelid, which might come later, which might mean they were getting somewhere. Normally Eldridge wouldn't attend, normally he would continue his work at the Yard and wait for the reports. This, however, was different; this might lead to Sleeper.

What's going on? Gray thought. What the hell's happening? He began to reply, to confirm the details. Stopped. Tried to work out what he should say and where it would lead him. Already no response, the watchers and listeners noted. Provo training. Been through the mangle and come out the other side.

'Yes,' he replied.

Something right or something wrong, the man next to him glanced at Eldridge. The interrogation began. How long had he lived in England? Where in Ireland was he from? Parents' names, occupations? Where did he go to school, who with? What happened to his schoolfriends? Why university, why LSE? Who said he should come to England, study here, get a job here? When was he last in touch with them? How often did he go home? When was the last time? What did he know about Sinn Fein, what names did he know in Sinn Fein?

The interrogators changed.

Where did he learn to shoot? What about the gun club? Why go to Essex when there were clubs he could have joined in London? Why the special arrangement with the farmer near Colchester?

It was time for a break. Not that Eldridge necessarily approved the provisions set out in the Police and Criminal Evidence Act, just that he had seen too many cases thrown out on a technicality.

Who ran him, gave him his orders? Who did he see when he went North? The interrogation resumed – it was late evening, night, early morning, Gray was no longer sure. But he'd said he'd seen the people from Sinn Fein – they threw the names back at him, twisted what he'd told them earlier, tried to lead him on. Who was his handler? What about the gun club, what weapons? What about a .357? Who gave him the details of the Mons job and how? When did he arrive in Mons, first spot the captain? How did he get the .357? He knew about .357s, of course, didn't he remember that he'd just told them? They played back the section of the recording where he had talked about the gun club and tried to catch him out again. How had he taken the weapon to Mons? If he hadn't, where was the dead letter drop? Who told him about the positioning of the getaway cars and the safe houses? When had he first picked up the captain? How many times had he shot him?

'You're saying I killed the army captain in Mons?' Gray was more tired than he would have imagined possible, the stubble on his face was itching and his head was thumping.

Now we're getting somewhere, Gerard. The interrogators changed, perhaps did not change. He wasn't sure, was no longer sure of anything.

How did he get to Mons? Why go there? Nice cover, Gerard, visit to Waterloo and interest in military matters. Too nice. They pressed on, gave him no respite. What time did he pick up the gun? Where from? Mag, suppressor, ammunition? They threw in the technical details he would have known anyway from his membership of the gun club, manoeuvred him into confirming them and took him on from there. So what did he do with the gun after the killing? How long after he shot the captain did he leave Mons? What did he do before, after?

217

'You're saying I killed the army captain in Mons?' he asked again, tried to stop the waves sweeping over him, tried to stop drowning. 'What if I can prove I didn't? What if I can prove I'm innocent?'

What's he playing at? Eldridge studied Gray's face on the video screen. What the hell's he going to say?

Tell us: the interrogator's silence said it all.

The first detail, they all knew, the beginning of the end for Gray, the start of his downfall. The first thing they had not suggested to him, the first piece of information he had given them. The first thing they could check on. Come back at him on, build on.

'I met someone there.'

So? The interrogator's look was of deliberate bemusement. What does that mean? How does that prove anything?

'I was in the Grand Place. We had a drink together.'

He hadn't denied being in Mons, Eldridge thought. Had admitted it right from the beginning. Had no option, of course, especially after they'd shown him the hotel record. But why was he registered at the hotel anyway?

What time? How could he be so certain about it? Convenient, wasn't it, that it gave him an alibi for the precise time the captain was shot? How did he know what time the captain was shot?

Tell us anyway, Gerard. Tell us about the friend you met. Tell us his name and how you know him.

Actually it's a woman. I met her at work.

But if she worked with him why was it such a surprise seeing her? Hadn't he told her he was taking a weekend in Belgium? Hadn't she told him? Didn't they discuss it before and after?

No, she didn't work with him.

But he'd just said that she did.

No, he'd said he'd met her at work. She was with Price Waterhouse. Not with them. On a consultancy with them.

'So what happens when we interview her, Gerard? What will she say?'

'That we met in Mons. That we had a drink together.'

'And how does that prove anything? How does that prove that you didn't kill the captain?'

Eldridge knew what Gray was going to say. Check the story out, he told the superintendent next to him. Get the details and phone Price Waterhouse. Get her address and phone number and find out what she says.

'Because if I was in Mons to kill someone, then I wouldn't call across the square and invite her to have a drink. I wouldn't do anything to draw attention to myself, would I?'

Who was she, Gerard? What was her name?

Philipa Walker.

Saunders left the flat at ten. Walker gave him thirty minutes, checked with the *Mirror* that he'd arrived, pulled on the gloves and let herself in. The sun was playing through the windows of the lounge and into the hallway. She confirmed that the apartment was empty, went to the room Saunders used as a study, and sat at the desk. It was interesting that Saunders didn't appear to be using passwords, she had noted two nights before, the implication being that he wasn't security conscious, or that he had nothing to hide. She opened her briefcase, took out the portable tape streamer, and placed it on the desk to the right of the computer, then took out the floppy, snapped the case shut and placed it on the floor.

This was what the security services or police would do if they ever suspected her, she was aware; this was the reason she had taken such care over her own computer security. Because at the end of the day there was virtually no such thing as computer security, at least for a PC. Depending on the level of security built in to the computer, all you normally needed was a portable tape streamer (price between £500 and £2000, but in her case a top-of-the-market Interpreter TapeXchange), a programmer's toolkit (price £200 to £500, but in her case a Norton Utilities), a DOS operating system boot disk – and the right technical background. Then you could bypass all the security measures on the C drive and get into the hard disk. If the security measures were built into the BIOS chips, you simply replaced them or physically removed the hard disk and copied it. And the hard disk contained not only the information a user had stored in the computer, but all the material he or she thought they had deleted but which had not been written over – totally or in part.

The streamer was contained in a small metal box, the tape on to which she would record Saunders's material already in it. The power sockets were behind the desk. She unplugged the printer lead from the back of the computer, plugged in and switched on the streamer, put the boot disk in the A drive of Saunders's PC and switched the computer on. The system booted from the A drive, bypassing the C drive, and the A prompt appeared on the screen. She keyed in the back-up command and watched as the files were copied from the secrecy of the hard disk. As each file was copied its name flashed on the screen. It was interesting, she thought as she had thought two nights before, that none of the names indicated even the remotest possibility of a royal schedule.

Four minutes and seventeen seconds later the screen flashed back to the A prompt and the process was complete. Walker took the streamer lead out and put the printer lead back in. If she was being careful, if she was concerned about her security, she would leave now, would shut up shop and return to Primrose Hill, examine the Saunders files in the privacy and safety of her own flat. At any other time, perhaps, in any other operation, that was what she would have done. But this was different. This was PinMan. And she wanted to know. Whether Saunders was the key. Whether, concealed in his computer, he had given her the way in.

She telephoned the *Mirror* and confirmed that Saunders was still there.

The boot disk was still in the A drive and the A prompt was still on the screen. She leaned forward, keyed in the C prompt, and called up the disk edit programme. The screen flashed and a hex display appeared. To a non-expert the screen would have seemed an incomprehensible mass of numbers and letters; what it now showed her was the beginning of all material stored on the hard disk, byte by byte. She selected TOOLS from the disk edit, and the pull-down menu appeared, superimposed over the hex display. She selected the FIND option and typed in 64 69 61 6E 61 – the hex value for diana. Because there were different hex values for lower and upper case, she selected the IGNORE CASE option, then pressed carriage return to activate the programme searching across the hard disk for the sequence of hex values she had specified.

Ninety seconds later the search stopped at its first find. The name of the file which contained the reference was displayed at the bottom of the page. She checked the words on the right of the hex values – the beginning of an article about someone called Diana becoming a godmother – noted the details of the software package Saunders was using – Word Perfect – then the file name, and continued the search. She was calm but excited, knew the search would not take long but would appear to take for ever.

Saunders hadn't built in any obvious security measures, but the file references were more organized than she had expected. Perhaps he had built in more subtle security measures, given his files innocuous names, even hidden them. She felt the adrenalin, almost the thrill. Twenty-three minutes later she came to the fifty-second reference to Diana. Of the previous fifty-one, thirty-nine had been to the Princess of Wales but none appeared to be what she was looking for, though she would check each file later. Automatically she noted the file code and name from the bottom of the screen – c:/wp51/DATA/SOCCER – then glanced at the numbers and words on the right. The date first, then the times, only then the words.

23.04.93. 9.00AM. Diana. Great Ormond Street Hospital for Sick Children.

It was time to go, she told herself, the place to search the files was in the safety of her own flat. One last check, she decided.

She called up Word Perfect, selected the RETRIEVE FILE option, and scanned the list for the file named 'soccer'. The file was not listed. She exited Word Perfect, went to the sub-directory indicated by the file code, and called up CHATT from the A drive. The screen flashed, then displayed every file contained in the sub-directory, the file names down the left of the screen and a series of classifications across the top. The third classification from the left was *hidden*. Most of the files were flagged 'null'. The 'soccer' file, however, was flagged 'Y'.

You son of a bitch, Saunders – the thrill screamed through her head, the excitement mixed with the chill. Two security measures of his own: giving the royal schedule an innocent and unrelated name, then hiding it.

She changed the 'Y' to 'null', hit escape, called up Word Perfect and accessed the 'soccer' file. In front of her was the royal schedule. Not the NPA version, not the Wednesday List of formal functions where the protection would be massive; the informal personal details where the protection would still exist but where it might allow her access.

She exited the file, went back into the sub-directory, called up CHATT, found the reference to the 'soccer' file, and changed the 'null' back to 'Y' – thereby hiding the file again and disguising the fact that she had been inside.

There was one more thing to do. She called up disk edit, as she had done with the search for the royal schedule, selected TOOLS followed by the FIND option, typed in the hex value for Walker and activated the search. The programme stopped only once, for the file titled 'Contacts' from which Saunders had deleted her name. She checked that Saunders had spelt her name correctly, then over-wrote the hex values for Philipa Walker, and her telephone number, with the hex values for another name and telephone number. As she keyed in each new value the name and number on the right of the screen changed, the number of new hex values exactly matching hers, so that when she finished there was not even the slightest indication of her name and number, and no indication that anything had been changed. Then she escaped disk edit, exited the computer, made sure it and the desk were as she had found them, and left the building.

The children were playing on the grass and the car was parked twenty yards from the house which contained her flat. She saw it the moment she turned the corner. BMW, two men sitting in the front. Police: she felt the sudden jump in her pulse rate. Not just police. Special Branch or Anti-Terrorist Squad. Outside her flat, therefore waiting for her. Calm it, she told herself. Assess the situation and work out the options. Not much time to think about what to do, she was suddenly and frighteningly aware, not much time for anything. Walk straight past and go inside, or turn now and walk away. But if they were waiting for her they would have her photograph, would be looking for her, probably see her turn. Yet if they knew her they would also know who and what she was and why they were waiting, and if they knew that they wouldn't be sitting how and where they were.

And even if the men in the car didn't see her the others would. Assuming there *were* others. Part of her mind was in turmoil, part was calm, working coolly and analytically. Perhaps they weren't sure, perhaps they'd put the car outside to panic her into making a mistake. So how did they know? What did they know?

She walked past the BMW, not slowing or looking at it, and into the house. Thirty seconds later the intercom from the front door rang. She wasn't expecting them, she reminded herself, wasn't expecting anyone. 'Yes?'

'Miss Walker.'

So why were they asking, why were they calling her Miss? 'Who's that?'

'Police. May we have a word?'

There was still time to get out, except that if they'd placed the

222

BMW in front they'd have the back covered as well. 'I'm sorry. Give me your names and which station you're from.'

Logical, the inspector thought: no woman on her own would – or should – let someone in without first checking. So the woman on the pavement was Walker, he also thought. Nice. No wonder Gray was pleased to see her in Mons. As well as the fact that she gave him an alibi. If she confirmed his story. Pity if she did, but Gray hadn't felt right anyway: wrong answers to their questions and wrong preliminary results from forensics. Still worth checking his alibi out, though.

'Detective Inspector Hughes and Detective Sergeant Griffith. Phone New Scotland Yard and ask for Superintendent Henderson.'

'Which department?' Give me a clue, confirm who you are.

He gave her the extension.

She dialled the number and asked for the extension.

'Henderson.' It was a hard voice. SO 13 or SB, she confirmed.

'My name's Walker. I have two men outside who claim to be your officers.'

'Names?'

'Inspector Hughes and Sergeant . . .' She made herself appear to hesitate. If she was too much in control, too sure about the names, she might tell them something about herself, her state of mind.

'Sergeant Griffith,' the superintendent suggested.

'Yes.'

'They're my men. It's okay to let them in.'

She was unsure whether or not to ask why they were visiting her: whether it would appear more normal to ask or not ask. What it would suggest on her part.

'Sorry to have troubled you, but you can never be too careful.'

'Of course not.' The voice had changed. 'You did the right thing.'

She thanked him and went to the window. The BMW was empty. Therefore the same men, she assumed, therefore only two of them. She pressed the intercom, unlocked the front door, and told them to come up, third floor. There was still time to try the back, she knew, still time to make a break for it. Stay in place, she told herself, don't give them anything. She opened the door and waited for them. Both men were tall and well-built. Anti-Terrorist Squad, she knew. 'Sorry, but you can't be too careful,' she said again.

'Quite correct,' Hughes reassured her, showed her his warrant card, confirmed she had spoken to Henderson.

She took them in to the lounge and offered them coffee.

'No, thank you.'

So why were they here? The way she looked at them asked the question. What did they want? They were all in a hurry, she sensed – Hughes and Griffith here, Henderson at Scotland Yard. Make a mistake, she prayed, give me a clue so that I can get my story straight before you ask me anything.

'You were in Mons two weekends ago.'

Christ, she felt the jump in her composure and knew it showed.

'Yes.' One of the advantages of working for oneself, she began to plan ahead. Work hard when you have to, take time off when you want. Not what a normal person would say, she told herself. 'The weekend that poor soldier was shot.' She shook her head. So how could she explain why she was in Mons, what she was doing there?

'You bumped into a friend?'

She hesitated, appeared to hesitate. Partly genuine, partly to give herself more time.

'Gerard Gray.' It was the man on her left.

She laughed – sort of laughed. 'I wouldn't say he was a friend. But yes, I bumped into him.' She tried to remember the conversation, tried to work out the questions which might rise from it.

Here by yourself? Sort of, sort of with friends. Which friends? they would ask. Who were they? Names and addresses. *How about dinner tonight? Nice try, Gerard. Have to go.* Go where? they would come back on her. Where had she stayed? Why wasn't her name on any hotel or pension listing?

'What time did you see him?'

Both were armed, she assumed, but that wouldn't be a problem. Neither had been through the heat of the desert days and the cold of the desert nights. Neither of them had killed before. She knew by the way they were sitting, the way they were looking at her.

'Mid-afternoon, four, four-thirty.'

Enough to give Gray an alibi, she suddenly realized. That was why they were here. For some reason they were checking on Gray, not her.

'And what happened?'

'I was crossing the square and he saw me, asked if I wanted a drink.'

'How long were you with him?'

Don't assume they're checking on Gray, she told herself; don't relax, keep on the edge, keep ahead of them. How long had Gray said, she wondered, how long should she say? 'Ten minutes, perhaps fifteen.' Give or take, it was in the way she said it, might have been slightly less, might have been slightly more. What then? she was aware of the follow-up. What did she do and where did she go? 'Bastard had a cheek.' She threw them in the other direction. 'Asked me out for dinner.'

Why bastard? she saw it in their faces. Why cheek?

'I meet him when I'm doing a job at the bank where he works. Working lunch, a couple of drinks with others, dinner one evening. All friendly and straightforward, most of it business.' She knew they understood what she was going to say. 'Then he asks me away for the weekend. River party or something. No problems, he says, plenty of single beds.'

So? It was in their faces.

'So I say I'll think about it and the next day he tells me he can't make it. Probably decided I was serious about single beds and took somebody else. The departmental secretary, I imagine. Why do you want to know?' She decided it was the right time to ask. 'Why are you asking about Gerard Gray?'

'Routine,' the inspector's voice was bland. 'Would you mind if I used the phone?'

The men had both relaxed, she was aware. Partly out of anti-climax, as if something they had been expecting or hoping for had come to nothing. Thank Christ she hadn't allowed herself to panic, thank God she'd made herself face up to them.

'Private?'

'If you wouldn't mind.'

'Use my office.'

The flat was quiet. Walker connected the tape streamer to the computer, inserted a floppy, and transferred on to it the file containing the royal schedule. Then for the next four hours, perhaps closer to five, she went through it, brain concentrating and excitement building. It was strange, she would think in retrospect, how once she'd found it it was so obvious. She ran through the rest of the schedule to make sure there was nothing better, then went back to the beginning and cross-checked. It was strange, she would also think later, how low-key even that moment was. How the thrill dissipated and her mind switched into auto-pilot, accepting that she had the information and deciding how to use it.

She made coffee and checked the street map of London, then she went to the filing cabinet and took out a copy of Kelly's street guide, which was publicly available, plus the edition of the reverse telephone directory covering Mayhill Street, which was not. Mayhill Street was totally residential – no shops or offices. The plan was forming, developing. She turned to the next stage. Kensington was embassy territory, therefore there would be a high police profile – armed stationary and mobile units of the DPG, the Diplomatic Protection Group, in addition to the RPG minders PinMan would be carrying. It was something to build into her computation, something which might mean a slight change of plan. Not something which might invalidate the plan completely, however, unless there was an embassy in or near Mayhill Street. The following day, therefore, she would check the embassy addresses in Yellow Pages, plot the locations of all those in the area, and plan her route in and out.

It was almost five in the morning. She slept for three hours, left the flat shortly before nine, secured the floppy and streamer tape in the bank deposit box, then took the underground to South Kensington and walked the half-mile to Mayhill Street.

The street was lined with trees, no leaves on the branches yet; the pavements were wide and the houses slightly set back, with steps to the front doors, semi-basements below and three storeys above. The odd numbers were on the right as she walked east to west, even on the left. The road itself was some thirty feet wide, residents' parking down one side but parking prohibited on the other. The pavements were almost empty, a nanny pushing a pram towards her, nobody else.

This is where it will happen – she passed number 29. This is where she would win or lose. She checked across and up and down the street, looked for the vantage points where the snipers and marksmen might be waiting for her. Which way would the PinMan car come in, where would she herself be standing. What was more important – to disguise the pick-up as it came in or to give it the easiest run out?

It was a pity she couldn't be there to see Conlan's face when he received the information she would send him, she thought. A pity she couldn't be there when he saw the date she had decided.

8

THE ONLY ILLUMINATION CAME from the desk lamp, the dark green shade protecting his eyes from the glare, the walls of the study lined with books and the rest of the room in darkness. So many shadows, so many more yet to come. One more trip into Europe, then Sleeper would be ready. Conlan slit open the envelope, took out the three sheets of paper folded inside, and began the process of decoding them.

Doherty was getting thinner, he thought. The Chief of Staff's cheeks were slightly hollowed and the pockets round his eyes were deepening. The others had also noticed, already the first whispers had begun about who would succeed Doherty, already Quin had begun his lobbying.

It was eleven at night, the doors of the house bolted, even the door to the study locked. He worked carefully, occasionally noting a recommendation – even more occasionally smiling at a detail. After an hour the decoding was complete. He poured himself a Black Bush and read the message from Sleeper: the date, the details, the probable cost. But above all the date.

It was a pity Sleeper hadn't been able to tell him personally, he would have liked to have seen her face when she told him. But Sleeper knew that both he and Doherty would enjoy it. The Chief of Staff would look at him and ask him to repeat the date, would begin to chuckle, then the chuckle would become a laugh and Doherty would pour them each another whiskey.

He pushed the image aside and considered the other aspects of Sleeper's plan. Funding would be no problem, there was enough money in the coffers. Not just money, clean money, the laundering operation going well. And now the IRA were about to go into property.

He moved on to the next stage of Sleeper's outline: the moment on Mayhill Street and the hours which would follow it. On the date

227

in question the Prince and Princess of Wales had separate appointments until the evening, when they would attend a charity gala
together. The authorities might be able to cover that one, but the
next day would be different. By the next day they would not be
able to cover a thing and it would all be over. Then he would know
whether or not Sleeper had pulled it off . . .

*. . . the bedroom was dark and smelt of musk. The curtains were
drawn and the woman lay still on the bed. Half an hour earlier
Siobhan McCann had received the last rites from the priest who
was her son. Conlan cleared the room and sat by the bedside. The
photographs of her dead husband and her other son were on the
table and the rosary was clasped tight in her fingers. He leaned
over and kissed her on the cheek, saw the way she smiled.*

*Daithi and Eamon are waiting for you, the priest had told her,
soon you'll be with them. Soon you'll be with the family.*

*One secret she was carrying to the grave, Conlan knew, one
torment still tearing at her.*

*'You're thinking of the girl.' His face was close by hers, and his
voice was so quiet even he could barely hear it. One hand holding
hers and the other stroking her face. 'You're thinking of little
Siobhan.'*

*She nodded, afraid to admit it yet afraid not to, as if admitting
it would absolve her from the guilt.*

*'You're wishing you'd never given her up. You're wishing she
knew. Wishing the two of you had met.'*

The nod again, weaker now, the strength ebbing fast.

*'She knows about you and Daithi, about why you and she had
to part.' The woman was sliding away, gently and peacefully. The
sort of words a priest would use, he knew she was thinking, kind
and gentle but meaning nothing, giving her nothing she could hold
on to. 'She knows, Siobhan. She found out and came home. She
and you have met.'*

The face turned, eyes looking at him.

*'The night we laid out wee Eamon. The night we all came to pay
our respects. The one I came back with after, the one you all
assumed was Army Council like the others. That was little Siobhan.'*

The eyes were suddenly bright and young again.

*'She's here now. You've brought her?' The hands were firmer
and the grip harder though the voice remained pitifully weak.*

'That I could not do.'

Why not? the eyes said what the voice no longer had the strength to ask. Why have you not brought her here tonight?

'You remember when Daithi and you and I were young. How we talked of a new Ireland. Of how we would achieve it.'

She nodded, smiled slightly, remembered her husband. But what is this to do with my little girl – the head turned slightly, painfully – why does this mean you can't bring little Siobhan to say goodbye to me? How could you deny me the chance to ask her forgiveness?

The time was almost gone, he knew, even now he was still undecided. 'When you made your sacrifice to protect Daithi you began something which none of us could ever see, could ever plan for.'

What do you mean? Her eyes were clouding again, the mist drifting over the brilliant blue.

'Siobhan cannot be here tonight because we have to protect her just as you had to protect her father.'

Tell me. It was not even a whisper. Tell me the truth.

'She's on active service in London. Not a bomber or a gunman but something else. Something we've all been waiting for.'

Even though he was bent over her and speaking in a whisper, it was as if he was standing upright, shoulders square and hands behind back.

'In three months she will change the course of history. In three months she will achieve the Ireland we dreamed of when we were young.'

The mother's head was still and the face calm. As he held her hands two tears welled in the eyes and rolled softly down her cheeks. Even on his own deathbed Liam Conlan was not sure whether they were tears of pride or tears of sorrow . . .

. . . Doherty would have swept the room before he arrived. He had always been careful, more so since the PinMan project. So he would have closed the curtains, locked the doors, and personally ensured that the room was not bugged. The two men sat in armchairs, the leather worn and soft, the standard lamp behind Doherty and slightly to the left, the glasses of Bushmills resting on the chair arms and the bottle to his right, the top off.

'Sleeper's finalized his plans.'

Doherty listened carefully while Conlan went through the details. 'And how much will it cost?'

'House prices are down, but it might still come to a quarter of a million.'

And how many guns, explosives and surface to air missiles could we buy for that? Conlan knew Doherty was already rehearsing his argument for the Army Council – except, of course, that the Army Council would not be privy to such detail.

'There's one thing which troubles me.' Doherty shifted slightly. 'God knows how, but suppose the Brits found out about Sleeper. What could they do?'

'It depends what they knew. If they knew his identity then presumably they would seek to take him out and the operation would end.'

'But suppose they knew of Sleeper but they didn't know who he was. What then?'

'They could seek to stop him through those running him.'

'Either by removing you, or removing the entire Army Council.' The thought had grown like a cancer in Doherty's mind.

'So what do you suggest?'

The next Council was in two weeks.

'Authorize Sleeper now. Don't wait for the Council. Let me sort out any problems when and if they arise. Tell Sleeper that's the final order. That from now on any order about PinMan must be negative. That he goes ahead with the operation unless we tell him to cancel it.'

And that way, even if the Brits sent the SAS to stiff them all, they wouldn't stop Sleeper. That way, even if the SAS succeeded in taking out the entire Army Council, the only thing they would achieve would be to guarantee Sleeper's attack on PinMan.

'Done.'

'Anything else?'

'Sleeper has not only decided the details of the operation, he has also decided the date.'

'And what date is that?'

Doherty was totally unsuspecting, Conlan thought, Doherty still had no idea. He had anticipated the moment, savoured it, delayed it slightly.

'What date would you like?'

Doherty shrugged. Any date was as good as another.

Doherty will enjoy this, Conlan thought. Doherty will go to his Maker with the smile still on his face.

'Orange Day. The twelfth of July. That's the day Sleeper has decided. That's the day he goes.'

Doherty sat back, head tilted and face to the ceiling. Orange Day – he was beginning to smile. The brollies and bowlers, the drums beating and the batons curling in the air. The Protestants beginning their marches, the Brits doing nothing to stop them. And Sleeper taking out PinMan in the centre of London.

The smile became a chuckle and the chuckle became a laugh. He reached over and poured them each another Bushmills.

The authorization to Sleeper, coded in the personal column, was published in the *Irish Times* two days later. That morning she walked the streets of London – Trafalgar Square, the Mall, Piccadilly – the streets famous in history and steeped in British imperialism. From now she was on her own, from now on the Army Council would instruct her only if they were calling her off PinMan. Of course she and Conlan would be in contact, of course there would be messages via the dead letter drop. But from here the road led beyond the horizon to a point she could not even begin to understand. In a way she was frightened by it, in another not. In a way, she understood, it was the beginning of the end. Even if she accomplished what she was setting out to achieve, there would be no coming back. It was what she had become accustomed to since she had stood on the stairs of the house in Orpington a decade and a half before.

That afternoon she booked an air ticket to the United States, travelling Virgin, leaving for Boston in two days and returning from Los Angeles in mid-August, two months away. That evening, over dinner, she informed Patrick Saunders that she was leaving for America and thanked him when he said he would like to see her to the airport.

The following day she travelled to Paris and placed a credit card and false UK passport, both in the name of Matthews, in a safe deposit box in the Banque Atlantique in the Boulevard Haussmann. On her return she arranged for the telephone to be temporarily cut off, and notified the bank of her plans, making sure that the various standing orders would continue to be paid. On the evening prior to her departure she also informed her neighbours. The following morning Saunders collected her at seven and drove her to Gatwick, standing beside her while she checked in and insisting on a bottle of champagne before she went through. Forty minutes before her flight was due they walked to the entrance to departures.

'Send me a postcard.'

She laughed and kissed him on the cheek, looked back at him once as she showed her passport and boarding card at the first check, then passed through security and passport control.

Virgin flight VA617 landed in Boston three minutes early. She took a cab to the city centre and checked in at the Howard Johnson. The following morning she left her passport in a safe deposit box at the Boston Federal Bank and collected a Canadian passport from a deposit box at the Neworld in Quincy Market. At ten minutes past four she took the Amtrak to New London, then the sleeper to Montreal, arriving shortly before eleven next morning. That evening she took an Air France flight to Charles de Gaulle, arriving at eight the following morning Central European Time. She collected the British passport and credit card from the Banque Atlantique, left the Canadian passport in their place, then caught the late morning boat train to Victoria. Sixty-six hours after leaving Gatwick she was back in London. She took a cab to the Novotel in Hammersmith and checked in using the credit card as deposit but explaining she would pay cash. The following morning she collected £10,000 from the dead letter drop in Abney Park cemetery, then visited a unisex salon in Chelsea and had her hair cut and radically altered. If anyone – a friend, or Saunders – saw her close up they would recognize her, but from twenty yards away she looked totally different. Then she returned to the hotel, placed £9000 in a sealed envelope in the hotel safe, hung the *Do Not Disturb* notice on the door handle of her room, and slept for the next fifteen hours.

Next morning she woke at seven, feeling fresh but knowing the jet lag would overtake her by mid-afternoon, and breakfasted in her room.

The PinMan plan required a house or flat, purchased or rented on a long-term lease. For either, however, she would need a bank, and to open a bank account she would need an address. At 9.30 she began telephoning accommodation agencies, stating that she wanted a well-appointed service flat for three months. By lunchtime she had arranged four visits, using the name Matthews, the first two that afternoon and the others the next morning. By eleven the following day she had made her decision and agreed terms – monthly payments in advance, two months' notice when she left. She paid

£500 deposit in cash and told the agency that she would pay the balance by cheque. Then she went to the Lloyds Bank in Kensington High Street, opened an account – again in the name of Matthews and using the address of the flat – paid in £5000 cash and agreed a special fee for delivery of a cheque book by the next morning. Over the next four weeks Conlan would transfer into that account a total of £250,000, broken down into six payments and made through a series of front companies he had set up for such purposes. At the manager's suggestion Walker would transfer the bulk of the payments into high-interest accounts. The following Monday she checked out of the Novotel, paying cash and retrieving the credit card slip she had signed as deposit, and moved into the flat.

The flat itself was off the Old Brompton Road, far enough from her own in Primrose Hill for the chances of meeting someone she knew to be almost negligible.

The next day she began the visits and telephone calls to estate agents. She was a cash buyer, she told each – she would not need to sell a property in order to buy another and in a housing slump, therefore, was a valuable client. The property could be a house or flat, freehold or on a lease, though there was one requirement which would have to be rigorously met. The property must have a garage which was part of the premises, so that she could enter the house or flat from the garage without having to go outside. If possible the garage itself should have an electronic door, though she was prepared to fit one herself if necessary. Given the rising incidence of attacks on women living alone, she explained, a girl couldn't be too careful.

Quin knew the moment Doherty brought the meeting to order: that Doherty and Conlan had talked and agreed; that Conlan was giving Doherty his chance of a place in the history of the Movement. He looked at both of them, saw it in their eyes. And in return Doherty was placing his money on Conlan as his successor. But Doherty wouldn't pin his colours firmly on Conlan until the PinMan operation was over and had succeeded. If he lived that long. The Big Man was speaking slightly slower nowadays, his eyes were less bright, and he seemed to need to pause more regularly for breath. Of course he covered it, gave the impression he was pausing for effect. He was, after all, the consummate pro. But perhaps the Big Man was going out faster than he admitted even to himself. So

233

what if Sleeper's plans were not as advanced as he feared? What if Doherty's body failed him before Sleeper took PinMan?

They came to the third item on the agenda.

'Sleeper's plans are finalized. He has a location and date for Pin-Man. He has another two weeks, perhaps three, of preparation. Then he's ready.' Conlan sat back in his chair, as if that was all he intended to say on the subject.

'And you still feel that we should know no more than you have told us?'

The question, from the quartermaster, was what Quin wanted asked but which he knew he could not ask himself. Correct, they all knew Conlan was going to say. Instead Doherty leaned forward, arms resting on the table and hands clasped.

'There's something that's been worrying me. Hypothetically of course. At the moment only two men know Sleeper's plans. Liam here, and Sleeper himself. And only Liam knows who Sleeper is. Even I don't know the details. Nor do I have any wish to. But suppose we decided that Liam should tell us the details. That would mean that seven men would know. And suppose the Brits smelt something in the air, suppose they had an inkling of Sleeper.'

Doherty knew, Quin felt the sudden fear: what he'd done and who he'd been talking to.

'And just suppose they decided that they didn't know enough about him and therefore tried to find out by getting at those who did know.'

Doherty didn't know, Quin felt the relief; but Doherty was setting them up for the kill and Doherty was going to win.

'With just Liam knowing, their chances of getting the right man are slim. If we all knew . . . '

'Suppose something else.' It was a member of the General Head-quarters Staff. 'Suppose they stumble on Sleeper, as you say. Suppose they know of him but not enough to know who or where he is. But suppose that they try to stop him by cutting off his line of command.'

'Suppose they try to stop Sleeper by sending the SAS after us?' The intelligence officer expressed the feeling which had descended upon them all.

They've played into Doherty's hand, Quin realized. Doherty and Conlan have discussed this already, have already given Sleeper his instructions.

234

'What do you suggest?' The Chief of Staff looked up.

'We change Sleeper's orders. Instead of telling him he should wait for our final approval we give him that approval now. Tell him that he should go ahead *unless we order him not to.*'

O'Connell Street was busy. Quin walked to the telephone kiosks at the side of the Post Office, inserted the phone card and dialled the direct number in London. The connection took eight seconds. He stood patiently, apparently casually but always checking around him, then heard the ringing tone. The number in London rang four times then switched to an answerphone.

'This is Jacobson. Leave a time when you'll phone back.'

'This is Joseph.' He cupped the mouthpiece slightly closer to his face. He could arrange the meeting now, he thought, tell Jacobson the time and place. Except that Jacobson might not get the message in time. 'I'm calling at ten in the morning, Tuesday the fourteenth. I'll call again tomorrow morning at eleven. That's zero eleven hundred, Wednesday the fifteenth.'

Michaelmass returned to London at six. For the previous 24 hours he had been at a security conference in Bonn. Penrose was waiting. He went through the checklist for the Home Office meeting the following morning, confirmed there had been no developments with Cobra, and wished Penrose good evening. Then he sat alone, as he did every evening, thinking back through the past 24 hours and forward to the next, automatically flicking through the files and checking the answerphone on the direct number he had given Quin.

He heard the change in tone the instant it happened – the empty hollow buzz of the tape, then the sudden click as the machine was activated and the voice began. *This is Joseph.* Sleeper moving, he thought. Perhaps he had hoped as they had all hoped: that Cobra hadn't found Sleeper, that McGuire hadn't led them to Sleeper, either because Sleeper didn't exist or because he'd been pulled off. He listened to the rest of the message, checked his diary for the next 36 hours – assuming already that Quin would suggest a meeting – then called for his car and was driven home. The evenings were lighter and the first leaves were on the trees which lined the street; for thirty seconds he stood looking at them, lost in thought, then went inside.

At seven the following morning he was at his desk. By nine, when Penrose and the rest of his personal staff arrived, he had cleared his paperwork for the day, informed the Home Office that he would not be able to attend that morning's conference, and requested a car on stand-by in Dublin. No driver, Walther PPK, SAS plus tracking gear if they weren't able to get close enough to whatever location Quin would suggest. Assuming that was why Quin had telephoned. It was as if he was preparing for Armageddon, he thought. For the next hour and fifty minutes he tried to busy himself. At ten to eleven he told his secretary he would take no calls for the next half-hour, then he locked his office doors, switched off the answerphone on the direct number, connected the tape recorder, and waited. It was eleven o'clock exactly. The phone on the direct number rang three times before he picked it up, the pause deliberate.

'Yes.'

'This is Joseph.'

'This is Jacobson.' Is this for real, Quin? Or you running a sting? Is it all a come-on? What are you really playing at?

'There's been a development. Perhaps it's time we had another meeting.'

'When?'

'Whenever you want.'

'I could catch an early-afternoon flight.' Or if it isn't that important I could come tomorrow, the intonation of the voice implied.

'The car park at Brittas Bay. Four o'clock. You'll make it easily.'

The line went dead. Michaelmass dialled his secretary and asked for his car, then telephoned the Director General's office and was put through immediately.

'There could be a development with Sleeper. My contact's been on the phone again. I'm seeing him this afternoon.'

'Protection?' The possibility of a trap was a still a prime consideration.

'It's at four.' It had been a balance: tomorrow for his own safety, today if the matter really was that important and he needed to take risks. 'The location's also difficult. It's a car park at the top of a beach, not much cover if we wanted to put someone in and not much time to do it.' And Quin himself might already have it covered.

'Tracking gear on you and the car, I assume, SAS following you.'

'Already arranged.'

'You'll be back tonight?'

'Yes.'

'I'll be waiting.'

*

The beach at Brittas Bay swept in a long and gentle curve between Jack's Hole to the north and Mizen Head to the south; the sand was fine, though not as fine or as white as on the west coast, and marram grass grew on the sand dunes which circled the top of the beach.

Michaelmass turned off the coastal road and bumped the Sierra down the lane. The car park was almost deserted, only one other vehicle there, the driver sitting alone and looking across the dunes to the sea. The afternoon was warm, a faint breeze coming off the sea and the tide out. Michaelmass parked the Sierra fifty yards from the Audi, facing away from the sea and towards the road, then he locked the car and walked over the dunes and down the beach.

'Good day for it.' Quin joined him and they turned right, walking along the water's edge.

The waves lapped against the shore and the gulls circled in the sky.

'Sleeper's in position. He has a target, a date and a location.'

Christ, Michaelmass felt himself almost freeze and fought to hide it.

'You have three weeks. After that he's on go.'

'Anything else?' Even now, even here, they did not face each other. Instead they walked side by side, hands in pockets and facing in front, almost as if they were not holding the conversation. 'Any indication of who or what or when?'

'The target is male. That's all I know.' And even then Conlan had not wanted to tell him, Quin remembered: Doherty and Conlan had needed to be tricked into revealing even that item of information.

It was always going to be either the Queen or the Prince or Princess of Wales, Michaelmass thought.

'How do you know?' How do you know if you say you haven't been given any details?

'Because the man referred to PinMan as *he* or *him*.'

And because PinMan was of the male gender.

The Prince of Wales, Michaelmass confirmed.

'What else?'

Quin shook his head. Your job now, it was as if he was telling Michaelmass.

You've told me nothing, Michaelmass knew he could say, make

237

the outburst deliberate and calculated. You phone, fine. You get me here. Also fine. Then you tell me nothing I can go on. What's the game, what are you playing at? Except that if Quin reacted it would be in the same calculated way and that would get him nowhere. Except that his intuition told him that Quin really had told him all he knew.

They walked on, the water shimmering to their left and the sand rippled with the tide. Without warning Quin stopped, bent down, and dug his hands into the sand.

'We used to dig for cockles when I was a kid. Not here. Some-where like here. When we were on holiday. Then the old man would build a fire and the old lady would boil them, us kids sitting round and singing, the sea air on our necks and the light of the fire on our faces.'

It was a strange memory for a man of violence. Michaelmass would always remember; an incongruous image for a man who had just told him that he was party to a plot to assassinate the future king of England.

'There's one other thing you should know.' Quin straightened and brushed the sand from his hands. 'It was suggested that if you knew about Sleeper but couldn't get to him, you might try to stop him by getting at those who give him his orders.' They began walking again. 'It was therefore decided that Sleeper's orders should be changed.' Michaelmass knew what he was going to say. 'Sleeper's been given the green light. The only order he might receive from us in the future is the order to stop.' So if you decide to take us out, the warning was clear, if you decide to send the SAS after us, then you close perhaps the only route you have of stopping Sleeper. You guarantee that Sleeper goes against PinMan.

'I might need to get in touch.'

'A coded message in the personal column of the *Irish Times*.'

'Fine.'

Michaelmass turned up the beach and across the line of dunes to the car park. The only time he looked back Quin was still walking, hands in pockets and head down. Feet wet and looking for cockles. In the dusk, still three hours off, Michaelmass could imagine the fire crackling and the boys singing.

The Audi and the Sierra were still the only vehicles on the beach. A gull was pecking at the ground in front of the Ford. As Michaelmass unlocked and opened the door the bird screeched as if

238

suddenly frightened, flapping its wings and rising in the air, then circling above the bonnet of the car. Michaelmass settled in the driver's seat and slid the key into the ignition. The gull was circling lower. He turned the key. The gull was straightening, wings back as if it was going to land.

He hadn't checked under the car – the realization hit him. He'd been thinking about the Prince of Wales and kids digging for cockles on a beach like this and had let his defences slip. Hadn't looked for the bomb under the chassis or in the wheel arch. The gull was closing on the bonnet, legs stretched down. Don't land, Michaelmass almost shouted, don't touch the bonnet, don't detonate the bloody bomb. The engine was running, the gull closer. Nice day for it, nice evening to go. The sun in the sky and the sand on his shoes. Too late now. If there was a bomb, if Quin was going to kill him, he'd be dead by now. The gull squawked and veered off. He pushed the Sierra into gear, took the handbrake off, and began the drive to Dublin.

At eleven that evening Michaelmass briefed the Director General; at ten the following morning he addressed the emergency meeting of the Cobra committee. The only person not able to attend at short notice was the Brigadier, Special Forces, who was in the Middle East, and who was therefore represented by the colonel commanding 22 SAS.

Michaelmass's account of his conversation with Quin, whom he did not name, lasted just under two minutes.

'And we think he's serious?' It was the Home Secretary.

'I don't think we have any room to think otherwise.'

'What about McGuire?' Sinclair wrote the name on the pad in front of him, as if it added to his efficiency.

'Still nothing. Two days ago he travelled from Newcastle to Glasgow.'

'But we still think he might be our man?'

'That's the problem. Can we afford to think otherwise?'

'You said that Sleeper has been given the green light.' The SAS colonel looked at Michaelmass. 'That the Army Council will only issue an order for him to stop, rather than for him to proceed.'

'My contact never actually specified the Army Council, but the assumption is correct. And yes, that's what he said.'

'So we can no longer stop Sleeper by negotiating the Army Council?'

'It would seem not.'

'So do I bring my men out?'

Before anyone found out, before someone made even the smallest mistake which might blow up into a major scandal. Except that Catcher was waiting for the man calling himself Donaldson to appear at one of the car hire offices; the SAS also waiting as a back-up in case Donaldson somehow slipped through Catcher's net. But the longer the SAS stayed in the Republic the greater the chance that someone might spot something was wrong. And even now there was no guarantee that Donaldson would show again, no connection whatever between Donaldson and Sleeper.

'Possibly.' He hedged his bets.

Perhaps they should look again at what the contact had told MI5, the head of Special Branch suggested. Perhaps he should lead the discussion, Sinclair came back on him. Hamilton played with his pencil and ignored the slight, drew patterns on his pad as he spoke.

'One: he identified the target as male.'

They discussed the point and the probability which came from it that PinMan was Prince Charles.

'Two: he said that Sleeper also has a date and a location.'

'Yes.'

The discussion was suddenly between Michaelmass and Hamilton, as if they were alone, as if the rivalry between MI5 and Special Branch had suddenly surfaced.

'What does he base that on?'

'What does who base what on?' Sinclair asked.

Michaelmass ignored him. 'Information.'

'And where does Sleeper get that information?'

The Prince of Wales's schedule was known in advance, Sinclair again tried to intervene; where the hell were they leading?

'A leak.'

'Somebody on the staff.' Needn't even be deliberate. They needn't even know what they've done. The sort of detail either not normally issued, or not issued in time for Sleeper to have made his plans already. Perhaps a more private function than an occasion of State.

'So what do you suggest?' Sinclair reasserted his chairmanship.

'Police and security forces to liaise on tracing a possible leak by a member of staff of the Prince and Princess of Wales. Look for a link or a pattern. As we've said, it needn't be deliberate, almost certainly isn't. Full background checks, personal politics, family, friends. Bank statements and telephone records. Telephone taps on from lunchtime, personal surveillance when we've narrowed the field. The teams on the leak enquiries obviously separate from those on the Sleeper investigation.'

Hamilton was genuine, as concerned with Sleeper and PinMan as the rest of them, they all knew. But he was also protecting Special Branch, staking a claim for its lead in the Sleeper investigation and therefore the future.

'Homes or office?' Sinclair was thinking like a politician.

If they tapped the offices of those concerned it meant they were tapping the phones at Buckingham Palace and Kensington Palace.

'Perhaps not offices for the moment. What about friends?'

'No.' Sinclair was adamant. Telephone surveillance on the royal staff was delicate enough; he might just survive it if it ever became public. But authorize surveillance on friends of the Prince and Princess of Wales and it got out, then he would be finished. 'Not friends.'

'Why not tell them?' It was Eldridge from the Anti-Terrorist Squad.

'Why not tell who what?' Sinclair's decision had been made and his manner reflected it.

'Why not tell the Prince and Princess of Wales and ask for their co-operation?'

'Negative.' Sinclair gathered his papers in the manner which meant he was closing the meeting. 'Excellent,' he nodded at Hamilton. A victory for Special Branch, they all sensed, small but significant. 'All agencies to contribute,' Sinclair rose and half took it away. 'MI5 to act as co-ordinator.'

The code appeared in the Tuesday edition of the *Irish Times*. By lunchtime Logan had rearranged his appointments for the next three days and made a telephone reservation at the Westbury. The following morning he drove south, reaching Dublin at midday. He left the car in the hotel garage, checked in, took his travelling case to the room on the fourth floor, changed, ruffled the bedclothes and used a towel. Then he removed the false driving licence and credit card from the hiding-place in the briefcase, left the hotel and took a cab to the airport. The afternoon was sunny and warm, the smell of aviation fuel hanging in the air. As he paid the driver a 747 lifted into the sky.

Nolan's telephone rang at twelve minutes past three, according to the log she kept on the case.

That morning there had been trouble – the story was already circulating round Lisburn, the twists and exaggerations creeping in, but the main theme with the ominous ring of truth. The night before a leading member of the Provisional IRA in Belfast had been gunned down by a Protestant hit squad. Which might have been fine, except that by breakfast the rumour had begun, albeit within a small and confined circle, that the UFF intelligence officer who had planned the hit was an undercover agent for the FRU, the Forward Reconnaissance Unit based at Lisburn which ran the undercover wing of British Military Intelligence. Questions were already being raised: had the informant passed a warning to the FRU; if he hadn't, why not; and if he had, why hadn't Military Intelligence passed the intelligence to the RUC as was required by the so-called police primacy in such cases.

So what would she do if Frank Hanrahan reported to her that an assassination was about to take place? Nolan remembered she had asked herself that after the Flynn shooting. What would she do if the victim was a known Provo or UFF killer whom she knew had been involved in murder but wasn't able to prove it?

What would she do if the target was RUC or army? She took the question on a stage, turned what had happened the previous night on to its head. What would she do if the target was a member of the security forces?

Not her problem, thank God. At least not today. She crossed to her desk and answered the telephone.

'Tiger's running.' Tiger the code for Logan.

'Where?'

'Blue Three.' Blue the code for Dublin airport, three for the Hertz desk.

'When?'

'Fourteen fifty-six.'

She checked her watch. Less than twenty minutes ago.

'Vehicle details?'

She wrote them down.

'Well done.'

She tapped the rest and dialled Farringdon's extension. 'Catcher. Tiger's surfaced.'

'Teams on stand-by?'

'Yes.'

If Donaldson repeated his previous routine then he would return the car between ten in the morning and five in the afternoon of the next day.

'Send them south, I'll notify Cutler and tell London to get their people across.'

She gave him the details and alerted the teams.

Cutler's scrambler call to Michaelmass was connected immediately.

'Tiger's running.'

'When?'

'Thirty minutes ago. Our teams go in twenty minutes.'

'Those from London will be there by tonight.'

The Brigadier, Special Forces, was still away. Michaelmass took the details, told Cutler to wish Catcher good hunting, and telephoned the colonel commanding 22.

Nolan reached Dublin shortly before seven. That evening she briefed the teams, confirmed the formations and codes they would use, and answered or deflected the questions they asked. That night she slept for four hours, spending the other two lying awake in the safe house and staring at the ceiling. Why was she really following Donaldson, why was the original SAS report blocked? It was six in the morning. Why had the SAS been sent south in the first place, why was the SAS staking out the Army Council? It was seven. So who was Donaldson and where was he leading her? She showered and went to breakfast.

The call from Farringdon came through on the scrambler at 8.14. 'Tiger's moving, heading east on the N6.' There was no indication where he had been seen or who had seen him. So why was he so important, she thought. Not him, she knew, the man he had been seeing. Why were there men in OPs, SATCOM to Hereford, scrambler lines from Hereford to London, London to Lisburn and now Lisburn to her in Dublin? It was as if she was being eased into a secret. As if, step by step, she was being led closer to the Holy Grail. So what was so important, she asked herself again. Or who.

She called the teams together and briefed them for the last time, pulled three teams – one motor-cycle and two cars – from the city centre and relocated them on the N6 close to the city, then confirmed she still had the centre covered, albeit more thinly, in case Donaldson used a different route in.

The morning was passing slowly. Nine, nine-thirty, still not ten o'clock. ETA eleven-thirty. Give or take. It was ten-thirty, ten forty-five. She checked with each of the teams. Eleven o'clock. Forty-five minutes to go. She ordered radio silence.

'Yellow Three. Blue Four.' Donaldson on the motorway at Lucan, west of Dublin: Donaldson early and closing. Entering the net. The mood in the car was different, suddenly on the edge, live with adrenalin.

'Yellow Four. Blue Five.' Donaldson off the N4 and at the toll booths on the M50. No point in issuing instructions, the tails knew their job. Would be changing, pulling away, car taking over from bike, bike handing over to car, sometimes in front, sometimes behind.

'Yellow Five. Blue Six.' Donaldson stringing his way through the north Dublin suburbs. Nolan's driver swung into the car park of the Forte Hotel between the motorway exit and the airport.

'Yellow Two. Green Four.' Donaldson on the M1 and heading for the airport. 'Black stand by.' Nolan alerted the vehicle and foot tails in the car park and arrivals lounge. 'Repeat. Black stand by.'

Ahead of him Logan saw the roundabout which marked the end of the M1: first left for Santry, second exit to the airport, third left and the N1 for Belfast. A hundred yards in front of Donaldson a red Sierra turned third left for Belfast; two hundred yards behind an Astra turned first left for Santry. Only after the roundabout had disappeared from his rearview mirror did the Kawasaki 900 ease left and follow him in.

'Black One. Purple One.' Logan parked the Mercedes 190 in the Hertz area and went inside.

'Black Two. Purple Two.' He smiled at the Hertz assistant, handed over the hire form, waited while she computed the fee, paid cash, and tore up the credit card slip he had signed as a deposit.

'Black Three. Tiger at Purple Four.' Logan settled in the back seat of the cab and asked the driver to take him to the city centre. The driver pulled away from the airport terminus towards the exit road. A hundred yards in front the Astra accelerated south on to the M1.

'Yellow Four. White Five.' The cab stopped outside Switzers department store on Grafton Street. Logan paid the driver, hurried inside, took the escalator to the second floor then the stairs at the rear to the ground, and left by the emergency doors on to Clarendon Street.

'Yellow Six. White Seven.' Tails in front and behind, the vehicles tracking along the parallel streets.

Logan crossed Clarendon Street, strolled apparently casually through the Powerscourt Town House shopping centre, glancing at the shops and checking behind him, then left through Mahler's Wine Bar.

'Yellow One. Probably going to White Nine.' Black team to White Nine, Catcher ordered.

'Black One. Tiger at White Nine.' Logan entered the foyer of the Westbury. One more move and she had him, Nolan thought. Unless he was using two covers, unless he was being really careful.

'Black Two. White Ten.' Logan walked to the concierge's desk on the first floor and asked for his room key.

'Your name, sir?'

'Logan.'

Yellow One to rear exit, Catcher ordered and checked the street map. Yellow Three to garage. Black team out of foyer, Blue in.

Logan packed his travelling bag, concealed the false driving licence and credit card in his briefcase, and went back to the main lobby.

'Blue One. White Ten.' He checked out, paying by American Express, and took the lift to the garage.

'Blue Two. White Eight.'

Logan dumped the bag and briefcase in the boot of the Scorpio and drove out of the car park. Fifty yards behind the Kawasaki 900 slid into position.

Catcher dialled the scrambler to Lisburn and spoke to Farringdon. 'Vehicle check.' She gave the details. It would take the Vengeful computer ten seconds. 'Vehicle listed as Ford Scorpio,' Farringdon came back almost immediately. 'Registered owner Michael Logan.' He read the address. Same as the hotel details, Nolan thought; perhaps he really was using only one cover, perhaps she really did have him. Hold, Farringdon told her; the check to see if Logan was on the security file.

'No record. What do you need?'

'Tiger seems to be coming home. Our vehicles are carrying Republican plates, therefore we need tails with Northern plates from Newry. Teams on his house as well.' Plus phone taps and checks, she was already thinking, knew Farringdon would be thinking the same.

'Done.'

Farringdon put the telephone down, spent the next ten minutes organizing more vehicles, then informed Cutler. Two minutes later Cutler informed Michaelmass.

By three that afternoon Logan was back in his own house and the surveillance teams which had located and tracked him in Dublin had returned to London and Belfast. For the next thirty hours Nolan pored over the data which was being pulled together on him, trying to see the pattern which might tell what he had done in the past and what he would do in the future. At eleven in the evening on the day following Logan's return from Dublin she went back to the flat in Malone Park, by midnight she was asleep. So what was Logan playing at – even when she was asleep the question circled in her brain. Who or what was the Holy Grail? The telephone rang five minutes short of seven hours later. She reached for it and realized it was the portable with the scrambler.

'Tiger's moving. Just phoned for a minicab to take him to the airport.'

'He's covered?'

'Yes.'

'And the other teams have been called in?'

'Yes.'

The bag was already packed; she showered, dressed and drove to Lisburn. For the next thirty minutes she briefed the team which would follow Logan on to whichever flight he checked on to. McGuire had gone to England and she had been taken off the case, the suspicion lingered in her mind. Not this time, she told herself. She telephoned Farringdon and left for Aldergrove.

At eight o'clock Logan took the Jersey European Airways flight to Leeds. For the next two days the tails shadowed him as he went from business appointment to business appointment. A cover, Nolan told herself, told the teams. Bloody good cover, though, if that was what it was. On the morning of the third day Logan left his hotel in the centre of Southampton, where he had arrived the previous midday, and took a cab to the airport. The LO returning to Belfast, she supposed, the tail apparently wasted. Except that the early flight to Belfast had left and the next wasn't till five that afternoon. She drove past and waited in the car park. Logan paid the cab driver and went inside. The tail in the bookshop, to the left of the entrance, watched as he crossed the lounge to the KLM desk.

Amsterdam – Nolan received the message. Logan going into Europe, doing something they hadn't predicted. Except that the records suggested that Logan's profession sometimes took him to the Continent. But by leaving Britain he was also leaving her jurisdiction. Europe was overseas, therefore the domain of MI6 and the security services of whichever country Logan might visit. She ordered three tails to buy tickets for the same flight and informed Lisburn of the development. Two minutes later Farringdon passed the information to London.

If he played according to the rules on this one, Michaelmass understood – if he informed MI6 and passed Logan on to them – then the probability was that Six would feel obliged to hand Logan back to them as soon as he returned to Britain. And therefore he would have strengthened his hand in the game with Six in Northern Ireland. Ten minutes later Nolan was instructed that Logan should be shadowed on the plane, but that Six and the Dutch would take over once Logan arrived in Amsterdam.

Orders were orders and rules were rules. Five was under obligation to pass the matter to Six once Logan left the UK, and Six were similarly under obligation to pass him back when he returned. Unless he returned direct to Northern Ireland, in which case Six might not. Before she boarded the shuttle to Belfast, therefore, Nolan requested a priority watch for Logan's return at all points of entry to the mainland and Northern Ireland, by sea or air.

Perhaps it was a face seen twice, perhaps it was instinct. Perhaps it came from problems created by an operation involving the security services of a number of different countries as Logan moved between Holland, Belgium and Germany, with no service knowing in advance when it might be called upon to participate. Perhaps, in the end, it was none of these. Perhaps it was that Logan was a professional who took certain precautions even when he was not aware that the tails were sitting like the shadow of death upon his shoulders.

For three days he moved routinely, making and keeping business appointments. On the fourth the pattern became slightly more irregular and the tails began to lose their grip on him. By the sixth they thought they had him again. On the morning of the seventh he kept a breakfast appointment in Bremen, then checked out of his hotel. Somewhere in the next twenty minutes he disappeared. The next time he was picked up was when he made a telephone reservation for a flight to Manchester two afternoons later, giving as a contact number a hotel in Hanover, subsequent enquiries confirming that for the period when he had appeared to be missing Logan had, in fact, been at the Inter Continental in the city.

At no point, therefore, and in no record, was there the slightest indication of his visit to Berlin and his meeting there with the leader of the Provisionals' ASU in Europe.

'White Two. Blue Three.' Logan left the plane, cleared immigration and customs, and made his way to the car hire offices on the ground floor of the car park opposite the terminal. Catcher sat in the Vauxhall Carlton and waited. MI6 *had* informed them, but Logan's flight *was* to the mainland, and the computer surveillance she had requested had informed her of his flight details ninety minutes before the notification had come through from Six.

'White Three. Blue Four.' Logan leaving the airport and heading for Manchester city centre, the evening light already fading.

Despite the information, there had been problems. No teams were available in Britain, and not enough cars. McGuire – she had heard the rumours. Stretching the net around him even more and Cobra fearing the worse, throwing everything at him. Therefore her teams would have to spend longer on the target than she might have wished, use the same vehicles more than they would have liked.

Logan using the cover of Donaldson twice – she sank back in the seat and tried to see the pattern.

'Green Two. Black Five.' Logan checking in to the Britannia Hotel, the hire car in the NCP car park at the side.

Logan was the key, but what was Logan playing at, where was he leading her?

'White Four. Black Eight.' Noon the following day, Logan attending a business lunch in the city centre and the teams tiring slightly because of the extra pressure upon them.

'White Two. Black Six.' Logan leaving his lunch engagement and picking up his hire car. The afternoon was humid, the threat of drizzle in the air. Logan 200 yards in front of Nolan's Carlton and the tail vehicle 50 yards behind it, afraid of losing it.

'White Two. Static. Am going past.' Nolan saw Logan's Granada pull in to a parking space on the right, the tail Sierra driving past.

The Carlton suddenly the only tail vehicle, the Sierra out until Logan forgot it, the Nissan refuelling and the Escort ahead in the one-way system and not able to turn back. 'Pull in here.'

The driver swung across the road and stopped. No parking zone, Nolan registered automatically, double yellow lines. Fifty yards in front Logan locked the Granada and went into a newsagents. The woman in the back of the Carlton pulled the collar of her windcheater up, left the car and followed him.

Nolan stared at the Granada and began to plan ahead. A break-in at Logan's house or office, or at the offices of the company for which he worked; tell the plumbers to look for any documents which might indicate his movements – photocopies or photos of personal or business diaries and expenses sheets if they struck lucky; hotel, restaurant or petrol bills if they didn't. The things Logan would remember, but the small items which even a professional might temporarily overlook.

There was a tap on the driver's window. Not a tap, more authoritative. She looked across and saw the policeman. The driver wound down his window and looked out

'What's the problem?' The policeman was in his mid-twenties, big build and confidence bordering on aggression.

'Sorry?' The driver was polite, neutral.

'Can't read?' The constable indicated the 'no parking' sign five yards in front.

He's going to make the driver get out, Nolan thought. Make him stand on the pavement and ask him what the double bloody lines are for.

Ex-squaddie, she saw the medal ribbon on his uniform. The green and dark blue, almost purple, for General Service in Northern Ireland. Single tour, she looked at it and remembered the nickname. One inch of glory.

'If you would be so kind as to step out, sir.' The words were polite, slightly mocking.

Fifty yards away Logan returned to the Granada. If he stayed they were in trouble, if he moved they might lose him. The driver glanced at Nolan and saw her nod.

'Priority check on the registration number of this vehicle, constable.' His voice was suddenly hard and unyielding. 'Make it fast.'

The policeman half-understood. CID, he supposed, DS – Drugs

249

Squad – or Customs and Excise. He pressed the transmit button of his radio and asked control for an immediate check.

Vehicle number blocked, Nolan did not need to hear the reply, saw it on his face. Sorry, he began to say. Logan was pulling out. No problems, the driver told him. They let Logan go thirty yards then followed him.

Two hours later Logan returned the Granada to the Hertz office at Manchester Piccadilly railway station and caught the 5.30 train to London. The following day he would return to Belfast. At 6.30 PC Michael Hendrick returned to the divisional headquarters building on Bootle Street for his evening break. The station was busy and the canteen was crowded. He helped himself to steak and kidney pudding and sat at a table with a sergeant from the control room and two other constables, one from traffic.

'What was that about this afternoon?' It was the traffic PC.

Even though Hendrick was the same age as the others his army background, and the fact that he had served in Northern Ireland, gave him a credibility he was not reluctant to exploit.

'Vehicle check, that was all.'

Behind him a canteen assistant cleared a tray of dirty plates, to the right someone from CID was talking to a civilian, to the left two electricians who had been rewiring the second-floor offices were finishing mugs of tea.

'Vauxhall Carlton. Two-litre model.' He enjoyed the way the other policemen at the table were impressed.

'Registration number?' The traffic PC took up the challenge.

Hendrick told him, did not need to check it in his notebook.

'So why the fuss?'

'Blocked, that's why. Control checked and were told to lay off. Somebody up to a bit of naughty in Manchester today.'

'CID? One of ours?'

Hendrick shook his head. 'Wouldn't be blocked if it was one of ours. Security services, I reckon.'

He sat back, basking in triumph.

'How'd you know that?'

Hendrick tapped the green and blue ribbon on his chest. 'Northern Ireland. Seen it all before.'

The code was in the *Irish Times*. Walker read it at nine. At ten she viewed the flat in the mews off Dunton Street. In the past two weeks she had seen six other properties, none of them meeting her requirements. The estate agent was waiting; he was in his late twenties and smartly dressed, a Toyota Supra parked outside.

The mews itself was some fifty yards long and entered through an archway. The centre was cobbled and the flats on each side had been converted without losing the character of the coaching yard the mews had once been.

The flat in question was priced at £225,000. On the ground floor was a garage, an inner door leading from it to a narrow hallway. A separate front door also led into the hallway. On the first floor was a lounge, a kitchen at the rear; and on the second were two bedrooms and a bathroom.

'I'd like to look at it by myself.' They were standing in the centre of the lounge. 'Like to get a feel of the place.' Her voice was friendly, a smile on her face. 'Give me fifteen minutes.'

'I'll wait downstairs.'

'I said I wanted to look at it by myself.'

'Fine.' He tried to smile. She watched as he crossed the yard and disappeared through the archway, then she went to the garage, took the tape from her pocket, and measured the height of the door. A Volkswagen camper was between seven and eight feet high, depending on the type of roof, and the door was seven feet six. She walked round the yard and looked at the other apartments. No curtains moving, no one peering to see what was going on, who the new neighbour might be. A yuppy mews if the expression wasn't out of date, but the same types living there. Young and professional, no children, at work all day. She went back inside. The rear windows overlooked a tangle of back yards, she noted, nothing and no one overlooking the flat. Curtains of the rear bedroom window drawn, she was already planning, easy to build a solid wall inside to form a containment area.

The agent came up the stairs. 'How's it going?'

'What's the asking price?'

'Two two five.'

'One five.'

He flinched, tried not to show it. 'They might take two twenty.'

'I'm a cash buyer. The legal search could be done in a week. I'd be prepared to exchange and complete the same day.'

So, he almost did not dare ask.

'Tell them I'll go to one sixty.'

251

There was no point wasting the Movement's money: £65,000 would buy an awful lot of anything in today's arms glut.

'I don't think they'll take it.'

'You have a car phone?'

He nodded and went downstairs, returned five minutes later. 'Two ten.'

'One seventy.' It was not her money, except that it was now a matter of principle.

'Perhaps I should suggest two hundred thousand.'

She shook her head and began to leave.

'One nine five?' He followed her down.

'One eight. Ten per cent deposit now, refundable if the legal and property checks are unsatisfactory.'

She hadn't mentioned surveyors' reports, he noted. He smiled again, as he had been smiling all morning, and went to the car. A hundred and eighty thousand, he confirmed when he came back.

The following morning Walker checked with the bank and solicitors that the various legal and financial arrangements she had set in motion were proceeding satisfactorily, then took the Victoria Line to Finsbury Park and walked the two miles across the sprawl of north London to Abney Park cemetery. The church in the cemetery seemed dirtier than before, even though it was spring, and the weeds were growing at the base of the wall which concealed the dead letter drop.

Three days later Tighe received the instructions from Dublin. Tighe and the men he commanded were not an active service unit. The most secret and secretive department of the GHQ of the Provisional IRA in Dublin was that dealing with English operations, and the most sensitive of that department's operations were those concerning not the ASUs, which might have been expected, but the flying columns.

The flying columns were small in number, and were the only PIRA units allowed to be fully armed 24 hours a day. Whilst most people had heard of the active service units, the ASUs, few outside the General Headquarters staff of the Provisional IRA had heard of them; even within GHQ their details were a closely guarded secret. The men in them were hand picked and intensively trained, and most were from South Armagh. On the mainland the flying columns were under orders to immerse themselves in the population, and were reserved for special operations. Thus Tighe and his men wore business suits, operated out of Holland Park, and the last operation they had undertaken was the escape of two IRA men from Brixton prison.

The instructions which Tighe received, therefore, were interesting for two reasons, first because they signalled a major operation in the future, and second because they came not from GHQ but from the Army Council itself. And then not from the Army Council as a whole, but from one member of the Council, the order emphasizing the secrecy of the instructions, and that secrecy confirmed by the Chief of Staff.

The orders were also specific. He was to acquire two cars – modern and large, Granada, Carlton, 505; he was to take them west, have them serviced and tuned, then he was to conceal them in a manner which could not be traced.

He was also to acquire two Volkswagen campers.

The first would be in good condition and should have a fixed rather than elevating roof. He would purchase it in Brick Lane, in the East End of London, where students and other travellers from Australia and New Zealand bought and sold the vehicles which would take them across Europe. He would use the registration document to buy a twelve-month road fund licence, then he would have the vehicle serviced and tuned, and return it to a specified location two weeks after purchase. He would lock the vehicle, but leave a spare set of keys in a magnetic key box in the front off-side wheel arch.

The second Volkswagen would be of a similar age, though the condition would be irrelevant. He would buy a twelve-month road fund licence for the vehicle, plus a set of new number plates. He would replace the old plates with the new, then resell the vehicle in Brick Lane. He would leave the road fund licence and the old plates in the first vehicle.

The day after he received his instructions he went to Brick Lane.

That morning Walker left for Berlin.

It was late afternoon, the office clearing.

Nolan spread the documents on the desk and tried to identify the one thing about them which would give her the pattern to Logan's behaviour – MI6 surveillance reports, plus those from the various countries Logan had visited, on the left, and photographs or photocopies of material which the plumbers had acquired from their visits to Logan's house and office on the right.

The surveillance reports were in two sections: the overview of Logan's movements, and the detailed day-to-day notes of the surveillance teams. She read them again then put them to one side and turned her attention to the material acquired by the plumbers: diaries, appointments books, business expenses. She checked quickly through the diaries and appointments, then singled out the expenses for the last three trips and scanned down them. Logan had already submitted his expenses for the first two; for the third, however, the bills and receipts had been placed in an envelope, as noted in the plumbers' report.

The starting point; she imposed the discipline upon herself.

Within days of what she assumed were his briefing visits to the Republic, Logan had made business trips away from Northern Ireland. In both there was a pattern, and the patterns were the same: two or three days in England, up to nine in Europe, then another two or three in England before returning to Belfast. So Logan was a businessman, Logan's job required him to travel. She checked back through the diary entries. In the preceding twelve months Logan had made an average of two trips per month to the mainland and an average of one trip every six weeks to Europe. But those trips were of two or three days' duration compared with the eight to ten on those following what she assumed were his visits to his political and military masters in the Republic.

The afternoon drifted into early evening, the office quiet.

For the next two hours she studied the documents relating to the first trip, then the second, still looking for the pattern. The light outside was beginning to fade. She took two sheets of paper, wrote a day-by-day diary of the two trips, then pinned them side by side on the wall to her right, shifted the chair back, and studied them. So what did she see, what was she looking for? She leaned forward, adjusted the desk lamp so that it was shining up and on to the lists, then looked at them again.

Nothing.

Logan was either very careful, or he was genuine. But if he was genuine he wouldn't have changed his identity in Dublin, wouldn't have been in contact with a member of the Army Council of the Provisional IRA. She cleared the desk top, spread the surveillance reports of Logan's most recent trip across it, and began the same process, writing her diary of the surveillance on Logan, the day-to-day minutiae, then pinning it with the others on the wall and sitting back in the chair, studying it, concentrating on it. Walked round the room and glanced back at it, looked at it from a different angle.

Christ, she suddenly thought.

Every day was full of detail. Except a day and a half, almost two days, towards the end. The pattern was so clear it screamed at her. For more than 36 hours Logan had gone missing. For almost two days, from when he was last seen in Bremen until he made the telephone booking for his flight back to Britain, there was no record of his movements other than the fact that he was resident at the Inter Continental in Hanover. The tails had let him give them the slip: the full horror of what had happened descended upon her. And when he had reappeared they had thanked God and covered themselves.

So what did it tell her, where did it suggest she begin looking? She wasn't there yet, was nowhere near. But at least she was at the beginning. She swivelled in the chair, turned the lamp back on to the desk, cleared the top again and spread out the expenses sheets for the two trips after he was known to have visited a member of the Provos' Army Council, plus the receipts which accompanied them.

Still nothing.

She was missing something, she reprimanded herself. Assume Logan has a pattern, assume Logan thinks it works and therefore repeats it. So what was the key? On the last trip the tails missed Logan for 36 hours. Fact or fiction? Had they missed him or had he really been holed up in the Inter Conti for the entire period?

She cleared the desk again, spread out the expenses sheets and bills and receipts relating to the second trip, and concentrated on them. Then she did the same with items relating to the first trip, separating the bills and receipts into days then concentrating on each day in turn, beginning to see it. The key, she reminded herself – for 36 hours towards the end of the third trip Logan might have gone walkabout.

For the first time she felt a tinge of excitement.

For the blocks of days at the beginning and end, all the bills or receipts were similar – hotel bills, restaurant or petrol, most of them computerized and therefore giving locations and dates. But for one short period between they were different. Hotel bills, of course,

255

entered on the computerized sheets, but only those which Logan could order in advance or which he could incur without actually being there. And the others. They were the giveaway. She sat up in triumph. They were where Logan had tried to cover his tracks but failed.

Except for the hotel bills, all the bills for the period when Logan might have gone AWOL were either undated, or if they were dated the date had been handwritten. She leaned forward again and checked the bills against the town or city where Logan was supposed to have been during the period in question. Of six bills, three carried the name and address of a restaurant in the correct location, but were handwritten – and therefore could have been written by Logan himself – and the remaining three carried the correct dates and were not written in Logan's hand, but were what she called generic bills, with the name of a beer or lager across the top rather than a specific restaurant or bar, and could therefore have come from anywhere.

It was almost midnight.

She made herself a coffee and looked for the pattern in the expenses for the second trip, found what she was searching for. Then she repeated the process for the third trip – even though Logan had not yet submitted an expenses claim – and confirmed the pattern again.

So what did it tell her; what was Logan doing? It was gone two, closer to three, her mind and body were tired and her eyes felt like sandpaper.

What was Logan? A financier, a purchaser of weapons, a link between the Provos and other terrorist groups in Europe? He had no security record, he was clean, yet Logan was in regular contact with a member of the Army Council.

Jesus Christ. The realization jerked her awake. Logan was an LO, a liaison officer. One of the men who ran the shooters and bombers. And not any LO. The LO for the ASU thought responsible for the killings in Venlo and Mons

Logan in, then goes missing. Logan in touch with the ASU. Logan pulls out and when he's safely home in Belfast the ASU murders some poor Brit.

She checked the expenses sheets. There was no record of him having been anywhere near either place, but there wouldn't be. Logan was a pro; he wouldn't make that sort of mistake.

Logan making a third trip, the horror mixed with the excitement,

Logan going missing again. Therefore another hit coming up.

She made herself a fresh coffee, laced it with Bushmills, and examined the seven receipts which she had singled out as covering the missing 36 hours on that trip. Logan had already made one mistake, had allowed her to spot him, therefore he might have made another. In two hours it would be light, in three she could go for breakfast. She topped up the mug with Bushmills and concentrated on the receipts.

When the plumbers had broken in Logan hadn't had time to go through them; in his neat and methodical way he had just transferred them from his wallet to an envelope. By now he would have filled out his expenses and discarded those he did not need or which might give a clue to where he had really been. But the plumbers had got there first. She stopped rubbing her eyes and concentrated on the photocopies of the receipts.

Two were from restaurants in Bremen, the name and address across the top, which might have suggested that he had not left the city, except that they were undated and could have been acquired at any time. Three others were for snacks or meals, but carried the name of a brewery or type of beer across the top or bottom. The fourth was also a bar receipt, though with a difference. The front was like the other three, advertising a beer or lager – in this case Kronenbourg – across the bottom, but was blank. On the back was a series of drawings and figures.

Six receipts for the target period, two traceable and four not. She left the office, went to the washroom and splashed cold water over her forehead and cheeks. She was wrong. The water trickled down her face and the realization hit her. Two weren't traceable, three were. The third because it was different, even though it didn't have a restaurant or hotel name on it. And that was where Logan had gone wrong; he should have paid it, torn it up, and dropped it on the floor or burned it in the ash tray. But because he assumed he was clear, he had not done so.

She hurried – almost ran – back to the office and looked at the bill.

In the top left corner was the number three. In the centre of the top was what appeared to be a flag. Down the left side were a series of drawings, figures opposite them on the right. She focused on the drawings. On the first line were what seemed to be two pots, bowls, she wasn't sure. On the next a bottle, below it shapes similar to the

257

first but not identical, on the next what seemed to be two plates, something on them. Then two coffee cups and two wine glasses. Not wine glasses, brandy glasses.

Two bowls of soup and a bottle of wine. Salad, then steak. Another bottle of wine then coffee and cognac. She checked the figures on the right and the total below them. Reasonable, she thought, depending on the food.

She looked at the image in the bottom left corner.

A set of snow-capped peaks, trees in front, sun rising behind. *Hand made* down one side, as if stamped on. *Merci* handwritten at the bottom.

She looked at the top of the paper. The number three on the left – table three. The flag in the centre. The Union Jack, she realized, and smiled at the irony.

A French restaurant somewhere in Germany. Germany or Austria, she corrected herself. Or wherever they sold Kronenbourg. A big place, Europe.

*　　　*　　　*

Two targets, the instructions from Conlan had said, both lance-corporals assigned to one of the British intelligence units stationed at the Olympic Stadium. Saturday evening, the Irish Pub in the Europa Centre in the middle of what had been West Berlin. Their photos, plus details of their standard movements on Saturday evenings, would be in the dead letter drop in the Tiergarten.

It was the last job before the spectacular and probably the most difficult. For that reason she had arrived by train a day early, slipped unnoticed through the station at the Zoo Gardens and checked in to a small pension. For that reason she had already recce'd the locations and would recce again in the morning.

She crossed the square at the east end of the Ku'Damm, entered the Europa Centre, and went down the stairs to the Irish Pub.

Heinz Dombrowski had been second-in-command of the BND office in Berlin for three years. Dombrowski was 35 years old, married with two children. He was extremely efficient, which was to be expected for a man with ambitions for high office, yet at the same time possessed of a flexibility of mind that sometimes singled him out. That morning, therefore, when the request for assistance had been forwarded to his office by the BND officer liaising with British Intelligence in the city, it had seemed perfectly logical to Dombrowski that he should do three things.

The first was to circulate the item in question in his own department and the second, which may have been influenced by the fact that in 24 hours he would begin two weeks' leave, was to delegate responsibility to one of his section leaders. It was the third course of action, however, which singled Dombrowski out. His men operated at one level, but there were others who knew the city better, who slid in and out of the bars and cafés and restaurants just as his moved in and out of the intelligence world. For that reason he had sent copies of the restaurant bill which the British were trying to trace to the Drugs Squad and criminal investigation.

It was a long shot, he had thought when he had received the request. French restaurant with Kronenbourg beer and an interesting way of doing the bill. The sort of place you'd stumble across in five years' time and realize *that* was what the Brits had been looking for, except that by then it would be too late. It was interesting, though. Not just the copy of the bill, but the fact that he had received two other copies that morning. One from Military Intelligence and the other from MI6.

The phone rang while he was fetching coffee from the machine along the corridor. Fuchs on line one, his secretary told him.

'*Ja?*' He sat down, spilling some of the coffee on the desk, and took the call.

'The restaurant bill.'

'Which restaurant bill?'

'The one the English want.'

'What about it?'

'We've got it. Somebody from Drugs Squad is on his way.'

The undercover agent arrived fifteen minutes later. He was in his mid-twenties, thin and casually dressed in Levis and jacket. Dombrowski and Fuchs offered him coffee and closed the door.

'The place you want is the Ty Breizh Café, in Charlottenberg.'

'Any drug connection?'

'No. I know it because I live round the corner and eat there regularly.'

'What sort of place is it?' Dombrowski assumed the British would ask.

'A crazy place. Does Breton food, hence the name. Good chef and mad owner. He's the guy who does the bills. Good music, he sings to it, sometimes switches it off and sings alone. People come in and sing for their supper, take a hat round after. Sounds casual but he must turn over one hell of a profit.'

He pulled a book from his jacket and handed it to Dombrowski. It was a volume of poetry, slim and hardback, bound in cloth. *Matthias Knoll. Der Bogen.*

'Last night the owner spouted a speech from some French play, then this young guy got up and quoted a poem. Sold us all a copy of his book after, of course.'

Crazy people, Berliners, Dombrowski thought, crazy city. He opened the volume at random. The poem was titled 'Riga', two lines standing out: *Coming home, find no sleep in the dark*, and below those another: *The unmistakable voice of humankind.*

'Sure.' He closed the book and gave it back to the undercover policeman. No sleep in the dark for the British, he thought, not too much humankind either if they were as worried as they seemed to be. He thanked the Drugs Squad agent and telephoned the British section at the Olympic Stadium.

Overnight Berlin had changed. Not obviously, and not to those who did not know. But suddenly Berlin was tight, security everywhere. British and German.

Walker sat at a table in the Irish Pub and glanced round her. She was wearing a dress and loose-fitting coat with large pockets, and had spent the early part of the evening changing her appearance. It was two in the morning, the bar packed, the targets sitting where the instructions had said they would sit, to the left of the bar, and the eyes were all round her. At least three Brits, she had counted, probably military police judging by the way they sat, glass of Guinness made to last all evening and shoulders slightly hunched to help conceal the weapons they were carrying. Plus two from the German GSG-9, younger and more casually dressed. Spot them a mile off if you knew what you were looking for, the sheer physical feel of them, the almost aggressive fitness which exuded from them. Twice that evening one of them had peeled off and followed a suspect from the bar.

It was twenty past two, the targets finishing their drinks and calling for the bill. Clockwork routine, the instructions had said, arrive at ten, leave at 2.30, Ford parked behind Wittenbergplatz.

She left the bar. Unmarked surveillance car behind the Europa Centre, she noted, two men in the front, dead giveaway. The targets passed the car, turned off Wittenbergplatz and stopped at the Ford. They were laughing, singing quietly. The driver fumbled for his keys, opened the doors and they tumbled in. The night was quiet. She waited till she heard the engine turn over, then walked down the street, stopped by the car, and bent over by the driver's door.

'Going to give us a good time?' The soldier laughed and wound down his window.

'Perhaps.'

She raised the Ruger and fired four times.

9

RODDY FAIRFAX LEFT MÜNSTER shortly after two in the morning. May was going into June, the night was warm, the speckled black of the sky merging into the purple of the countryside. The soft top of the Porsche was down and the wind whipped through his hair. South on the A43, then west past Duisberg and Venlo – the route and times were clear in his mind. Coffee at one of the service stations between Eindhoven and Antwerp, just as the light was coming up, and Calais by six, seven at the latest. Coffee and cognac, then the 0730 ferry to Dover. No point in getting the earlier one and sitting for the next two hours in the jam of idiots trundling into London in the morning rush hour.

The 944 was barely ticking over at a hundred and five.

The flat in Onslow Square, quick shower, then lunch at Kensington Palace. They'd love the thought that he'd just driven non-stop across Europe. A couple of hours' kip late in the afternoon, and the Tower that evening to view the Ceremony of the Keys with an American contact. Then the rest of his week. Lunch with Saunders the day after; a few items of regimental business he'd promised to sort out, polo at Cirencester on Saturday, though he didn't play, then the drive across to Highgrove. Special guests only, he'd been given to understand, though Charles hadn't quite used that expression. Then the late night dash on the Sunday: the midnight ferry to Calais and the drive through the night to make the adjutant's parade at 0800 Monday morning.

Christ, how he loved it.

The night was warm. He rolled a sweater across his shoulders and left the top down.

The battalion had been in Münster since February. It was the standard tour, standard exercises. Except that the bite had gone out of it all. Now that the Berlin Wall had come down, Germany was reunited and the Soviet empire totally disintegrated into republics, the whole thrill and tension of exercises under the noses of the enemy had evaporated. Germany was still a nice little tour, of course, good jumping-off spot for winter skiing, plus the glaciers in the summer. But it was no longer a soldier's posting.

Nowhere was any more. Except Northern Ireland.

Perhaps he should start thinking about his future, seriously consider the various offers he'd had from the business and banking contacts he'd built up over the years.

Bloody Northern Ireland. In the mess the night before there had been talk of what the tours there would be like in the future now that the government was cutting back on everything. He remembered his first tours there, the tension building up, tightening, as the hunger strikers queued up to die. What was the name of the first one, the bastard who'd started it all? McCann. That was it. Eamon bloody McCann.

Cobra met at ten. The mood was always serious, always tense, but this morning, Michaelmass thought, the atmosphere was more brittle, the faces and voices tighter. His own included. His own especially.

It was a fortnight since Quin had told him that in three weeks Sleeper's plans would be in place, therefore in one week from today Sleeper would be ready to strike at the royal family. Yet in the past fourteen days he and his people had turned up nothing. The same with Special Branch and the Anti-Terrorist Squad.

Plus himself, Sinclair would have added. Because at the end of the day, unless they pulled something out of the bag, it was he as Home Secretary who would have to stand in Parliament and take the flak, who would be called upon to resign.

'Right, gentlemen. Let's get on with it.' Sinclair sat slightly hunched, arms on the table and hands folded. 'This evening the PM sees Her Majesty. What does he tell her?' They knew he hadn't finished. 'I myself am briefing the Prince and Princess of Wales. What do I say to them?'

The look at Michaelmass, Eldridge and Hamilton was deliberate, almost accusing, certainly aggressive. *You* raised the whole matter – at Michaelmass. *You* have failed to find Sleeper – at the three of them. God help you all if we don't find him. The eyes came to rest on Michaelmass. You were the one who got us into this mess, who came up with the intelligence that the IRA was plotting against the

263

royal family. And if you hadn't we wouldn't be sitting like this now. Except that if you hadn't we wouldn't know of the possibility of a royal threat – Sinclair was not in the mood to be generous. But God have mercy on your soul and your future, or lack of it, if this whole affair is a scam.

'You have to tell them the truth. That, so far, we have been unable to come up with anything.'

'Updates?'

The agenda was familiar – no leads or information on Sleeper, McGuire was still stretching the surveillance teams but taking them nowhere, forensic evidence on the Berlin shootings confirmed that the weapon was that used for the Venlo and Mons killings. So where do we go from here, Michaelmass wondered, what new lines do we follow?

'Any suggestion of a connection between Europe and Sleeper?' It was the Brigadier, Special Forces.

'Nothing that we've been able to establish.' Michaelmass considered how he should phrase his next remark. 'Although there is close co-operation between the various agencies involved, such incidents are not the responsibility of MI5. Therefore we can't conduct our own investigations.'

Although the bastards would like to, Hamilton was tempted to whisper to Eldridge.

It was Catcher who'd tagged McGuire and made the connections which led them to Logan, Michaelmass suddenly thought. Perhaps he should bring her to London, listen to whatever she came up with. Not that he would tell everything, of course, not that he *could* tell her much.

'And how are the royals reacting to the increased protection?' Sinclair changed the subject.

'They're not exactly happy.' Denton had debriefed the members of the Royal Protection Group personally. 'They understand that it's necessary but object – quite naturally – to the increased intrusion into their lives.'

'And would therefore like it off as soon as possible?'

The Home Secretary trying to cover himself both ways, Denton thought. 'Yes.'

'What about the royal engagements over the next months? Do any of them indicate where Sleeper might strike? If, of course, the threat is real.'

The last phrase was unnecessary, thought Hamilton. As if Sinclair was berating the Opposition in the Commons rather than addressing senior members of the police, army and security services at a meeting of Cobra.

They discussed the possibilities, neither rejecting nor opting for any. It was that stage of an enquiry, they all understood, the doldrums, knowing a lead was unlikely but hoping to hell something would turn up.

Sinclair began to wind up the meeting.

'There is one other matter, Home Secretary.'

'Yes.' The turn of the head was sharp, almost as if Sinclair objected.

'The enquiries into the possible leak of the royal schedule.' It was politically delicate, Hamilton was only too aware, the sort of issue the politicians didn't want to dirty their hands on. 'So far we've come up with nothing.'

'So?'

'At our last meeting you decided that friends of the Prince and Princess of Wales should not be included.'

'Correct.'

'I wonder, given the circumstances, whether we should reconsider.'

The Home Secretary closed his file and stood up. 'No.' He left the room.

He would speak to Cutler this afternoon, Michaelmass decided, arrange for Catcher to be sent over. A long shot, of course, but nothing to lose, nobody else had come up with anything. Worth bringing her over for a morning anyway. He wished the others good morning and walked to his car.

Time to forget the niceties, Hamilton and Denton would agree as they walked back to New Scotland Yard. Time to ignore the restrictions the Home Secretary had imposed upon them in their search for Sleeper. Time for the police service to show solidarity in the battle with MI5.

The Cabinet offices off Whitehall are 600 yards from the concrete and glass tower which houses New Scotland Yard. Hamilton and Denton left the meeting at 11.20 and arrived back at their offices at 2.10, their route having taken them via the rear bar of the Phoenix public house, close to Buckingham Palace. By 6.30 the first list of names of the personal friends of the Prince and Princess of Wales had been collated from the men who were their bodyguards and passed to Special Branch. At seven Hamilton briefed the team he had personally selected to conduct the enquiry. As with the checks into the royal staff, the team were given no intimation of the PinMan threat. All day, 24 hours a day, he told them. When he left his office at ten the team were converting the material they had already gleaned into computer format.

The last thing that Nolan checked before she flew out of Aldergrove, and the first thing she confirmed when the shuttle touched down at Heathrow, was that the surveillance on Logan was running smoothly. Then she left Terminal One and took the underground into central London. Why had she been summoned, she wondered. Something to do with the Donaldson affair, she assumed, something to do with the fact that she had made the Logan connection but hadn't covered her tracks sufficiently. Except that the meeting that morning was with Michaelmass, and Michaelmass was the Deputy Director General.

She changed trains, took the Victoria Line to Warren Street and walked to Gower Street. The morning was warm and sunny, the noise of London all around her. She turned into the anonymous building which was the headquarters of MI5, showed her identification at the security check, and was asked to wait in a small and sterile anteroom on the first floor. Three minutes later Penrose came in and shook hands.

'Good to see you again.' The office boy with the immaculate suit and accent, she remembered. 'Show you upstairs right away.'

They left the anteroom and took the lift. 'Good flight over?' He was slightly anxious and talking too quickly, Nolan thought. She didn't know why she'd been summoned to London, but he knew even less and it worried him. 'Fine.'

They left the lift and walked down the corridor. This isn't Belfast, the feeling crept up on her, this isn't Lisburn, where the tension seeps in from the streets and permeates everything. This is calm and controlled and so very British. But this is power. Permeating the walls and rising from the carpet. Not required to answer to the public which it serves, not even accountable to the politicians who are supposed to be its masters.

Penrose stopped outside the third door, knocked firmly but politely and held it open for her. The room was the domain of a personal secretary, one door leading off it to the left and closed, and another to the right, which she correctly assumed was Penrose's. The woman at the desk was in her mid-forties, attractively though soberly dressed. She glanced at Nolan, the merest hint of a nod acknowledging her, and pressed the intercom.

'Your appointment has arrived.'

It was an interesting term, Nolan thought. *Appointment.*

Penrose knocked on the door to the left and opened it for her.

First impressions, Nolan thought. Hers of Michaelmass, Michaelmass's of her.

The Deputy Director General looked sharp; comfortable and relaxed, but everything concealed by a veneer. The mahogany desk dominating the room and Michaelmass dominating the desk. He looked up from the report he was studying and indicated that she should take the chair in front of the desk.

'Coffee?'

Everything totally functional and efficient, Nolan thought, no handshake because that would imply the meeting was social, no courtesy of rising as she entered because he would not have risen for one of his male officers.

'Milk, no sugar.' So why was she here, why had she been summoned to the inner sanctum?

'Good trip?'

'Fine, thank you.'

Why was one of the most powerful people in British Intelligence offering her coffee?

'Good work in Belfast recently.'

Penrose's return with a tray saved her an answer. Michaelmass waited till he left the room.

'You were responsible for the McGuire and Logan operations. In retrospect, what are your impressions?'

Michaelmass was not asking for impressions, Nolan knew: impressions didn't count. What mattered was analysis. Taking a case beyond the point where others might stop. Even using other people's finishing point as your start.

'You're asking three things to begin with.'

'One: what are McGuire and Logan up to? We know Logan is connected to the killings in Europe, but I don't know about McGuire because I was taken off the case.

'Two: is there a connection between the two?'

She wondered how far to go.

'Three: is there a connection between one or both of them and something that you know about but I don't?'

Michaelmass looked at her calmly. 'I'm asking a great number of things.'

So what is it that you know, Nolan wondered. What is it that you've brought me to London to tell me?

'The starting point is that something is either wrong or missing.'

How? The question was unspoken, his eyebrows raised slightly.

'McGuire first. There was something wrong with him from the very beginning. We had no option except to do what we did in Northern Ireland, and you had no option to do anything other than what you did on the mainland.'

'How?' he asked aloud this time.

'You've operated in Belfast?'

Nolan was not here to ask questions, Michaelmass thought. Especially to ask such questions. 'I was Director of Intelligence there.' So even though others might not understand, he would.

'Over a period of three days, six known Provos start moving. Not just Provos, men known to have been associated with previous bombings and shootings. The opposition know that's the sort of thing we're looking for. At the same time McGuire, a known LO, goes missing. Then McGuire surfaces, temporarily and in the dead of night, then he goes on the gallop, at first in the North and finally on the mainland.

'Three possibilities follow from this. The first is that the six Provos and McGuire are unrelated. The second is that the six were ordered to start moving in order to disguise whatever McGuire was up to. The third, however, is that everything – McGuire included – was a scam to cover something else.'

Michaelmass was worried, she thought. Michaelmass was close as you could get to God Almighty – unless you were the Director General, the Virgin Mary or the Angel Gabriel – and he was worried witless. Something else happened at the time that McGuire began moving, something that was the reason for everything.

She moved the argument forward.

'Logan was different. Let's assume we were supposed to spot McGuire. We were never supposed to spot Logan. He was using cover, he was always a pro. McGuire was as well, of course, but let's suppose McGuire's job was to be spotted, lead us on. Logan never intended to be spotted. Witness the way he slipped his tails on his last time in Europe.'

But something else was running, she did not say. Something else happened which led you, a Deputy Director General of MI5, to put the SAS into the Republic. And the SAS saw something nobody anticipated. And then, thank God, somebody made a mistake; circulated something on a report that they weren't supposed to. And that led me to Logan. So what is it, Mr Deputy Director General? What's up and running and so important that even you are frightened?

She took the argument to its next stage.

'Logan is connected to the killings in Europe. We know that, we've established a link. A number of strands are possible from that point.'

She counted them on the fingers of her left hand.

'Logan is an LO running a Provo active service unit in Europe and his trips there are to instruct them on the next target. The assumption which follows from this, of course, is that it is the ASU which is responsible for the killings in Venlo, Mons and Berlin. We should seriously question that assumption.'

'Why?' Michaelmass wondered how far Catcher would take it and how much he would tell her.

'Provo killings in Europe in the past have been random and haphazard. They've used a Kalashnikov, sprayed a British service car with bullets, got a soldier if they were lucky but also wives and tourists. The same with bombs. The recent killings, however, are different. Very cold, very calculated. Same weapon, same technique. Which doesn't automatically rule out an ASU, of course.'

But . . .

'ASUs aren't trained for those sort of killings.' She was aware that she had crossed the Rubicon, the thin divide between what she had thought through before today, what she had analysed and assessed, and what she had not previously considered.

'So?'

'Suppose Logan is handling not just one unit but two. That the killings are being done by a gunman who isn't part of the ASU. That Logan's trips to Europe are to liaise with the ASU. That the ASU help set up the targets, safe houses, weapon drops, ways in and out. And then Logan sends in the shooter.'

Sleeper, Michaelmass suddenly thought.

'There's something more about the shootings, almost a second pattern.'

It was as if she was sitting alone at night, the office empty and the coffee laced with Bushmills.

'Assume they're the work of one man, then look at them again. The first was easy: no one was expecting it, it took place in an isolated part of a car park which was itself fairly deserted. The second was more difficult, again a single target, but this time an officer, who presumably should have been looking out for such things, and it was in a more public place.' And then Berlin, they both knew. 'Berlin was in a different league altogether. Two soldiers, Intelligence Corps, in the front seat of their car, at a time when they had been warned of possible attacks and the city was tight with security.'

Sleeper, Michaelmass thought again. If Catcher was right then they'd almost got Sleeper in Berlin. 'So what are you saying?'

She was unsure what she was saying. 'That the gunman is being trained up.' She corrected herself. 'That the gunman is a pro, but that he's being taken to the edge. Almost as if they're building him up.' For something big, she suddenly thought. For something so big it was unthinkable.

'So what's your theory?'

'Hypothesis, not theory.'

'Hypothesis, then.' Michaelmass was not used to being corrected.

The Prime Minister, she suddenly thought. The Provos had almost got Thatcher when they'd bombed the Grand Hotel in Brighton during the Conservative party conference, now they were going for the PM again. But this time differently, using someone up close.

'That McGuire is a cover. That Logan and the ASU have been setting up targets in Europe. And that the gunman the Provos are using is winding up for a spectacular.'

Michaelmass sat back, considering what he should say.

You know what he's winding up for, Nolan suddenly thought. That's why you broke the rules and sent the SAS cross-border. And there, by the grace of God, was your stroke of luck. Because that was how we stumbled upon Logan and found the key to the Europe killings. Except that it won't do us any good, because whoever's behind it has built in his cut-outs. All we know about is Logan. And not even Logan – especially not Logan – knows the identity of the gunman or his ultimate target. Logan won't even be aware there is an ultimate target.

Michaelmass leaned forward, arms on his desk. 'Last August we received intelligence about an operation the IRA was planning in this country.'

The same time as McGuire began to move, Nolan thought, therefore a possible link.

'The intelligence stated that an IRA gunman had been ordered to plan an attack on a target in Britain.'

Who received the intelligence? Nolan almost interrupted. What was its source and reliability?

'The information was passed direct to me from a source established when I was DoI in Belfast. Because of its nature we are obliged to treat it as reliable, though there is always the possibility it is deliberate misinformation. The source is a member of the Army Council.'

He was still undecided how much he would tell her.

'The gunman's codename is Sleeper. Three weeks ago we received additional intelligence that Sleeper had finalized his plans, including a date and location, and was about to complete his preparations. That's all we know. Apparently not even the Army Council has been informed of the identity of Sleeper or any details of his operation.'

There was more, Nolan sensed.

Michaelmass sat back in his chair. 'Questions?'

'Why do you refer to Sleeper as *he*?'

'Because that's how the man planning the operation refers to Sleeper in the Army Council.'

'Why is the report that led to Logan important?'

'It had been hoped that McGuire was Sleeper's handler and would lead us to him, but McGuire has simply been a drain on resources. The possibility was then considered that if we weren't able to access Sleeper, we might stop him by removing those controlling him.' He was still unsure how far he would go. 'The SAS was therefore sent South to make sure they had the relevant information should that option become necessary. The report from which you traced Logan came from one of the SAS teams involved.'

'What was the name of the Army Council member being observed by the SAS team which sent the Kelly report?'

'Conlan.'

'Conlan is on the Army Council. Through him we spotted Logan. Logan is the handler for the Europe shootings.'

271

'There's a logic in that.'

'If our analysis of those shootings is correct, then the gunman might be Sleeper?'

'Possibly.'

'Therefore Conlan would appear to be the man running Sleeper.'

Michaelmass sat without moving, hands in front of his face and fingers playing with his lips. 'Yes.'

'So why not order the SAS to negotiate him?'

'Because according to our source the Army Council's last order to Sleeper was that he should proceed *unless they called him off*. If we remove one of them, especially the one running him, all we do is make sure that Sleeper goes ahead with his plan.'

And the Brits joked about what they called the Paddy factor, she thought. One last thing, she knew, one more thing Michaelmass was holding back, still undecided whether he should tell her.

'We know of Sleeper.'

'Yes.'

'Do we know his target?'

What should he do? Michaelmass asked himself for the last time. Had he gone so far down the road that he had to go the whole way?

'Yes.'

'And who or what is Sleeper's target?'

She was staring at him, did not take her eyes from him.

'Not what,' he told her. 'Who.'

'So who?' she came back at him.

'Sleeper's target is codenamed PinMan.'

He was still undecided.

'And who is PinMan?'

He looked her straight in the face.

'Every indication is that PinMan is the Prince of Wales.'

There was something about London on a summer's day, particularly early summer. Probably because the evenings were getting lighter, Midsummer's Day still a couple of weeks off, and there was plenty to look forward to. Saunders left the *Mirror* building and took a cab to the White Tower. Polo at Cirencester on Saturday, hope the photographer gets a good shot of Charles, hope Charles does something worth snapping. He paid the cab driver, wondered when he might get a postcard from Philipa Walker in America, and went

272

inside. Roddy Fairfax was waiting. They ordered mezes and discussed where each would be spending his summer holidays. Between courses Fairfax passed to him the computer disk with the updated diaries of the Prince and Princess of Wales.

The office which Nolan was assigned was at the rear of the building on the fourth floor. It was grey and impersonal, the desk and filing cabinet metal and the chair plastic, and was all she needed. The corridor outside was equally anonymous. In the next days she would meet only three people she knew: one from The Fort and two who had passed through Lisburn. The flat off Portobello Road, where Penrose had driven her, was equally functional: kitchen, bathroom, lounge and bedroom, each with the antiseptic feel of a hospital ward and the transient atmosphere of an airport lounge in Middle America.

She would report directly to him, Michaelmass had told her. She was looking for anything the others might have overlooked, anything they hadn't recognized as significant but which might stop Sleeper taking out PinMan. She would continue to lead the Logan operation, and she would have access to whatever she needed. But she should not confer with any of the teams already analysing the material in case what he called their conventional wisdom rubbed off on her; and she would inform no one of her orders.

Why not, she had asked. Because, he had told her, with the exception of the Prime Minister, the Queen, and the Prince and Princess of Wales, she was the only person outside Cobra to know Sleeper's target.

The only thing she had requested at the end of the briefing was the Browning Hi-Power locked in the top right-hand drawer of her desk in Lisburn, which she could collect when she returned briefly to pack a bag. It was unlikely she would meet anyone who might recognize her from her undercover work in Belfast, but if she did she did not want to go down like a sacrificial lamb.

The Special Branch team assigned to investigate friends of the Prince and Princess of Wales moved in to a new office in the corner of one of the upper floors of New Scotland Yard twenty hours after the private agreement between Hamilton and Denton. There was no indication that the team belonged to Special Branch, and the combination on the door lock had been changed.

Hamilton left his own office, took the lift to what he called upstairs, walked along the corridor and keyed in the new code.

The room was filled with desks, most of them with computers, the superintendent in the corner nodding at him but the others not bothering to acknowledge his entry. It was a philosophy he sought to imbue in every officer he recruited. If a man or woman was doing a job, and unless protocol or politics dictated otherwise, there was no need to waste time on formalities.

'You'd pay millions for this view.' He stood by the superintendent's desk and looked out, then turned back and sat down. 'What's new?'

Nothing was new or Bailey would have informed him immediately. The two inspectors who were part of the team joined them, one sitting in a chair and the other on a desk to the side.

'We've divided the list into those who are closest to the royal couple, those who might have access to their official and personal diaries, and those on the fringe.' He passed Hamilton the computerized sheets. 'Obvious things to start with. Background checks on friends and acquaintances. Personal and financial details. Bank statements, investments where we can find out, clubs, cars. Telephone records, of course, sexual relationships, heterosexual or otherwise.' None of it would tell them what they wanted to know, but something somewhere might provide the lead.

'A hell of a job.' Hamilton's comment was half to himself. 'Sorry I can't spare anyone else.' He'd spent half the morning arguing resources and knew he'd lost. Bloody accountants taking over everything. 'So who're you starting with?'

'Charles's guest list for this weekend. Eight of them on it. More than usual.' He gave Hamilton a separate sheet. 'Any ideas who we should concentrate on, or who we might leave off, would be appreciated.'

Hamilton lifted the telephone, dialled Denton's extension and asked for his comments, jotting notes on a pad.

'Concentrate on those.' He indicated three names, one male and two female. 'The RPG boys say there are worries about their sexual proclivities.' Therefore vulnerable to possible blackmail, they understood. He pointed to Fairfax's name. 'You can drop him. He's army. Apparently doubles up on security when necessary.'

He left the office and went downstairs.

*

274

The night was black, no moon outside and no light through the curtains. Hamilton lay on his back and stared at the darkness. The telephone rang, he snatched at it and heard the voice. 'PinMan is down. Repeat. PinMan is down.' The panic filled him, the realization that it had all been in vain, that they had all failed. That Sleeper had got through, taken out PinMan. The other voice came at him from the void. 'What's wrong? You all right?' He recognized it as his wife's, heard the low hum of the dialling tone in the telephone. 'Bad dream. Sorry I woke you.' Even now he was unsure what was real, whether he was in his office. Whether PinMan was down. Whether his wife had woken and spoken to him or whether that, too, was part of his dream.

He was standing stiffly, feet slightly apart and head bowed. The darkness was around him. Not darkness, the muffled grey of state mourning. The coffin was behind him, English oak and lead-lined, the Union Jack over it and the crown on the flag. The guard of honour at each corner. Himself, Denton from the Royal Protection Group, Eldridge from the Anti-Terrorist Squad, Rhodes from Special Forces and Michaelmass from MI5. Plus Sinclair, of course. Grieving deeply but enjoying his moment nevertheless. Cobra standing guard at the lying in state of His Royal Highness The Prince of Wales. Sinclair at the head, standing by himself. Five other members of the Cobra committee, but only four corners of the coffin. They were shuffling round, the music playing then stopping, four taking their places and the fifth trying to find his. They were all moving again, the music stopping again and the five of them rushing for a corner, knocking each other out of the way.

It was three o'clock in the morning. He slid out of bed, pulled on his dressing-gown, went to the kitchen and made a pot of tea. Don't just go for those who are obvious simply because they should be included, he suddenly thought, also go for those who are obvious because they should be excluded. He poured himself a cup and ran through the guest list for Highgrove that weekend. Instinct or self-preservation, he wondered. The cordless telephone was in its holder on the wall. He picked it up, went back to the table and dialled the direct line into the team investigating the friends of the Prince and Princess of Wales. The voice that answered seemed remarkably fresh.

'Hamilton. Just having a think. Anything doing?'

'Sorry, guv.'

'Fairfax, the army chap we dropped from the list this afternoon. Put him back on.'

Mervyn Davis had been in Special Branch for six years, promoted to inspector within the squad three years ago. In his teens and early twenties he had played rugby, the bend in his nose a reminder of that time. At eight o'clock he contacted the liaison officer and requested the telephone records of Major Roderick Fairfax. The list was faxed to him at eleven; he photocopied it and passed it to the two men assigned to Fairfax. Jenkins had been on the squad two years and Miller eighteen months.

'You're in luck, not too many calls from his flat.' Davis dropped the three sheets of fax on the desk the two were using and glanced over Jenkins's shoulder. ' Apparently he's been in Germany since February.'

Miller was entering data into the IBM computer; he turned in his chair and examined the list of numbers, eliminating some. 'Wellington Barracks, Kensington Palace and Buckingham Palace,' he explained to Davis.

In the rest of the room other teams were doing the same for the other people on the royal list.

At noon the teams stopped their individual enquiries and sat informally round the office, discussing the various leads which each section was developing and looking for a cross-match. At one Jenkins and Miller went to the Tank on the ground floor, each carrying a bleeper in case they were needed. The club was crowded. Miller found a table while Jenkins waited at the bar. 'Two pints of best,' he asked, waited slightly impatiently while the barman began to pull them. 'Forget them,' he suddenly told the man, and pushed his way back to Miller.

The office was quiet; Davis was sharing sandwiches with the superintendent.

'You got a minute, guv?'

'As long as you don't want any of these.'

Jenkins and Miller sat down. 'Barry and I were thinking.' Bailey and Davis waited. 'We're checking the royal circle to see if any of them might be the sort who would targeted by someone wanting inside information.' Bailey and Davis had stopped eating. 'There's one obvious group.'

'Who?'

'The rat pack.'

The journalists who earned their living off the royal family.

Bailey looked at Jenkins. 'And I thought the Met only recruited Welshman because they played rugby.'

At 2.30 the superintendent briefed the team leaders on the suggestion, at three he informed Hamilton. By 4.30, and based on their telephone records, the first source of a leak to the press had been identified, within the next hour two more. By the time Hamilton next visited the section, shortly after seven that evening, the list had grown to nine, some of whom appeared to be leaking to only one press contact, but others to several. The fifth name on the list, he noted, was that of Major R.E.F. Fairfax, and the journalist linked with him was Patrick Saunders of the *Daily Mirror*. If they had this many after such a short time, he thought, God knows how many they would end up with.

'Polo at Cirencester tomorrow,' he told Bailey. 'I assume most of the rat pack and their sources will be there. Stand by at six, we go in as soon as they leave home. I'll arrange the paperwork now.'

Bailey led the final briefing at seven on the Saturday morning. Hamilton sat against the rear wall, listening but not speaking. Wonder what's going on in his head; Davis looked across the room at him. Wonder what this is really all about.

Overnight the list of those members of the royal circle whose telephone records showed calls to the press or to authors had grown to eleven. Six of these had been confirmed as attending the polo at Cirencester that day, plus eight of the reporters or writers to whom it was assumed they were leaking information. Stake-outs were already in position outside their houses or flats to alert the search teams once the targets left. When the search team was safely inside the technical people would join them, other specialists on stand-by in case they were needed. Where possible each search team would deal with those they had been investigating. Other targets were also under observation in case they also left their places of residence.

They left the team room and went for breakfast. By 9.30 they were in position, the back-up teams in unmarked cars keeping the premises under observation for the moment the targets left, and the break-in teams also in unmarked cars and each with a driver who would remain outside, the first of the technical teams hovering within two minutes' drive.

Hamilton was tempted to stay in the operations room and listen to the reports as they came in, knew that was Bailey's job.

'You remember the fuss about the press just before and after Charles and Di separated?'

'Which particular fuss?' There had been many.

'The suggestion that some of the leaks the press received were approved by the royals.'

'What about it?'

Be ironic if it was one of those which set up PinMan for Sleeper, Hamilton began to say. Remembered that Bailey's teams knew nothing about the Sleeper operation.

'Nothing.'

He waited another two minutes.

'I'll be downstairs.'

'Right, boss.'

'Red Three.' It was the stake-out team outside the house of a lady-in-waiting. 'Leaving now. Premises secure.' The first of the break-in teams slid from its waiting point.

Hamilton left.

'Green Four. Target leaving now. Premises secure.'

By 10.10 three teams were inside, by 10.25 four.

'Blue Two.' It was the back-up car outside Fairfax's flat. 'Leaving premises. Starting car. He's gone. Repeat. He's gone. Premises secure.'

The Cavalier slid past the back-up car and stopped outside the flats in which Fairfax lived. Davis and Thompson left the car, walked across the pavement and up the steps. Both men were casually though smartly dressed, Davis carrying a briefcase. The front door was locked. Thompson opened it with a skeleton key and they went inside, Thompson taking the lift and Davis the stairs. The block was quiet, only the faintest sound of music somewhere along the corridor. Thompson opened the flat door.

'Blue One. Inside.' Davis placed the briefcase in the hallway and they walked round the flat, familiarizing themselves before they began their search. Eight minutes later the technical team arrived.

'White Two.' It was the team outside Saunders's flat. 'Leaving now. Premises secure.' Within nine minutes Jenkins and Miller were inside, the technical team assigned to them twelve minutes later.

*

278

Fairfax's flat was as Davis had expected, the mix of regimental and bachelor life-styles reflected in the clothes which hung in the fitted wardrobe in the bedroom and the photographs and paintings on the walls. Davis ignored the two men installing the listening devices and began his search, Thompson examining the rest of the furniture, both men taking care to replace the items they moved exactly as they had found them.

The safe was behind a limited edition of regimental uniform prints on the lounge wall.

'Blue One. Wall safe.' He gave the make and model.

A quarter of an hour later a Sierra pulled up and a man in his mid-forties hurried inside; within nine minutes the safe was open. Davis took the portable copier from his briefcase and began to copy the documents found inside, working methodically and carefully and glancing only occasionally at the material in front of him.

Saunders's flat was neater and larger than either Jenkins or Miller expected, and better furnished. Must be making a bomb, Miller joked.

'White One. Computer.'

Jenkins settled at the desk and began to go through it, not even turning the computer on. The bank statements were in a file in the bottom drawer on the right. He flicked through them, then began copying them.

The lounge was neat and well-furnished. Miller began with the bookshelves and storage drawers of the furniture, checking for a safe either in the floor or the wall.

An Astra drew up outside and a woman hurried up the steps. She was in her mid-twenties, colourfully dressed, and had a canvas bag slung over her shoulder. Jenkins opened the door and heard her running up the stairs.

'Fitter than I am.'

'Wouldn't take much doing.'

She sat at the desk, took the tape streamer from the bag, replaced the printer lead with the streamer lead, inserted the boot disk into the PC and switched it on. Easy when you knew how, Jenkins told himself. No obvious security precautions, the woman noted, therefore no need to replace the BIOS chips or take out the hard disk. The file names flashed on the screen as the material on Saunders's hard disk was copied. Jenkins ignored it and went slowly and meticulously through the rest of the material in the office.

'You want to see what's there?' The woman interrupted him.

He was always amazed that the process only took minutes.

'Why not?'

'What name?'

'Try Charles.'

She went into disk edit and began the search.

The technicians had almost finished. Miller left the lounge and went into the bedroom, searching in a set pattern for the stubs and bills which people often overlooked but which might tell him what he was looking for or where he might find it.

'Interesting.'

'What's interesting?' Jenkins leaned over her shoulder and looked at the screen.

'This one.' She pointed it out to him. 'Contains Charles but the file name's "soccer". You want to look at it?'

'Yes.'

She accessed the files on the C drive. 'Even more interesting.'

'Why?'

'It's not there.'

'But you said it was.'

'It is.' She called up CHATT from the A drive, sat back as the screen displayed every file contained in the relevant sub-directory, then pointed to the 'Y' symbol. 'It's hidden.' She unhid the 'soccer' file and called up Word Perfect.

Miller left the bedroom and went into the kitchen. The champagne in the wine rack was Bollinger. Making a bomb, just as he thought. The notice board was on the wall above the wine rack, a telephone hanging beside it and notes and postcards pinned on the board. He checked the messages and looked at the pictures on the postcards – St Petersburg, Cyprus, Val d'Isère, Tangiers, Venice. He unpinned them and began to read the messages on the other side.

'Barry.' He heard Jenkins call to him. 'Have a look at this.' He left the kitchen and went through to the office. On the computer screen were the engagement schedules of the Prince and Princess of Wales.

10

THE AFTERNOON HAD BEEN WARM — the first warmth which came with early summer — but the evening was cold. Conlan poured himself another coffee and looked at the single shattering piece of information which Doherty had passed to him the night before.

British Intelligence had been tailing somebody in Manchester at the time that Logan had been in the city. The report itself did not make the connection, and no one other than Conlan knew of Logan's role or his presence in Manchester that day. All the report said was that a police officer had stopped a car and that the occupants were security service shadowing someone. There were no details of the source of the report. Perhaps a conversation overheard in a police station, he assumed, an office cleaner or canteen worker. Perhaps one policeman telling another in a pub. Perhaps a police officer on a reporter's payroll tipping him the wink for a good story. It didn't have to appear as a security leak, of course; the person who had begun the chain might have been totally unaware of the significance of what he or she had said. Except that it had somehow got into the system, and the system had eventually brought it via the GHQ staff to Conlan. Except that it disclosed something which should not have been disclosed. Except that it was so accurate that it even gave the make, model and registration number of the car the security forces were using.

So where did it leave Logan — there was no guarantee the tail involved Logan, but no doubt in Conlan's mind.

There was one way to find out, of course. Send Logan back and put his own tail on him, see if his tail spotted another. Logan had been a good and faithful servant, but in the end everyone was expendable. Himself included. Thank God he had built in the cut-outs, though; thank God that even if the Brits pulled Logan and tore him to pieces he could tell them nothing about Sleeper.

But where did it leave Sleeper?

Put Logan back in, use him as a bait, but do it in a way that the Brits would know that he knew they were tailing Logan. And if the Brits knew that, then they would suppose that Logan was expendable. And if Logan was expendable, so were the projects he was handling. Therefore Logan could not be associated with Sleeper. Except, of course, that the Brits didn't know about Sleeper.

The surveillance team into Manchester on Monday, he began to plan anyway. Logan in on Wednesday or Thursday, the timetable and locations precise so that the team knew when and where to be looking. The mule a nice good-looking girl, good figure and smiling eyes. And the Clock-Maker primed and waiting.

If they spotted a tail. If the report from Manchester was correct.

11

COBRA CONVENED AT ELEVEN, at twenty minutes past Hamilton began his briefing on the progress made by Special Branch since the last meeting.

Investigations were under way of those identified as recipients of royal leaks, though the list might be lengthened when the premises of all of those suspected of passing information to journalists or authors had been searched. Telephone taps were now in place on both informants and recipients, and Special Branch was now concentrating on what Hamilton called the third phase – those with whom the recipients of leaks had been in contact, defined initially by their telephone records, contacts books or, as in the case of the *Mirror* journalist Saunders, names and telephone numbers found on his computer.

Special Branch capitalizing on its fast footwork and the Home Secretary buoyed up by what he clearly considered the successes of the weekend, Michaelmass understood. Typical Sinclair. The Home Secretary hadn't approved anything, and in so doing had covered himself in case anything went wrong, but because it had gone right he was now in a position to share the credit. The politicians probably had their own word for it.

Special Branch had done a good job and now MI5 was trying to catch up. Nolan sat at her desk in Gower Street and imagined the man hours and resources being consumed on investigating the contacts of the various people to whom information on the royals had been leaked. For the next 36 hours – including one session which ran until five in the morning – she pored over the details in the reports, then she drew up her own list of individuals whom she considered prime targets. Two were responsible for leaks and two were recipients; three were on the list because of aspects of their background, and the fourth was the journalist Patrick Saunders because of the exactness of the royal schedule found on his computer. The next morning she asked for a meeting with Michaelmass and requested access to the houses or flats of each. Authorization was granted immediately.

Eamon Doyle received the telephone call at 11.30.

Doyle was 38 years old, thin build with a slight stoop of the shoulders. His hair was long at the back and thinning at the front. He wore gold-rimmed spectacles – the frame of the right lens scratched where he clipped the magnifying loupe – a suit and old-fashioned shirt, the type with detachable collar, preferring to remove the collar when crouched over his work.

Doyle was a craftsman in both the professions he practised.

The first, in the single-fronted shop on Johnson's Court, a narrow alleyway lined with jewellers' and silversmiths' shops off Dublin's Grafton Street, was that of clock repairer. Not just repairer, and not just of any clock. Customers who spent fortunes on their passion insisted that the only man they could trust to repair their Tompions or their Harrisons was Doyle. In the back room, the bow of the front window protruding slightly on to the alley, he bent over the Knibbs and the Beckers with a devotion and precision he also practised in his second profession.

That of bomb-maker for the Provisional IRA.

Doyle constructed his works of destruction with the same love of his skill as the craftsmen of The Hague had made their Huygens, or those of Paris their Breguets. In terms of bomb-making Doyle was technically unrivalled, yet perhaps the single characteristic which lifted him above all others was his recognition that the role of the bomb-maker did not begin and end with the process of construction and destruction, however detailed and intricate. Rather, that the skill he practised was merely part of a game, continuous and ongoing, so that he should never consider himself in isolation.

Other bomb-makers left what those hunting them called their calling cards or their prints. Not the whorls and curves of the fingertips, or the arches and ridges of the palm – all wore surgical gloves to avoid such a possibility. Yet somewhere others left the slivers of clues which might enable a hunter to trace a bomb to them, or at least to say that a range of bombs, even of different types and at different dates, had been made by the same man – the use of certain parts, the type of timer, the way a wire had been cut or soldered.

It was one of Doyle's greatest strengths that he recognized this, so that although an individual bomb might give the hunters one part of one jigsaw, it never provided a link, either to another part of the same puzzle or, more importantly, to another jigsaw. The only exception – outside his control – was the source of the explosive he used.

He was cutting a pinion when he heard the ringing. Outside the sunlight pierced the alleyway and a handful of tourists looked in the window. He switched off the lathe and picked up the telephone.

'Mr Doyle?'

He recognized the voice. 'Yes.'

'I have a Becker from the Freiburg factory I'd like you to look at. Possibly this week, perhaps next.'

With the bracket clock on his bench Doyle had felt one kind of thrill, now he felt the other.

'Of course.'

It was a long time since the slip of an English university student had knocked on the door and asked for the priest. Since they had sat in the armchairs in his sitting-room and she had declined to tell him why she was trying to trace a Siobhan O'Connell. Since he had pulled her away from the animals which comprised the British army. Since he had sent her back to her hotel on the River Fane and telephoned Conlan. Since he had stood near her at the funeral of her brother. Then she had disappeared and only Conlan knew what had become of her.

McGinty left Rathmeen and drove south. By four he had finished his meeting with Conlan, in a room in Trinity College Dublin. At five he had his next, in a pub off the Quays.

Blanchard was dressed in a suit and carrying a briefcase. He was in his mid-thirties, with slightly greying hair neatly cut. The instructions which McGinty gave him appeared straightforward. The following morning he was to fly to Manchester, which McGinty said he understood Blanchard knew well. He was to establish six locations from which vehicles passing for a given period of time – say fifteen minutes – could be easily watched and their details taken, without the observer being seen. The locations should be the kind which someone making a business trip to the city might normally pass. He should also place on stand-by a team of three people.

Blanchard returned from Manchester 72 hours later. His meeting with McGinty was at six; by nine Conlan had approved his suggestions and built them into a timetable. The following morning the new instructions were passed back to him.

He and his team would be in position in Manchester the morning after next. He should divide the locations he had selected between them, assigning two to each member. The first set of observations would take place at 10.00, 11.15 and 12.30, the second at 2.00, 3.15 and 4.30. Each member of the team should be equipped with a pair of binoculars and a pocket-sized dictaphone – there would be no time to write down the details required. They should record the make, model, colour and registration number of every vehicle, including motor-cycles, passing north to south or east to west at their location, from five minutes before the specified time to ten minutes after. After each location they would hand the cassette to Blanchard and move to the next. After collecting the cassettes Blanchard himself would transfer each to a laptop computer he would carry with him. When the lists were complete he would key in a cross-match programme and look for registration numbers which appeared on more than one list. Then he would report to McGinty, who would also be in Manchester.

They were trying to spot a tail, Blanchard knew immediately. Trying to see whether an ASU or a gunman or a bomber had picked up a shadow.

If any vehicles appeared regularly, then he and his team would be assigned a second task – to tail one of them to where it was parked during the hours of darkness. The fox turned hunter, he thought with relish, the quarry tracking the pursuer. And then the ASU would slip in – Blanchard had no way of knowing the details though he might have assumed them. Then the Clock-Maker would hand his precious charge to the active service unit and the ASU would attach it to the car, either to a cavity in the bottom or under the wheel arch. Probably to the Vauxhall Carlton, Conlan had already told McGinty.

The first three flats on her list had been interesting – if you could say that autographed photographs of the royals were interesting – but sterile. Nolan sat in the rear seat of the Toyota and waited. Lonsdale Square was quiet, the forward car from the plumbers parked inconspicuously and the woman who did the cleaning for Saunders still in his flat.

'Black Two. Premises clear.'

Nolan and the two plumbers left the Toyota and turned into the square. Although the morning was warm Nolan wore a jacket, a camera with built-in flash in one pocket and the Browning Hi-Power in the shoulder holster. They passed the lookout car, noted the other watchers strung discreetly along the street, and went up the steps to the front door of the flat. Someone had left it open. The plumber shrugged and they divided, one of the men taking the lift, Nolan and the second the stairs. As they reached the flat the door opened and the first man let them in.

'Black One. Inside.'

The flat smelt of fresh polish. One of the plumbers remained in the hallway, just inside the door, and the second sat in the lounge, neither speaking. Nolan went to each room, standing quietly and looking round, familiarizing herself with the layout and trying to see where she should start looking, then went to the room Saunders used as a study. Bookshelves, desk, computer. She registered the items and went to the main bedroom. There was no point in going through the clothes hanging in the wardrobe: Special Branch would have been through them already, included every scrap of paper in their report. She went to the kitchen and glanced round: morning mail unopened on the dresser, telephone on the wall beside the notice board, personal notes and half a dozen postcards pinned on to the board. She went into the lounge.

'You want me to leave?' The plumber stood up.

She had explained as they waited in the car – that she wanted to be alone, that she didn't know what she was looking for and didn't want anyone else present whilst she was looking in case it distracted her.

'Not yet.' She went back to the study and sat in front of the desk.

So what was she looking for? she asked herself. Nothing unusual. Something – anything – that appeared totally normal and routine but that she could feed into the computer of her mind and see if there was a match with anything else. The small thing that was so obvious it would be overlooked but which might not add up, which might tell her which path to take.

She leaned forward, switched on the computer and noted the modem plugged in at the side. If Saunders was Sleeper's source and Sleeper had visited or broken into Saunders's flat, and if he did the same again, they had the flat covered. And if he tried to confirm the royal details by hacking into Saunders's computer, which she assumed would not be difficult, then they could trace him.

She left the study and went into the lounge. The plumber looked up at her.

'If you don't mind.'

'Of course.' He went into the kitchen.

There was no point in looking along the bookshelf but she did it anyway, taking each book down and shaking it for the piece of paper that might fall out but which Special Branch would already have found. Then she went through the telephone directory and the magazines on the coffee tables, looking for the mindless doodles or occasional word or name.

The flat was quiet, not even traffic noise from outside.

She left the lounge and went back into the kitchen, smiled her thanks as the plumber slipped out. Bollinger champagne, she noted: perhaps journalists were even better paid than she'd imagined. She went through the drawers and read the notes pinned on the notice board. Nice collection of postcards, she thought. She looked at the photographs then took them off one by one, noting the position of each, and read the messages. One from Venice, a second from the ski resort of Val d'Isère, a third from Tangiers. *Couldn't resist a day trip. Soukh amazing.* Automatically she noted the date. St Petersburg. Interesting five years ago when it was called Leningrad, she thought, took the details anyway. Cyprus – the alarm bells began to ring. Seemingly ordinary. Full of tourists and apparently innocent. But still *the* meeting-place for the Eastern Med. For the nameless people who came in the night from Beirut and Iran and Iraq, from Syria and Israel, from the former terrorist sponsors of North Africa.

She laid the cards on the kitchen table and began to photograph them, had almost finished when one of the plumbers came into the room. Saunders back early, she thought, either that or the cleaning woman had forgotten something. Except that if it was that sort of problem the plumbers would have had her out of the flat by now.

He gave her his microphone and earpiece.

'Tiger's moving.' She recognized Farringdon's voice. 'Going South. The tails are on him.'

Fifteen minutes to Gower Street to pick up a passport then Heathrow – she was already planning – flight to Dublin, one of the team waiting for her; the Westbury Hotel and the car rental offices already covered.

'On my way.'

The postcards were still on the table. She finished photographing them, placed them back in position, and left the flat.

Aer Lingus flight EI 159 landed at Dublin two minutes before schedule. Nolan cleared immigration and customs, passed the tail and walked through the arrivals lounge, allowing him to overtake her, then followed him to the short-term car park.

'Where is he?'

'Work. He's gone to his head office.'

A cover, she told herself. They pulled on to the N1.

'How long's he been there?'

'An hour.'

They entered the city.

'Blue One. Green One.' Logan leaving the office.

'Blue Two. Green Two.' Logan collecting his car.

'Blue Four. Yellow One.' Logan at the beginning of the N1. Going back to Belfast.

The disappointment crept in like a fog, cold and deadening. No change of identity therefore no trail, no trail therefore no Sleeper.

Ninety minutes later Logan cleared Dundalk and slowed for the border, tried to shake off the panic which had wrapped round him like a shroud the moment he had read his orders. The fact that the meet was at head office should have warned him. The fact that there was no meet. Just the instructions concealed in the cistern of the toilets on the second floor.

So the Brits were on to him.

It was clear from the orders, from the fact that he was to return to Manchester, the precise details of timings and locations. He was being used as a bait, see if the tails really were sitting on him. Where the hell had he gone wrong, how had they fingered him? He had always known he was not immortal, joked about it – to himself, of course, never to anyone else. But he had never really believed it. Believed in the last great mortality, but that wasn't what he meant. And now The Man was sending him back into the lion's den. Bastard, part of him thought. Bastard, the rest of him thought but in a different way. The Man knew that once he'd read the instructions Logan would understand. No tail and he was clear, tail and he was finished anyway. So it was better to know. But if he was picked up, if he was tailed in Manchester, then The Man was not only giving him his way out but also his last great glory. It was between the lines, of course, but clear as crystal. The first day he would follow the pattern, the second he would hole up and hardly move, except for the last two hours of the afternoon when he would repeat part of the pattern, though in a different order and at different times. That evening he would take dinner in the hotel restaurant, booked beforehand and in the company of the woman hired from an escort agency to give him an alibi. And next morning he would fly out. But not to Belfast. To Dublin. And there was the rub, there was The Man telling him what he was going to do but making sure he was out before it was done. Making sure he was safe in the Republic before The Man blew the bloody Brits to kingdom come.

At one that afternoon Eamon Doyle closed and locked his shop, took a cab to the station and caught the 1335 train to Rosslare. The only luggage he carried was a worn leather holdall. In Rosslare he bought a ticket for the 1700 ferry to Cherbourg, paying cash. When the *St Killian* berthed in France eighteen hours later, he took the train to Calais via Paris, overnighting in a small hotel in the town centre. The following morning he caught the 1015 ferry to Dover, arriving at midday and passing unnoticed in the flood of tourists. Then he took a National Express coach to London and settled into a nondescript but comfortable hotel off the Cromwell Road, no trace existing – other than the 'closed' notice on the door of the shop in Johnson's Court – that he had even left Dublin.

At four that afternoon the three members of the Provisional IRA active service unit covering the north were ordered south from Glasgow. The team consisted of two men and one woman. As individuals they had taken part in a total of three bombings and eight shootings in Northern Ireland. Collectively, as an ASU, they had been responsible for three bombings in England over the preceding nine months. By eleven that evening they were in the safe house in the south of Manchester.

The office in the Lisburn complex was quiet, stale cigarette smoke hanging in the air. London was London and Belfast was Belfast: each was real, yet the two realities were poles apart. Northern Ireland always had this effect, Nolan reminded herself. Not just on her. On everyone. You got on a plane and left behind a world where life was peaceful and ordered. And you stepped off at the other end and you were on the wire. Except that once you were there you didn't notice it. Until you got on the plane again and stepped off at the other end and saw the police without guns. She was tired, she told herself: tired because she was worrying about Sleeper, because Logan had returned to Belfast without slipping into the pattern she had drawn for him. She arranged for the film she had shot in Saunders's flat to be processed and prints run off, spoke to Brady about Frank Hanrahan, and returned to her apartment in Malone Park.

At six the next morning she was back in the office. The telephone call came at 7.10.

'He's moving. Just been picked up by minicab.'

The airport. Logan heading for the mainland. Blue team to Aldergrove, she ordered, red and green stand by, yellow keep with him. She left the barracks and was driven to the airport. Manchester, boarding in ten minutes, she was told; two tails in front of him and three behind.

She bought a ticket and spoke to Lisburn on the scrambler, requesting back-up and vehicles on their arrival, plus personal weapons for the surveillance team, herself included, who would shadow Logan on the plane.

Flight BA 5281 landed at Manchester on schedule. Logan cleared security and baggage collection and walked briskly to the arrivals lounge. One tail was ahead, among the first off the plane, checking that the cars and back-up were in place, another twenty yards in front of Logan and the rest melting away. The tension of Belfast, Nolan remembered she had thought, the way you lost it once you stepped on the plane at Aldergrove and stepped off at the other end. Not always. She hurried through the hall to the control car. Vauxhall Carlton, same vehicle as before. Bad, she thought: McGuire presumably still tying up everything. In the building opposite Logan stopped at the Hertz desk and hired a Granada.

For how long?

Two days.

Returning it here?

Yes.

He collected the car and drove to the Britannia Hotel.

'Blue One. Green Two.' Logan leaving the hotel, Logan on the gallop.

It was ten minutes to ten. The first spotter checked the dictaphone, focused the binoculars, and waited. Five minutes to ten. He began to dictate the vehicle descriptions into the machine. Ten o'clock exactly.

'Blue Three. Black Five.' Logan opposite St Mary's Hospital on Oxford Road, travelling south. One tail three cars behind him, others in front or on parallel streets, and motor-cycle at rear.

Ten minutes past. The spotter stopped taking the details, removed the cassette from the dictaphone and left his position. Blanchard was waiting in a Renault Espace 200 yards away. The spotter gave him the cassette, then left and made his way to the afternoon location he had been assigned. Blanchard drove the three miles to the second morning location, parked the Espace, shifted to the rear seat, placed the laptop and dictaphone on the table, and transferred the list of vehicle descriptions and registration numbers on to the computer.

It was ten minutes past eleven. The second spotter checked the time, raised the binoculars and held the dictaphone close to his mouth.

Eleven-fifteen precisely. 'Blue Six. Black Nine.'

Twelve-thirty. 'Blue Three. Black Four.'

The tail behind Logan pulled off and the Carlton slipped into place.

It was four-thirty. 'Blue Two. Purple Four.' Logan turned off Moss Lane and returned to the Britannia Hotel. At four forty-five the third spotter handed Blanchard the last cassette and the Provisionals' surveillance team returned to their safe house.

Blanchard made a point of congratulating each member, then shut himself in the bedroom at the rear of the house, fed in the final surveillance notes, and ran the cross-match programme for the last time. Eight matches in total, he confirmed, one bait and seven tails. He plugged the laptop into the printer and ran off a single copy. Then he told the team he would be back in two hours and drove to the bus depot in Chorlton Street. McGinty was waiting in the café, at a table by himself and against the wall, the hookers and rent boys already on the street outside and in the coach terminus itself. Good conditions for a tail, Blanchard thought, except that today *they* were the tail.

'This one.' McGinty indicated the Carlton. 'At seven tonight our man will leave the Britannia Hotel and drive to Piccadilly Station. He'll wait for twenty minutes as if he's meeting someone, then return to the hotel. He won't leave again tonight.' McGinty spoke quietly, so that even though he was sitting close to him Blanchard could barely hear. 'That should give you time to pick up the Carlton and find where it goes. Tomorrow morning, seven o'clock, you let me know.' Neither of them had touched their tea. 'At ten our man will leave the Britannia. He'll pass points two, three and five, this time going in the other direction than before. That should give you the chance to confirm the Carlton is still with him.' He gave Logan the times. 'He'll return to his hotel at six. He won't leave. We assume that the Carlton returns to the same overnight spot, but you confirm this to me at eight.'

At seven precisely Logan left the Britannia, drove to Piccadilly Station, parked the Granada and went inside. There was something about him; Nolan could not shake off the unease. As if he was simply passing time. Abruptly Logan left the station, collected the Granada, and drove back to the hotel. Forty minutes later the tail inside reported that he was taking dinner in the restaurant.

Blue Two to remain in position in case Logan left unexpectedly, Nolan ordered, Blue Three to relieve them at two in the morning, the other teams to pull out for the night. She left the hotel and drove to the safe house in Rutherford Street, one of two which the teams had been allocated in Manchester.

The package was waiting – the negatives and prints of the film she had shot in Saunders's flat and which Farringdon had ordered to be sent to her. She ate supper, checked on the radio with the team in position at the Britannia, then spread the prints of the postcards on the bed of the room she was using and studied them. Cyprus was the one to concentrate on, she knew, plus whoever had sent the card from St Petersburg. Look for other things, she reminded herself, the simple things which she could check even though they wouldn't lead her anywhere. Not just the two on the suspect cards. See if a cross-match existed with any of the other files compiled by MI5, Special Branch or the Anti-Terrorist Squad. Check whether the people in question, assuming they could be identified, really were out of the country on the dates in question; whether there was a Pavarotti concert in Venice on the date in question; whether the friend who'd talked about superb skiing at Val really was a skier; how one managed a day trip to Tangiers.

*

The street was quiet. Three of the tail vehicles, including the Carlton, parked together. So easy, Blanchard thought. Pity it wasn't on for tonight, pity they had to wait till tomorrow. Good planning, though, caught the bloody Brits with more than their trousers down.

McGinty left the boarding house at ten and walked to the public telephones two streets away. The first call he made was to the Clock-Maker, Eamon Doyle, in the hotel off the Cromwell Road in London, and the second was to the safe house where the ASU was waiting. The following morning he woke at five, the sun pouring through the thin curtains of the hotel room and the sounds of the traffic outside. At seven, with the city still waking, he met Blanchard at Chorlton Street bus station. The café was open, early morning workers replacing the hookers and rent boys, and the smell of bacon sandwiches in the air.

'Rutherford Street. The Carlton was there, plus two others.'

'You know what you have to do today?'

'Yes.'

'I'll see you this evening.'

There was something about the other man, Blanchard thought as he watched McGinty leave, an inner calm which he envied yet which also frightened him. As if he was close to God Almighty. Or the Devil. Probably both.

An hour later, McGinty sat at a table in a transport café on the Rochdale Road. At 8.15 exactly Riley came in, ordered a breakfast, and joined him.

Martin Riley was 29 years old and built like a Cork bull, though deceptively fast on his feet. In addition to the three shootings for which he had been responsible, he had also headed a PIRA punishment squad, during which time he had carried out a number of knee-cappings. As head of the ASU in the north of England, he had brought to the organization a ruthlessness which was admired and welcomed in Dublin. The second member of his team, Jimmy Nugent, was 25 and had begun his IRA career by passing information on British army patrols to his local PIRA intelligence officer when he was still in his mid-teens. The third, Moira Galvin, was a 20-year-old former nursing student from the Bogside area of Londonderry, or Free Derry as she herself called it.

'Rutherford Street, tonight.' McGinty's tea had passed from hot to lukewarm. He stirred it anyway, though he did not drink. 'A Vauxhall Carlton.' He gave Riley the details, including the registration. 'I'll check it myself first, then telephone you to confirm.' They agreed on the code. 'The man is on his way, he'll be with you at eleven. He knows the address, but only you should meet him.'

'What sort?'

What sort of bomb, he meant – remote control, timer, tilt device?

'Timer. Set for eleven tomorrow morning.' Conlan had been specific. By then Logan's flight would have touched down in Dublin and the LO would be secure. 'I'll leave it to you what time you go in.'

Of course you'll leave it to me, Riley thought. Good the way the man said it, though. No bullshit, like some. Or fear, like others. As if there was no problem about it, as if the man had done his job and now Riley could do his.

'Probably between eleven and twelve tonight. Give them time to settle.' It was interesting that they were bringing in a specialist to put the device together, he thought; he himself could have done it. A big one, he understood; not a spectacular but something important.

'Excellent.' McGinty rose and left. No *cheerios*, Riley noted, no *good lucks*. A pro doing his job, just like himself; melting into the crowd just as Riley and his team would disappear.

Eamon Doyle checked out of the hotel at 6.30, paid cash, took the underground to Euston and the Pullman north. At Manchester Piccadilly he bought a city map, then took a cab to a street 600 yards from the safe house, walking the rest of the way and spending thirty minutes confirming that the premises were not under surveillance before he approached. Only when he was sure did he cross the road and ring the door bell. Not even the closest and best-trained observer would have noticed that he did so with the knuckle of his right hand, therefore leaving no fingerprint. The Clock-Maker was that careful.

Riley opened the door.

'I'm come about the ad for a room to let.'

'It's not in the paper till tomorrow.'

'A friend told me about it.'

Riley stood back and let him in, then locked the door behind him and shook his hand.

'The others are upstairs, they won't be down.'

'Good.'

Doyle placed the leather travel bag on the floor, took a pair of surgical gloves from Riley and put them on. Even though he was disciplined, even though he knew his life and his liberty depended on that discipline, he was aware that not even he could guarantee he would not touch something without noticing.

The man's the best, Riley remembered he'd been told. That's why we've put the two of you together. He led Doyle into the kitchen.

'Coffee?'

'Please.' Doyle hung his coat on the back of the chair, removed the collar from his shirt, cleaned his spectacles and fitted the magnifying loupe to them, and focused his attention on the items Riley had prepared for him.

Semtex plus digital timer, magnet to attach the bomb to the chassis – the requirement was straightforward, not like some he'd worked on. He'd be finished by two and take the 2.30 from Manchester to London, even get one of the evening ferries from Dover to Calais. Be out of the country by the time his little toy went off.

'She's yours.' He handed Riley the package, almost as if he was a priest handing the bomber his daughter at a baptism.

'You want a lift?'

'I'll walk.'

He locked the travel bag and followed Riley to the door. Only when they were at it did he pull the gloves off and give them to the other man to dispose of. Anyone searched by the police and found in possession of such an item would come under suspicion, probably of housebreaking. An Irishman, however . . .

Good luck – it was in the handshake, in the nod of the head – we'll see each other again. Riley opened the door for him, seeing the concentration on Doyle's face and in his eyes, the bombmaker maintaining his concentration and avoiding the last-minute mistake which would leave a palm- or fingerprint anywhere on the premises.

Doyle left the house, turned left and walked quickly away, not even looking back. Only after he had been walking for twenty minutes did he even contemplate stopping a cab.

Logan breakfasted at eight, telephoned the escort agency at nine and left the hotel at 9.30. His first business appointment was at eleven and his second at three, each lasting longer than his meetings the previous day. He returned to the Britannia at six, smiled at the porter and asked for his key.

'Could you book me a table for two in the restaurant for eight-thirty?'

'Of course, sir.'

He went to his room, showered and waited.

Tiger apparently eating at hotel tonight, the tail reported, booked a table for two. Nolan stretched her legs in the front seat of the Carlton and wondered how long the game would last. At 7.55 one of the tails in the hotel reported that Logan had left his room, two minutes later a second reported that he was in the cocktail bar. At eight o'clock exactly a cab stopped outside and the woman entered the hotel, walked confidently through the foyer and made her way to the bar. She was in her early thirties, tall and good-looking, wearing an attractive and expensive blue dress. Logan rose from the stool. Often in the evenings he preferred to relax, to put on a pair of casual trousers and take his time over a drink. Tonight, however, he was smartly dressed in suit and tie.

'Michael Logan?'

'Mike. You're Sarah.' The agency had given him the woman's details that morning.

'Yes.'

'Good to meet you.' They shook hands.

'My pleasure.'

'I've booked dinner for eight-thirty. Perhaps you'd like a drink first?'

What the hell was Logan playing at, Nolan wondered. Logan was careful; wouldn't do anything that might expose him to any pressure or blackmail. Logan in the hotel for the rest of the evening, therefore with an alibi – the instinct was too subconscious at this stage for her to sense it. She ordered one team to remain on duty, a second to replace it at midnight, and pulled the others back to the safe houses.

Rutherford Street sloped slightly, the pavements on either side lined with trees and the houses set back slightly from the pavements, each house with a small raised garden and steps to the front door, cars parked on both sides.

McGinty walked casually – not quickly, not slowly – hands in pockets and whistling to himself. The Vauxhall Carlton was positioned exactly where Blanchard had told him. Correct registration number – he checked without even slowing – the vehicle parked midway between street lights and the foliage of the trees shading the light anyway. It was a rough area, he thought – hoods, hookers and dope-dealers. He walked four hundred yards before he found a telephone that worked.

'Patrick?' It was the first line of the code.

'Hang on a second, Micky, I'll turn down the television.' The second.

'I've got a job come up. Need a couple of brickies. I was wondering if you might be interested.' The suggestion of work and the operation was on, the statement that a job had fallen through and it would have been off.

'Sure I'd be interested.'

'You'll be having a drink this evening.' Confirmation that the operation was for tonight.

'I'll see you there.'

McGinty put the phone back on the rest, took a bus to Piccadilly Station, and caught the 2145 to Sheffield. Riley put the phone down and went to the kitchen. The package was in a holdall by the door and the others were looking at him.

'We're on.'

The call from London came through at ten. Someone working overtime, Nolan thought. Reference her requests that morning: three of the names she had given from the postcards had been identified and enquiries had begun on the travel movements of the individuals involved, the names had been run through the computer but no cross-matches with other files had so far been found.

Win some, lose some. 'What about the other points?'

There *had* been a Pavarotti concert round the date in question, she was informed, and the day trip to Tangiers – assuming it was from southern Spain – would have been made from Algeciras or Tarifa.

'That day?' The question was reflexive, instinctive. There was no point checking the exact date of the Pavarotti concert because the postcard hadn't specified a particular day. The card from Tangiers had given a specific item of information for a specific date.

'Yes. They go every day.'

'But did they go *that* day?' She did not even think about it, was thinking about Logan.

'I'll check.'

'Thanks.'

Logan and the woman had finished dinner and gone upstairs, the tail reported.

Rutherford Street was quiet, the smell of blossom in the air and the sounds of the city in the night. Riley and Galvin approached from the top, her arm in his as if they were a courting couple, the Star pistols in their belts and the bomb in the holdall which he carried, the zip undone. Fifty yards away Nugent approached from the bottom. The street was empty and the night was still, the faintest sound of traffic.

Riley and Galvin slowed down and laughed, joked, stopped at the Vauxhall Carlton. He put the holdall down and she turned into him, arms apparently round each other as if embracing. A yard, less, from the front door of the Carlton. Riley facing up the street and Galvin down, safety catches of the Stars off. Nugent reached them, the street empty. He took the bomb from the bag, slid half under the car, and felt for the place where he would attach the package.

What the hell was Logan playing at? Nolan lay on the bed and tried to shake the thought from her mind. She was still fully clothed, the trainers on the floor and the Browning Hi-Power on the table. It was all too neat, too slick. Logan had been so obvious, so easy to tail. Almost too easy. Now he was safe and sound and tucked up in bed for the night.

Everything signposted, she suddenly thought, everything tele-graphed. Either Logan really was tucked up in bed, really was out of the action for the next six hours, or he was giving himself a cover. The woman in his bed possibly drunk or drugged – so easy she wouldn't even notice, not even feel any side-effects – but saying he'd been with her all night and believing so, the Granada left untouched and Logan slipping out through a back door for a meet.

Theory, pure speculation. But possible. No chances, she told her-self, no way she would risk the bastard putting one over on her as he had done with the others in Europe. Blue Five to the hotel, she decided, double the cover, front and back. Christ, Logan didn't even need to leave the hotel, the contact could already be there. She herself would check, no point sending the boys into the night if she wasn't prepared to do it herself. She woke her driver. 'We're moving in five minutes. Simply a precaution. I'll see you at the car.' She slipped the Browning into the shoulder holster and pulled on her jacket.

'Almost there,' Nugent whispered. He made sure the undercarriage was clean of mud, set the timer and pulled out the safety pin. 'Plenty of time,' Riley told him, no one around, no problems. He was still looking up the road, Galvin down. Nugent held the bomb in position and felt the magnet clamp on to the metal.

Nolan shut the door and walked down the steps, turned right.

Nugent was half under the car, easing himself out, head and shoulders clear.

Great evening, Nolan thought, great night to be on the beach on the west coast.

Someone coming, Riley saw, whispered to Nugent. Get back in.

Someone by the car, Nolan thought. Two people, man and woman, courting couple.

Trouble, Riley sensed, began to move.

A third, head and shoulders visible, pulling himself back out of sight. Holdall on ground. Somebody breaking into the car, Nolan thought, nicking something from it.

Shit. Riley knew, swore, began reaching for the Star. Galvin reacting, beginning to turn, Nugent coming up.

Not taking something from it. Putting something in it. On it. Under it. Putting a fucking bomb under my fucking car. Nolan was already moving, automatically, instinctively. Gunman One hand to jacket inside. Gunman Two, the woman, turning. Gunman Three on floor and rising. Nolan was reaching inside her coat, taking out the Browning, safety off. She saw the gun in Riley's hand.

Three on one. The Hereford training overtook everything. Two shots at One, make sure he was out, then move to Two and Three. Or one shot each, then go back. She was not even thinking, was reacting instinctively, dropping into a combat position, Browning held firmly and on target, finger squeezing trigger. First gunman chest shot. She moved right, found a minimal cover behind the wall of some steps. Second gunman, the woman, still turning, two shots, both to the chest. She was still in the crouch position, went back down the line. First gunman, second chest shot. Third, on pavement, chest shot, difficult because of his position. Second chest shot, third. Third shot at first gunman, third at the woman. She dropped to one knee and changed magazines, even though there were still rounds in the first, full mags in left pocket, used in right. Rose and came forward, still in a semi-crouch, finger on trigger and Browning trained on the bodies on the ground. First body, no movement. Second, no movement. Third, on the pavement, slight movement. Right arm and hand still partly under car. Possible bomb under car, no indication of detonation system, therefore possibility of remote control by Three. She fired again, three shots, four, kept firing till the figure stopped moving. She dropped to one knee again, reloaded. Fresh mag from left pocket, used into right. Crept forward again, full mag in Browning Hi-Power. Heard the footsteps behind her and spun round, almost fired. Saw her driver and two of the tails.

The police would be there in minutes – her mind worked as quickly and automatically as her body had fifteen seconds before. Play the game according to the rules, leave the location as it was and everybody would know. Or break the rules and conceal the operation, conceal everything. Keep her options open and give herself time to decide.

'Leave the Vauxhall, there's probably a bomb under it.'

Get the bodies out but conceal the secret of the safe house – she was still assessing, planning. So what was going on, how did they know?

'Put these in the Sierra and get them out of here fast.'

If they were going for her then they knew she was tailing Logan. And if they knew she was tailing Logan then they knew she was looking for Sleeper.

Riley's chest no longer existed, the blood soaking through his shirt; Galvin's chest and shoulder had been torn away where the soft-nosed rounds had struck her as she turned; the blood covered the top part of Nugent's body and the hair round the bullet wound to his head was matted and sticky with dark red-brown blood. They lifted each body and dumped them on the back seat of the Ford. The tail slid into the driver's seat and pulled away. Nolan watched as he turned out of sight, then went back into the house.

Forty seconds later the first police car turned into the street.

Nolan sat at the table, the telephone on her right and the checklist she had drawn up in front of her. So what was happening, how did the IRA know – assuming the people by the car had been IRA – how did it affect the hunt for Sleeper? She pushed the thoughts aside and concentrated on the list.

Michaelmass:	to confirm the decision she had already made;
Police:	Michaelmass to square things with them;
Logan:	still in the hotel and the tails tight around him;
Bodies:	in the second safe house;
Doctor:	too late;
Pathologist:	no dispute over cause of death but get in anyway;
Forensic:	to remove anything from the bodies which might be useful;
Bomb Disposal:	to deal with bomb;
SAS:	in case the bomb disposal people didn't make it in time or weren't inclined to do what she wanted.

It was ironic, she thought, that in order to protect the British system of government people like the SAS were even required to kill those who were already dead.

One of the tails put the mug on the table.

'Thanks.' She sipped the tea, dialled London on the scrambler, asked for Michaelmass to contact her urgently, and requested priority back-up, listing her requirements.

'Keep Logan covered.' She turned to her second-in-command. 'Make sure the bastard doesn't even blink without us knowing.'

Michaelmass came through on the secure line ninety seconds later. Three people, two men, one woman, presumed Provisional IRA, had been observed at the side of one of the tail cars outside a safe house – her briefing was succinct, omitting unnecessary details. Each was armed and each had been shot dead. A bomb was believed to be under the car. The bodies had been removed but the car was still in place. A police patrol, presumably reacting to an emergency 999 call, had arrived in the street two minutes later but had found nothing.

She stated the options which might explain the events without commenting on them, and the facilities she had requested.

'What do you propose?'

'Either we go open with it, in which case the Provos will know we know about them. Or we put the lid down tight.'

'But if we put the lid down the Provos will be wondering what's happened to their people.'

'Easy. We give their people back to them.'

After we've done all we can with them. After the photographers and the fingerprint boys and the forensic scientists have stripped their mortal remains of anything worth saving.

'How?'

He knew how.

'An own goal.'

'The Chief Constable will need sorting. I'll speak to him myself. He'll probably insist on being around, which might not be possible to prevent.' Or politically expedient, she understood by his tone. 'He thinks he's God, if he plays silly buggers tell him to contact the Home Secretary. I'll clear it with Sinclair now.'

She thanked him, left the first safe house and was driven to the second.

Haslam answered the telephone on the first ring.

'Ops. Now.'

Give me a clue. He was already getting out of bed, trying not to wake his wife.

'No big deal, you'll be home for breakfast.'

When he reached Stirling Lines the Gazelle was already warming up. Within four minutes he and Phillips had been briefed, collected the equipment they needed, and the helicopter was lifting off into the night sky, the navigator already plotting the course for Manchester.

The bodies were laid out on polythene sheets, one in the bathroom and two in the kitchen, the procedures around them as calm and methodical as if they were taking place in the controlled environment of a hospital mortuary. First the photographer, then the forensic scientists, stripping off the clothing and tagging each item before placing it in a polythene bag, then working their way over the bodies. As they finished each corpse the fingerprint team moved in, wiping the ink from the skin and leaving no trace. Bomb disposal ten minutes away, Nolan was told, SAS airborne. She watched as the pathologist took his place. Make sure all the rounds are removed from the bodies, she reminded him.

*

The carpet of light stretched as far as Haslam could see. The pilot brought the Gazelle into Manchester; he and Phillips picked up the bags they had brought with them and hurried towards the car.

Logan was still in bed, Nolan confirmed. The minder at the front door allowed the bomb disposal team in to the safe house and a second showed them into the room she was using as a command centre.

'Two things you should know.' She turned in the chair.

'The first is that we have three IRA members dead. We think they were placing a bomb under a car. For a number of reasons we haven't been able to check. If there is a bomb we therefore don't know what sort it is. The labs would obviously like it intact, but that's your decision. One of my people will show you the vehicle in question but we're running short of time.

'The second is that in two hours the bodies of the IRA men will be put back in position then they, and the car in question, will be blown up. Your decision about how you deal with the bomb will obviously determine what we do. If you think you can move it safely, then we replace it with our own charges. If you think you can't, then we detonate it. Questions?'

'I assume the area is sealed off?'

'No.'

Because this one was being kept under wraps, they understood.

'You want us to do it?' There was no prejudice or dissent in the question, simply a request for information.

'I'm assuming everyone is going to be busy. The SAS are on their way in case you have your hands full.'

SAS just arriving, she was informed, Chief Constable as well. She closed the briefing and the bomb team left the safe house.

The Chief Constable was just inside the door of the kitchen, looking at the two bodies there. Haslam recognized him, even though he was wearing civilian clothes. The pathologist extracted the last bullet from the first body and moved to the second. The bodies were naked, neither had been cleaned. Haslam knelt down, examined each in turn, then examined the body of the woman in the bathroom, and returned to the kitchen. The first male with the wounds to the chest, as if he had been facing whoever had killed him. The woman with wounds to the chest but also to the shoulder, as if she had been turning. The second male also with wounds to the chest and head but the angle different, as if he had been crouched. He knelt again by the second male. The man planting the bomb, the body still moving after the initial shooting and someone taking no chances.

'Chief Constable, I'm from the security services. Thank you for coming.' He heard the voice and turned slightly. Have to get the politics over first, he understood she would have told him if it had been possible, have to get the obstacles out the way. 'Could we have a word in private? I'd like your advice on something.'

Fifty minutes later the bomb disposal team confirmed they had removed the package from beneath the Carlton, ten minutes after that Haslam and Phillips replaced it with their own.

The night was quiet, almost peaceful. The Sierra drew up behind the Vauxhall, the bodies of the IRA team were lifted out and placed against it, then the Sierra slid quietly down the street and the area round the car was cleared.

Nolan stood next to the Chief Constable, the lookouts in the shadows at both ends of Rutherford Street. It was one hour and forty minutes to dawn. Haslam checked that the street was clear and detonated the one and a half pounds of PE4.

The item was on BBC Radio's *Today* programme.

'More on last night's explosion in Manchester. According to police three people were killed when a bomb exploded under a car in the city. A report from our correspondent at the scene.'

Philipa Walker rolled over and turned up the volume.

The explosion had happened shortly before four, the reporter said. Three people had been killed, believed to be two men and a woman. The area was sealed off and police were conducting a detailed search of the area. Little remained, either of the vehicle itself, or the people concerned. Police had so far refused to comment, but the presence of Anti-Terrorist Squad officers suggested that the IRA was involved.

An own goal, she thought automatically, an ASU blown up as they were planting a bomb. Not that it would affect her. Everything was in place: the room at the rear of the flat had been sealed off, a partition built in front of the window; the VW camper was in the garage downstairs, the false plates and other items ready, and she had finalized the route. All that was left was the waiting.

An own goal, Conlan knew. All the signs were there: the time of night, the numbers involved, the reported sexes – two men and one woman.

305

So what had gone wrong? It would be nothing to do with the bomb itself, the Clock-Maker would not have made any mistakes. Doyle would be as puzzled as he was. But where did it leave Sleeper?

He made fresh coffee and thought through the alternatives.

The Brits knew about Logan and were tailing him, Blanchard's surveillance had established this. And now the Brits knew that the Provisionals knew. They would cover up the details of the car, of course, the public would never know the truth. But MI5, or whoever was tailing Logan, would know that but for the grace of God one of their surveillance teams would have been taken out. But – again – where did that leave Sleeper? What if they knew about the PinMan operation? What if they were tailing Logan in the hope he would lead them to Sleeper? But nobody knew about Sleeper, other than the members of the Army Council. And not even the Council knew of the Logan–Sleeper connection. Yet what if the Brits *did* know about Sleeper? He made himself think about the unthinkable. How did the deaths of the Manchester ASU affect PinMan?

In a way one of the objects of the Manchester operation had been achieved, though not in the way he had planned. The Brits had still been made aware that the Provos knew Logan was being tailed. Therefore the Brits would assume that Logan was expendable. And if Logan was expendable then the projects on which he was working, and to which – as LO – he would have been crucial, were also expendable.

So nothing had changed. Sleeper remained unaffected. Unless they picked Logan up on the way out, unless they were so desperate and had so much on Logan that they could risk lifting him. But even then there was no link. It was part of the game, he decided, the part some would call Chance, even Fate. And either you allowed it to scare you off or you ran with it, welcomed it when it went your way, and put two fingers up to it when it didn't.

Logan woke shortly after seven, the woman beside him.

'You'll stay for breakfast?'

Some clients were happy enough to smile with her over dinner, she thought, but only too anxious to be rid of her by the morning.

'That would be nice.' She slid her arm across his chest and lay closer to him. 'You'll be back?'

'I hope so.' There was no way he could come back, no way he could set foot in the North or on the mainland ever again.

'Ring me when you do.' Not through the agency, she meant, not for the money like last night. She kissed him and went to the bathroom.

Leave the hotel at 8.30, Logan confirmed. Airport by 9.00 and the flight to Dublin at 9.50. He leaned across the bed and switched on the radio.

'More about the bomb explosion in Manchester last night.'

The words hit him. Thank Christ the woman was in the shower, thank Christ she wasn't there to see his fear and his panic. What the hell had gone wrong, what had happened that the bloody bomb had gone off while he was still in Manchester and not safely back in the Republic? Thank Christ the nameless man in Dublin had thought about the escort agency, given him an alibi for the night.

Calm it, he told himself, work it out. Get it right before the woman came back. There were two places the Brits would pick him up. At the hotel or at the airport when he checked in for the flight. If they picked him up. If they had enough on him. But if they had enough on him they would have been here already. They could still lift him, probably kick the shit out of him. And in the end they would let him go, probably exclude him under the terms of the PTA, because in the end they had nothing on him. He had been that careful.

Play it out, he decided: commercial trip to Manchester, the business appointments to back his story up, plus a cast-iron alibi for last night. In a way he had no option. The woman came out of the bathroom. Her hair was glistening wet and a towel was wrapped round her. An own goal, he suddenly thought, the bloody ASU had blown themselves up and dropped him right in it.

Tiger in the restaurant, Nolan was informed.

Alone? she asked.

With company from last night.

So what the hell was going on, what game was Logan still playing and what was his role in it? She had discussed it on a secure line with Michaelmass at six, a hot thick bacon sandwich on the plate in front of her and a mug of sweet steaming tea beside it. The Provos had set her up. Not her personally, but the operation. And not the Provos. Conlan, the man behind the PinMan operation. If she was correct. If Logan had been the handler for the European hits. If the European jobs had been a warm-up for Sleeper.

Conlan had used Logan as bait, to see whether he was being tailed. Somehow someone had spotted them, traced the surveillance cars back to the safe house and put the bomb under the Vauxhall. The bomb due to detonate twenty minutes after Logan had landed at Dublin and cleared the airport.

But by placing the bomb the Provos had let her know that they knew there was a tail on Logan. Why? What did that tell her about Sleeper?

If Conlan had used Logan as bait, then Logan was expendable. And if Logan was expendable then so were the projects he was handling. So perhaps she was wrong about Sleeper and the European connection. But perhaps that was what Conlan intended her to think, why Conlan had been prepared to blow Logan. Except that Conlan didn't know that the Brits knew about Sleeper and the PinMan plot. But perhaps he would have blown Logan anyway, simply to put the Brits off.

Everything was speculation, she knew, only one thing was certain.

Logan was closed down and Logan was her only lead to Sleeper. So by closing him down Conlan had also closed that lead. Even if he didn't know that the Brits knew about Sleeper.

So what to do with Logan?

Pick him up, put him through the mangle for the seven days allowed by the Prevention of Terrorism Act, then they would have to let him go, or exclude him, because they had nothing on him.

Let him go, on the other hand, and the bastard who'd tried to blow her off the face of the earth would walk free. But he would walk free anyway and she would have wasted time. Nothing personal, she knew he would have said, even meant it. Part of the game. Except that she would have been the one splattered over the car park at Manchester airport.

'Blue Two. Black Three.' Logan on his way.

Let him go. It was what she and Michaelmass had agreed unless something came up, unless she suddenly thought of a reason why they should detain him.

It was eight hours later, on her own flight from Manchester to Heathrow, that she realized the mistake they had made.

12

THE MEETING TOOK PLACE in an upstairs room of the Hope public house in Matchett Street, in the Protestant Shankill area of Belfast, the three men seated round the table in the centre of the room and the stairs discreetly guarded. Two nights before the Provisional IRA had shot dead a Protestant politician with alleged links to the UFF, five nights later they would kill another.

'This is the target.' The intelligence officer gave them the photograph.

The gunmen studied it. Neilson was the best IO the UFF had, the older of the two knew. Sometimes he wondered how Nielson managed to get the material he gave them and how he managed to get away with so much.

The address was in the Falls area of the city. He gave them the details and a photograph of the house.

'What time will he be there?'

'Wednesday night's always the same. He and his missus go for a drink up the road. They leave the bar between ten-thirty and ten forty-five and are back home fifteen minutes later.'

Nolan's debriefing with Michaelmass began at eight. She had spent the day dealing with what they had casually called the loose ends in Manchester, he with the political flak from the police, Home Office and Downing Street. Cobra was meeting the following morning, he told her, and he needed whatever she could give him to cover his back.

For the first fifty minutes, therefore, they discussed in detail the events in Manchester. How the IRA might have known about the tail on Logan, how the Provos were able to mount an operation against an MI5 surveillance team, and the implications for the PinMan/Sleeper affair which followed from this.

'We made one mistake. We were correct in everything else we did, but we should have picked Logan up.'

'Why?'

Surely that would have played into their hands, confirmed that we knew about Logan. The way we played it we left the confusion in their minds, left them not knowing whether we knew about Logan or not.

'Our prime interest, our only interest, is Sleeper.'

'Yes,' said Michaelmass.

'The Provos don't know we know about Sleeper.'

'Correct.'

'But what would they do if they did?'

He saw the mistake they had made and what they should have done.

'We should have picked Logan up, held him for the full seven days, given him a hard time. And sometime during that period we should slipped in something about Sleeper.'

And then we should have released him, then the bird would have flown. And somewhere in the long hours he would spend being debriefed he would remember that the Brits had asked him about something or someone called Sleeper.

And then Conlan would not know what to do, then MI5 could sit back and watch the ripple effect, see where it took them. See if it persuaded the Army Council to call off Sleeper.

Michaelmass sat back in the chair, hands held palms together in front of him, almost as if he was praying, fingertips playing with his lips. For five minutes he held the position, not looking at Nolan and Nolan not interrupting, occasionally nodding to himself, as if he was working something out, as if he was going through the options and deciding which he should choose. As if, deep in the quagmire of information he was fed daily, he was searching for the one option he needed.

'We can still do it.' He looked up sharply, hands down and body language different.

Not Logan. Logan wouldn't be leaving the Republic, and even if he did it would be too obvious.

'One of the people you're running in Belfast.' Michaelmass was looking straight at her. Like a fox, she suddenly thought, eyes bright and close together, like a predator closing for the kill. 'Hanrahan. You put him in the Provos' security section.'

'Yes.'

'So we use him instead of Logan. We brief Hanrahan. Then we lift somebody, he'll have to be reasonably high up, interrogate him, drop something about Sleeper into the questioning, then let him run. He reports back to the security section that he's been picked up and Hanrahan debriefs him on the details of his interrogation.'

And that way they were covered, no matter which game Hanrahan was playing or which side he was really on. If he was straight, if he really was working for the Brits, then he could report back to his IRA superiors that the Brits were chasing someone called Sleeper, and the fact that that information had come from someone he had debriefed as part of the security section would give him his cover. And if he was still a Provo, if he was playing a double game, then he would report back immediately on the fact that the Brits were asking about someone called Sleeper.

'I'll call Lisburn now.'

The gunmen had been waiting eight minutes when they saw the target and his wife appear at the top of the street and enter the house. One was armed with a Spanish Star pistol and the other with a Colt 45, and on the back seat of the car – stolen from the city centre two hours before – was a sledgehammer. They would have taken the man in the street, the younger of the gunmen assumed, except that – even though they had his photograph – they could not be sure of his face. It was his second job and he felt the excitement as he waited, did not understand why they had teamed him with the older, more experienced man. They slid forward and stopped outside the house, pulled the balaclavas over their faces, moved for the front door. Two smashes of the sledgehammer and they were inside the hallway, the older man first, turning right into the first room. The target was half-way across the room, his wife trying to haul him back, protect him. Even as the gunmen opened fire on him he was pushing her out of the line of fire, moving away from his son and daughter so they would not be hit, going for the gunmen even as the rounds pounded into him.

The morning was bright and sunny, and the flight was on time. Nolan cleared the checks at Aldergrove and walked through the terminal to the car park. Brady was waiting for her; his skin was grey and his face was grim. She dumped her travel bag in the back seat, sat in the front and waited. Brady was not even looking at her, was sitting in the driver's seat with his hands clenched round the steering wheel and his eyes staring straight ahead.

311

'Frank's dead. The UFF took him out last night. Two gunmen, in front of his wife and kids.'

She was fighting against the void which suddenly engulfed her. So she didn't know – neither of them knew – whose side Frank was really on. But she'd got round that, had worked out a different set of rules for the game. And now Fate, Chance – call it what you bloody liked – had come back at her, reminded her that it, not she, made the rules. That it, not she, ran the game.

They drove out of the airport. Two minutes later Brady pulled into a lay-by and gave her the shoulder holster and Browning Hi-Power he had collected from stores.

'What else is it?'

She had seen Brady when he was up and running, when he was under pressure, when he was sitting in a forward stake-out car with the IRA or UFF all round him. Had seen him when she had gunned down McKendrick and he had run the Opel over Rorke. But she had never seen him like this.

'Something was up last night. Something was wrong.'

She waited for him to tell her.

'Frank was gunned down at eleven, give or take a minute either side, his wife couldn't be sure.' He was staring ahead as he had stared ahead in the car park. 'Lisburn logged two calls last night.' Two specific calls among the many. 'The first was at ten fifty-five, asking for an extension in one of the closed sections. When there was no answer the caller asked if there had been any incidents.' An army patrol passed, the soldiers glancing at them; Brady ignored them. 'The second call was at eleven three. The caller, apparently the same man, asked for the same extension. When there was no answer he asked if there had been a shooting. Not an incident, the log is specific about this, but a shooting.'

So . . . Nolan did not say, waited again.

'You remember the rumours over the McMullen shooting.' The senior IRA man gunned down by the UFF four weeks earlier. 'You remember the whisper that the job was set up by Sammy Nielson.' The intelligence officer for the UFF in Belfast, she knew, knew what Brady was going to say next. 'You remember the other whisper, that Nielson was being run by the FRU.' The Forward Reconnaissance Unit based at Lisburn, the wing of Military Intelligence running agents within the ranks of the IRA and the UFF. 'The extension that the caller asked for last night belongs to the FRU.'

So either the FRU knew Hanrahan was being taken out and hadn't checked with the other police and security agencies, or an agent they were running was out of control. Either way Frank was dead. The one man anyone had ever got into the Provos' security section, the man Gower Street was relying on to stop the attack on PinMan. And now the Brits had killed him or allowed him to be killed.

Christ, she thought.

They left the lay-by and drove to Lisburn.

Cobra convened at ten.

The Hanrahan ploy would have worked, Michaelmass knew. Catcher would have briefed him this morning, this afternoon the security forces would have lifted a middle-ranking Provo, someone they knew had been through the mill. And sometime tonight, probably on the graveyard shift when the suspect thought that his interrogators assumed he was getting tired and therefore more likely to make a mistake, they would have slid in the question about Sleeper.

To his left the head of Special Branch briefed Cobra on the latest investigations into contacts of those reporters and writers who had received leaks of royal information.

By tomorrow morning they would have released whoever they had chosen to lift – Michaelmass's mind was half on what Hamilton was saying, half on what might have happened in Belfast. By afternoon Hanrahan would have been debriefing him and reporting to the officer commanding the North Belfast Brigade. By the morning after the IRA's Northern Command would have been informed, and by the end of the same day the Army Council. Except that sometime in the past 24 hours some idiot had overstepped his jurisdiction and blown the whole thing.

Hamilton came to Patrick Saunders.

'Wasn't he the one with the royal schedule on his computer?'

'Yes, Home Secretary.'

Perhaps it was then that the seed was sown. 'I wonder if you could remind us of Saunders and his source.' The idea was only an embryo, still needed time to mature and develop.

'Of course,' Hamilton nodded. It was unlike Michaelmass to ask such a question, Michaelmass was always well informed and sharp as a razor. 'Saunders's source is Roderick Fairfax, a major in the First Battalion the Grenadier Guards. He's unique in that he's always been liked and trusted by both the Prince and the Princess, even after the separation. When Cobra was first notified of the Sleeper threat Fairfax received a partial briefing and doubled up on the security arrangements when Charles took his skiing holiday.'

If Fairfax was responsible for the leak to Sleeper, however indirectly, he might also be the key to stopping him. Even though most would find the solution as immoral and abhorrent as the act it would prevent.

'Fairfax's telephone records suggest that he's in contact with Saunders, and Saunders's telephone records confirm this. In addition Fairfax's details were on the computerized list of names, addresses and telephone numbers found at Saunders's flat.' Hamilton did not need to consult his notes. 'He has substantial private investments. Banking records, however, show no financial connection between Fairfax and Saunders.'

All it involved was adapting Catcher's original idea and taking it one stage further. And even if Fairfax wasn't responsible, he was a soldier, had signed the oath. So that, in a way, he would understand.

'We're currently checking the other names on Saunders's contact list in an attempt to establish the next link in the chain to Sleeper. Assuming the Fairfax–Saunders link is how Sleeper got his information. We are also pursuing similar lines of enquiry with other recipients of royal leaks.'

It would be useful if Fairfax had been responsible for the leak to Sleeper, of course. Michaelmass had no trouble with conscience. In a way he was doing no more than the generals who had sent the men over the top in the 1914–18 war. Yet it would be nice to know he was right, that some form of justice still existed. And there still remained the problem of how to play it.

'But you still think that Saunders is the way to Sleeper?' The Home Secretary's question was brusque and to the point.

'Yes.' Hamilton's response was clear and unequivocal.

'Excellent,' said Sinclair.

Cobra broke shortly before midday. Fifteen minutes later Michaelmass was back in Gower Street; ten minutes after that he had arranged for the advertisement to be placed in the personal column of the *Irish Times*:

'Joseph Jacobson. Father ill. Phone home urgently.'

*

314

The telephone message on what Michaelmass mentally referred to as the Sleeper line was logged on to the answerphone at three minutes past two the following afternoon.

'This is Joseph for Jacobson. Will phone again at six this evening.'

Quin's accent was as neutral as ever, Michaelmass thought, perhaps the hint of menace in it which came with the territory. Or perhaps because he was looking for it. There was a chance Quin wouldn't buy it, of course. Except that he would be as desperate as Cobra to solve the problem. Assuming that Quin was on their side, but that was the risk he'd known from the beginning. He checked the times of the Dublin flights that evening, and booked himself on the last.

The call came through at fifteen seconds past six.

'Jacobson.'

'This is Joseph.'

'We need to meet.'

The conversations on the telephone – like all their conversations – were functional and stripped of unnecessary detail.

'When?'

'As soon as possible.'

'Tomorrow.'

'Same place. What time?'

'Early.'

Jacobson in a hurry, Quin understood. Despite the way he tried to disguise it, the way he tried to keep his voice matter-of-fact. Probably already booked on a flight that evening.

'Seven?'

'Fine.'

Brittas Bay was deserted. The car park above the sand dunes was empty, the ice cream kiosk was locked and shuttered and the night tide had swept the beach clean even of footprints.

It was 6.55.

Michaelmass checked the package in his pocket, locked the Ford, then walked through the gap in the dunes and on to the beach. The tide was out. He turned right and walked, hands in pockets, along the water's edge towards the headland a thousand yards away. He was half-way there when he heard the second car stop. At the headland he turned and walked back. Quin was coming towards him, hands also in pockets. What should he say about Manchester,

315

Michaelmass wondered. Nothing, he decided. Manchester was about Logan, Logan was about Sleeper, and Quin knew nothing about Sleeper other than that he existed.

They met without shaking hands and turned left.

'We're not getting any further with Sleeper or PinMan.' So what do you want me to do, Michaelmass almost expected Quin to ask, but knew he would not. Sleeper was both their problems – as long as Quin wasn't lying, as long as Quin wasn't trying some sort of black propaganda game. 'There might, however, be a way out.'

'How's that?' It was the first time Quin had asked him anything.

'Sleeper doesn't need a green light. The only order the Army Council would give him from now on is a red. The order to stop.'

'Correct.'

'So the problem is persuading the Council to change the order.'

Quin nodded his agreement.

'What if you were able to present them with evidence that we knew about Sleeper and were about to pick him up.'

'How?' How would I be able to do that without cutting my own throat?

'I feed someone the stuff that would make the Army Council pull Sleeper out. Then I hand him over to you.'

'Where?'

'It'll have to be in the North.'

Jacobson running a scam, part of Quin's defensive instinct warned him, luring him into the North so they could pull him. But Jacobson coming up with the way out for both of them, he knew.

'Specifically?'

'I brief him, then arrange for him to be sent to Northern Ireland on a task related to Sleeper, and you lift him. He'll obviously need to take a number of men from his own regiment with him, otherwise questions will be asked on your side and mine.'

'As long as it's not the entire British army.'

He himself would need to be present at the interrogation – Quin was already thinking ahead – but he would also have to cover himself, make his presence appear a coincidence.

'Will he talk?'

'I shouldn't think so.'

They reached the headland then turned back along the waterline. June gone, the thought barely registered in Michaelmass's mind – already a quarter through July. Soon the summer would be over and Christmas would be coming up at them. Christ how time flies.

'You'll need to let the boys have him for a few hours, then give him this.'

Michaelmass took the envelope from his pocket and dropped the contents into Quin's hand. The bottle was small, no more than two inches long, a screw top concealing the vial inside. Both the label on the bottle and the box in which it was contained stated it contained a brand name ear drop.

'Sodium pentothol. Applied by injection. He'll talk within thirty seconds.'

They walked on, Michaelmass allowing Quin the time to plan.

'The Halfway House, between Mowhan and Whitecross. Nine o'clock in the evening. There's a car park outside. His minders stay in the car and he goes inside. There's been no trouble there, so that'll be in order.' Quin already knew how he would arrange it, how he would guarantee that he himself would attend the interrogation, how he would explain the sodium pentothol. 'He'll have to stay inside twenty minutes.'

'When?'

'When can you get him there?'

'Two days. The evening of the tenth.'

Fairfax reported missing that night and the proverbial hitting the fan in Belfast and London on the morning of the eleventh; they both began their calculations. The Army Council meeting on the twelfth. Sleeper called off on the thirteenth.

'It might be unwise to be in contact after today.' Quin stopped and looked out to sea.

'Only contact me if anything goes wrong.' Michaelmass stood beside him.

The fishing boat crossed in front of them, the gulls circling above it.

'One other thing.' Quin looked at the boat. 'When this is over, it's back to square one.'

Back to war.

'Of course.'

Cobra met at two.

'Thank you for coming at such short notice.' Sinclair was in his customary chair at the head of the conference table. 'This meeting has been convened at the request of the Deputy Director General.

317

I therefore suggest that he explains.' He sat back and glanced at his watch. As quickly as possible, the gesture said, I'm a busy man.

'Thank you, Home Secretary.' Michaelmass flicked down at the pad in front of him, then looked up. 'With your permission, I would suggest that this discussion is not recorded in the minutes.'

Why? the glances asked. The discussion is secret, even the existence of the committee is known only to a few.

'Agreed.'

He nodded his thanks. 'Sleeper and PinMan.'

Of course. Sinclair's show of irritation was deliberate. We know that. Get on with it. I'm seeing the PM at six.

'Late yesterday afternoon I received a telephone call from my contact in Dublin.' Economical with the truth, he recalled the expression. 'We met this morning. It could be there's a way round our little problem.' Already there was the suggestion that the solution had originated with the contact, rather than from himself. 'The instructions to Sleeper are that he goes ahead with his assignment. The only order which the Provisionals' Army Council will issue to him from this point is to abandon the operation.'

We know this – there was exasperation on Sinclair's face. I'm the Home Secretary, I'm the poor bastard who has to resign if the Prince of Wales is chopped.

'There are two circumstances under which the Army Council might do this. The first is if they thought they would suffer politically or militarily from it, which they would have already considered and rejected. And the second is if they thought we were on to Sleeper and about to lift him. Then they might pull him out to save him.'

He allowed the thought to sink in.

'How do we persuade them of that?' It was the head of Special Branch.

If it had been an internal M15 job they would have done it without a second thought. Not quite without a second thought, but it would have been cold and calculated and agreed immediately because that was the nature of the war in which they were engaged. Come into the open, however, be required to liaise with politicians and civilian police officers who might not subscribe to the same sub-code of ethics, or the same code of sub-ethics, and you ran into problems.

'We brief somebody. Tell him what we want the Army Council to hear, and give him to the Provisionals.'

He waited for their reaction.

318

You can't do that.

You know what they'll do to him.

Betraying our own.

Impossible.

Immoral.

The reactions were as he had expected, the discussion swinging as he knew it would.

Yet consider what was at stake.

The options running out, and fast.

The implications if the Provos succeeded in taking out a member of the royal family.

It swung a little further, began the dangerous slide from ethics to logistics.

Then Michaelmass's contact could be informed.

Report back to the Army Council.

But how would Michaelmass's source know?

How could they guarantee it was the source who was informed?

The discussion moved from logistics to security.

Wasn't there a danger the whole thing was a sting by the Provos to get their hands on a British army officer?

How could they guarantee that the officer concerned knew no more than they wished him to divulge?

How could they guarantee that he divulged it?

They came to the final point.

Who?

The Home Secretary looked round the table, then focused on Michaelmass. Not that we've agreed, of course. But tell us anyway.

Michaelmass opened his hands, as if unsure, as if asking the committee their recommendation. Someone from the military, he saw it in their faces, someone from Intelligence. Otherwise there would be no credibility. Otherwise the Provos wouldn't go for it.

'Who leaked the royal schedule?' It was the Cobra member sitting two seats to Michaelmass's right. 'Wasn't he military?'

'Yes.' The member to his left.

'What was his name?'

'Fairfax.'

The meeting broke at 5.40. As the others left Sinclair asked Michaelmass to remain.

319

'You'll cover yourself?' You'll cover us all? Set it up so that it can't be traced back?

'Of course.'

Fairfax was informed at five, 1700 hours in the military jargon in which he mentally logged the last hours of his life. Special job in London – the orders were equally brief and functional, partly because that was the manner to which both he and the lieutenant-colonel giving them were accustomed, partly because that was all the commanding officer had been told. Select eight men, chopper to Gütersloh and RAF transport to Northolt at 2000 hours. Briefing at MoD 0900 tomorrow.

The following morning he woke at six. At 6.30 he led the men he had brought with him from Germany in a twelve-mile run in Hyde Park, then he showered, changed into uniform, breakfasted and was driven to Whitehall, arriving at the Ministry of Defence at five minutes to nine. Two minutes later he was escorted to the third floor. The porter knocked, waited for an order to enter, then held the door open for him. Fairfax went in and the porter closed the door behind him.

The room was small and spartan, three military watercolours on one wall and a large oil of the Battle of Waterloo facing them. The desk, which occupied two-thirds of the floor space, was of metal. One of the two men seated at it was in uniform and the second in a civilian suit.

'Major Fairfax.' The brigadier invited him to take the remaining chair. 'Thank you for coming. This gentleman is from the security services. I'm afraid you aren't allowed to know his name. He'll be briefing you.'

He rose.

'You're not staying?' Fairfax was slightly surprised.

The brigadier shook his head. Only when he had left did Michaelmass reach across the desk and shake Fairfax's hand.

'Sorry about that. Nose a bit out of joint, I think. Security clearance not high enough. Shouldn't worry about it.'

There was no file on the desk, Fairfax noticed.

'Before we start I have to tell you one thing. You're being asked to volunteer for an operation in Northern Ireland. There is an obvious element of danger, but you should make it through without too much difficulty. The problem is that you have to agree to volunteer before I'm allowed to tell you what you're volunteering for.'

Typical military, Fairfax thought. 'Agreed.'

'Good.' Michaelmass changed his posture slightly, drumming his fingers on the desk. 'This briefing has the highest security classification. No details of it can be repeated to the men you will command over the next few days. Your commanding officer is also excluded. Given the nature of the subject, it is closed for ever.'

'Understood.'

Michaelmass's hands were still.

'For some time now we've been in possession of intelligence that the Provisional IRA has activated a hitman on the mainland. His codename is Sleeper, only the man running him knows his real name or any personal details.

'His target is codenamed PinMan.

'For several weeks now we have also been aware that he was close to finalizing his plans. Eight days ago we discovered a safe house which Sleeper had been using. From items found there we have established his identity. We know that the Provos' Army Council has given him the green light on the assassination. From other material we now know the location, time and method of the attack.'

So what was this to do with him, Fairfax wondered, what had it to do with what was obviously an undercover job in Northern Ireland?

'Sleeper is responsible for a number of killings in the North and in the Republic, though using different covers. There is a meeting with a contact tomorrow night and that contact is in a position to tell us about these operations, though he is obviously unaware of Sleeper's latest operation or why we want the information.'

'Why not use the normal people?' Fairfax asked. If anything was normal in the world of terrorism.

'You're close to the Prince and Princess of Wales.' Michaelmass was looking straight at Fairfax.

'Yes.' It was no secret.

'You accompanied the Prince and his sons on the ski trip to Klosters last winter.'

Again no secret. 'Yes.'

'You provided extra protection?'

'Yes.'

'I said earlier that Sleeper's target is codenamed PinMan.'

Fairfax waited.

321

'PinMan is the Prince of Wales.'

Oh Christ, Fairfax felt every sinew of his body tighten.

'So now you know.' Michaelmass folded his hands in front of him. 'The contact point is a pub, probably tomorrow evening, time and details to be confirmed by me to you once I have them. You should take back-up. Obviously.'

Obviously, thought Fairfax.

'They are to remain outside. Only you are to enter the premises.'

They began the details.

At eleven Fairfax briefed the men he would take with him. At 2.30 they took off from Chelsea Barracks in a Puma helicopter, refuelling at Anglesey and landing in the military section of Aldergrove.

Logan was out of bounds in Dublin and Hanrahan was even more out of bounds in the morgue, both her leads in to Sleeper removed in one grim twelve-hour period. Nolan sat back and wondered what she might do next, where she might start looking again. She had returned to London that afternoon and spent the next hours reading through the range of reports and analyses from MI5, Special Branch and the Anti-Terrorist Squad, reaching the inevitable conclusion that nothing took them any closer to Sleeper. Michaelmass hadn't been looking as grim as she had expected when they met briefly at four, though; perhaps that was an attribute of leadership – put on a good show for the troops when you knew they were flagging.

The telephone rang.

'Yes.' Even within Gower Street she never identified herself.

'Your query reference the Tangiers ferry.'

What Tangiers ferry enquiry? She was slightly puzzled: she'd lodged the enquiry and received the reply, hadn't made another. 'Yes.' Her response was automatic and her mind on Hanrahan.

'You were right. On the date in question the ferries from Algeciras sailed on schedule but the ferry from Tarifa was cancelled because of an engineering problem.'

So whose game were you playing, Frank? What side were you really on? No matter what the answer you were still the way to countering Sleeper. Don't worry about the boy and girl, Frank; I'll still stick to my part of the bargain, still see they make it.

She realized what the woman was talking about and what she had said. 'Tell me again.'

Someone wasn't where they said they were – she felt the excitement. Someone had written the card, probably written several, as a cover; given himself a location when he was elsewhere and handed the cards to a controller who'd arranged to have them posted. Except that something had gone wrong. Whoever had posted the card in Tangiers had been told simply to do that and nothing else. Didn't even know why they were doing it, and had therefore seen no reason to do any checking. *Couldn't resist a day trip. Soukh amazing. Another world.* She pulled out the photographs and checked the wording. Whoever had posted the card hadn't realized that on the day in question the ferry from Tarifa had been cancelled.

So all they had to do was establish the identity of *P*. They could pull Saunders, but that might alert Sleeper. Or they could run the initial against the names they had, cross-reference it against the other files.

It was suddenly too easy, too obvious. There was a multitude of reasons for the discrepancy. She wouldn't inform Michaelmass, therefore, but would run the check anyway. She telephoned the section and asked for a search to be run for names beginning with the letter P and a cross-match sought for any names found.

'First name, middle names or last name?' You know what you're asking for? The silence before the question said it all.

'First name.'

'Male or female?'' You know how long that will take us and how many other checks we're running?

Take a risk, she saw the temptation, cut corners. Especially as the lead was so tenuous and she wanted any intelligence from it in a hurry.

'Both.'

Quin began his journey north at nine, crossing the border clandestinely and changing to a car with Northern Ireland plates, then going to the house near Keady which the IRA security section used as a holding and interrogation centre for members believed to be working for the British or the RUC. When he moved on, at eleven that evening, he left at the house a vial of sodium pentothol, which he explained he had acquired from America, and which the interrogators might find useful.

*

323

The night was long, made longer by the isolation in which the unit was held. Fairfax lay on his bunk and rehearsed again the plans the nameless man at the MoD had given him. Pity the job hadn't been tonight, the nerves screwed in him, pity they weren't doing it now, hadn't already done it. Pity they weren't home and celebrating. He rolled off the mattress and checked the Browning for the third time that night.

At eight next morning Quin met the man commanding the North Belfast Brigade, at ten the Boss Man of East Tyrone, at noon the council of the Northern Command. At four, having established his cover, he was driven west for his meeting with the man commanding South Armagh.

Nolan received the call at ten. Overnight one of the computers had gone down and there would be a delay in getting her the information she wanted. What about the other computers, she asked. A second-ary problem was the decision that MI5 should collate all information from the other police and security agencies, the operator explained. Why, she asked. Because the other agencies were using different programmes, he told her.

'So where does that leave my enquiry?'

'If you could reduce the scope of the search, even temporarily, it might be possible to get you at least some of the material within the next twelve hours, fifteen at most.'

'In that case just run the cross-check for males.'

'Thanks.' The relief in the man's voice was unmistakable.

Michaelmass's call to Fairfax was made shortly before midday; ten minutes later Fairfax briefed his team. The location was the Halfway House, between Mowhan and Whitecross. They would use two cars, three men in one, himself plus two in the other, and everyone else on stand-by. They would arrive at the pub at 2030 hours; he would go inside immediately and would stay a maximum of 25 minutes. One car would remain in the car park, the other in the general area and in constant radio communication.

They all knew the problem. Fairfax needed a two-car back-up at least, but even one vehicle waiting outside was bad. Just hope to Christ that the pub was clean and the Provo activity in the area was currently as low key as the Int reports suggested.

*

324

The day had been hot and the sky a clear blue, not even the faintest hint of a change in the weather. At two it was announced in London that the bodies of the three IRA members blown up by their own bomb in Manchester would be returned to Northern Ireland the following day. At six Quin arrived at the farmhouse. The gunmen were in the yard and by the barn where Quin's driver parked the Audi, more in the hills and fields surrounding the meeting-place.

Martin Farrell was waiting in the kitchen. He was 41 years old, had commanded the South Armagh Brigade for the last seven, and appeared mild-mannered and quietly-spoken; after McKendrick, however, who was still remembered in the Movement for his attempted raid on the Crumlin Road prison the previous July, his reputation for violence was second to none.

'Good to meet you.'

The way in which Quin said it told the men around them how importantly Farrell was viewed in the councils of power, how impressive their own record was. For the next two and a half hours they discussed medium- and long-term tactics and strategies, the role of the armed struggle, the relationship between the bullet and the ballot box, and what Farrell saw as the need for action in the wake of the incident in Manchester.

The suggestion of a drink came shortly before eight, originated by Quin though in retrospect it appeared to have been Farrell who made it.

'Where would you be thinking of?' It was Quin again who turned the thought round, away from simply a glass in the kitchen, though the truth of the moment would be lost in the events of the night.

Farrell saw the glint in Quin's eyes and understood. The Brits would be tightening the screws, would be winding up the security for fear of retaliation to mark the homecoming of the Manchester ASU. So the Provos would be sitting tight and waiting for the storm to pass. Except that they wouldn't be. Except that the commander of the South Armagh Brigade and one of the Big Men from the Army Council would be sitting openly and defiantly, taking a glass together.

'Where'd you fancy? The Three Steps, the Bridge, the Halfway House . . .' He reeled off the names of the pubs in the area.

'The Halfway House.' There was the hint of a query in Quin's voice. 'I went there once with my father. How would that be now?' It did not seem an answer, merely a memory.

Farrell turned to his second-in-command. 'Check it out.'

The road was clear and the drive took ten minutes. The moment Mullins turned off the road and saw the Cavalier he knew. Two men, front seat. His first instinct was to turn and drive out, and his second was that that was what the bastards would be looking for. He parked the car and went inside. Another bastard was sitting by himself and supping a bloody Guinness. Thank Christ Farrell had sent him first, thank Christ they hadn't brought The Man here without checking. He asked for a pint, sipped it slowly, then thanked the landlord and left. The telephone kiosk was two miles away. He pulled off the road and dialled the number of the farm.

'For you,' one of the gunmen told Farrell. The brigade commander listened without speaking, then told Mullins to hold and cupped his hand over the mouthpiece.

'Problems?' Quin looked at him from the table.

'There's an undercover unit there. Two in a car, one inside.'

'RUC or Brits?'

'Brits.'

Pull The Man out of the area, logic appeared to dictate. Bit of a waste to let it go, Farrell saw the glint in Quin's eyes, shame to let the bastards off the hook when they were sitting up and begging to be taken. Sure we'll have to be careful, sure I might have to hang back a bit. But tonight of all nights. Tonight when the poor fuckers are lying cold and forgotten in their boxes in Manchester and the Brits think they've bloody won.

'We'll be there in fifteen minutes. Wait for us.'

Four cars, he gave his orders: Mullins and one other in first, take out the bugger in the bar, the others to deal with the bastards outside when they heard the shots from within. Himself and The Man in the last car and holding back slightly.

They began to leave.

Wonder what they're up to – it may have been himself, may have been Quin. Wonder why they're there tonight of all nights. Interesting to find out.

Mullin and one other into the bar, cover the bastard inside – Farrell changed his orders. Twenty seconds after they go in the men outside deal with the Brits in the car. As soon as he hears the shooting Mullins brings the other out. Rendezvous at Flannigan's – he gave the name of another farm – this one's too close.

The black was seeping into the purple of the hedges. The convoy stopped for Mullins, then the cars divided, the lead car 300 yards ahead, those carrying the gunmen in the middle, and the fourth carrying Quin and Farrell 200 yards behind.

The soldiers in the Cavalier saw the headlights turn in and tensed. The car stopped on the other side of the car park, thirty yards from them, then the two men got out and strolled towards the pub. Hands in trousers pockets and jackets pushed back, one of them talking and the other laughing. Going for a drink, the soldier in the passenger seat thought, couldn't be too careful though, especially with the major inside. Radio the back-up when they disappear into the pub, he decided, make sure they were on their toes. In front of him he saw the headlights – two cars, close together, turning in to the pub. Christ, he saw it. The two men at the pub door but a third still in the car, the car engine still running.

'Provos,' he warned the driver. 'Three cars, assumed Provos,' he called the back-up. 'In now. Repeat. In now.' Warn the major, every instinct told him, pull the major out now. He reached for his Browning and began to open the door.

The windows were down, the muzzles of the Kalashnikovs pointing out. Mullins's car clear and the Brits like sitting ducks. Fairfax heard the first crash of the submachine gun, dropped his drink and reached inside his jacket. Ran for the door. The driver of the back-up heard the request and smashed his foot on the accelerator even before the message was completed. The rounds ripped through the thin metal of the Cavalier, the two men inside dying immediately, the rounds still arcing across the bodywork and the figures inside crumpling. Fairfax came out of the door, Browning in his hand, saw the back-up hurtle into the car park.

'Behind' – the driver of the second Provo vehicle saw and shouted the warning. The back-up Sierra was coming straight at them, the soldier in the front seat firing through the windscreen and the driver wrenching the wheel over, trying to turn and give the men in the back a firing line. Mullins's driver car saw Fairfax running and shooting, and accelerated towards him. The Sierra driver did not turn quickly enough, felt the shock as the rounds from the Kalashnikovs in the second Provo assault car thudded through the side. Felt the shudder in his chest and realized the man in the seat next to him was firing back but wounded, one soldier in the back also returning fire and the second trying to roll out of the rear door and take a position behind the car from where he could shoot. Mullins's car struck Fairfax and bowled him over. The sound was deafening, endless. Fairfax saw the men coming towards him and tried to drag himself up, cursed, felt in his pocket for a fresh mag. Saw the gun on him and knew he was about to die. The fourth Provo vehicle turned into the car park. Christ, whispered Farrell, almost in glee. Perfect, thought Quin.

The cellar was dug into the floor of the barn on the edge of the farmyard, the hurricane lamp swinging from the wooden beam which supported the ceiling. The lower section of his right leg, four inches below the knee, was at an angle, and the blowtorch had been placed on the stairs so that Fairfax could see it.

Farrell crouched over him again. 'So what were you doing there?'

The Sleeper contact. Fairfax tried not to think of it. He knew what the bastard was going to do and tried to brace himself mentally for the pain. Farrell moved back and touched the right leg, watched as the pain shot through Fairfax.

'Like I said. What were you doing?'

Routine patrol, Fairfax told himself, no special reason for stopping there. Farrell moved his lower leg again. Fairfax felt the agony and tried to stifle the noise which came from him. Don't scream, don't say anything. He felt the pain again as Farrell held the leg again and twisted it to the right. Don't think of Sleeper, don't think of what you mustn't tell them.

He was lying crumpled against the wall, legs spread open, head on one side. The blowtorch, he tried not to look at it, could not stop his glance drifting towards it.

'Strip him.'

Mullins and two others manhandled Fairfax to his feet and ripped off his shirt, trousers and pants, as well as his shoes and socks, ignoring the broken leg, then dropped him.

Farrell nodded.

Mullins picked up the cattle prod and held it close to Fairfax's chest, not quite touching. Quin watched and waited. So what did the man he knew as Jacobson tell the poor bastard on the ground, he wondered; how had he managed to set it up? Mullins touched Fairfax with the prongs of the prod. The pain shot through him, Mullins still holding the prod against him. His body was convulsing, leg twisting grotesquely. Mullins lifted the prod off and he felt the relief. Farrell nodded a second time and Mullins reapplied the prod.

It was going well, Quin thought, better than he had hoped. The trap sprung and nobody the wiser.

Mullins lowered the prod and held it against Fairfax's genitals, against the break in his leg. The pain was searing, consuming. Fairfax had not known what pain was like before now, could not even think about it, only felt it. Did not know what was worse, suffering it or waiting for it, knowing how much worse it would be each time. Mullins took the prod away, gave him a moment of relief, then reapplied it.

Quin checked his watch. It was midnight. Farrell nodded and Mullins put down the cattle prod. Fairfax watched him and knew what he was going to do.

Calmly, almost deliberately, Mullins walked to the stairs and picked up the blowtorch. Two men held Fairfax down, one on each shoulder, so that he was half-sitting half-lying against the wall. Mullins turned on the torch and smiled, then he struck a match and held it to the gas. The flame was bright, a brilliant mix of blue and orange. Mullins adjusted it and held it close to Fairfax's face. Fairfax felt the heat sear across his eyes and tried to control the way he was shaking. Mullins smiled at him and turned the flame downwards, held it across his chest. The scream was different, the mix of pain and horror affecting even those around him.

'So what were you doing?' Farrell asked again, nodded again.

Mullins directed the flame on to Fairfax's stomach, the angle oblique, the flame cutting across it and burning the flesh.

Routine patrol, Fairfax fought not to tell, tried to convince himself, knew he was screaming. Whatever you tell them don't tell them about the contact. For God's sake don't tell them we know all about Sleeper. Don't ever tell them we know his name and details. The flame cut across him again, he felt the pain and smelt the burning. Don't ever tell them we know where the safe house is. That we know the time and place of the hit. For God's sake never say that we're about to lift him.

'You know you're going to tell us.' He heard the words and saw Farrell close to him. The face disappeared and the flame scorched across him again.

He knew he was crying. Not outside. Outside he was still screaming. Was crying inside. Because he could no longer take the pain. Because he was about to tell them. I was there to meet the Sleeper contact, he began to say, thought he was beginning to say. Felt the relief that it was done, that it would soon be over.

'He's not going to talk.' Quin stepped forward and stopped Mullins. It was getting like a barbecue, soon there wouldn't be enough of the bastard left to tell them anything, even if he wanted to. 'They have something at Keady. It'll take me half an hour to get it.' The security section's interrogation centre, Farrell knew. Pity he couldn't use the sodium pentothol now, Quin thought, but then he would need to explain why he was carrying it, then the cover would be jeopardized. 'Somebody look after him, make sure he doesn't do anything stupid.'

He left the cellar and went upstairs, Farrell and Mullins following him.

'Don't touch the bastard till I get back.'

'Why? What can you get?'

'Some sodium pentothol.'

Quin made a show of hurrying for the car.

Why hadn't he mentioned it before, Farrell thought. Meaner than he looked, Quin. Actually enjoyed putting the bastard downstairs through it.

The cellar was empty, the thinnest beam of light through the gap where the guard had left the trapdoor partly open. Fairfax huddled in the corner like an animal. No more blowtorch, please God. I can't stand any more. I almost told them once. I know I'll tell them next time. Even before they start next time. Anything to save the pain.

They were going to kill him anyway, so whatever he said wouldn't help him. Except that it would save him from the pain. He looked down his body, the flesh and muscle singed black. Christ, how the pain was burning through him, as if he was in a furnace, as if the fire and the flames were still on him. No more, dear God, stop them now.

You're a soldier, he told himself. You're Brigade of Guards.

The pain was fiercer, hotter.

One duty, Fairfax. Not to tell them about the reason for the operation, not to tell them that London knows about Sleeper.

No more, dear God, no more pain.

You're a soldier, so do what you have to do.

Please no more pain, no more suffering.

He peered through the dark of the cellar. Table and two chairs, nothing else. No clothes, nothing to hang himself with. Nothing he could use to strangle himself, nothing to cut his wrist.

Christ, the bloody pain.

No point smashing his head against the wall and trying to break his skull. They would see, hear; would know he was trying to protect something. And if they didn't stop him in time there was no guarantee it would be fatal. The pain, the Christ-making ball-breaking pain. He gave up and rolled himself into a ball, wrapped his arms round him. Tried to comfort himself, tried not to let his arms touch his body. Please God help me. Please God save me. Please God take me now.

You or the Prince of Wales, Fairfax. You or the next king of England. No one will ever know, of course. Except you. And when you stand before your Maker you're the only one who matters.

He turned slightly, facing the corner, so that if the guards looked down they would not see. His body was shaking. He held his left wrist in his right hand and turned the left so that the palm and inside of the wrist were facing up, wrapped his fingers round the wrist and felt for the pulse. Then he lowered his head, and closed his mouth on his left wrist, began biting, gnawing through it. The flesh was slimy, sickening; he knew he was going to vomit and stopped himself, made himself keep biting. His teeth snapped through the cartilage and tendons. Almost there, Roddy, worst part over. The fire was still eating him, devouring him. Last bite, old man. Didn't let the side down. Bloody proud of you.

Quin's car pulled into the yard. Farrell hurried outside to meet him, then they walked the twenty yards to the barn. The guards were by the trapdoor to the cellar, the door itself slightly open and the light shining down into it.

'Any problems?'

'None.'

Quin took the vial of sodium pentothol and the hypodermic from his pocket. 'Two minutes and we'll know.'

The guards pulled the trapdoor open and they went down.

Fairfax was in the far corner, bent double and still, facing away from them. Curled like a dog, Quin thought. The first gunmen reached up and lit the hurricane lamp. The floor round Fairfax was red and sticky. Quin crossed the cellar and turned the body over. The torso and face were drenched in blood, the walls coloured where it had spurted up. The left wrist was jagged and torn, as if a wolf had ripped it open, and the last blood had pumped from it minutes before.

He let the body drop and went upstairs.

The night was black, a myriad stars but no moon.

So what the hell to do – Quin sat back in the seat and tried to work out his options. Get back to Dublin, he had decided, at least to the Republic; let Jacobson know the bad news. Bloody Farrell, he cursed, bloody guards, slipping out of the cellar for a smoke when they should have stayed with the bastard in the corner.

The car was moving quickly.

They rounded the corner and saw the lights of the army road block. No problem, Quin thought, nothing on him or the driver, nothing on the car. Nothing to connect him with the carnage at the Halfway House.

Perhaps it was because of the increase in tension in anticipation of the return of the Manchester bombers later that day. Perhaps because of the news over the radio of an ambush of an undercover patrol and the death of five soldiers. Perhaps because it was the end of their tour and they were due home the next day. Perhaps because Quin's driver was going too fast and did not see the lights soon enough, did not slow quickly enough. Perhaps because the man at the road block was the least experienced of the patrol. Perhaps because they were paras, trained to the edge and pumping aggression.

The lights of the car were coming at him, headlights full on. The soldier had heard the car a minute ago, the gear changes in the night still, yet was not expecting it, had assumed it was going somewhere else. Was only aware of the car swiftly and suddenly – more or less in the time it took to shout for the sergeant and bring up the SA80.

The car was not slowing, coming straight at him. He was shouting the standard warning, suddenly aware he was standing in the middle of the road, dead in front of the road block. Unaware that the driver had not heard the warning.

The car was still coming at him, the other paras huddled over the brew in the ditch suddenly alert and moving fast. Moving too late, he assumed.

The car was still not slowing, the headlights blinding him. He flicked the safety off and pressed the trigger, the copper-jacketed rounds penetrating the engine space and smashing through the windscreen. The car veered right, struck the bank and bounced over, turned upright again.

The first para reached it five seconds later, the SA80 trained on it and advancing cautiously. Quin was lying at an angle, his face and head through the windscreen and his neck broken. The driver was jammed in his seat, one round through his head and the column of the steering wheel through his chest.

Trouble, the sergeant knew. Board of enquiry, the Irish bleating on about indiscriminate shooting, and the paras getting it in the neck again. The end of the tour, and a bad one at that, and the poor fucker who'd done the shooting getting married tomorrow afternoon. Another week in this God-forsaken country at least, probably more. And all the hassle that would come with it.

The others were looking at him. Good guys, he thought, guys who'd been through it together. Guys he could trust. To cover his back. To keep their mouths shut. Guys who relied on him to pull them out of the shit.

'Lose the motor.' He turned to them. 'Take it on to someone else's patch and torch it. Make sure nothing's left of it or the stiffs.'

The Army Council met at ten. Doherty's eyes were sinking fast, Conlan thought. But Doherty would see it through, would get his place in history. The Chief of Staff looked round the table.

'Sleeper is set. Unless there are any last-minute problems Sleeper is on go.'

The only problems might have come from Quin and Quin had not made the meeting. In Belfast the bodies of the Manchester bombers were on their way from Aldergrove to their family homes.

'One message to Sleeper.' It was the oldest member.

Doherty turned his head.

'Wish him good luck.'

Three hours later McGinty left Dublin with the messages which would activate the London flying column and enable Sleeper to contact them.

The Cobra committee met at twelve. The Home Secretary was looking relieved, Michaelmass thought, as if a weight had been lifted from his shoulders. As if his political future was assured.

'No fresh news on the killings at Mowhan last night?'

'No.'

'And nothing on Major Fairfax?'

By now Fairfax would be dead.

'No.'

'And nothing from your contact?' The contact only to be in touch if anything had gone wrong.

'No.'

'In that case, gentleman, and with the greatest regret, we have to conclude that Major Fairfax's mission was successful.' The Home Secretary closed the file. 'The Prime Minister has an audience with Her Majesty this afternoon. He will take the opportunity to inform her that the Sleeper threat no longer exists. I myself will inform the Prince and Princess of Wales this evening.'

13

THE PICTURES OF THE KILLING of five soldiers at the Halfway House pub near Mowhan the night before had been on breakfast television. Later that morning the coffins of the IRA men apparently blown up by their own bomb in Manchester would be flown back to Belfast. Equations, Nolan thought: three of yours for six of ours. And the Sleeper enquiry stood down. Yesterday the world was hitting the panic button, or so it seemed, and today everything was fine. Today it was as if Sleeper had never existed.

She had telephoned Lisburn immediately she had heard. Five shot dead *and one missing*, she had been told – the last information not disclosed to the media. Not five of ours, she had asked in horror, not five of the guys from 14 Int? Five of ours wouldn't get caught like that. In from London the afternoon before, she had been told; held incommunicado, no indication who they were or what they were working on. Then suddenly they were off, and two and a half hours later they were dead. So why bring someone fresh in from London, she had asked, why not use the boys from 14 Int, them and/or the SAS with whom they customarily worked. And what about the guy who was missing. Who and what was he? What the hell was he up to?

Of course the Sleeper hunt hadn't been abandoned. Everyone was still looking for him, she herself would be reinstated to it after she had sorted out the loose ends about Logan and Manchester. Michaelmass had said so at their meeting. It was simply that the heat had been turned down on the hunt for Sleeper. Almost as if they had a respite, almost as if someone had pulled something off which nobody else was allowed to know about.

It was a shame no one had produced the cross-match which would have taken the hunt a stage further, though, a shame the apparent anomaly of the postcard date had got them nowhere.

The computer section had done well, but in the end their work had come to nothing. Of the total number of males listed in the various police and security service enquiries collated by MI5, fifty-seven had names beginning with the letter P. Twenty-eight of these could be eliminated because they were in the wrong age profile, and none of the remaining twenty-nine could be cross-matched under even two headings of the Sleeper hunt.

The summer moving on, she thought. Tomorrow the marching season in Northern Ireland would be in full swing. Tomorrow was the twelfth of July.

The images on the mid-morning television news bulletin were grim: the bodies of the five undercover men killed in what was being described as an IRA ambush being driven away, the places where they had died in the car park marked in chalk; the coffins of the three IRA bombers en route to Manchester airport.

Walker watched the bulletin in one of the television shops in Tottenham Court Road, then caught the tube to St James's Park and walked to the wine bar. The Tapster was in the basement of a modern office block a hundred yards from New Scotland Yard and three hundred from the Home Office. Its walls were red brick, with tables in a raised dining section furthest from the door as well as in alcoves along the sides, separated by wood partitions. Most of the customers already crowding the bar were businessmen, civil servants or policemen.

The table in the alcove on the right side of the dining area had been reserved in the name of Mills three days before, and the choice of position had been deliberate. The man now sitting at it was in his early thirties, dressed in a city suit with a monogrammed brief-case on the floor beside him and a copy of the *FT* folded on the table. She glanced at the initials on the briefcase and noted the way he checked hers.

'Sorry I'm late.' The first line of the code.

Tighe looked up, slightly surprised but covering it. They told me to expect the organ grinder not the monkey, he might have said under different circumstances. Good place for a meet, though; the security services would never expect the head of a Provo flying column and the courier for a hitman to meet in such a place. Except, he thought again, that he had been expecting the man himself.

'I've only been here five minutes. I've ordered a bottle of dry white. I hope that's all right.' The second line.

'Some mineral water as well.' The code was straightforward and simple.

'With or without gas?'

'Without.' The last line of the code.

A waitress took their order.

'The job's tomorrow.' Walker waited till she had left them. The briefing was public but secure; totally in the open but no one being able to hear because of the position of the table in the alcove and the position of the alcove in the wine bar. 'You bring the cars in from the West Country tonight.'

A courier, a messenger girl, shouldn't know about the cars. Tighe felt uneasy.

'Whoever got the documents for the VW did a good job.'

Time to get out, Tighe began to think, too little security in the operation already.

'You collect the first VW this afternoon.' She gave him the keys and the location. 'It's blue.' He wondered why she told him the colour. 'Inside are strips of Fablon, already cut to fit the body panels, plus spray cans. This evening you put the strips on and spray them orange. You also smoke the windows.' What the hell is this, Tighe was thinking. 'You put on the false number plates from the other VW; you put them over the originals, and in a way that they can be quickly and easily removed. You also put on the road fund licence for the other VW, but you keep the original behind it.'

Tighe saw it. One VW with two identities. The orange one, false plates and vehicle licence for the hit, then the reversion to the other soon or immediately after, the number plate and vehicle licence matching in case they were stopped by police. Not only matching but genuine, except that the vehicle to which they correctly belonged would be half-way across Europe by now.

The waitress served their smoked salmon.

'You have the Cellnets and the weapons?'

'Yes.' It was the first time he had confirmed anything other than his identity.

'You and I meet at the Café de Paris near South Kensington tube station at nine-thirty, confirm everything is in order.' At least the courier was businesslike, Tighe thought, but when did he meet the man, check through the plans with him?

Walker took the street map and blow-ups from her briefcase. 'The target area is Mayhill Street, number 29.' She indicated the position

337

on the first blow-up. 'The target is scheduled at eleven-thirty. Her car will arrive and park outside two minutes before. It'll be an Escort XR3i and there'll be a back-up behind, probably a Rover. I'll be in position here, begin walking down Mayhill Street at twenty-eight minutes past, arriving at number 29 the same time as the Escort.' She indicated the position on the blow-up.

You'll be in position. Tighe realized he was almost thinking aloud: *you'll* time your walk to reach the firing zone at precisely the time the target arrives. *You're* The Man.

'You plus two are here in the first car.' She indicated the position. 'You watch my movements carefully, your timing will have to be precise.' Of course, he almost said. 'The target will be carrying a bodyguard. I drop him, immobilize the two men in the back-up, then concentrate again on the bodyguard.' She was cold, Tighe began to think. 'At that stage there will two other people on the pavement, plus me. You time your run-in with two objectives: to finish off the men in the back-up, and to lift the two people I'll be with on the pavement. You get them in the car, rear seat, I get in as well.'

It wasn't a hit, he understood for the first time, wasn't someone being gunned down. It was a kidnapping. In broad daylight and in the centre of London. Someone important enough to be carrying protection and back-up. Christ, he thought.

'There are two vehicle switches. The first is here.' She indicated the location on the street map, then on the second blow-up. 'We stop here. There's an alleyway running to here. There are parking meters here.' She indicated the street at the other end of the alleyway. 'You park the second car there first thing tomorrow morning. Jam the meter so you don't get any trouble with a traffic warden. We leave the first car, go down the alleyway, and take the second. During that time you're in charge of the target. The streets and alleyways are quiet at that time of day, so nobody should see us.

'The second switch is here.' She indicated the location on the street map and on the third blow-up. 'It's a derelict factory site, known locally as the Fax. The fourth member of your team drives the VW there and stays with it. When we arrive we switch from the second car. There's a lock-up area there. We hide the second car in it, so nobody associates the VW with it. After that there's one more switch.'

'The VW back to its original appearance.'

Walker nodded. 'There are three potential locations for this.' She indicated and described each in turn.

And then? Tighe did not ask.

'Then we go to the safe house.' Himself and the others, including the target, hidden in the back, Tighe knew. Garage part of the safe house, so they wouldn't have to go outside to enter the house, electronic doors on the garage. The communication systems already worked out and the timetable from that moment on as precise as that which had preceded it, he assumed. Christ, she was good.

'How long do we have then?'

'Maximum eighteen hours, could be as little as four.'

'And we'll get out okay?'

'That will be part of the deal.'

There were a number of questions, asked and answered quickly and efficiently, mainly about the routes but also the guns they would carry. The boys had time for a dry run tonight, Walker suggested, but they shouldn't make it too obvious, just a quick look to familiarize themselves with the key points. Except Mayhill Street was taboo: not even she would go near it. You have something for me? she asked as they left.

Tighe gave her the package. Inside was a Ruger, shoulder holster, suppressor, ammunition and fast loader. Plus Semtex and detonators, the instructions meeting her specific requirements and planned by the Clock-Maker.

'Two other things. You should have a woman's coat, headscarf, sunglasses and shopping bag in the first car.' The disguise might seem irrelevant if anyone saw the guns they would be carrying, but if they could keep the weapons hidden there was every point in at least trying to hide the target.

'And the second?' Tighe asked.

'This afternoon I want you to buy me a dog. Collie would be good, not too young but still frisky.'

Why, he began to ask, then understood.

The first television pictures on the one o'clock news were of the car park outside the pub near Mowhan, and the second were of the coffins of the Manchester ASU arriving in Belfast. Nolan left Gower Street and walked to Regent's Park, the sun hot and the frustration growing in her.

Something about the postcard, except that they had checked

339

everything and come up with nothing. Therefore something wrong with their observations and their logic.

The band of the Royal Marines was playing 'Greensleeves', their buckles and medals sparkling in the sun and the music drifting through the trees, the circles of deckchairs round the bandstand, people eating and drinking and enjoying the day.

Not something wrong with their observations and their logic, something wrong with their assumptions. Even hers. Especially hers.

She was back in Saunders's flat, going into the kitchen, looking at the notice board, at the postcards on it. Cyprus was the one, Cyprus was still the crossroads for international terrorism, still the jumping-off point for the faceless men from the Middle East and the even more faceless men who ran them.

Except.

A man wouldn't have signed a postcard with the initial P. A man would have signed his name. Or used both his initials. Unless he and Saunders were intimates, and nothing in the checks suggested that Saunders was that way. Therefore a woman – with whom Saunders was having an affair or who had something to hide.

They had considered the possibility of a woman's involvement, as a cover or a courier, then they had rejected it. Because Sleeper would have trusted no one except himself, would have done his own research and made his own plans.

But suppose.

Just suppose.

That Sleeper wasn't a man.

That Sleeper was a woman.

She rejected the notion, left the bandstand and walked back through the park. Asked herself why she had rejected it.

She had rejected it because Michaelmass had always referred to Sleeper as male, and he had done so because that was how his contact referred to Sleeper. And the contact in his turn had done so because that was how the unnamed Army Council member running Sleeper – presumably Conlan – had always referred to him.

She was walking faster.

But suppose that had been deliberate. Suppose Conlan had always referred to Sleeper as 'him' as part of the veil he had drawn over him, part of Sleeper's cover.

She was running.

It fitted, she thought. In Venlo the police had come up with nothing: no description, nobody seen near the scene. In Mons they had concentrated on descriptions of men seen near the location and again come up with nothing. In Berlin the authorities had been watching for a gunman and seen nothing. Yet two squaddies had been shot dead in a car less than 200 metres from a police patrol. A couple of hookers operating as a pair, plus one by herself, but at night in Berlin that wasn't unusual. And two squaddies wouldn't open their car door or window to a man when there was a security alert on. Especially two squaddies with service in Northern Ireland. At two in the morning a typical squaddie would only open his car door for one thing and one sort of person.

She was running faster, across Euston Road and down Gower Street. The computer section hadn't come up with a cross-match, but somewhere there was one, somewhere she had already seen it. She entered the building, cleared security, ignored the lifts and ran up the stairs to the office. The corridor seemed quiet. She telephoned the technical department, asked for a handwriting expert and was told one would contact her within the hour. Then she telephoned the computer section and identified herself.

'The Sleeper enquiry. The search of names beginning with the letter P. You gave me the list of names you ran for a cross-match.'

'Yes.'

'How long would it take to run a similar check on females?' Or was the computer down again, she did not dare ask.

'We'll give it priority. Cross-match or just a list?'

'A list first, then a cross-match.'

The graphologist telephoned ten minutes later. She explained her requirements and arranged delivery of the photograph of the postcard. When the list arrived from the computer section she closed the door of the office and concentrated on it.

At three she completed what she termed her first division – those individuals whose positions or backgrounds appeared to single them out for special attention – the list of royal staff first investigated by Special Branch, then the lists of friends. At four she finished her second division – contacts of staff members and friends of friends. At five her third.

She stopped for coffee, then began again. The fourth division, not even the fourth division – those whose names were on the list because of some twist of Fate. Who had been mentioned in

341

connection with a suspect, had once had a drink with one, had happened to be in the wrong place at the wrong time.

The Saunders documents.

The killing at Venlo.

The shooting at Mons.

She telephoned the Anti-Terrorist Squad, identified herself and asked to speak to the officer who had headed the British investigations into the Mons shooting.

'The suspect Gray. He gave the name of a witness, almost his alibi. I wanted to check a couple of things with him and wondered what her telephone number was.'

'I'll phone back. Give me a number.'

The man would check with Eldridge and the head of the Anti-Terrorist Squad would call Michaelmass for confirmation. Unless SO 13 wondered why MI5 were asking and decided to check themselves. She gave him the number and knew he would ask for a name. 'Catcher.'

The computer section came through and informed her they had found no cross-match. They wouldn't have, she knew.

Eight minutes later the Anti-Terrorist Squad passed her the address and telephone number. When she tried it the number was unavailable. She dialled the British Telecom liaison officer, requested an immediate check, and was informed that the name and address were correct, but that the number had been suspended for three months at the subscriber's request. Why? she asked. Holiday, she was told.

She telephoned the Anti-Terrorist Squad again and spoke to the detective inspector who had talked to the witness.

'It ties in.' He spoke with a South London accent. 'She was self-employed, systems analyst, I think. I got the impression she liked it because it meant she could work when she wanted and take time off when she felt like it.'

'Sounds as if you approve.'

'Why not, if you can work it?'

Why not? she thought. She thanked him and put the phone down. So why hadn't she asked about the woman, what she looked like, how she moved? Because the connection was too thin, too tenuous. And because the lead – if it was a lead – was hers and she didn't want anyone screwing it. She checked the address in the *A to Z*, took the Browning Hi-Power and shoulder holster from the top right-hand drawer, notified Operations where she was going, then walked to Tottenham Court Road and waved down a cab.

The street was on the edge of Primrose Hill, sloping slightly and lined with trees, children playing in the park on the other side of the road. She checked the list of names at the side, confirmed the name and pressed the buzzer.

Why was she bothering? The woman was innocent, the only reason she appeared in the file was because she happened to know a man whose surname was spelt the Irish way. So why was she wearing the Browning, Nolan asked herself.

She pressed the buzzer again, then tried the flat above. Again there was no answer. She tried the one below and heard a woman's voice.

'Sorry to trouble you. I'm a friend of Philipa Walker's. She told me to drop by when I was in London, but her telephone isn't working and I'm getting no answer from her flat.'

'She's in America.'

'Sorry?' The hint of surprise in her voice was deliberate.

'She's on holiday in America.'

She could easily be checking the place out for a burglary, Nolan thought, knew that was what the woman would have suspected if the caller had been male.

'When did she go?'

'Couple of months ago.'

'Any idea when she's due back?'

'Sometime in August, I think.'

'Thanks.'

She left Primrose Hill and returned to Gower Street. So Sleeper wasn't Walker, except that there was no one else and Walker cross-matched. Walker didn't cross-match, she reminded herself: Walker's name appeared on the Mons file, but there was no confirmation that she was the *P* on the postcard in Saunders's flat. The Cyprus postcard was the key, the suspicion still lingered, but so far the Cyprus postcard had led them nowhere. She checked the number of the *Daily Mirror*, dialled, and asked for Patrick Saunders. The extension rang six times before it was picked up.

'Saunders.' The voice was confident.

'I'm sorry to trouble you. My name's Katie Donald.' She hoped her Irish accent wouldn't throw him. 'I'm a friend of Philipa Walker's. I was wondering if you'd heard from her since she's been away.'

Philipa Who? she expected him to say, picked up the hesitation. *How do you know I know Philipa Walker? What do you know about me and Philipa Walker?*

'Sorry, what did you say your name was?'

'Katie Donald. I had a card from the Rockies a month ago, but nothing since.'

She sensed the moment he relaxed.

'Sorry, I haven't heard anything at all.'

A cross-reference, the alarm bells were ringing, the excitement mixing with the ice.

'Thanks, anyway. I hope you didn't mind me calling.'

'Not at all.'

The graphologist telephoned at 6.30.

'The handwriting belongs to a woman.'

'Tell me.'

So Walker was a cross-match, Walker knew Saunders and was in Mons at the time of the SHAPE shooting. But what did that mean? A cross-match would point them to Sleeper, Walker was a cross-match, therefore Walker was Sleeper. But Walker was their only cross-match, therefore they should avoid turning possibilities into facts simply because there were no other runners at this stage. She moved the telephone to one side, placed a sheet of paper in the centre of the desk, and wrote out the arguments.

Walker was out of the country and not due to return for six weeks, confirmed by witnesses and British Telecom. So Walker couldn't be Sleeper. Except that was what she herself would do if she was Sleeper. Give herself a cover by leaving the country, then return with a false ID, do the job, leave again with the false identity, then return openly and apparently innocently with her own.

Walker's name wasn't on Saunders's contact list, either on the computer file or the hard disk. But if Walker was more than a friend Saunders might have deleted it and Walker herself might have over-written it on the hard disk.

And Walker wouldn't expose herself by sending Saunders a card and having a drink with the man called Gray in Mons. Except that when she sent the card – if it was Walker who sent it – she needed a cover for her real destination, and at that time there was no reason for the man running Sleeper to suspect that his plan had ever been betrayed. Except that when she was waiting to do the hit

344

in Mons there was no reason for her to expect to see someone she knew.

The fog settled on her. The freezing, mind-numbing neutrality which insisted that it was impossible.

She would request a team be assigned to the lead, Nolan decided, request preliminary enquiries overnight.

Because Walker was a cross-match. Because Walker had been in Mons when the army captain had been shot dead. Because Walker was known to Saunders and Saunders was believed to be the unwitting conduit for the royal leak to the IRA. Because it was the only lead they had.

Except there was no reason why Walker should be Sleeper, no explanation of how a respectable professional Englishwoman should be an IRA hitman.

14

THE DRUMS RATTLED LIKE DEATH and the pipes echoed like penny whistles. The sun rose slowly, casting its early sheen across the waters of the docks, the cranes and derricks like matchsticks against it. In the Protestant strongholds the bowlers were brushed, the umbrellas tightened and the banners unfurled. In the Catholic heartlands the men and women woke grim-faced and hard-souled. In the streets between, the RUC and army erected the barricades.

Belfast, 12 July.

The Princess of Wales breakfasted at 7.30. For the middle of the week, especially during her sons' term time, the meal itself was slightly unusual and therefore all the more enjoyable. Partly because her eldest son was present – she had collected him from school the evening before. Partly because the day itself was of personal significance to the two of them, the single appointment of the year which she insisted William keep. Not an appointment as much as a family tradition, simple yet important.

At eight the Prince of Wales left Buckingham Palace and was driven to the RAF station at Northolt, west of London. From there he would pilot a Sea King to Falmouth, where he would officially bid farewell to the clipper *Trelawney* and set her off on her round-the-world trip. It was a long way from the first planning meetings in the office overlooking the Thames at St Katharine's Dock, he thought as his car entered Northolt, a lifetime since the paraplegic former SBS commander had first suggested the operation to him.

It was good to be free of the massive security which had been thrown round the royal family over the past months, he thought, good to have the relative pleasure of being accompanied merely by his personal bodyguard. The additional protection was still in place, the head of the Royal Protection Group would have told him, despite what the Home Secretary had said and the Prince believed. But only where it would not be noticed, and then only at the more formal occasions he could plan for.

He shook hands with the crew of the Sea King and climbed aboard.

Conlan woke at six. If, that was, he had slept at all. He walked to the window and opened it. Even here he could hear them, even here the drums and the pipes haunted him. He turned away and checked the equipment he had assembled. The Cellnet phones, the recording equipment, the back-up to each item, and the telephone numbers into Downing Street.

Walker woke at five, surprised that she had managed to sleep, and checked the items laid neatly on the table. The Ruger, sound and flash suppressor, soft nose hollow point ammunition and fast loader; the balaclava, holes for eyes and mouth but able to be rolled up so that it appeared to be a stylish lightweight turban. The Cellnets and recording equipment, small and compact. Each item except the weapon with back-up, in case any failed. Most she would leave in the flat, on the assumption that the morning went according to plan; some, however, she would carry in the shoulderbag in case something intervened and she did not make it back. The last item she checked was the slim leather wallet, the Semtex packed neatly into it and the dual detonating system connected to it, which the Clock-Maker had prepared to her specification among the Huygens and Breguets of his shop in Dublin.

The nerves ate at her stomach. They were a good sign, she told herself, would melt the moment she went into action.

Nolan was at her desk in Gower Street by six. The preliminary reports of the teams drafted on to the enquiry overnight were on her desk: Philipa Charlotte Louise Walker, place and date of birth; parents' names and address, father's occupation and related family details; education and career. The details were skeletal, the barest outlines from which they would begin working. It would take weeks before all the avenues were identified and explored in the hope that one would provide the glimmer of a clue. Then Walker would reappear from America, confirm her alibi, and they would start looking somewhere else.

She telephoned the number of the department dealing with

positive vetting, was given the number of the liaison at the General Register Office, dialled the number and stated her requirements. Five minutes later the liaison officer informed her that the Orpington district office of births, deaths and marriages was expecting her call, and gave the number of the direct line.

'Last name Walker, first names Philipa Charlotte Louise. Date of birth 12.3.61.,' she told the woman who answered.

'Will you call back?'

'I'll wait.' She sat back in her seat and wondered why she was wasting her time, where else she should start looking for Sleeper.

'Sorry, no record of that name here.' The check had taken ten minutes.

'Thanks anyway.' Presumably Walker's parents had moved to Orpington after she had been born and her birth was therefore registered somewhere else. She telephoned the liaison officer again, was given a number at St Catherine's House and told to telephone it in two minutes to allow him to clear her call.

'Philipa Charlotte Louise Walker,' she said simply. 'Date of birth 12.3.61. Registration district unknown.'

The wait was a little under eight minutes. No record, she was informed. She spoke again to the liaison officer and was given a third number, the instructions the same as before. When she dialled the number was engaged. She allowed another five minutes and dialled again.

'Philipa Charlotte Louise Walker, date of birth 12.3.61.'

How urgent? she expected Southport to ask. Not especially urgent, she was inclined to say, sometime today.

'Fifteen minutes. Give me your number.'

Sinclair left his London house at eight and was at the Home Office by 8.20. He divided the next sixty minutes between a meeting on the future of British broadcasting and a second on the annual renewal of the Prevention of Terrorism Act, then prepared his brief for the morning's Cabinet. At 9.40 he was driven to Downing Street, waiting with the other members in the corridor leading off the front lobby. At ten the Prime Minister joined them and they filed after him into the Cabinet room.

Walker left the flat at 9.15. She wore Levis, trainers, light sweater and loose and slightly long summer-weight jacket, the pockets larger than they appeared. The jacket was reversible, pale unobtrusive green on the outside now, bright yellow on the inside. In the inside pocket, zip fastened, she carried the wallet the Clock-Maker had prepared for her; in the leather shoulderbag the Ruger and Cellnets, a tape recorder, a pair of soft cape leather gloves and the woollen turban.

Tighe was waiting at the Café de Paris, the dog sitting under the table. She ordered coffee, neither of them drinking.

'Everything ready?'

'Fine.'

'The boys managed a walk-through last night?'

'Only the locations for the vehicle switches, nothing else.'

'See you later.'

She paid for her coffee and left, taking the dog with her.

The call from Southport came at 9.25.

'Date and place of birth: University College Hospital, London, 12.3.61.' The voice was impersonal, almost uninterested, reading the details in chronological order, left to right, as if the enquiry was routine.

The parents had moved, Nolan thought. Obvious really. So where else could she start looking? The postcard from Cyprus, she knew. If the clue was somewhere on the cards, which was not necessarily the case.

'Christian name Siobhan.'

Wrong, she thought, wrote down the detail anyway.

'Father's name and surname.'

Walker, Phillip John.

'No details listed.'

A mistake; the contact in Southport had pulled the wrong file.

'Mother's name and maiden surname.'

Walker, Joan Mary.

'Siobhan O'Connell.'

They'd got the wrong Walker.

'Rank or profession of father. No details.'

Either that or there was something wrong with the computer.

'Signature and description of informant. S.M. O'Connell. Mother.'

'It's not what I expected.' Could you explain, she meant. Are you sure you haven't made a mistake or the computer hasn't gone haywire? Why would she be called Walker if her mother is listed as having the name O'Connell?

'Weren't you told the register you were calling?'

'No.'

'This is the Adopted Children's Register.'

She did not react, felt no excitement, not even surprise.

'Could you confirm the details?'

The man read them again. 'You want a fax?'

'Yes.' She gave him the number. 'Thanks for the help.'

'Interesting,' he said as an afterthought, so that she almost missed it.

'What's interesting?'

'The mother gave a wrong detail.'

Which cancelled everything, Nolan knew. 'What detail?'

'The birth certificate is for 1961. After 1969 the mother was required to give her own place of birth, before that she merely had to give her place of residence at the time she had the child.'

So . . .

'The child in question was born in London, therefore the mother should have given a London address for herself. Instead she seems to have given somewhere else.'

Her own place of birth. So that one day, if her daughter discovered she had been adopted and if she wanted to trace her natural mother, then the girl would at least know where to begin. And in so doing the mother had given the security services the way in to the daughter. If the daughter was Sleeper.

'Where?'

'Rathmeen.'

'Thanks again.'

Possibly Ireland, probably Scotland. She found a road atlas and checked.

Northern Ireland. And not just Northern Ireland. South Armagh.

Even now there was no excitement, no reaction, simply the concern with the arrangements which would have to be made for the information to be checked. Somewhere, somehow, there had been a mistake, sometime soon the lead would be cut off as the others had been cut off. The 1130 shuttle to Belfast – her mind was still devoid of emotion, as if she was preparing herself for the moment when the mistake would be corrected. She called for a car to take her to Heathrow, telephoned Farringdon in Lisburn, asked that Brady be

350

waiting for her at Aldergrove, and requested an immediate check on Siobhan O'Connell, age approximately 50, place of birth Rathmeen.

If O'Connell was still alive then she might be on the security computer, even though O'Connell was probably her maiden name. And even if she wasn't then somebody in Rathmeen might know something. If the details from Southport were correct. If Walker had gone looking for her past. Except that when she and Brady arrived in Rathmeen they would find the mother and daughter living quietly and happily, and the message from Gower Street that the computer at Southport was out of service.

It was time to tell Michaelmass, to cover her back, even though the lead was tenuous. She telephoned his office and was intercepted by his secretary. The DDG was with the DG and couldn't be disturbed, the woman informed Nolan. With the Director General, representatives of MI6 and select officials from the US embassy, she didn't see fit to say. It was probably for the best, Nolan decided, there was no point informing Michaelmass if the lead had collapsed by lunchtime.

Conlan watched from his bedroom window and waited for the telephone call. Eleven o'clock – he checked his watch. The first of the Cellnets rang.

'Yes.'

'Just seeing how the shares are doing today.'

Sleeper checking in.

'Going up.'

'Then we should sell.'

Sleeper in position, Sleeper ready to go.

'I'll arrange it.'

The back-up telephone rang and the conversation was repeated.

'Good luck.'

It was ten minutes past eleven.

Walker sat in the small park 200 yards from Mayhill Street and confirmed on a Cellnet that Tighe and the flying column were in position, the conversation also coded.

Eleven-fifteen. She put the telephone back in the leather shoulder-bag, checked the Ruger, patted the dog on the head, pulled on the gloves and hat, and left the park. The nerves had gone from her stomach.

*

351

The Ford Escort XR3i left Kensington Palace and turned right. The Princess of Wales was a good driver, accelerating confidently and quickly and ignoring the surprise of the occasional motorist who recognized her. Prince William sat behind her, glancing between her shoulder and that of the man sitting next to her. Hugh Wilson was 34, married with two children, and had been with the Royal Protection Group for two years, the last eighteen months with the Princess. In a shoulder holster he carried a Walther. Twelve years before a gunman had attacked Princess Anne as her official car was being driven along the Mall towards Buckingham Palace; the bodyguard's gun had jammed and the detective had been shot when he stood in front of the attacker. If it came to it, Wilson knew that was what he himself was ultimately paid to do. To stand between the gunman and his target. To be the bullet stopper. He checked the rearview mirror and saw the back-up Rover slide into position.

Nolan hurried through Terminal One to the ticket desks and check-in for Belfast and Dublin flights. There was more than the usual security, she noted, more armed police, the increase due to the bomb incident in Manchester and the killings of the undercover men in Northern Ireland, she assumed. July the twelfth, she suddenly thought, Orange Day. In Belfast the drums would be beating and the marches beginning. A year ago today the Provos had launched their attack against Crumlin Road prison, a year ago today she had waited in the forward observation car in Beechwood Street. A year ago today she had shot McKendrick dead and Brady had run over Rorke.

Something about 12 July: the first tentacle of doubt insinuated itself. Not about the past, about the present.

She stopped at the ticket desk and asked for a return to Belfast, glancing anxiously round her and wondering what was wrong. Control it, she told herself, or someone would spot her, ask her to step aside and question her about why she appeared so agitated. The clerk took her Amex card and began the routine questions.

'Any baggage?'

'Only hand baggage.'

'Did you pack it yourself?'

'Yes.'

She was wasting her time, would find the mother and daughter

352

and the telephone call saying that the Southport computer had gone AWOL. It was worth checking, though, worth eliminating the possibility.

'Are you carrying anything for anyone else?'

'No.'

Who was Siobhan O'Connell? What was her background? If O'Connell was her maiden name, was she married? If so when and to whom? Was she connected at all with the Republican movement? With the IRA?

'Has anyone asked you to carry anything for them?'

'No.'

Assuming the registration department at Southport was correct. Not only about Walker being adopted but also about the Irish connection of her blood mother. And even then something must have happened to Walker, something more than just the realization that she was adopted and that her mother was Irish.

The clerk handed over her ticket and Amex card, and she walked through the first check and towards the baggage X-ray.

One hell of a cover for Sleeper if the information was correct, though. Everyone looking for an Irishman and Sleeper was English. Everyone assuming it was a man and Sleeper was a woman.

She placed her bag on the roller and stepped through the gate.

July 12th, the worm still nibbled at her subconsciousness. What the hell was it about July 12th?

The Sea King crossed the thin silver strand of the River Tamar, the Prince of Wales at the controls and the south coast of Cornwall to their left. In front of them Charles saw the mouth of the Fal, the villages tucked along its banks, then the town itself, the *Trelawney* moored in what the locals called the Roads. He circled her twice, glancing down. Spread along the yardarms, some of them seventy feet above the deck and all in immaculate white, were the men and women who would crew the clipper for the next three months. Half these people are disabled, he thought, half these men and women have been discarded by society. Now look at them. He circled the ship a third time and saw them waving, then turned for the granite outline of Customs House Quay, bringing the helicopter down slowly and confidently, the mayor and the welcoming committee stepping forward to greet him.

Around him the close protection squad scanned the faces of the

353

crowd, members of the squad in the buildings around the quay and on the docks 300 yards away. One Russian and two Liberian-registered tankers, Charles's personal bodyguard noted, well within sniper range. Hope to Christ the boys have them covered.

Nolan cleared the security gate and raised her hands while the security guard frisked her. Lucky she wasn't carrying the Browning, she thought. She felt naked without it, without the familiar weight on her waist or below her shoulder. She collected her bag and made her way along the corridor towards the departure lounge.

Incredible discipline on Conlan's part. Assuming he was the Army Council member running Sleeper and that Walker was Sleeper. Always to refer to Sleeper as 'him'. Must have drilled himself even to dream of Sleeper as a man.

July 12th, bloody July 12th.

The entrance to the Belfast departure lounge was at the end of the corridor, a Special Branch check in operation and armed police in the corridor and the lounge itself.

If Conlan had been so disciplined over Sleeper, perhaps he had been equally disciplined over PinMan. Nolan was not sure where the thought came from, only that it was suddenly there.

The line shuffled forward. She glanced at her watch, hardly noting the time other than to confirm that she would catch the 1130 shuttle. The Belfast check-ins were always the same, she knew from experience, especially when there was a security alert in place.

If Conlan had always referred to Sleeper as 'him' as part of Sleeper's cover, perhaps he had done the same with PinMan. And if Sleeper was a woman, then perhaps PinMan was as well.

Supposition, she told herself, pure hypothesis.

The line moved forward again.

But if the supposition was right, then PinMan wasn't the Prince of Wales, as they'd all assumed. PinMan was the Princess.

She was back in Saunders's flat, back at her desk in Gower Street, sitting at the computer and running through the royal schedule Fairfax had leaked. Not just the formal occasions, but the seemingly insignificant entries in the personal diaries.

Oh, Jesus Christ.

She broke from the queue and ran to the desk, reached into the inside pocket of her jacket. The only thing the armed police saw was a woman behaving abnormally, pushing past the queue and confronting the Special Branch detective at the desk. The only thing the Special Branch man saw was a woman coming towards him. Late twenties, early thirties, casually dressed – jacket, jeans and trainers. Hand going into jacket inner pocket. The police were moving, whispering the alert into their radios and their hands moving towards their guns.

'I need a telephone. Now.' Nolan held the ID in front of the SB officer.

'Just a minute.' He was checking the name of the man at the front of the queue. 'You'll have to wait,' he stalled. 'I've got these people to deal with. If you wouldn't mind re-joining the line or standing to the side.'

'Priority.' The way she said it terrified him. He saw the ID for the first time and looked at the wording on it.

'This way.'

The people in the line were staring, the woman ignoring both them and the armed police suddenly round her. He began to walk with her to the office at the side. 'I said priority,' she told him. He broke into a run. 'Secure line?' 'Not here. In the main office.' She checked her watch. Twenty-seven minutes past eleven. No time to get to anywhere else. 'Outside line?' she asked. He nodded, confused. MI5, he mouthed the words to the armed policemen who had followed them. 'Shut the door,' she told him, dialled Michaelmass's direct line, still standing, no time to clear the office. She heard the ringing tone, then the slight click as the call was re-routed to Michaelmass's secretary.

'This is Catcher. Is he there?'

'No.'

'Transfer me. It's urgent.'

Her brain worked calmly and automatically.

Sleeper a woman.

PinMan a woman.

The hit today.

Except that it wasn't a hit. It was a kidnapping. And not just the Princess of Wales.

July 12th. Orange Day. The day the Protestants celebrated the victory of King William at the Battle of the Boyne.

The Princess of Wales and the future King William keeping their annual meeting with his former nanny, unseen and virtually unprotected.

355

'I'm afraid I'm not allowed.' He's with the DG, Michaelmass's secretary did not say, express orders not to be disturbed unless the world was falling down, and then only if it was really urgent.

'Take this message. Pass it to him immediately.'

The secretary glanced up as Penrose came into the room. Catcher, she cupped the palm of her hand over the mouthpiece and whispered.

'PinMan is the Princess of Wales. The strike is at Mayhill Street at eleven-thirty. It is not an assassination. It is a kidnapping. Inform the Royal Protection Group and Anti-Terrorist Squad immediately. You have that?'

Perhaps it was because she was not accustomed to such pressure, perhaps because she was accustomed to pressure of a different type. Perhaps it was because Penrose distracted her, perhaps because she was concerned with passing on what she considered important. Whatever the reason she took only part of the message, as her notes would testify later. *PinMan – Princess of Wales. Mayhill Street 11.30* A M. *Kidnapping.* The next words – *inform RPG and Anti-Terrorist Squad* – she missed. Either did not hear them because she was already turning the notepad so that Penrose could read it and begin to act on it, or because the words which preceded them were so devastating.

'Yes,' she replied. 'I have that.'

Still time, Nolan thought, checked the clock on the wall. Still two minutes to pull PinMan out. 'Message logged at eleven twenty-eight.'

She put the phone down and turned to the SB man. Double up on the warning, she suddenly thought, contact the RPG and Anti-Terrorist Squad herself.

'You have a panic line to the Yard?' she asked.

'Yes.'

'Who's head of SB?'

'Hamilton.'

'Get him. Priority.' You heard the message, she did not need to say. You know what's going on.

He began to dial the number. The door opened and the SB inspector in charge of the section pushed his way through the armed police. The detective on the telephone heard the ringing tone.

'Who's she? What's going on?'

'Commander Hamilton, urgent,' the man on the telephone began to say.

'I said who's this and what's going on?' The inspector almost pushed Nolan aside.

MI5, the detective put the phone down and began to explain.

Nolan held the ID in front of the inspector. 'There's a security alert for the Princess of Wales. Possible kidnap in ninety seconds. You've just lost us thirty of them.' She turned to the man by the telephone. 'Hamilton. Now.' The detective glanced at the inspector, lifted the phone and dialled. The number was engaged. He cursed and dialled another.

The first line to the Director-General's office was engaged. Michaelmass's secretary tried a second and said a silent prayer when her call was answered. 'This is the DDG's office. I know he's in conference, but we need to speak to him urgently.'

'I'm sorry. The DG has said that under no circumstances can they be disturbed.'

Penrose heard and ran. The lift was on the second floor, going down. He ignored it and raced up the stairs.

Edgehill Crescent, bordering Mayhill Street, was virtually empty. 'Shares going up.' Walker spoke to Tighe on the Cellnet and approached the corner.

'In a position to buy.' Tighe sat in the front passenger seat of the Granada, Megahey at the wheel and Murphy in the rear, the Stars in their belts and the AKs and Ingrams with their folding stocks concealed beneath their coats. Funny that the boss was a woman, he thought. In a way he still could not accept the fact. Except that she was good. Better than anyone he had ever met. Brilliant concept and meticulous planning. Just wonder what she's like when it comes to it.

In twenty minutes they would be tucked away in the flat in the mews off Dunton Street and Conlan would be telephoning Downing Street and asking for the Prime Minister, and by tonight it would all be finished. Walker put the Cellnet in the bag, transferred the Ruger from the bag to her coat pocket, fastened the bag, then slung the strap over her right shoulder with the bag itself hanging on her left hip. The dog was on its lead, held in her left hand. It was twenty-eight minutes past eleven. She slid her right hand into her pocket, closed her fingers round the Ruger and turned the corner into Mayhill Street.

*

357

The DG's secretary was still arguing with Michaelmass's office. Penrose burst past her and into the conference. The eight men seated round the oval mahogany table turned as one.

'Sleeper.' He saw Michaelmass. 'Now.'

'Excuse me.' Michaelmass offered his apologies to the DG and followed Penrose from the conference room. The secretary put the phone down and began to protest. Michaelmass held up his hand and silenced her, turned to Penrose.

'Tell me.'

'Catcher's just come through. PinMan is the Princess of Wales. It's a kidnapping. Mayhill Street at eleven-thirty.'

Penrose didn't know what Catcher was talking about, Michaelmass thought, but at least he'd reacted. He checked the time: 11.29.

'You've informed Scotland Yard: RPG and SO 13?'

That was the second thing Catcher would have told them if she couldn't get through to him personally. First the message, then the orders to warn the Royal Protection Group and the Anti-Terrorist Squad.

The colour drained from Penrose's face. 'No.'

Royal Protection Group first, Michaelmass's mind worked automatically, get them to pull Di and her minder out of the area; then either SO 13 or DPG. He reached for the telephone and punched the number of the RPG, heard the ringing tone. The Diplomatic Protection Group he decided, the Anti-Terrorist Squad wouldn't have anybody in the area, but the DPG would because of the embassies. He scribbled the number and handed it to Penrose.

His call to the RPG was answered.

'This is MI5.' There was no time for niceties or formalities, no time for anything. 'There's an attack on the Princess of Wales, Mayhill Street, eleven-thirty. Pull her out now, then confirm with Commander Denton.'

Identical warning coming in from Special Branch, he was told. Catcher doubling up just in case, he understood. He terminated the call and took the other telephone from Penrose.

'This is MI5. There's a political kidnapping on Mayhill Street at eleven-thirty. All cars there. Confirm details with Eldridge at SO 13.' Eleven twenty-nine and thirty seconds. He ended the call and dialled the Anti-Terrorist Squad.

*

358

Wilson didn't like it when the Princess was driving. She'd done the course and was fast – sometimes too fast for his liking. But if a car swerved in front of them or a push-chair rolled off the pavement, the Princess's reaction would be to slam her foot on the brake instead of the accelerator. To stop instead of to get the hell out. No matter what the consequences, no matter who or what was hurt. And that was the difference. Because at the end of the day the only people who counted were the Prince and Princess of Wales, plus the boys. Nobody else mattered a damn. Not even himself.

She stopped in front of the house. Even before she had pulled on the handbrake and switched off the ignition he had left the car and swept the street for problems. Mayhill Street was empty – virtually. No cars on the move and only one person on the pavement. A woman, young and attractive, shoulderbag across her body, hand in pocket, and dog. That was what did it. The dog. Border collie, full of beans and pulling at the lead. If the woman had been alone he would have looked a second time; if she'd been pushing a pram the hairs on the back of his neck would have stood upright and his hand would have moved a shade nearer the Browning. But the dog told him the woman was no threat. Not told him, just planted the relaxation in his brain. He turned away from her and checked the rest of the street again.

The Rover pulled in.

The Princess climbed out of the Escort and walked round the front. Wilson held the door open for William – left hand on the handle, right hand always free – still looking round him. The boy was on the pavement, his mother just in front of him, the group tight together. Wilson began to close the door and heard the beginning of the radio message to him on the earpiece.

The Princess of Wales looked up and back – even in retrospect she would not know why. Perhaps it was the woman with the dog, perhaps the way the dog was barking and William was laughing at the animal.

'Go.' Tighe whipped the blanket off the Uzi. Megahey slid his foot off the clutch and the Granada slipped away from the pavement and down the street.

The bodyguard's back was momentarily towards her, the Princess and Prince less than three yards from her, and the Rover to her right and slightly behind her, the two men remaining in it. Walker let go of the dog's leash and took her right hand from her pocket, left hand pulling the balaclava over her face. Wilson was straightening, beginning to turn slightly. The Ruger was pointed at his back. Walker thumbed back the hammer and squeezed the trigger, pivoted round and thumbed back the hammer again, barrel pointing at the man in the front passenger seat of the Rover, squeezed the trigger. Moved slightly, fired at the driver, knew she had hit both men in the car and swung back to the bodyguard on the pavement. Wilson was falling forward, almost on the boy. The Princess looked round and realized, pulled her son away from the gun. The bodyguard was still moving, the Ruger now on the Princess and Prince. The Granada stopped by the Escort, Tighe already out and shooting at the two men in the Rover. Murphy out as well, Tighe suddenly with him, the balaclavas over their faces, grabbing the Princess and Prince and bundling them into the back seat, sitting either side of them.

'Mayhill Street in one minute.' The sergeant in the front passenger seat of the DPG vehicle radioed their position and pulled on the bulletproof jacket. No sirens, he told the driver, nothing to alert the opposition. So what was in Mayhill Street? No embassies, he knew, no one who was on the IRA or Arab hit lists. 'Mayhill Street in thirty seconds.' In the back seat the third man in the car unlocked the metal box, took out the Heckler and Koch sub-machine guns and passed him one.

The bodyguard was still moving. Walker bent forward slightly and shot him in the head. Megahey was already moving the car forward. She ran round the front, jumped in to the passenger's seat, and Megahey pulled away. As they turned the corner the unmarked maroon Sierra screamed past them.

'Turning into Mayhill Street now.' The Granada passed them, travelling in the opposite direction. On the pavement the first blood trickled from Wilson's body and the dog cowered in fear by his side.

'Warning passed to PinMan's minders,' Eldridge received the information from the Royal Protection Group and relayed it to Michaelmass. 'No acknowledgement.'

'Something wrong with the radios?'

Not with two radios, they knew. 'Perhaps.'

The street was empty, the cars parked under the trees and the engine of the Sierra still screaming. 'Mayhill Street quiet. No movement.' The Hockler was in his hands, safety off. 'We use the motor as cover,' he told the other two men. 'No risks.' 'Shit,' he heard the driver curse, felt the force as the Sierra passed the Rover and braked hard by the Escort, saw the body on the pavement. He was already out, ducking slightly and looking for the opposition. Knew whose car it was, had seen it on the television. Christ. Oh, Jesus Christ. He checked the Rover, ran round the back of the Escort and bent over the body on the pavement, the second man covering him. Check it for ID, the sergeant told the man with him, ran back to the car. The driver was pulling on his bulletproof vest. 'Silver Ford Granada . . .' the sergeant grabbed the radio and tried to remember the details.

'Radio report from DPG.' Eldridge's voice was calm. 'Ford Granada seen leaving Mayhill Street. DPG are giving a description and approximate registration number.' No indication that they were too late. Michaelmass knew anyway, knew what the man on the scene was doing. First priority any information on suspect persons or vehicles, only after that the details they all feared.

'What else?'

'Nothing yet.'

Eldridge waited, one telephone on open to the Diplomatic Protection Group and another to Michaelmass.

'Second message from DPG vehicle. Ford Escort XR3i at scene and confirmed empty. Two men dead in Rover motor car, third man dead on pavement.' They still hoped against hope. Eldridge received the next message and passed it to Michaelmass. 'Body on pavement is that of Detective Sergeant Hugh Wilson, member of the Royal Protection Group. Details established by his warrant card. DPG back-up vehicles and Met Police armed response cars are being directed to the scene. Scotland Yard has put out an alert for the Granada, with instructions for it to be tailed but not stopped.'

'What about the house? Is she there?'

'No. The Princess of Wales is not inside.'

Neither the Princess of Wales nor her son had spoken, neither of them had made any noise whatever. Megahey cut past a Datsun parked slightly off the kerb and stopped at the mouth of the alleyway between the houses.

The maroon Sierra turning the corner into Mayhill Street as they left, Walker thought. Three men inside – she had seen the blur as the vehicles passed – dark blue uniforms, no caps. Diplomatic Protection Group. What the hell were they doing there so quickly? And why DPG? If it had been an emergency call from the house or a witness, the first vehicle would have been an area car. Something had gone wrong, the authorities had found out. But if the authorities had found out they would have acted sooner.

Murphy was already out of the Granada and running down the alleyway, checking the Carlton. In the back seat Tighe pulled the coat and headscarf on to the Princess, pushed the sunglasses on, and hooked the shopping bag over her arm. At the bottom of the alley-way Murphy waved that the Carlton was ready. The Princess and her son were still in shock, reacting automatically and doing what they were told without even realizing. Street clear, Walker checked round them. 'Go.' Whenever she spoke it was with an Irish accent. They bundled Diana and William out of the Granada and down the alleyway, the figures tucked between them. The doors of the Carlton were already open and the engine running. They pushed them into the back, Tighe and Murphy again on either side of them, and Megahey slipping into the driver's seat. Even as they closed the doors he was pulling away.

The second maroon Sierra slammed to a halt by the Escort. Any moment now and people will start to appear, the sergeant from the first car thought. And once people started to appear it wouldn't be long before somebody made the connection and telephoned the newspapers and television stations.

All the rules dictated that he did not disturb what the Hendon CID course would call the scene of the crime – guard on the cars and the bodies, then the green canvas screens around both and the white-coated men and women from Forensics sifting their way slowly and carefully through the evidence. But this was different. All the indications were that the Princess of Wales had been taken hostage and the one thing you did not do was allow this information to leak to the public.

They could explain the Rover, he was thinking fast, could say it was an armed gang or a bunch of politicos, but they couldn't cover the XR3i, the press would know whose that was in a flash. 'Put Wilson's body in the back seat,' he told the crew of the second car. 'Get it away before anybody sees it. One of you take the Escort.'

The Granada had a minute's start, he was calculating, almost two by now. If the Granada had been involved. The dog was still whimpering on the pavement, the collar and lead on it. That was how the gunman did it, he suddenly understood, that was what the gunman used for cover. A bloody dog. 'Him as well,' he shouted to the second car. He had barely closed the door before the driver pulled the Sierra in a tight circle and screamed it back down the street.

The speedometer of the police BMW touched 145 miles an hour, its lights flashing and its sirens blaring. The driver slowed slightly for a Jaguar XJS to slide into the central lane, then accelerated again.

'Message for Catcher. Repeat. Message for Catcher.'

They were a mile from the end of the M4, Heathrow behind them and Chiswick coming up at them fast.

'You?' The observer turned to the woman in the rear seat.

'Me,' Nolan confirmed.

'Catcher receiving.'

'Message for Catcher reads: *PinMan is down. Repeat. PinMan is down.*'

'Message received.' He turned in his seat again. 'Got that?'

'Got it.'

The Granada was slewed at a slight angle in front of the Datsun.

'That's it.'

The driver of the area Rover saw it a second after the observer. Tail but do not stop; he remembered the instructions and drove past, then realized it was empty. Even before he had completely stopped the observer was out the car and running down the alleyway.

'Whisky One. We have located the Granada. The vehicle is abandoned at Glashner Street. Alleyway to Arbroath Street. Occupants may have second vehicle waiting.'

The observer reached the end of the alleyway. An armed robbery, something involving the Serious Crime Squad, he suddenly thought and slowed slightly. What if they're changing motors, what if he reached them before they got away? He turned the corner.

The parking space immediately to his right was vacant, two women coming out of the newsagents twenty yards to the right, one opening a packet of cigarettes and the other pushing a pram.

'A car just pulled away. Did you see what it was?' He was overweight and breathing badly.

'Sorry, love.' The women began to walk away.

'The Vauxhall, you mean?' The till of the newsagents was just inside the door, the shopkeeper leaning over the counter and peering at him.

'Yeah.'

'Vauxhall Carlton, been parked there all morning.'

'Registration number?' He knew he was expecting too much.

'Sorry.'

'Colour?'

'Dark blue, I think.'

'Which way?'

The shopkeeper indicated with his thumb.

'Thanks.'

The maroon Sierra screeched to a halt. Dark blue Vauxhall Carlton, he panted. Registration unknown. Heading west.

Something had gone wrong. Somehow someone had known she was going after PinMan. Worse than that. Somehow someone had worked out the details of the operation, the time and place. But Conlan had suspected nothing. And the Brits could not have known or they would have sealed the Princess of Wales off, not let Walker anywhere near her.

Except the Sierra was from the DPG and had stopped by the Princess's Escort.

Something had gone wrong. And once one thing went wrong others followed. Then the tide turned against you.

Walker's mind was calm, the thoughts almost detached. She glanced back at the Princess and her son, squeezed between Tighe and Murphy, and began to plan ahead. It was thirty seconds to the next switch. Megahey slowed and turned right across the main road and into the streets leading off it. As he did so a police Montego turned left, out of the road into which he now turned, and headed in the direction from which they had just come.

No problem, Walker told them, next switch coming up. And the last – the change of colour and registration number of the VW – between two and four minutes after that, depending on which location she chose.

'Right here.'

Megahey swung into the cobbled street, the grimy walls of deserted buildings on either side, then right again through a set of iron gates hanging open and lop-sided on their hinges. Kennedy was waiting in the VW. The Princess and her son were bundled into it and the door slid shut. Kennedy drove the Carlton into the dark area at the end of the factory, slammed and padlocked the door, then ran back to the VW and jumped in, and Megahey pulled away. The cobbled street was still empty; they turned out of it, stopped at the junction with the main road, and right again.

'They've switched vehicles. Are now believed to be travelling in a dark blue Vauxhall Carlton,' Eldridge notified Michaelmass. 'Tactical Support Group are already in the area, eight cars from the DPG, two helicopters are up and all patrol vehicles have been notified.'

Sleeper had been so organized and they themselves so lucky, thought Michaelmass. If Catcher hadn't spotted it, if the DPG had arrived thirty seconds later and not seen the Granada, if someone hadn't noticed the vehicle they'd switched to. One more piece of luck, dear God. Don't abandon us now.

WPC Jenny Watson had joined the Metropolitan Police three years before and was due to sit her sergeant's examination the following week.

'Three to Control.' The area had always been a black spot for the personal radios to the local station, hard to hear anything or get anything heard. 'Three to Control.' The main road was busy, the pavements full and cars and lorries taking the detour which avoided one of the North Circular's hold-ups. 'Bravo Four Five to CCC.' She used the car radio to the Central Communications centre at New Scotland Yard.

'CCC. Go ahead, Bravo Four Five.'

She was on the six to two shift, boring but at least she could get some study in after work. The visit to what was known locally as the Fax, the deserted area of factories off the High Street, was routine, sometimes slightly scaring – the place where the addicts and glue sniffers hid out. The previous January someone had lit a bonfire there and almost burned that part of the patch down.

'Bravo Four Five. Reference Vauxhall Carlton. Vehicle answering description seen turning off High Street and into Fax area.' She passed on the registration details – had repeated them to herself from the moment she had seen the Carlton turn across the road until the moment she had pulled in fifty yards away from

365

the junction, entered them in her notebook before making the radio call.

The car she'd seen wasn't the one they were screaming about on the radio, of course, they didn't even have a registration number for the one they were looking for. But it was a dark blue Carlton, a number of people in it, and you didn't normally see cars like that turning into the Fax.

'CCC to Bravo Four Five.' Message received and thank you, she knew New Scotland Yard would tell her: enough of the cowboy stuff, now just get back on patrol. 'Remain in position but do not approach. Repeat. Do not approach.'

'Understood.' In her rearview mirror she saw the orange VW camper pull out of the turning behind her and drive away from her.

The blue lights were moving fast, even in the sunlight she saw them 200 yards ahead, coming towards her. White patrol car, unmarked cars behind it. Going like the clappers, she thought, two of them on the wrong side of the road and the first car almost opposite her already. She checked behind her and ran across the road, tried to wave the first car down, knew it was too late. The maroon Sierra coming fast behind it just managed to stop, the brakes screaming and the smell of burning rubber suddenly filling the air, another behind it. Fifty yards on the patrol car began to reverse.

'Dark blue Vauxhall Carlton?' she asked, saw with a shock that they were armed. Not just armed. Submachine guns and bullet-proof vests.

The sergeant was already out of the lead Sierra. 'Where?'

She indicated the side road to the Fax. 'Down there three minutes ago. Full of people.' It wasn't necessarily the one they were looking for, she told herself, told them. She checked her notebook and confirmed the registration number.

'Any other ways out?' the sergeant asked. What's up, she wanted to know, what the hell's this all about?

'Not by car. It's an old factory area, lots of disused buildings. Couple of footpaths out the other side if you know where to look.'

The driver was already relaying the details over the radio, asking for back-up, the sergeant running back to the open passenger door. In the sky above she heard the sound of a helicopter.

'Something else. May or may not be connected. A minute after the Vauxhall went in a VW camper came out. Faded white top, orange bodywork, smoked windows.' She gave him the registration number. 'Turned down the High Street.'

The driver had relayed the information before she finished speaking.

'Got that?' The sergeant turned to the driver of the area patrol car, made him repeat the details. 'You follow the VW, see if you can spot it. We'll check the Fax.'

The last switch was ninety seconds away.

'You know we've picked up a tail.' Megahey checked the side mirror again.

'I know.'

The white patrol car had been four vehicles behind them for the last 800 yards. Now a maroon Sierra had joined it.

If she tried the change there was an outside chance it might work, but if the tails really were on them they'd spot it immediately. And if she tried the switch all but one of them would have to get out of the VW. One man with the hostages would have been fine if everything had gone to plan, but not now, not with the rest of them outside the vehicle and therefore exposed to potential snipers. And if they stopped, the tails might prevent them from leaving. Probably wouldn't close in on them, just seal them off.

Killing time.

Choose her own ground, she decided, don't let the opposition choose it for her. Give Conlan the time he needed, even though it wouldn't be the limitless time she had planned. He didn't need that time anyway. Two hours, three at most. Then it would be done.

She came to the last decision.

There was little chance of reaching the safe house. In some ways, therefore, it might seem better to stay in the VW. That way they could see all round them, make sure that no one closed on them. Psychologically, however, that would be bad. They would feel exposed and in the hands of the opposition. And that would change the balance. That would mean she had lost at least part of the control.

There were shops on either side of the road. Typical bedsit London, she thought, and checked the street name.

'Block of flats fifty yards ahead on the left. Pull in there.'

Tighe knew what she was going to do and nodded.

Megahey stopped and she waited to see how the tails would react.

The white patrol car passed them, none of the three men in it even looking at them. They were wrong, she thought for a moment, there wasn't a tail. Fifty yards on the police car pulled in. Almost immediately another car drew up in front of it. She checked in the mirror. Forty yards back the maroon Sierra had also stopped.

She looked at Murphy. 'You go first, open a flat for us. We'll give you thirty seconds. Use the stairs so we don't miss you. Front flat if you can, so we can see the street.' She looked up at the flats – eight floors, she counted quickly, no front balconies, the angle preventing her from seeing the roof. She looked at the flats opposite and assumed they were the same – flat roof angled slightly in front with dormer windows to the top flats. 'Second or third floor, no higher than fourth.' Therefore difficult for the SAS to abseil down unless they came from the flat immediately above – she was thinking as she knew the opposition would be thinking – but the absence of balconies would limit the positions from which they could launch the attack against her, would mean there was no place they could balance on to set the window charges. They could swing through the windows, of course, but that was for the movies. That way they couldn't synchronize their entry, make sure that the gas canisters and stun grenades went in simultaneously, that the teams went in in precisely the right sequence.

Murphy left the VW and disappeared into the apartment block. Someone will walk past soon, her training told her, someone in plain clothes but walking like the bastard he is because he's not used to anything else. She looked at the name of the block and checked the pavements again.

'Now.'

She slid out of the front seat and opened the side door. Tighe and Kennedy bundled the Princess and Prince out, keeping them between them, and half-pulled half-pushed them up the four steps and into the building, Megahey in front and Walker guarding the rear. The hallway was clean and smelt of fresh polish, a lift at the rear and the stairs winding up the side. The two hostages were still locked in shock. They reached the first landing, then the second. Where the hell's Murphy, she thought. Someone's going to come out. Someone's going to be leaving a flat and see us. She made herself slow down and look around, examine the layout of the floors and how many flats there were on each, whether they were at the back or the front.

Murphy was standing at an open door on the next floor. Front flat as he had been instructed, Walker noted, another door along the same side suggesting another flat at the rear. They hurried the Princess and Prince inside and shut and bolted the door. The curtains were full-length and partially closed. She crossed the room and looked out, barely moving them. In the street below a man in civilian clothes slowed as he passed the VW and glanced inside.

The Princess of Wales sat on the sofa without being told, her arm round her son. The numbness, almost the dizziness of the shock was receding, the fear and the panic seizing her. Remember the course at Hereford, she told herself, remember what they told you to say and not to say, remember what they told you to do and not to do. Thank God William was still dazed. She smiled at him and stroked his hair, remembered the day he had been born and the night she had sat at his bedside after he had fractured his skull at school, told him it would soon be all right.

She had fifteen minutes before the authorities began to organize themselves, Walker calculated, therefore fifteen minutes to organize herself. She told Tighe that the Princess and Prince were not to move then went to the kitchen, taking the shoulderbag with her, closed the door behind her, and tapped the number on the Cellnet.

Conlan answered on the second ring.

'Good news and bad.' It was remarkable how calm her voice was, he would think later, though it was no more than he expected. 'PinMan is with us. Unfortunately we didn't make it home. They seemed to know we were coming and arrived just as we were leaving.' He wondered how, knew it no longer mattered. 'We're now in a flat. They're outside.'

'But PinMan is with you.'

'Yes. PinMan is with us.'

And therefore she had won. Even though the plan had gone wrong and the full force of the British security system would soon be outside. Because in the end, and no matter what they did, she had PinMan. And that was the one thing the Brits would not be able to admit – that the IRA had kidnapped the Princess of Wales and the boy who would one day be king.

The old man would like to be here now – she thought of her father – the old woman as well. Better to be here than rot away in a prison cell as her brother had done.

'Two hours, then you'll be out,' Conlan told her. 'Give me the details.'

She finished the call and inspected the flat.

The door from the landing led into a hall, two yards wide and some eight yards long, the lounge overlooking the street at the other end. On either side of the hall were two rooms. On the right, as she walked from the door, was a kitchen then a bedroom. On the left a bathroom then a second bedroom. The apartment was tidy and well-decorated, rugs on the floor and paintings on the walls.

Walker walked through once, then a second time with Tighe, considering the security implications. The door to the landing was secured by two locks and a chain. In the kitchen, on the right of the door, was an air vent, another in the bathroom opposite. In both bedrooms there were small windows into the lounge to provide some form of natural lighting.

The primary entry points, therefore, were the door and the windows in the lounge. Plus through the walls. Furniture inside the door and in front of the windows, she told Tighe. In the case of the windows allow space for us to see the street, but make sure no one can get in that way.

The Princess of Wales was thinking, calculating – Walker saw the look in the woman's eyes. Trying to disguise it, but working out the options. She would have done the course and would know what to expect, what was expected of her.

The woman in front of her had planned everything, Diana thought, saw the eyes looking at her though the holes in the balaclava. But something had gone wrong. And therefore the situation was more dangerous than if everything had gone to plan. Remember what they had taught her at Hereford, she told herself, remember what they needed to know.

The Cabinet had been in session an hour and fourteen minutes, the Prime Minister sitting at the centre of the conference table and facing the walled garden at the rear. There was a knock on the door and an aide slid behind the row of the chairs facing the window and placed a folded note in front of him. To the Prime Minister's right the Foreign Secretary was discussing the latest developments in what had once been the Soviet Union. The Prime Minister indicated that he was still listening, opened the note, read it and nodded to the aide.

The scrambler was handed to him. 'Yes.' There was no indication to whom he was speaking, or the nature of the information being passed to him. The person seated opposite, his back to the windows, was the Chancellor. For one moment he saw the vein on the Prime Minister's left temple flicker, then the Prime Minister put down the telephone and looked across the table.

'Ladies and gentlemen. With your permission I would like to end this meeting. The Home Secretary, Foreign Secretary and Northern Ireland Secretary to remain, plus Sir William.'

The others round the table tried to work out what was happening. The first two were the PM's senior colleagues, the presence of the Cabinet Secretary suggested something of major political or constitutional significance, and the request that the Northern Ireland Secretary remain pointed to something involving the IRA. They collected their papers and filed from the room.

The Prime Minister stared across the table and through the windows to the garden beyond, then he shifted to his right slightly and looked at each of them in turn.

'The telephone call was from the Commissioner of Police. He informs me of the possibility that the Princess of Wales and Prince William have been kidnapped by the IRA. The Princess's car has been found abandoned. The body of her personal bodyguard was alongside it. He had been shot. Two other officers are also dead. Both the Princess and Prince are missing.'

He looked at the Home Secretary. *You headed the Cobra committee into Sleeper*, the eyes said it all. *Your responsibility, Home Secretary. The end of your political career. No matter what happens.*

'There is a possibility that the group concerned is holding the Princess and Prince in a flat in west London. The police followed a car there and have surrounded the location, though they cannot be sure that the Princess is involved.' The details would come in the next minutes, they all knew. 'Until it is proved otherwise, we have to assume that the report is correct.'

He straightened the sheaf of paper in front of him and began to itemize the points which required their immediate attention:

'News blackout immediately.

'Cobra to convene here, myself in the chair. The Home Secretary to take charge of the operations room when it's established.

'The Northern Ireland Secretary to advise on relevant issues.

'The Foreign Secretary to draw up a list of those with whom I should consult.

'Sir William to advise on the constitutional issues which might arise, as well as to serve as administrative head of the operation.'

He turned to the Cabinet Secretary.

'Emergency centre in this room. I'll need to speak to Her Majesty and the Prince of Wales. I also assume the IRA will be telephoning Downing Street. If the report is correct I have no option but to talk to them. Unless any of you think otherwise.' He glanced at them, then continued. 'Therefore alert the switchboard – no details, of course – plus recording equipment installed as priority.'

He looked at each of them again. No questions at this stage, they understood.

'Reconvene in five minutes.'

The others left the Cabinet room. The Prime Minister sat silently for twenty seconds, then lifted the telephone and asked the switchboard to connect him on the scrambler to the Brigadier, Special Forces.

The sub-skimmer had been submerged for thirty minutes. Haslam watched as a trooper brought it to the surface. Telephone, one of the mechanics told him.

'Haslam.' He was still looking at the sub-skimmer.

'AT room. We're on.'

As he crossed the barracks he heard the distinctive whine of the Pumas being started. By the time he reached the anti-terrorist block half the teams had already removed their kit from the crew room. In the corner of the room the squadron major was briefing a captain.

'Hostage incident, central London.' He saw Haslam and turned. 'Presumed IRA. Third-floor flat.'

'Who have they got?'

'One of yours.'

One of the people he'd trained, one of those he'd put through the killing room.

'Who?'

'The Princess of Wales and her son.'

Oh Christ, he thought. 'Which son?'

'William.'

July the twelfth. Orange Day.

'London teams in attendance?'

'Two minutes ago.'

He took charge. 'Blue and Red teams in full kit now.' There was

372

no point in not having some teams ready to go the moment they arrived. Equally there was no point in leaving no one dressed apparently normally for surveillance. 'Where are we landing?'

'Heathrow.' There were landing zones closer to the location, but the run in along the M4 was fast and the airport offered the security and anonymity lacking elsewhere.

'Three Hertz rental vans to meet us. Plus some furniture and white overalls as cover when we go in and come out. Full briefing when we're in the air.'

The Prime Minister's inner committee – the Wise Men, as they were later referred to – reconvened at 12.25. In the intervening period the Prime Minister had received a further briefing from the Commissioner of the Metropolitan Police. He relayed the information to the men seated round the Cabinet table and received in turn the information and advice each had prepared for him.

The first five points were matters of detail.

One: confirmation that the Princess of Wales and Prince William had been taken hostage. Two: police and first SAS teams were in place at the flat where they were presumed to be held. Three: the presence of police and SAS was discreet, nothing had so far been done to alert public suspicion. Four: the IRA were assumed to be involved, though no communication had been received from them yet. Five: security and phone traces were in place should the IRA contact Downing Street as expected.

The remaining two were issues to be discussed.

Six: the government response should the IRA make any demands. Seven: public information on the kidnapping, and government response if the IRA notified the media rather than contacting Downing Street.

'My feeling, Prime Minister, is that the question goes far beyond the immediate point of what we tell the press at this moment in time, whether or not we confirm or deny the situation should anyone enquire.' It was the Northern Ireland Secretary.

'Please explain.' The atmosphere was calm and controlled.

'It's simple. Can we afford to admit that the IRA – if it is the IRA – have kidnapped the Princess of Wales and Prince William? That the IRA are holding hostage the future king.' He sat forward, elbows on the table and the tips of his fingers forming a bridge. 'There are a number of scenarios.

'One. The IRA make certain demands and we agree to them.

'Two. The IRA make certain demands and we reject them.

'Three. We storm the flat and rescue the Princess and her son.'

Four, the Prime Minister thought.

'Four. We storm the flat but the IRA kill the Princess and her son, or they die in the rescue attempt.'

'No hostages died in the Iran embassy siege in 1980.'

'I think you might find that the SAS say they were lucky that day.'

In the end it came down to two simple and basic questions, the Foreign Secretary suggested. Whether they were prepared to negotiate over the lives of the Princess and Prince, and whether they should ever admit to what had happened.

'What about the Princess's car and bodyguard? Did anyone see those?' It was the Cabinet Secretary.

'No. The first DPG officer on the scene had them removed.'

The blue telephone rang.

'The call. He's coming through on the direct line in ten seconds.'

Conlan confirmed that the recording equipment and back-up were both functioning and dialled the Downing Street number. The call was answered immediately.

'Private office.' His accent was official and the request matter-of-fact, the switchboard putting him through without question.

'This is the Provisional IRA. I need a direct number for the PM. I would imagine he's expecting this call.'

'I'm sorry?' The duty clerk was one of those who had not been briefed. 'Who is this?'

'This is the Provisional IRA. If you don't know what I'm talking about then give me someone who does.'

Someone passed the clerk a slip of paper, the instructions written on it. Behind him someone was calling security. 'Transferring you.' The clerk passed the call to the Prime Minister's Principal Private Secretary and breathed a sigh of relief that whatever it was the responsibility was no longer his.

'One moment.' The Private Secretary turned as an assistant gave him a number. What the hell's going on, he thought, what's happening? He read the number to Conlan.

'Thank you.'

It couldn't have been the IRA, the duty clerk thought. The voice was too educated, too sophisticated.

Conlan wrote the number on his notepad, a thin sheet of metal beneath the page so that it would not indent the page beneath, checked the recorder was still working, and dialled. The call was answered on the second ring.

'Prime Minister?'

'Yes.'

'I'm speaking on behalf of the Army Council of the Provisional IRA.'

The technicians began the trace.

'I assume that you are also recording this conversation.' Because I am – the statement was implied.

'Perhaps you should tell me what this call is about.' Of course they both knew what the call was about, he implied, otherwise he would not have taken it. Felt obliged, for protocol's sake, to ask anyway.

'The incident at Mayhill Street. We have one simple demand.' Conlan read the prepared statement.

'Impossible.'

'I understand that is what you have to say, Prime Minister.' It was almost a discussion between diplomats, the analysts would think later. 'May I suggest that you consult those whom I assume you have already assembled, and that we speak again in fifteen minutes. May I also tell you what we propose to do if you do not agree to our demands.'

First the diplomacy then the threats, the Prime Minister understood.

'We have no wish to harm those involved. Neither, however, do we have any wish to see our own people harmed. If, when we speak next time, you are no nearer being able to agree to our demands, our first step will be to inform the press that the Princess of Wales and Prince William are in the hands of the IRA.'

You can't, the Prime Minister almost interrupted. And even if you tried we'd stop you, bang a D-notice on everyone, quote the security of the state and the unending wrath of God.

'We are aware, of course, of the pressure you would quite understandably bring to bear on the British press.'

And therefore we would inform the foreign press – again implied. So everyone except the British would know. And the British press would feel obliged to respond.

But then it was only the word of the IRA against the British government, the Cabinet Secretary thought. Except for the simple fact that the bastard had played it quite beautifully – there was no admiration in the acknowledgement, only frustration. The Prime Minister had no option but to take the call, but in doing so he had effectively confirmed what he might later wish to deny.

'Of course you could invent a reason for the Princess's failure to appear at Great Ormond Street this afternoon, or her charity gala engagement this evening. Tomorrow, however, might be more difficult.'

It was like a game of chess, the Foreign Secretary thought, except that the bastard at the other end was playing both sides.

'Then again, you might decide a rescue attempt would in order. We assume the London units of the SAS are already in position, and that back-up teams are already airborne from Hereford. But what happens if something goes wrong? How would you explain to the British people that the blood of the Princess of Wales, and of the future king, is on your hands?'

Outside the Cabinet room the sky was blue and the birds were singing.

'Thank you for listening, Prime Minister. We'll speak again in fifteen minutes.'

The line went dead.

Give me twenty seconds to work out what I think, the Prime Minister prayed to his colleagues, give me time to even begin to decide how I respond.

He turned to the Home Secretary. 'Cobra's assembled?'

'Ten minutes ago.'

'I'll need a military assessment before he phones back.'

There was a knock on the door and the head of Downing Street security entered with one of the intercept technicians.

'We can't trace him.'

Whoever had made the call would already have moved, they knew, the second call would be made from a different number at a different location.

'Why not?'

'He's using a Cellnet.' And because Cellnets were designed to be mobile he could be anywhere.

'But he has to own a unit.' And therefore they could trace him via the number or the ESN – the electronic serial number – of the unit he was using and through which each item, including the numbers called, would be computer-logged. Except there would be a catch, they all knew. If the IRA were using a Cellnet, they would have taken measures to circumvent the possibility of a trace.

The technician shook his head. 'That's what we're doing at the moment. But the chances are that it's not going to get us anywhere. Either they've duplicated a number of ESNs, which would be difficult, if not impossible. Or the Cellnet's been stolen. Or they've bought units using false IDs, addresses and bank accounts.'

And there was no point cancelling the number, because the IRA would have other units or duplicates, and in any case they wouldn't wish to cut off the telephone link with the Provisionals.

'What about establishing the general area from which the calls are being made?'

'Calls are routed through EMXs – electronic mobile exchanges. There are five in London alone. Outside London it's even more vague. Calls from Southampton, for example, are routed via an EMX in Bristol.'

'Thank you.' The Prime Minister nodded and waited until the two men had left the room. 'The demand,' he said simply.

The four men around him waited.

'They haven't made a specific demand.' He saw the confusion on their faces. 'What they want is round-the-table negotiations, discussions between the Provisional IRA and HM Government.'

Impossible, he knew how he himself had initially reacted, how the others would initially react.

'Nothing more?' It was the Foreign Secretary. 'Nothing specific?'
'No.'

There was no way they could hold talks with the IRA, they knew. No way they could sit down face-to-face with the IRA – the first way out began to seep in.

The Prime Minister turned to the Northern Ireland Secretary. 'I'll need precedents for holding such talks, even through an intermediary.' Not that we're giving in to them, it was understood. He turned to the Foreign Secretary. 'Those I may need to consult?'

'Where possible they're already on their way here. Where not possible they're awaiting a telephone call. Lines are being made secure.'

He turned to the Cabinet Secretary. 'A transcript of the conversation, plus a separate transcript of their demands, as soon as possible.'

'I'll get it done right away.'

'If you don't mind, I'd prefer it if you typed them yourself.'

'Of course, Prime Minister.'

'One thing before you do.'

Even under such circumstances there was a protocol, and protocol demanded that although the call to the Palace would be from the Prime Minister, it should be through the Cabinet Secretary to the Queen's private secretary. The others left the room and the Cabinet Secretary dialled the number.

'Sir Robert. This is Sir William at Downing Street. The Prime Minister would like to speak to Her Majesty.' The call and the request outside normal channels, therefore something of major constitutional or political significance, the Queen's private secretary understood. The Cabinet Secretary waited while the other man informed the Queen, then handed the telephone to the Prime Minister, so that although the Queen was waiting for the call, the Prime Minister was waiting for her.

'Your Majesty. I'm afraid I have some terrible news.'

The conversation lasted a little under five minutes.

'Has the Prince of Wales been informed?' The Queen's voice was a mix of personal grief and public self-discipline.

'No, Ma'am. I thought it best to speak to you first.'

'I'll tell him now.' She remembered the moment in Tree Tops, the safari lodge in Kenya, when she had been woken in the night and informed that her father had died and that she was queen.

'If I may make a suggestion, Ma'am.'

'Yes, Prime Minister.'

'Perhaps I should speak to him first. It may be that he would appreciate a call from you after he's heard.'

For the briefest of moments the conversation had changed, was no longer a discussion between head of government and monarch, was a conversation between a father and a mother.

'Thank you, Prime Minister. Your understanding is appreciated.'

He waited for the Queen to end the call, then asked the Cabinet Secretary to telephone the Prince of Wales.

The Fal was glistening in the sun, the river speckled with sails and the white hull of the *Trelawney* gleaming against the blue of the water. The equerry took the call, clamped the scrambler on the mobile, punched in the security code and informed the Prince of Wales that he was wanted urgently.

Charles spoke to the Prime Minister in the seclusion of the master's cabin, at the stern of the ship. For thirty seconds after he had been given the news he sat slumped, trying to surface against the vast emptiness which engulfed him, the Prime Minister not speaking, allowing him his time.

'So what do you recommend I do?' The Prince spoke at last.

The message, and the genuine sympathy which accompanied it, had been delivered, now it was time for the affairs of state to be met head on.

'Because of the constitutional issues involved, the Cabinet feels it best that news of the kidnapping should not be allowed to reach the public. Despite the personal grief which you are suffering, therefore, I have to ask that you continue your programme as if nothing had happened.'

He should be in London, the Prime Minister knew the Prince would probably say. Waiting. Supporting his younger son.

'Of course, Prime Minister.'

He ended the conversation, called for his equerry, and asked him to telephone the Palace. Ninety seconds later he spoke to the Queen, both of them alone. For two minutes they spoke as mother and son, for another two as monarch and monarch-in-waiting, for the next three as mother and son again.

'What will you do?' The office in which she sat suddenly seemed vast, empty.

'Stay here, continue as normal. The Prime Minister's suggestion. I'd like to be in London but I agree with him.' He paused. 'It's strange. I always thought that if they came it would be for me.'

Nolan reached Gower Street forty minutes after leaving Heathrow. She cleared security and went immediately to Michaelmass's offices. Penrose was waiting for her. The DDG was at Downing Street, he explained, then passed on to her the limited information available to him, plus instructions from Michaelmass. She went to her office, arranged blow-ups of the various photographs of Philipa Walker which she had collated, and contacted Downing Street, requesting that Michaelmass be interrupted in the Cobra meeting and briefing him on the possible identity of Sleeper. Then she spoke to SO 13, SB and RPG at the Yard, and SAS in London and Hereford, receiving from each the latest information on the kidnapping, passing to each the same information, and informing each that photographs were on their way. Then she took the Browning Hi-Power and holster from the desk drawer, collected an armoured vest from stores, left Gower Street and was driven to the operations centre close to the hostage location.

The waiting would be the worst, Walker had always known. Even if it had been in the flat off Dunton Street. Tighe stood by the window, looking out; Kennedy and Murphy close to the hostages; Megahey near the hallway. On the sofa against the right-hand wall of the lounge the Princess of Wales sat with her arm round her son.

Diana would have done the course, Walker thought again, therefore would been told how to behave and how to expect her kidnappers to behave. Would know the jargon and the techniques backwards, would have carried them with her every day of her life, despite the stylish skirts and the winning smile. Stockholm Syndrome – they would have drilled it into her at Hereford – the relationship which developed naturally between hostage-taker and hostage, the sympathy, almost the empathy, growing between them. Work on it, they would have told her, develop it, but be aware of it. Try to turn it to her advantage.

Therefore the Princess would talk to her, therefore the Princess would be friendly. If not friendly then neutral. The Princess seeking to use the Stockholm Syndrome against her. Therefore she and Conlan would use it against the authorities.

'I'm sorry about all this. It wasn't supposed to happen this way.'

She sat on the arm of a chair two yards from the Princess.

Of course it wasn't supposed to happen this way, Diana felt the anger. Of course you weren't supposed to kidnap us. Of course you weren't supposed to kill the sergeant.

The Stockholm Syndrome: she remembered the instructions. Don't antagonize the people holding you. Talk to them if necessary, try to get them on your side. At least try to build the first bridge between you. So that when the time comes they might hesitate. Might think twice about shooting you. Talk to them and give the men outside a clue, any clue. Talk to them so that the microphones which would soon be in place would have something to pick up.

She stifled her natural response and said nothing.

'Perhaps you or Prince William would like to use the bathroom?'

The politeness was deliberate.

The Princess nodded.

380

Tighe took them to the bathroom, opened the door for them, allowed them to shut it behind them. The inside lock had been removed. Listen to me, she told William: everything will be all right, they mean it when they say they don't want to hurt us. She looked round the room for a way out. Of course there was no way out, of course the gunmen wouldn't have allowed her and William to be by themselves if there was. She splashed some water over her face and told herself that it made her feel better, washed William's and told him again that everything would be okay.

'Make them some tea,' Walker told Murphy, saw the way he glanced at Tighe and knew what he was thinking. We're holed up in a flat, police and SAS outside, and she tells me to make fucking tea. Tighe nodded. Nothing was unplanned, he was aware. Except the fact that someone had rumbled them, and even then the Bossman had been calm, consulted the flying column leader when appropriate and made the right decisions. And now she had reverted to what he supposed was a timetable, even though they were in the wrong place and surrounded. So why had she told Murphy to make tea? He checked the street again – all quiet, nothing to suggest that anything was wrong – and turned back.

Walker opened the shoulderbag, took out the Sony Professional Walkman, placed it at the side of the bag so that although the cassette recorder was concealed its microphone would pick up any conversation in any part of the room, and switched it on.

The Princess of Wales and Prince William came out of the bathroom and returned to the sofa.

'I don't know how long we're going to be here.' Walker sat again on the arm of the chair. 'It shouldn't be more than this afternoon.' Murphy came out of the kitchen and placed the tray of tea on the low table in front of the sofa.

'Perhaps Prince William would prefer something else, orange juice perhaps?'

'Tea will be fine, thank you.' The boy's voice was frightened yet clear, unmistakable. Walker changed her tactics and directed the conversation at him.

'How's the head now? The fracture's mended okay?'

'Yes, thank you.'

'You were a bit brave then. Tell me about it.'

He told her – of the innocent game at the prep school at Berkshire, the fractured skull after he had been knocked on the head, the rush to hospital and the operation which followed. The way his mother had stayed at his bedside, the day she had driven him home.

It was all part of the ammunition, Walker thought, all part of the pressure Conlan would bring to bear on the British government.

'I'm sorry about the bodyguard.' She turned her attention to the Princess. 'Had he been with you long?'

Stockholm Syndrome; the Princess of Wales fought her natural revulsion. Don't give anything away, but talk if you think it will help your situation.

'Eighteen months.' They were the first words she had spoken in the flat, other than the low whispers to her son.

'What was his name?'

'Hugh Wilson.'

'Was he married?'

'Yes. Two children. Little girls.'

Walker allowed the silence to dilute the memory.

'A day off school for you, then.' She spoke to Prince William.

'Nanny's birthday. I always have lunch with her on her birthday.'

Walker turned her head slightly, questioningly, towards the Princess, as if she did not understand.

'William's first nanny. She retired four years ago. We're all still close to her.'

The first Pumas landed at Heathrow, the Hertz trucks and police escorts waiting for them in one of the cargo areas and the area sealed off. Ten minutes behind them another group brought in the advance party of armourers and communication specialists, the rest already en route from Hereford by road.

Haslam confirmed the arrangements, then he and the squadron major who would act as operations officer were driven by police BMW to the apartment block close to the siege flat where the operations room was being established.

The Home Secretary's armour-plated Rover swung through the security barrier at the end of Downing Street, the back-up Rover close behind, and turned right along Whitehall. In five minutes the Prime Minister would leave the Cobra committee and return to the Wise Men seated round the Cabinet table, Sinclair knew; in ten he would take the second call from the IRA. Then he would consult with his Wise Men. And he – the Home Secretary – was out of it.

Of course he was in command – of the control centre. The lackeys would be running round him, trying to impress. But in reality he was merely a messenger boy, the point of communication between the decision-makers and the action-takers. It was the end of his career. If the operation succeeded – whatever the Prime Minister decided to do – then it would be the Prime Minister who took the credit. And if it failed it would be he as Home Secretary who would be the scapegoat, who would be called upon to resign. Who would stand in the House and take the wrath and scorn which would be poured upon him.

The BMW stopped fifty yards from the entrance to the building housing the operations room. Haslam and the major walked into the flats and up the stairs, the security present but discreet. The captain in charge of the London teams and a number of police officers were waiting for them, plus two men from London HQ. Early days, Haslam knew, the cordon unseen round the siege flat but nothing else yet in place. The captain led Haslam and the major to a small room off the main control room and briefed them.

'The ASU and the hostages are here. Flat at the front of the building, on the third floor.' He indicated the position on the first of the maps. 'We're setting up an ops room here.' He indicated the position on the same map, then turned to the architectural drawing. 'Layout of the flat. Entered by door off landing into a hallway. The hallway is approximately eight metres long and slightly less than two wide. Two rooms on each side; on the right a kitchen then a bedroom, on the left a bathroom and a second bedroom. The lounge is at the front.' Some captains didn't know what they were talking about, Haslam thought, thank God this one knew his way round. 'Obvious access points are the front window, the door from the landing, or the walls of the lounge.' Probably correct, thought Haslam. 'The kitchen, bathroom and bedrooms might be eliminated because of the time needed to get from them into the lounge, where we assume the hostages are being held.' Worth checking, but probably correct again. 'It's also probable that they've blocked the hall door, and they may have blocked at least part of the window.' And in any case he wouldn't want a four-man assault team jammed together in a space as confined as the hallway, Haslam thought. Which left the walls of the lounge.

383

'We have access to the flats above, below and on either side. The owners of the siege flat have been located and are being brought here to advise on internal layout.'

'Surveillance?'

'The police already have laser surveillance on the windows, but the curtains are drawn most of the time. They expect the first microphones to be in place in an hour, perhaps slightly longer. Video when they can.'

Sieges were normally long and drawn out, Haslam knew, the surveillance technology taking time and care to install, nothing being done to alert the gunmen. The SAS were not normally involved until the police had exhausted all other possibilities, and even then not until something like the shooting of a hostage had taken place and been confirmed, even though they would be on stand-by. And sieges were also normally public, in that the public was aware something had happened without knowing all the details. But this was not normal: by the time all the normal procedures had been applied, the technology in place and the system up and running, this one would probably be over.

He left the provisional ops room and walked along the street. Apparently flat roof, slightly sloping in front, he noted, no balconies on the front windows. Third-floor flat out of eight, an abseil down the front was possible, the men tying off before they received the order to go in through the windows, but highly public. Whoever was in charge of the hostage-takers had either been lucky or had thought it through, even under the most extreme of pressure. The latter, he knew. He looked up and down the street then went into the block containing the siege flat. Nowhere was there any obvious sign that anything was amiss. He reached the third floor and stopped. The door of the flat to his left opened and the eyes looked at him over the Hockler.

Access into the lounge through the adjacent flat, he decided. As long as the surveillance confirmed that was where Di and Willy were being held. Right or left wall after he'd talked to the owners and knew the furniture layout. Harvey WallBanger rather than explosives. Explosives might blow back at them or blast the debris into the siege room and injure the hostages. He left the block and went next door to the flat adjoining the siege flat; the furniture had been cleared from the separating wall and a team was standing by. Incoming teams to stop outside number forty-seven, he radioed the ops room. Nothing to move till he was back, he told the teams in the room. Then he went downstairs and waited for the first of the vans.

Sinclair shook hands with the major in charge of what would be the operations room, and with the range of army and police officers present, then he was taken to the adjoining room and the position explained to him using the maps on the table there.

Any minute now and the PM would be taking the next call, he glanced at his watch. Then the PM would inform the Wise Men and – separately – the members of Cobra. And the Cobra committee which he himself had instigated would in turn inform the PM of its advice. And he would not be present. He, who as Home Secretary should have been at the PM's right hand, who as Home Secretary and senior member of the Party was one of the most powerful men in the country, was now effectively powerless. He, who should be chairing Cobra, now enjoyed the trappings of office but the function of a messenger boy.

Except that he was not powerless. As messenger boy he had more power than he could ever have dreamed of had he still been in the confines of the Cabinet room at Downing Street. As Home Secretary in charge of the control room he was at the centre of everything, the sole link between the decision-makers and the action-takers. The SAS would not be receiving their orders direct from the Prime Minister. It would be he, as Home Secretary, therefore, who would bear the responsibility of authorizing the transfer of power from the civil authority to the military, from the police to the SAS. He, as Home Secretary, who would bear the additional responsibility in the event of the PM hesitating or prevaricating, as he was known to do. Especially in the event of an opportunity suddenly presenting itself for the Princess of Wales and her son to be rescued and the PM locked in another of his interminable Cabinet discussions.

Stand by, stand by. The words drummed though Haslam's brain even though he was talking to the owners of the flat where the hostages were being held. *Stand by, stand by.* Four-man team, himself and Phillips tight together in front, other two tight behind them. He was listening to the ops commander activating the diversions, counting down the assault teams. *Stand by, stand by.* Harvey WallBanger taking out wall, through hole and into siege room.

Himself going right, Phillips left, clearing the hole for two men behind. Already sweeping his sector for gunmen.

He thanked the couple, told them it would soon be over, and went to the apartment adjacent to the siege flat. The couple had been nervous but helpful, had been told there was the possibility of an armed gang holding a bank manager hostage and had assumed that the man they were talking to was a policeman. He would enter the flat through the left wall of the lounge if he was inside the siege room and facing the window, he decided. Di and Willy presumably seated on the sofa against the right wall, the television to their right and the chairs opposite them.

The adjacent apartment had been cleared. He pulled down the balaclava, then the gas mask. There was no point in touching the wall, every reason not to – even the slightest sound or vibration might alert the gunmen. He nodded, and the WallBanger was edged into the room.

The call came precisely on time. The Prime Minister heard the click as the recording equipment switched on and allowed the telephone to ring three times before picking it up, the delay intended to convey his control of the situation. The men around him were listening on earpieces.

'Yes.'

'Good afternoon again, Prime Minister. I assume you have reached a decision on the Princess of Wales and Prince William.'

The voice was still calm and reasonable, they all noted.

'Because of the constitutional issues involved, I cannot give you an answer at this point in time.'

It was a response on which they had agreed, neither rejecting the demand nor agreeing with it. A politician's answer.

'I understand, Prime Minister.'

Why the constant reference to 'Prime Minister'? the Foreign Secretary thought. Because the PM could not deny it and by not denying it was confirming it. Confirming that the conversation which was taking place was between the British Prime Minister and a representative of the Army Council of the Provisional IRA. That the subject under discussion was the kidnapping by the Provisional IRA of the Princess of Wales and her son. That the IRA *did actually have the Princess of Wales and Prince William.*

'I have to remind you, however, of what I said I would do if you felt you could not agree.'

Inform the overseas press that an active service unit of the Provisional IRA are holding the Princess of Wales and her first son, Prince William, as hostages.

And the British government would deny it, he knew the Prime Minister would say.

'If you would allow me to play you something.'

They waited, heard the slight change in sound, the almost hollow echo of the cassette, then the voices.

Perhaps Prince William would prefer something else, orange juice perhaps?

Tea will be fine, thank you.

They knew the voice, knew who it was.

How's the head now?

They listened, horrified.

I'm sorry about the bodyguard. Had he been with you long?

Don't answer, they pleaded, for God's sake say nothing.

Eighteen months.

What was his name?

Hugh Wilson.

If it got out, if the Provos gave it to the press.

A day off school, then.

Nanny's birthday . . .

'One hour, Prime Minister. Then I give the overseas press the cassette.'

Starting with CNN, the 24-hour American television news channel. And CNN would use it. Not because they would sympathize with what was happening, but because unless they ran with it first someone else would.

'I'll telephone you five minutes before, of course.'

The Wise Men listened again to the recording, then the Prime Minister looked at them. 'Thoughts?' he asked.

'In a way the demand might be seen as a starting position for negotiation.'

'And what the IRA are doing is establishing the ground rules for negotiation?'

'Yes.'

'Precedents for HM Government holding direct negotiations with the IRA?'

'In the 1920s, of course. In 1972 the then leader of the opposition, Harold Wilson, met with the Provisional leadership in Dublin. The same year the RAF flew a Provisional delegation to London for secret talks with the then Northern Ireland Secretary, William Whitelaw. There have been other approaches since, always through an intermediary.'

'But.'

'But in each of those instances the Irish lost because they entered the negotiations from a position of weakness.'

The IRA always the bridesmaid, he remembered how someone had once described it, never the bride.

'Yes.'

'And in any negotiation resulting from today's occurrence it would be they, not us, who held the whip hand?'

'Correct, Prime Minister.'

'Even though those negotiations might not start, or at least be made public, for two, three years.'

'Yes.'

'So we've lost?'

There was a silence.

'Or we might have won.' It was the Northern Ireland Secretary. Why? He saw it on their faces. How? 'If whoever is behind this is able to control the Provisionals for the next five to ten years, able to keep the gunmen and bombers off the streets. If they're prepared to allow us the breathing space to break the circle of violence, prepared to allow a new generation of young people to come up, then we might be talking about a solution.'

'And you think that's what they're offering? And if that's what they're offering they can pull it off?'

The Northern Ireland Secretary shook his head. 'I don't know.'

It was ten minutes since the Prime Minister had talked to Conlan. 'So what do we do?'

Stand by, stand by.

The WallBanger was in position; behind them the back-up team waited. On the wall opposite were pinned photographs of the Princess of Wales and Prince William, Haslam and his team seeing them and familiarizing themselves with them each time they turned. Plus the blow-up photograph of the woman allegedly leading the hostage-takers which had arrived from MI5 ten minutes before. Haslam

388

removed his gas mask, wiped his face, and put the mask back in place.

Standing by, he told the operation commander.

'First sound surveillance in,' the SAS major told Sinclair. 'Bit rough, but at least we now stand a chance of knowing a little of what's happening inside.' He turned back to his planning.

Two diversions: the first through the door from the landing to the hallway and the second through the ceiling – explosives to open a gap then stun grenades in. Then Haslam's team through the wall.

No news from Downing Street, Sinclair thought, the Prime Minister still prevaricating.

The Princess of Wales glanced at her watch: they had been in the flat almost two hours. The police had followed them there; by now the SAS would have surrounded the place and the technical teams would have inserted their listening equipment, would be eavesdropping on anything and everything that was said.

Information – she remembered the instructions at Hereford. If you can do anything, say anything, which might help us.

'What went wrong?' She and William were still on the sofa, Walker in the chair opposite, two of the Irishmen close by her, the third by the window and the fourth by the hallway.

Walker shrugged.

'But you and the other four must have spent months in the planning.'

Good girl, the surveillance expert whispered, passed the information to Haslam and the assault team.

The woman was looking at her through the eyeholes in the balaclava. Almost smiling, the Princess thought.

They already know how many of us there are, she knew the woman was telling her. They counted us on the way in.

Walker crossed the room and checked the Cellnets: one in readiness for Conlan to contact her and a second always open and Conlan recording everything that happened in the room. So that even if the Brits sent in the SAS, even if the SAS killed her and the others, there was no way Downing Street could deny anything. And if the Brits sent in the SAS and something – from Downing Street's point of view – went wrong. If the SAS killed her but also killed the Princess of Wales or her son . . .

So that no matter how it ended, she would win. Not just in the long term, the political propaganda Conlan would be able to make out of the fact that the Princess of Wales had been kidnapped. In the short term as well. Even if they shot her before she managed to fire back she would still take some of them with her. The Clock-Maker had been that good and the device he had delivered to her that precise.

So this is what it was like at St Comgalls school, this was how her father had felt as he was defending the Divis. There was no emotion in her thoughts. This was how her brother had felt as he had waited for the nightmare before his death. This was how her mother had felt in the bedroom of the terrace house in Rathmeen.

At the end of her mother's days, Conlan had told her, just before the end, he had told her mother the truth, told her that her daughter had come looking for her. Told her that her sacrifice had not been in vain, that in a short time her daughter would change history.

She stood and checked through the window.

She was going to die, the Princess of Wales suddenly knew.

There was no way the government could admit that the IRA had kidnapped her and her son, yet no way the government could agree to the gunmen's demands, whatever they were. And therefore she was going to die. The realization shocked her, her mind suddenly spinning as it had spun on the pavement on Mayhill Street that morning, everything else suddenly irrelevant.

So think it through, she told herself, the calm suddenly descending upon her. If she really was going to die, work out what she could do and how she would do it. What should she be planning even though they may not have taught it her at Hereford?

She was unimportant. The important person was her son. No matter what the IRA planned for either of them, no matter how the IRA had planned the kidnapping should end, she had only one function. To save her son. To ensure that William lived. To put herself between him and the gunmen. To protect the future king. In the end, if the end came, she had one role and one role only. The same as Hugh Wilson. That of a bullet-stopper.

For ten minutes after they had reached their decision the Prime Minister and his Wise Men discussed the details of their response, for the fifteen minutes after that the Prime Minister consulted with the political leaders and statesmen listed by the Foreign Secretary, including the Leader of the Opposition. Then he left Downing Street, travelling unnoticed in a dark green MoD Transit van and entering Buckingham Palace unobserved, and informed the Queen of his decision. Ten minutes before the third and final call he returned to Downing Street.

Conlan telephoned precisely on time.

'I assume, Prime Minister, that you have been able to make a decision.'

The Prime Minister paused, staring at the prepared statement on the table in front of him and thinking of the other decisions taken in that room, how those who had taken them would judge what he was about to do. He looked up and read the statement.

'On behalf of Her Majesty's Government, and dependent on the safe release of Her Royal Highness the Princess of Wales and of her son Prince William, and dependent upon certain other conditions being met, I accept.'

'And your acceptance includes safe conduct for my people?'

'Yes.'

'In that case we have an agreement.'

'There are certain details to be worked out, including the release. I think it proper to inform Her Majesty of our agreement, as well as His Royal Highness the Prince of Wales.'

'I would also like to inform my people. And through them, of course, the Princess.'

'Agreed. You'll telephone again in ten minutes.'

'Yes.'

A long road, Conlan thought. Three hundred years long. Now perhaps the beginning of the end. Doherty's footnote in history. He terminated the call and keyed the number of the Cellnet.

'Yes.'

Walker's voice was calm, he thought.

'It's over. They've agreed. There are some details to work out, but it's finished. Your safe conduct is guaranteed. It'll probably be another half-hour, but you can tell the hostages.'

Something's happening, the surveillance team informed Control, telephone call coming in, the leader of the ASU is answering it. Her voice is different, more relaxed.

She'd won, Walker felt the thrill. She'd won and she was going to make it home. 'One moment.' She turned to face the others.

'It's over. They've agreed to our demands.'

391

She turned to the figures on the sofa. 'We've guaranteed your freedom. Your government has guaranteed our safe conduct out. It will take another half an hour.'

The Princess of Wales nodded, saw the way the guns came down and the group relaxed. Smiled at William, understood his fear and his confusion, even now, and tried to comfort him.

They think they've won, the Home Secretary heard the message. The leader seems to think the government's given in.

'How are they?' He stood beside the SAS major, the police commander in charge of the operation to his left.

'More relaxed, by their voices. As if they've lowered their guard.'

No word from Downing Street, Sinclair thought, no indication whatsoever from the Prime Minister or Cobra that what the IRA believed to be the case was the truth. Their defences down and the time to act. No time to consult with Downing Street. The SAS reacting only to his orders.

'Go,' he told the SAS major.

The operation was still the responsibility of the police, he was aware. The police commander handed Sinclair a notebook, Sinclair took it and wrote the authorization transferring control of the operation to the SAS, then gave it to the major.

'No indication from Downing Street, no time to check or we waste the opportunity.' He was firm and decisive.

'Standing by. Gunmen apparently off guard.' The operational major was isolated, expected and expecting to act upon the orders of the Home Secretary and knowing the Home Secretary would only act upon instructions from Downing Street. 'Going in twenty seconds. Radio silence.'

Stand by, stand by. Haslam and Phillips were at the wall, Scott and Davis behind them. *Stand by, stand by.*

'Fifteen seconds.'

First diversion: Harvey WallBanger siege cannon to blow the door of the flat away – Haslam rehearsed the movements in his mind. Second diversion: hole through ceiling and second stun in. He was rocking backwards and forwards, breath rasping through the gas mask and the voice of the major counting down in his earpiece. Second Harvey WallBanger taking out the wall. Phillips and himself through the hole, him going right, Phillips left, clearing the hole for Scott and Davis. Move right as soon as he was through, check his sector. Look for Di and Willy, look for the gunmen.

It's all right, the Princess told William. Very soon they'll let us go. It's all agreed. Nothing else will happen now.

'Ten seconds.'

So what would she do? Walker wondered. Safe conduct out then back to Ireland. Disappear to America and then what?

Five seconds.

So what the hell was going on, Haslam wondered, what had happened to make things move so suddenly? How did it affect what would happen once they entered the flat?

Three seconds.

Forget it, forget everything except getting through the hole in the wall and taking out the gunmen before they took out the hostages.

Megahey came back into the lounge, cups on the tray and a plate of biscuits. Kennedy and Murphy with their guns still in their hands, but the weapons no longer trained on her, Diana thought. The Stockholm Syndrome or the sheer exhilarating knowledge that they were all going to get out of it alive. She laughed at William and stood up, took the plate of biscuits and offered them round. Never trust the Brits, Walker thought. But Conlan had stitched them up, Conlan had made it impossible for them to win.

'Green go.'

The door to the hallway exploded and the flash filled the air. Walker's mind was spinning, the noise and explosion disorientating her, whirling her down a corridor. The room, the flat, the whole world spinning. Automatically she looked at where it came from.

'Red Go.'

There was an explosion from above, the shock waves pounding through her like the shocks of an earthquake. Just like the nightmare when Charles had taken the boys to Klosters, Diana thought, just like somewhere she had been before but could not remember where.

'Blue go.'

The second WallBanger blasted through the brick and plaster of the wall. Another stun grenade dropped through the ceiling and exploded, then a third.

Go. Haslam shouted it to himself. Was already through the hole, the world in circles through the eyepieces of the gas mask. The monsters, Diana remembered, the screams and flashes and explosions. Haslam moved right, clearing the hole, sweeping left to right. Phillips to his left and Scott and Davis coming in behind. Walker was turning, fighting to recover, reaching for the Ruger. Di

393

and Willy, Haslam looked, where the hell were Di and Willy? Gunman One going for gun. Haslam touched the trigger of the Hockler, three-round burst, saw the gunman begin to fall. Second three-round burst. Continued sweeping.

Bastard Brits, Walker's fingers closed on the Ruger.

Diana's head was suddenly clear. Not because the effects of the stun grenades had worn off. Because of the order throbbing in her head. William. Save William. She saw the Provo by the hallway beginning to react, beginning to raise his gun at them. She pushed William back and down, threw herself on him. Covered his body with hers. Haslam saw the gunman, turned. Three-round burst, second three-round burst. Diana heard the rounds above the rest of the storm. Knew they were for her, braced herself. Looked up, still covering William. Saw the gunman's chest redden. Walker's hand was on the Ruger. Gunman by window, Davis swept his sector: three-round burst, second burst. Gunman against far wall, Phillips saw, gun coming up: three-round burst, second burst. Christ he was still moving, about to fire. Prolonged burst, counting rounds down. Walker was turning. Seeing the black shapes turning towards her. Three-round burst, Haslam pressed the trigger, three-round burst. She felt the rounds, knew her body and head were exploding.

'Out.' Haslam swung round and checked. More men coming through the hole in the wall, forming a line into the adjacent flat. The other team members dealing with the terrorists, making sure they were dead.

Diana felt the hands on her and looked up, saw the monster. Clung even tighter to her son. Haslam flicked the safety of the Hockler on and swung the weapon over his back, tried to pull Di clear, knew he was making her clutch the boy even tighter. No time for messing around – he was operating automatically, instinctively, totally aware of everything. He hit her, knocked her out, felt her grip weaken and picked her up. Threw her to Phillips. Picked up William. Threw him in turn.

She was coming round, was spinning through the air, being tossed like a rag doll from man to man. Through the hole in the wall, into the next flat and down the stairs. William being thrown from man to man behind her.

Nolan ran up the stairs, ID hanging from her neck and Browning Hi-Power in hand. Past the line of men. The first body was thrown past her. The Princess of Wales. The second. A boy. William.

Haslam came past even though she did not recognize him, Hockler in hand again and gas mask still on. She reached the third floor, went in to the adjacent flat, through the hole into the siege flat.

Jesus Christ, she thought.

The five bodies were in shreds, tatters, guns in their hands and blood on the walls. Four men, she saw, one woman.

Behind her the Home Secretary came in to the room.

Haslam reached the ground floor. 'Di and Willy okay?'

'Okay.'

'Hostages secure,' he spoke into the throat mike. 'Van in front now.'

The Hertz rental van drew up, the crowd already gathering at the entrance to the next set of flats and paying no attention to it. The group of men left, white overalls over black AT-gear, the two figures lost between them. The men in front pushed the Princess and Prince into the back of the van, Haslam and three others jumping in with them, then the last man shut the door and the van pulled away.

Not Sleeper, Nolan thought, Sleeper wouldn't have let herself be taken out like this. She stood looking at the body, turned, saw Sinclair. 'Everybody out,' she ordered. 'Bomb disposal and sniffer dogs in now.' She pushed past Sinclair and walked down the stairs.

The van accelerated quickly, disappearing from the scene as inconspicuously as it had appeared. Haslam slumped on to the floor opposite the Princess of Wales and pulled off the gas mask and balaclava.

'Thanks, Dave.' Diana held her son close to her. 'Like I said, it'll be all right on the night.'

Nolan was on the second floor, turning for the stairs to the first. The image hit her. The Home Secretary. Standing in triumph over Sleeper. Bending down, pulling down the zip of her coat to examine the damage to what remained of her body.

The last game, the last come-on.

No . . . she turned, screamed the warning, began to run back.

The explosion from the siege room filled the air and vibrated through the building, down the stairwell and into the hall.

15

THE ANTHEM DRIFTED ABOVE THE NOISE of the traffic and lifted into the blue of the sky above Westminster. Michaelmass stood unnoticed amidst the public figures and looked around him.

The memorial service to the late Home Secretary, man of the people and hero of his time, receiving in death the accolades for which he had striven so hard, and which had so eluded him in life. The service was attended by Her Majesty the Queen, the Duke of Edinburgh, the Prince and Princess of Wales, and a phalanx of statesmen and politicians.

The previous afternoon, and less publicly, the memorial service had been held in the Guards Chapel at Knightsbridge for Major Roderick Fairfax, First Battalion the Grenadier Guards, killed in action, that service also attended by the Prince and Princess of Wales.

So who had won and who had lost, Michaelmass wondered. The British or the Provos? Himself or Sleeper? Perhaps they had each won, perhaps they had each lost, but in so doing had won anyway. Perhaps Sinclair's death, and the manner of it, had given those in the Provisional IRA who supported the bullet what they wanted, and in so doing gave a breathing space to those who believed in the ballot box.

The service ended and the crowd moved away. A strange day in London, Michaelmass thought, the security problem massive, yet it was as if there was no fear. Almost as if a truce had been called. He left Westminster Abbey, crossed Parliament Square, and walked unnoticed down the Embankment and along the Thames.

The cortège stretched as far as the eye could see. The piper in front, the five hearses, the guard of honour on either side – black berets, black jackets, black sunglasses – the drummer behind them beating the pace. Then the mourners, eight wide and thousands deep. The funeral of the London Brigade. The team that had taken out the British Home Secretary in the centre of London on Orange Day.

The procession turned into the cemetery at Milltown, the green, white and orange flags fluttering above the Republican graves, the coffins unloaded and the vast crowd filling the grounds. It was strange that it had been allowed, some had commented, strange that there was no security presence that afternoon. Almost as if an amnesty had been declared: you bury yours and we'll bury ours.

The coffins were lined up, then each committed. One by one, till there was only one left.

The tricolour was draped across it, the black beret on top, black gloves and belt folded in front. S.M. McCann, the words would say simply and noncommittally, and in Gaelic 'Freedom's Breeze', after the words of Colonel John Roberts before the battle at Lime Ridge 130 years before. S.M. McCann – already the name had a ring to it, already the legend had begun. No full name, the Army Council had announced, no details for reasons of security. The same surname as the hero of St Comgalls school, those steeped in the history of the Movement had noted, even the same initials as the hero's wife; no relation, of course, the hero who had helped save the Divis and his wife had only had two boys, one the priest who led today's service and the other the hunger striker who had given his life for the Cause a decade before.

The crowd waited, expectant. The men appeared from nowhere, dressed in military uniforms, SLRs ready. Conlan stood to attention, lost in the crowd. The first volley echoed into the sky, then the next.

For a Brit she didn't do that badly, Nolan thought. She went to her desk and opened the drawer. Even now the guard of honour would be firing into the sky above her coffin, any moment now they'd lower the coffin into the ground. Lisburn was quiet, the echo of footsteps at the other end of the corridor.

So who put the tail on McGuire? Conlan thought. Who saw through Logan and did the job in Manchester? Who was the one who almost stopped her?

*

397

Interesting that when she died she'd thought she'd won, of course. Nolan reached into the drawer and took out the bottle, poured herself a glass.

The echoes were hanging in the air, across the motorway on one side of the cemetery and the police station on the other. Conlan reached in the pocket of his jacket and took out a hip flask, the leather round it brown and worn. It was as if he was alone, as if he was sitting by the lough at Kilmore, the sun setting and the evening warm. As if he was sitting that first afternoon in the hotel at Fane. He opened the flask and raised it.

The office was empty, but she would have done it anyway. 'Sleeper.' Catcher raised the glass and downed it in one.

EPILOGUE

THE ANGEL OF DEATH stood in the graveyard and the priest waited at the door.

The Sunday afternoon was quiet, the faintest breeze stirring the foliage of the trees and rustling the hem of his cassock, and the faded red brick of the Church of St Mary and St Phillip lost amidst the colours of summer.

It was two years now since she had last come but still he felt it was his duty to wait. The afternoon drifted on, an English afternoon he would have called it, warm and restful, only the faintest sound of the world outside.

The day wore on, still warm. At five he left the steps and locked the doors. Perhaps it would be the last time he would wait, he thought, perhaps he would wait one more year. He left the church and walked through the graveyard, past the Angel of Death.

An interesting article in the *Sunday Times* of the previous week. Both sides had denied it of course, but both sides would, and in the end it would probably come to nothing.

For the past six months the Roman Catholic Church had been acting as intermediary for talks between representatives of the British government and the Provisional IRA.